THE
MINDBREAKER
ELIMINATION
MARINA EPLEY

The First Book in
THE MIND BREAKER Trilogy

PART 1

PART II

CHAPTER 1

I wake with senses on keen alert, picking up any noises coming from outside. I hear no sirens, no clatter of military boots against the sidewalk. Only a light rain tapping on the window pane.

It's all right, I tell myself. Elimination won't come for us today. They still don't realize we're among the mind breakers they're hunting.

My clothing is too old and worn to keep me warm enough in the morning chill. Shivering, I walk to the kitchen and open the cupboards, looking for something to eat. Empty. Only a few stale crackers and yesterday's teabag still in the cup. Today is only Wednesday and Friday is my payday. Two more days with neither food nor money. How in the heck are we gonna make it?

Hoping for a miracle, I check out the jar where we keep our change. Several dirty coins fall out on the scratched table. It's not enough to buy a real lunch or supper, but it might provide a small slice of pizza for Kitty and maybe a cup of coffee for myself.

I place the kettle on the oven to warm before going to wake my little sister. Entering the bedroom, I see her dreaming peacefully. She is only fifteen and looks like an angel while sleeping. Her unruly reddish hair curls into tight locks, covering her tiny shoulders. Obviously, Kitty doesn't suffer from the same bad dreams.

I touch her arm gently.

"Kitty," I say. "Time to get ready."

Kitty complains and shakes off my hand.

"Come on," I say louder. "You'll be late."

Finally, she opens her dark green eyes and props herself on an elbow, being groggy and angry.

"Why do I need to bother with that stupid school?" she asks. "Those brainless teachers just make me sick."

I sit down on her bed, preparing mentally for a long and tiring conversation.

"I know," Kitty says, rolling her eyes. "Education is so important blah-blah-blah. It will help me get a good job in the future and more blah-blah."

"Exactly," I say.

"Do you really believe all that?"

"I do. I may not always be around to take care of you. Remember what's going on in the world these days."

"Oh, lordy!" she exclaims. "You've forgotten we're breakers. We just need to stop hiding."

I frown, feeling uneasy. Our conversation has taken a dangerous turn.

"Get rid of any such thoughts," I say, "or we'll both end up in prison or worse."

The smile fades from her lips.

"I'm not scared of Elimination," she states. "I can protect myself and you as well."

"Get up and get ready," I answer. "Don't make me drag you out of bed."

The kettle whistles in the kitchen. I hurry to make two cups of weak tea, using the teabag found earlier. Placing the crackers on a plate near Kitty's cup, I take a sip of tea and can't help from wincing. Tasteless and smelly, it's much worse than I'd expected.

Dressed in a dark blue school jacket and a short black skirt, Kitty comes into the kitchen and plops down on the chair. Her hair sticks out in all different crazy directions, making her look scruffy. With another sigh, she takes a gulp of her tea and coughs.

"Oh my," Kitty expels. "No sugar?"

"Sorry," I say.

"Goodness," Kitty groans. "Why do we always have to do without? We can take whatever we want. I'm sick of hiding and living like rats. Actually, rats may be better fed."

"Stop it, Kitty," I say, raising my voice. "I told you to quit thinking that way."

"Whatever," she mutters, realizing that arguing is pointless. "So what do we do?"

I smile, pretending to be unconcerned.

"Don't worry," I say. "I'll ask Thompson at the bank for an advance."

"Maybe it would be easier to just rob your bank?" Kitty asks.

I work as a bank clerk, wearing the only suit I have and helping customers, which includes quite a few disagreeable ones. This job pays even less than what I make occasionally building fences, but does provide some benefits which are hard to come by nowadays.

Kitty is still waiting for an answer. Her lips stretch into a smile, but her eyes peer at me seriously.

"Let's just wait for my paycheck," I answer, ignoring her glare.

Kitty eats her crackers, thinking. She continues staring at me expectantly. What does she want? To risk everything and become a thief as so many others have? That's not what I wish for Kitty. Remaining incognito and living a peaceful life is a much safer way to survive for breakers.

I glimpse at the clock. It's a quarter after six. We need to get going.

"Finish your breakfast," I say sternly and head to the living room to change.

A howling wind bites coldly outside the building. At least it's not raining anymore.

I shiver, pressing my teeth together. I scan the street, checking for any sign of people wearing black uniforms. Elimination wears black, but thankfully I see none so far. Only wrapped in rags, several homeless men nearby are ripping into garbage bags. I glance at them in passing and quickly turn away. Less attention means less trouble.

At the bus stop I hand over most of the coins to Kitty, saying to get something for lunch. She kisses me on the cheek and walks away, both hands filled with books. I watch her leaving although the school is only two blocks away. She'll be fine.

The bus arrives within a few minutes and I clamber inside, looking for a place to sit. There are several empty seats in the back. I pick the one furthest away from other passengers.

A guy selling bus tickets walks toward me. Silently, I hand some coins to him. He counts, shakes his head no and asks for more.

"Wait," I argue. "It went up that much since yesterday?"

"Dude, they raised it," he answers. "Don't you watch the news?"

I don't. We have no money for a TV. I give the guy a displeased look while counting out more coins. He takes them, tears off the ticket and walks away. I know he has nothing to do with the increased price, but can't help feeling angry.

I stare out of the window, watching crumbling buildings and littered streets passing by. The trees grow chaotically and packs of rabid dogs roam freely, hunting for prey. Long before the Eruption, these same neighborhoods were booming and full of life. At least according to the historical books in the library. Having been born long after the volcanic and earthquake disasters, I never got a chance to witness all the prosperity myself.

Our Coastal Republic is little more than the miserable remains of that once great country here before. It now consists only of a few half ruined cities close to the Atlantic Ocean. The Eruption really messed things up. Thick layers of deadly ash covered most of our former territories. Lethal gas stretched for thousands of miles, killing multitudes more. The sky darkened for years afterward, with ash blocking the sun and altering the climate of the entire planet. The lack of food, shortages of water and fertile land led to long and brutal wars.

Now we're in a deep crisis and on the very edge of extinction. Our Republic is the last known country that still exists in the world.

Something catches my attention.

I notice a huge red slogan, painted on the wall of a tall building. "Kill a breaker, help save the world!" Might be new, I didn't see it yesterday. As the bus travels further into the city, more ugly slogans appear. They all have a common theme calling to fight, capture or kill the mind breakers.

Looks like Kitty and I being targeted.

The government apparently thinks we're the most dangerous threat to our society. A misstep in the human evolution chain, or so scientists say. Most ordinary people both hate and fear us, believing we're evil-doing freaks full of bad intentions. I can't blame them, really. Who wouldn't dread somebody with the capability to hypnotize with a glimpse or read all their memories?

Too many silly myths and rumors surround us, exaggerating our skills and intent. My method of hypnosis has nothing to do with my eyes. I have no clue how I do it. And it's hard, really exhausting. It hurts my head like crazy and turns my stomach nauseous. I've never been able to hypnotize more than one person or an animal at a time. Kitty and I only use it for self-defense in emergency situations when nothing else works. As for reading somebody's mind, it's total trash. I've no idea how to steal memories. Anyway, why would I do it? All I want for us is to have a simple life, earning enough money for food and necessities, and be safe. I didn't ask to become a breaker. I have never killed or robbed anyone. Do we really deserve all the hatred and anger?

Well, our government doesn't give a damn whether you're a good person or not if you're a breaker. Being a mind breaker is illegal, period. The Council of the Fathers created Elimination consisting of people resistant to hypnosis. The only purpose of Elimination is to catch, imprison and torture the breakers. One mistake and we could easily wind up locked behind bars or dead. That is the harsh reality of being a mind breaker. This is the world we live in.

It's warm and clean inside the bank. Brand new ceiling lamps fill the space with colorless light. The floors are freshly mopped. Being here, I get a feeling of having landed in a parallel universe. There's something unrealistic and odd about this place. Too sterile I guess.

As I walk down the hallway, a tall young man wearing a holstered gun stops me.

"Hey, you," he says roughly. "Do you work here?"

This must be our new security guard, who doesn't know me yet. Wordlessly, I show him my name tag. It has my picture and says I'm Rex Hunter, a bank teller. I've been using this name for years, erasing the real one from my head. The picture seems too serious for a person of my age. I've just turned eighteen, but look more mature and could pass easily for an older guy. A fake ID I have says I'm over twenty one.

The guard studies my name tag and finally nods. I pin it back to my shirt and walk into the large main office, heading to my desk.

The other employees arrive, seeming ruffled after a long commute. Nobody talks a lot in the morning. While preparing my desk for the day, I notice my friends, Tim and Mandy. I wave to them, but no response follows. They are too busy, drinking coffee and checking documents. No big deal.

At 8 am we open.

Instead of loans for business, nowadays most people come to the bank to borrow money for food and paying bills. Being helpless and in despair, they often tell you heartbreaking stories and cry. They may threaten and curse you, upon hearing a refusal. The problem is that in most cases we have no choice but to refuse, following the unforgiving rules of the bank.

By the time my lunch hour finally rolls around, I am dog tired and hungry. My empty stomach produces embarrassing growling noises. I count out the last coins in my pocket and get a cup of black coffee. As I enter the tiny dining room, I see Mandy and Tim eating sandwiches at the table.

"Where's your lunch, youngster?" Tim asks. He is a short arrogant guy, hardly older than me.

"I'm not hungry," I lie. "Ate a huge breakfast at home."

"I hate eating breakfast," Mandy says. "Although my mom gets angry with me, if I don't. She thinks it's the most important meal of the day."

Mandy is a chubby plain girl, who lives with her parents and doesn't have to suffer many hardships. Not exactly the sharpest knife in the drawer, she has a tendency for saying something really stupid at times. She seems all right, though. Kind of harmless and simple.

"Did you see Lola Great's show?" Tim asks.

"I did!" Mandy blurts out proudly. Her eyes sparkle with excitement. "It was terrific!"

I feel a chill creeping up my spine. They've just selected the worst topic possible. As part of her spectacularly sadistic show, Lola Great describes in detail the capture and processing of mind breakers. Man, they even orchestrate an execution complete with a dead body still convulsing from spasms. The show receives the highest rating in the network.

Now tensed up, I take a big sip of hot coffee.

"Are you all right?" Mandy asks. She's noticed a change in my expression.

I take a breath and force a smile, trying to relax.

"God!" Tim says. "Those darn breakers are real freaks. The last one killed two families with little kids after stealing all their money."

I raise my eyebrows in pretended astonishment of his revelations.

"I'm so scared of them!" Mandy says. "What if I meet one? He could do whatever he wants to me and I'd be totally helpless."

"You wish," Tim says, laughing. "No, just don't look into their eyes. Lola says they use their stare to manipulate people. If I ever meet one, I'm gonna poke out his eyes and smash in his head. Just keep punching the damn thing till he falls down and can't use his evil tricks on me."

I stare right into his eyes and nod, faking agreement. It sucks to be me. I have to adapt and live a lie every day in order to keep my secret. No true friends. No real trust. Anybody could turn on me at the drop of a hat, calling Elimination. Except Kitty, of course. Being a breaker like me, she's the only person I can believe in.

"Maybe all that's just for ratings and they aren't all evil," I suggest quietly.

Both mouths drop in surprise.

"Are you crazy?" Tim asks.

"Well, think about it," I say. "All breakers can't be the same. Some must be bad and some good. Just like us, normal people."

Mandy blinks, looking confused. Tim shakes his head.

"No way! They're not normal at all," he says. "Those stinking freaks can only kill and rob people. That's their nature. They can't resist all the temptations that their power brings. Just imagine if you can walk into a bank, take all the money and leave unnoticed. If you could ask a stranger to give away his wallet and erase your face from his memory." He shakes his head again. "No way can they resist doing it. It's too easy."

I shrug my shoulders, having no desire to debate.

"Maybe you're right," I say.

"Of course I'm right," Tim blurts out. "Anyway, why the heck are you protecting them?" He narrows his eyes in suspicion. "Maybe you're one of them, a freaking mind breaker?"

For an instant, I feel like I'm losing control. One incautious word might ruin my entire life.

"Oh, sure," I roll my eyes. "I'm an evil mind breaker," I say with exaggeration. "I'm gonna kill you guys and make off with all the cash. Right after I finish my coffee, which you surely would have paid for were I a breaker."

I smile slightly, then screw my face into a shocked frown. Tim and Mandy burst out laughing. Sometimes telling a half truth is the best way to hide.

"There's a new movie about mind breakers," Mandy says. "The preview looked really cool. Breakers and normal people falling in love all over the place." She suddenly gives me a strange look. "Do you wanna watch it with me?" she asks.

Everything tightens inside me. Is she asking for a date? I didn't see it coming. I can't let people get really close. It's too dangerous, too easy to reveal your secrets. People can get rewards, informing Elimination about hiding breakers.

"Well," I say to Mandy. "You probably won't enjoy when the breakers start blowing up heads in that movie. No, sorry. I'm too busy anyway. Have to take care of my little sister."

Looking away, Mandy seems upset. I can't help feeling a little guilty, although I shouldn't. I'm just protecting my life.

Our boss Mr. Thompson comes in grumbling that we're a couple of minutes late for getting back to work.

"Customers are waiting out there," he says strictly. "Let's get a move on."

I finish off my coffee quickly and hurry back to the desk. My head hurts. I'm tired with all this mumbling about evil mind breakers. Gosh, I hope my work day will end soon.

And it does end earlier. Only not the way I wanted.

The door slams open widely and three men dressed in military style clothes and black ski masks charge into the office with guns drawn.

CHAPTER 2

"Everybody, on the floor now! This is a robbery!" a harsh voice slices through the air.

Bullets crash into the ceiling, sending down clouds of white dust.

I flinch, startled. Adrenaline runs through my veins. My legs turn weak. I can't believe what's happening. It feels unreal, like something straight out of a bad dream.

The intruders point their guns at us, looking a little too eager to start shooting. Shocked and frightened, people collapse on the floor as ordered. Somebody screams. A security guy flings his arms up and stares at the gunmen. His eyes widen, full of terror. An intruder disarms him quickly and shoves him to the ground. Everything is happening too fast for the guard to react.

I'm the only one still left standing who hasn't complied. My fingers clench into fists. The splitting headache explodes under my skull. A well-known sensation, which usually means I'm ready to hypnotize.

"Hey, you idiot!" one of the intruders yells. "Can't you hear? I said get down!"

He slams the rigid barrel of a .45 into my chest.

Instinctively, I step back, eyes fixed on the deadly weapon. It's been a long time since anybody threatened me with a gun. This is turning into a really nasty day.

"Do you think you're freaking special?" the man shouts. "Get on the floor!"

His voice is assertive, but his hands are shaking. Possibly, this is his first robbery attempt. Being on edge, he may panic and pull the trigger at any moment.

I struggle with instincts that scream to hypnotize him. No, it's too risky. I can't reveal my secret. Too many witnesses around. Cameras on the walls to capture every move I make. I mustn't do anything foolish.

I kneel down slowly, my eyes glued to the barrel. The nervous perp watches me carefully. A large drop of sweat runs down his neck. I can hear his heavy ragged breathing. Avoiding jerky movements, I sprawl on the floor interlocking my fingers behind my head. This seems to satisfy the guy and he passes on by.

"Where's the money?" he yells in an unsteady voice, waving his gun in the air. The other two seem anxious as well. They fidget back and forth on their feet, pointing weapons at people. Tension fills the room.

I have a bad feeling about this. They could be on drugs, unpredictable and crazy.

Be still, I order myself. Don't do anything stupid. It'll be over soon.

Mr. Thompson raises a hand and gestures toward the teller drawers and vault. Two gunmen head over. As they pass the security guard, he scrambles onto his feet and charges into one of the intruders, tackling him. They both hit the ground, grappling. The security officer grabs the robber's arm, trying to yank the gun away. The second assailant comes from behind and puts a bullet into his head.

I shudder from the explosion.

A long spray of blood and brains covers the white floor. People scream in horror. Somebody sobs hysterically. The guard's body sags down and becomes motionless. Murdered!

I shut my eyes for a second, snarling in silent fury.

"Nobody moves!" comes a harsh command.

Agitatedly, the gunmen confront the hostages, waving their weapons. People are praying out loud, terrified. Panicking, our boss stands up. He has a frantic look on his face.

I feel sick to my stomach, realizing what may happen.

"Please," Mr. Thompson yells. "Please, stop it!"

Angered, the robbers fire their guns. The bullets strike Mr. Thompson, instantly opening holes in his chest. His mouth gapes open in a silent plea for help, as he falls over. I notice a growing blood stain on Mr. Thompson's white shirt and his still wide open eyes, although I guess he's very much dead.

"Who else?" one of the robbers shouts. "Who else wants to be a hero?"

I lie motionless, fighting the impulse to act. Stay still. Forget who you are. Don't be stupid. Pain pulsates in my head. Damn it! Where's the police when we need them so much?

The thieves verify containment of those on the floor and walk over to the safe. A huge metal contraption, built into the wall. It's securely locked, virtually impossible to crack.

One gunman, apparently the leader, approaches Tim, pointing a gun.

"You! Get up! Now open the safe!"

Sweating, Tim shakes his head. His eyes turn moist, as if on the verge of tears. I've never seen him like this before.

"I can't," he says.

"Oh, you'll do it all right," the guy threatens, smashing his face with the butt of the gun. Blood sprays from Tim's nose. He gulps, covering his head with trembling hands.

"I can't," Tim repeats. "I don't know the combination."

"You think I'm an idiot?" the robber asks as he pistol whips Tim once again. Tim lets out a short cry, his body shuddering from pain and fear.

This is insane. He's gonna kill Tim. I can't remain quiet any longer.

"It's true," I say. "Only the manager knows the combination to the safe."

"Which of you is the manager?" the robber asks.

"He's the guy you've just shot," Tim answers softly.

The robber glances at Thompson's unmoving body. Growling, he strikes Tim again.

"She knows the combination as well," Tim mumbles, gesturing toward Mandy. "She's a lead teller. She can open the safe."

I can't believe Tim just ratted her out. My heart sinks. Poor silly and helpless Mandy.

As the criminal approaches, Mandy cries out and begins to crawl away. He catches her long hair with one hand and yanks her into a sitting position.

"What's the combination, sweetheart?" he asks, giving her a hard slap across her face.

Mandy opens her mouth widely, sucking in air like a fish out of water.

"What's the combination?" the gunman repeats, shaking her fiercely.

I raise my head a little, watching in despair. What should I do? I have to protect myself and Kitty. Revealing my mind breaking abilities would be suicide.

"Answer!" the criminal says, slapping Mandy.

She stares at him with empty eyes. Her lips move, but no sound comes out. Paralyzed with fear, Mandy can't speak.

I have to do something so I cautiously get up. Two robbers point guns at me instantly. Time slows to a crawl and I feel my heart pounding in my chest.

"She can't speak," I say, keeping my voice steady.

"Shut your mouth!" the leader shouts.

"Just let me calm her down," I ask.

"Get on the floor!" he orders.

I kneel down again, lowering my head. I wait for bullets to pierce my body any second. One jerky movement and they'll shoot. But somehow I make it back down on the floor, having survived the moment. The robbers are too busy working on Mandy.

"Answer!" the criminal yells again. "You can know I'll freaking blow your head off otherwise."

He presses the gun into her forehead. Mandy manages only a few incoherent noises, eyes twitching as blood drips from her lips and nose. Mandy is completely in shock.

My head hurts terribly. I can't stand to watch it anymore, but unable to look away. I hear a click as the robber thumbs the hammer of the gun against Mandy's head.

"Just stop," I say, directing my thoughts toward the robber.

I can almost physically sense how I capture his mind. My psychic suggestion reaches his brain, momentarily grasping hold and tentatively controlling his will. It takes only a second. He turns toward me, puzzled. His eyes are glazed and inattentive. Thank God, I don't feel any resistance. Everything goes smoothly.

"Lower your gun and let her go," I say quietly, getting on my feet. "You don't wanna hurt her."

He blinks a few times, thinking, but can't understand what's happening. His grip weakens, letting Mandy free. She collapses to the floor, crying.

"Drop the gun," I command.

He hesitates only for an instant. Then his gun falls to his feet. The other two robbers stare in shock.

"He's a stinking breaker!" one of them shouts. "Shoot him and don't look into his eyes!"

I don't have time to pick up the weapon. The surprise wears off quickly, as both robbers backpedal, shooting. Fortunately, the fools believe in myths about breakers hypnotizing people by eye contact and turn away from me as they fire. They miss. I drop down and crawl behind my desk as a hail of bullets slam into the walls and furniture, splintering the wood. Not good protection, but at the moment I have no other place to take cover.

The hypnotized thief still stands motionless like a statue, peering into nowhere.

"Shoot them!" I yell to him. "They wanna kill you!"

He glances over at his partners, picks up the gun from the floor and fires. One of the other gunmen grunts, bending and pressing a hand into his stomach. His legs give out and he falls.

This is my chance.

I leap out from behind my desk, charging into the criminal still standing. I grip his wrist, preventing him from using the gun while slamming an elbow into his jaw. The robber clenches my shirt as he falls, pulling me off balance. We crash together onto the floor. I roll on top, smashing my fist into his ribs. I still hold his gun hand tightly, keeping the barrel away from my head. The guy begins choking me with his free hand. I grab his fingers and bend them back violently to breathe. Two fingers snap, breaking. The criminal cries out in pain.

I notice the gut shot robber rising up a few feet away, gun in hand. Apparently, he's survived.

"No, don't," I blurt out, concentrating hard. I've never broken two people at the same time. Maybe I've run out of strength and am unable to perplex his mind.

"Shoot him!" the robber underneath me yells. "Kill this stinking freak!"

"I'm your friend," I say. "He's a breaker. Shoot him." I move my head, gesturing to his partner.

The blast of the gunshot deafens me for a second. The bullet whistles close by my ear and smashes into the criminal's face. I roll away. A large puddle of dark blood spreads on the floor. The body stops moving.

Disoriented and trying to catch my breath, I turn around. The wounded robber stares in confusion at his gun. I scramble onto my feet and grab his weapon. He doesn't protest, still being under my hypnosis, which may not last. I slam the gun into his temple, knocking him out cold. Have I killed him or is he just unconscious? Whatever.

Swaying, I walk to the Mr. Thompson's body. I kneel down and check his pulse, not really expecting to find one. Surprisingly, I feel slight pulsation under my fingers. I can't believe it. How can anybody survive such a severe wound? His shirt stains red in warm blood.

"Someone call emergency!" I yell. "He's still alive!"

Nobody rushes to help. Nobody even moves. The customers and bank workers stare at me in stark utter horror.

"It's all over," I say. "You're all safe. Now will someone please call for help?"

People shudder at the sound of my voice and turn away. Some even cover their eyes. Suddenly I understand. They're frightened and intimidated by me, having made me as a mind breaker.

"Hey," I say. "This is just me. You're safe. I won't hurt you."

They don't care. I'm now a monster to them, a blood lusting freak of nature.

I hear sirens. Police are on the way. Somebody must have sounded a silent alarm. The cameras inside the building have recorded all my actions. There are also plenty of witnesses, and these people know my name and address. Only now I realize the scope of catastrophic trouble I'm in. Feels like I'm standing at the edge of a great abyss. My life has just crumbled within a matter of minutes, everything going to hell.

As I think of my next move, a well-armed SWAT team arrives at the scene. Seeing two gunmen dead and the third sitting on the floor in a stupor, the team spreads around the room, covering everyone.

"Everybody stay calm and remain on the floor!" they order, holding their assault rifles ready.

"He's a breaker!" Tim screams, pointing at me. Darn Tim! He's selling out everybody today.

They surround me in a semi-circle.

"Drop your weapon!" they order. "Face down, you're under arrest!"

To most, just being a mind breaker is worse than any crime I could possibly commit.

I've never felt so desperate and doomed in my entire life. Not knowing what action to take, I can only stare at all the gun barrels leveled at me. No choice but to drop the gun and get down on the floor.

If you give up now, you'll be dead, a thought swirls in my mind. They'll send you straight to Elimination where there's no mercy for breakers. You'll be imprisoned, tortured, and finally killed.

A jolt of excruciating pain in my head blinds me for a moment. I shudder as I project my thoughts toward the team. Attempting to hypnotize multiple people at the same time is something new and untried. I get the sense of tremendous power from within, triggered by basic survival instinct.

"Let me go," I hear my own rough voice. "Back off!"

The officers still aim their weapons at me, but there's an almost imperceptible change in their features. Eyes become blank, void of all expression.

"Drop your guns," I order, concentrating hard. There may be too many of them. These guys are tough. I have to transfer my thoughts with all the force I can muster to break their wills. My head is foggy. I'm running out of energy. I begin to sway on my feet, risking a blackout. My nose bleeds profusely, splattering onto my shirt.

The SWAT team stands unmoving. They're still holding the rifles tightly. Being too weak, I can't back them up or make them drop the weapons. At least I've broken their will to shoot me. Their minds are cloudy, not perceiving reality correctly. Good enough to escape if I hurry.

I take slow and unsteady steps toward the exit. The officers stand frozen like lifeless mannequins. I walk between them, holding my breath and trying not to accidentally bump them. Anything may snap their mind out of the hypnosis.

"Don't move," I say. "Keep still."

I feel their resistance. Some of the officers follow me with their glazed eyes. Then each face begins turning my direction. Bad sign. They may shake off their trance at any moment. I need to get the heck out of here!

Leaving them behind, I walk hurriedly to the rear door which empties into an alley behind the bank. Using the main entrance isn't an option. My legs are shaky, but I must move as fast as I can. The pain in my head is making me sick.

I have to find the fire exit located somewhere in the back part of the building. Hopefully, the police haven't blocked it yet. Sirens wail and I know that more are coming.

I run along the hallway. It seems endless. I hear rattling of gunfire behind. Still being drowsy and confused, the officers can't give chase yet, but they've apparently recovered enough to use their rifles. Several bullets crash into a nearby wall.

Don't stop, I tell myself. Keep moving.

At last I come to the fire exit and slam into the door. Locked! The sound of heavy footsteps is getting closer. Without looking, I fire a few rounds in the direction of my pursuers. Hopefully I didn't kill anybody. I didn't ask for this, but now have no choice but to fight and protect myself and Kitty.

Frantically, I kick the door hard. It cracks, but doesn't give. I hit it with my shoulder, putting all my weight into a motion. The door breaks, splitting open and the momentum throws me out onto the concrete. I land on my hands and knees, immediately looking around. No sign of cops. They haven't had time to cover all of the exits of the building yet.

My legs are aching and my nose is still dripping blood, but there's no time for rest. I have to run and put as much distance between myself and the cops as possible. If they see me, they won't simply use pepper spray or a taser. An armed breaker on the run? They'll shoot first and ask questions later.

I scramble back to my feet and take off running, not looking back.

I know of a park nearby with dense overgrown shrubbery which might provide temporary shelter. No one has gardened there for a long time. Nobody even walks there anymore. I run lightly, setting my sites on the park in hopes of shaking pursuit.

Reaching the edge of the park, thick bushes with gnarled thorns scratch my hands and face. When I'm far enough in, I fall on the ground and lie motionless, catching my breath. Seems I can hardly move. I hypnotized too many people back there at once and my strength is gone. How did I control the entire SWAT team? The extreme situation must have altered something in my brain, unleashing some kind of hidden reserves. Now my blood pressure is dropping. All breakers suffer some type of symptoms after hypnosis and I'm no exception. I press my aching head against the cold soil. I can't run anymore. I want to close my eyes and fall unconscious.

The sounds of approaching voices startle me awake. I can't give up now, especially after what's happened at the bank.

Gasping, I cross the park and come to a street with light traffic. As I enter the intersection, an angry looking young man in a sports car speeds up to act like he's gonna hit me. He slams on his brakes at the last second, skidding to a stop just inches away. I get a crazy idea. Suddenly I turn, brandishing my gun.

"Stop!" I yell as I pull the trigger, shooting out a headlight. "Get out!" I order, pointing the gun at the driver. I won't shoot him unless I have to, but he doesn't know that.

Having suddenly recovered from his bout of road-rage, the now scared guy steps slowly out of the vehicle, staring at me.

"I'm taking your car, start walking," I calmly say, continuing to wave the gun.

I watch the hesitant young man take a few steps away. I get in the car knowing I can't allow myself feelings of guilt. I have to survive and warn Kitty.

I've driven only a few times in my life, mostly on abandoned roads and that was farm machinery. The car is still running. I place my hands on the wheel. My foot finds the pedal. The sound of not too distant sirens urges me to act. I romp on the gas, making the vehicle leap forward. It's too fast and jerky, all over the road. Startled, I slam on the brakes and the impact of the car abruptly stopping smashes me against the steering wheel. The horn goes off, bringing unwanted attention to my growing predicament. Other vehicles are stopping, waiting for me to clear out from the middle of the road. The sirens are getting louder, too close now. I have to hurry.

Pressing the gas pedal more gently this time, I drive down the street. My fingers turn white from gripping the wheel and sweat drips down my neck. Navigating between other cars is one heck of a task at first. I have trouble with staying in my lane. Near misses begin to pile up with several instances of avoiding a collision by only a few inches. A large truck swerves out of my way and collides with another vehicle in a violent wreck. Police cars drive past them, now on my tail.

Miraculously, I drive through a busy intersection and come to the devastated part of the city. There's no other traffic around so I increase speed, trying to lose my pursuit. It doesn't quite work out the way I'd planned. I hit a pothole, sending the car into a crazy spin. The steering wheel jerks, jarring my wrists, and the world turns upside down. The front window crashes, spraying pieces of glass into my face. Something hard slams into my head as I'm swallowed by absolute blackness.

CHAPTER 3

I awaken to the stench of gasoline. When I open my eyes, everything is deathly still. The car lies on its roof while I'm stuck inside, upside down and unable to move. Pain racks my body. I feel like I've broken every bone. My chest hurts with every breath. Sirens fill the air around me. I see flashing red and blue lights through the broken window.

Two policemen jog toward the car, searching for me. They kneel, peering inside. I close my eyes and try to concentrate, overcoming the crushing pain in my chest and head. I have to twist their minds. It's my only chance to be free.

"He's not here," I say through clinched teeth.

Nothing happens for a few moments. I remain motionless, waiting. Time seems to stop. I don't know if policemen see me or not. Maybe I'm too weak to break them.

Then I hear a loud voice, "Negative on the suspect, he's not here!"

"Anybody see which direction he went?"

"Let's do a thorough search and send officers to check his place of residence."

It works. I take a deep breath in relief. One noise and police will understand that I'm still in a car. I have to keep silent.

Kitty! I need to find her. The cops already have my address. Searching for me, they will arrive at my apartment and find Kitty just returned from school. Unprepared, she'll be vulnerable. I can't let it happen.

I get an awful picture of my little sister being shot. The thought brings mental anguish to add to the physical pains I'm already suffering. I have to reach Kitty before the police.

Gasping for air and struggling with the seatbelt, I manage to crawl out of the vehicle through the broken front window. Taking a look around, I realize that this area is only a few blocks from home.

Limping, I stagger hurriedly in the direction of our apartment building. My left knee aches. My vision is blurry. I can see almost nothing with my right eye. I must have injured it as well. Convulsions shake my body and I fall, landing on my hands and knees. I close my eyes tightly for a moment. It's all too much. I can't handle all this pain and suffering on top of being hated and chased.

No, you can't give up, I tell myself. You can't fail Kitty. Now get up and move, you wimp!

The image of my sister snaps me back to reality. Grinding my teeth together and gathering all my will power, I push myself up and stand still for a few seconds. Keeping my head down, I wait for my mind to clear. Breathe, just breathe and regain your balance. There you go. Now move.

I limp along the street, swaying and stumbling like a drunkard. I haven't the strength to conceal my identity from any passersby. Thank goodness, only a few homeless are out wandering around. They could care less.

The sight of our apartment building sends goose bumps down my spine. Is she still alive or not? What if police have already arrived and shot her? I groan miserably at the thought. Regaining a second wind, I proceed.

I can't lose Kitty. She's my whole world. I can't let anything happen to her.

Breathless, I enter the building. It's dark and silent. No sign of the police. Maybe it's not too late? I rush up the dilapidated stairs leading to our apartment. They seem endless. The stairwell creaks with each step, ready to break.

Finally I see our door. I smack into it, turning the handle up and down. My shaky hands search for the keys in my pockets. I must have lost them in the accident, or during all the fighting and running before. Insanely, I pound the door with my fists.

"Kitty!" I scream at the top of my lungs. "Kitty, open the door!"

Panicked, I don't care about police who may be already waiting inside. Forget about any neighbors who might hear me yelling like a madman. I just want to see my sister right now. One more minute of waiting and I'll lose my mind.

The door opens suddenly and there she is…unharmed. Still dressed in her school uniform. Seeing such a mess standing before her, Kitty's jaw drops and her eyes widen.

"Holy cow!" she exclaims.

I push her back inside our apartment and shut the door behind. All the blood suddenly drains from my head and the room darkens. Not feeling my legs, I slide down the wall and sit on the hard floor, resting. I know there's no time for a reprieve, but can't help taking a moment to collect myself.

"What the heck happened?" Kitty asks.

I open my mouth, but can't speak.

"Hold on," Kitty says, running off.

My mind floats between a dream world and reality. All sounds seem muffled. Objects fade and silhouettes mix together. I drop my head down, fighting a bit of nausea rising in my throat.

Kitty wipes my cheeks and forehead with a towel.

"Wake up," I hear Kitty's voice. "Rex, wake up."

Her hand gently slaps my face. Kitty crouches beside me, holding a towel now stained with my blood.

"What happened to you?" she asks.

"The cops are coming. We have to get out of here."

Kitty thinks for a second. Her eyes darken.

"Do they know that you're a breaker?" she asks.

I nod.

"Damn it!" she cusses.

"I'm so sorry," I say. "I had no other choice. I had to save my coworkers. Those thieves would have killed them."

"Really?" Kitty says. "What about us? What about me?"

I don't know what to tell her. Kitty sighs and helps me get up.

"It's unbelievable," she says. "Why do you always have to be the freaking hero?"

She's right. I screwed up. I always thought it'd be Kitty bringing Elimination down on us. What a fool! I was so wrong.

"We gotta go," I say. "They could be here at any moment."

Kitty searches for her shoes. She's no longer scared. Her expression reflects only disappointment.

I change into an oversized hoodie and old pair of black jeans. The hood is large enough to hide half of my face. Hopefully, it will prevent people on the street from recognizing me.

The loud wail of sirens makes my heart skip a beat. They're already here! There's no time left. I feel like a cornered, wounded animal.

"Kitty," I call, running to her bedroom. She's ready, dressed in warm flat boots and a coat above her school uniform.

"Let's go," I say, grabbing Kitty's hand and pulling her toward the exit.

The door shudders from a violent strike. A few cracks split its wooden surface. I stop abruptly. It's already too late. I take a last desperate look around, trapped. Thick metal bars cross our windows, cutting off our last chance of escape. Nowhere to go. The police are breaking in.

"Help me put them under," Kitty says. "Make them think we're not here."

The door breaks down and several officers rush inside, brandishing firearms. I step to the wall and close my eyes, concentrating. We're not here, I repeat in my mind desperately, we've left.

I hear heavy footsteps and a dog barking. Every muscle in my body tenses so much that it hurts. I stand motionless, scared to move. If they see us, we're done for. If our ploy doesn't work, we'll be sent straight to prison or shot. I feel vulnerable and exposed. One simple thought swirls in my mind I keep repeating over and over. Not here, nobody home, they've already left.

A minute passes with nobody shooting or handcuffing us. Anxiously, I open my eyes and see policemen walking right past me, searching the apartment.

"Clear!" somebody yells from our kitchen. "He's not here!"

"Damn it," the policeman standing beside me spits out in anger.

I breathe out slowly and glance to my left, checking on Kitty. My sister stands propping her back to the wall. Her lips curl into a mocking smile. Unbelievable. She's enjoying it. Hypnosis seems to give her no headache.

Feeling my astounded gaze, Kitty turns to me and winks playfully.

"It's all right," she says. "We're holding them."

How on earth can she speak, while I can barely keep myself upright? My legs are weak and my head dizzy. Doesn't she feel any of that herself? Kitty must be an even stronger breaker than I ever realized.

The officers are trashing the apartment, opening closets and throwing our meager belongings onto the floor.

An officer with a huge German shepherd enters the apartment. Passing me, the dog stops, sniffing the air. Its ears twitch, listening closely.

"Hey," the officer says, yanking the leash. "What's wrong, boy?"

The dog emits a low growl and bares its razor sharp teeth. Relying more on instincts than logic, animals are darn hard to twist.

I'm sweating. Not here, I project, you can't see me.

The dog barks, rising up on its hind legs. The officer pulls back on the leash, almost falling off balance, but thankfully preventing this furious animal from attacking me.

"Bad dog," he says. "Stop!"

"What's wrong with Buck?" another officer asks.

"No idea," the dog owner answers. "He's been acting a bit strange today."

Buck continues going crazy, barking and charging toward me. His teeth snap at the air inches away from my leg.

The officers move closer, narrowing their focus. I concentrate even harder to keep their minds foggy. My headache is making me sick. I'm losing it. Their wills seem to strengthen with each passing moment. Their minds fight relentlessly against me, resisting continued suggestions. One of them puts his face close to mine and stares right at me. I hold my breath. I already know what's about to happen.

Suddenly the policeman flinches, letting out a short burst of surprise. He blinks a few times, shaking his head and not believing what he's seeing.

"What's wrong?" the cop with the dog asks.

"He's right here!" his partner screams. "Can't you see?" He shoves the gun in my face. "Don't move, punk!"

This is getting worse than any nightmare.

Kitty reacts instantly, pointing a finger at the officer in front of me.

"That's him!" I hear her screaming. "Get him! He's the breaker!"

The policemen turn their heads, raising their guns.

"No," the officer pointing the weapon at me says. "Don't listen to her. She's a breaker too!"

"Drop your weapon, freak," his partner orders.

"Run," I hear Kitty's demanding voice as her hand grips mine, pulling me away. Still overcoming nausea from the car accident, I follow along as fast as I can. The space behind me explodes into gunfire and shrill cries. They're shooting each other, I realize. How in the world could Kitty have confused them so easily?

No time to think. We need distance first, now running for our lives. The effect of hypnosis won't last after we leave. Their minds will clear within seconds and they'll be looking for us with a vengeance.

Outside it's cold and getting dark. The fresh air does bring some relief for my headache. I feel better and am able to jog again. Fast and full of energy, Kitty runs ahead leading the way. We change direction several times, stopping only briefly to catch our breath. The sound of sirens blare in the distance. Hopefully they've lost us.

"Where should we go?" Kitty asks.

I stand still, thinking. I haven't faced such a situation before.

"Let's try to get outside the city," I offer, concealing my doubts.

Kitty nods in agreement and we're off again. I pull my hood down low as I move, turning away from any random people crossing our path. My face might already be in the news so caution is warranted. I was considered a dangerous criminal, just being a mind breaker. Now after the incident at the bank and this run in with police, I may even become public enemy number one. The police are after us, and the Elimination force may already be tracking as well.

Finally, after passing countless blocks of dilapidated buildings, we reach the woods. It's quiet and peaceful here. I can no longer hear any sirens. Now we need to find some sort of shelter. I'm too weak and worn out to continue walking. Kitty seems tired as well. Arriving at an abandoned house, we decide to spend the night inside, although it's still very risky.

"I'm hungry," Kitty complains in a hollow voice. I nod in understanding. My stomach is empty as well.

We search the kitchen area for anything edible. This is an enormous two floor mansion where wealthy people must have resided long ago. Now it's empty, with looted rooms, broken windows and crumbling walls. We find nothing but trash.

Exhausted, we plop down on the floor to collect ourselves.

"So, what happened earlier?" Kitty asks.

I tell her about the robbery and killings at the bank. She listens attentively, offering no comments while I'm speaking. Her pale face is stone cold and insensitive. I have no idea what's going on inside her head.

"Let me get this right," Kitty says after I finish telling my story. "So the life of that silly, stupid girl meant more to you than mine."

"Kitty, please," I protest. "Why are you talking that way?"

We remain silent for a few minutes. Kitty bites her lower lip, deep in thought. Actually, she's right. I chose to protect others instead of protecting her. Guilt burns through me like fire.

"I'm sorry," I say. "I really screwed up."

"It's okay," Kitty answers. "I'm actually pleased that it's turned out this way."

"What?" I can't believe my ears.

"I'm sick and tired with all this hiding," she says. "Now we can do whatever we wish. True freedom! Just like I've been dreaming about."

"What are you talking about?" I exclaim. "Our lives are ruined and we're on the run. How in the world is that your dream?"

"Our lives were pretty miserable before," Kitty answers. "I hated that stinking apartment we could barely afford. I hated going to that nasty school where all those idiots were making fun of me every day just because I was poor. Hated to watch you counting out our last penny and tired of being scared all the time. That's all over with now. We don't have to lie or pretend to be people we aren't. We can fight them now and finally be ourselves."

"Are you insane?" I ask. "Whom are we gonna fight? Elimination?"

"Whomever stands in our way," Kitty says.

I just shake my head.

"You're out of your mind," I say. "An entire army of well-trained resistant soldiers are looking under every rock for us now. We need to find a safe place to hide and become scarce."

"Oh, my goodness," Kitty groans. "Why do you always have to act like this?"

"Like what?" I ask.

"Like you're afraid of being a breaker and hate trying even now, when it's time to soldier up," Kitty answers.

"Of course, I hate it," I say with exasperation. "I'm sick of being a freak of nature. I just want to be normal."

"I don't!" she yells. "We're not normal, Rex. And the time for worrying about it has passed. I love being a breaker. I enjoy having power to control people. Now that they've come for us, I'm gonna put that little gift to good use."

"Forget about it, Kitty," I say. "No more fighting. Tomorrow we'll head south toward some small town where we're not recognized, and start all over again."

"Oh, really?" Kitty questions. "And what if I don't want to go?"

"You'll have to go anyway."

"What makes you think you should be the one to always make every decision?" Kitty asks, her voice trembling. "Why should I have to do only what you want?"

"Because I'm your older brother and know what's best!" I answer in anger.

"You're not really my brother!" Kitty snaps.

Wow, I feel like somebody just dumped a bucket of ice water on my head.

"Don't say that!" I protest. It takes all my effort to keep my voice lowered.

Kitty jumps to her feet and stomps away as if she's frightened. Her eyes sparkle in the darkness, becoming moist.

"It's true!" she shouts. "I'm so sick of playing this stupid little sibling game. I won't pretend to be your sister anymore, Rex. Your real sister along with your mother betrayed you long ago. I'm not them and I'm nothing like them. I'll never abandon you."

Having spoken from her heart, Kitty turns and runs off. I don't follow. Being so angry, I could lose self-control and say something even worse. We both need time to cool down.

I sit on the floor, holding my aching head and trying to think. Kitty is the only family I have left. Four years ago I found her homeless in the street, scrawny and hungry. She was using her breaker abilities to steal money and food. I remember like it was yesterday.

I was on my way home, deeply immersed in thought. It was my first year in a new and sometimes hostile city. I was close to utter despair, having been rejected by everybody I had known before. I could trust nobody. No family or friends. A wall of distrust and fear separated me from all normal people. I felt like a freak and was lonely all the time.

She stepped out from the shadows walking toward me, tiny and pitiful. I stopped, stunned. Some features in her bruised hollow face resembled my lost sister. Her tangled filthy hair had the same reddish color. She had the same green eyes.

She actually tried to rob me, not knowing that I'm a breaker as well and not subject to her hypnosis. When she understood, Kitty turned and ran. I chased her for a long time. When finally I caught up to her, she hissed and scratched at me like a feral animal.

"Let me go," she pleaded. "I didn't know you're like me."

"Calm down," I suggested. "I won't hurt you."

"Yes, you will," she said accusingly. "Everybody tries to hurt me!"

I had no idea what she had gone through before, being homeless and facing dangerous strangers every day. Eleven-year-old Kitty was an orphan. Maybe her parents just abandoned her, upon learning she was a breaker. It happens often in our world.

I offered shelter and food. Kitty accepted, although she didn't trust me at first, even being scared to walk into the apartment. I had to bring food for her outside. After that first evening, Kitty began coming to me every day.

"You're like a kitty cat," I joked. "You come around only when you're hungry."

That was how she became known as Kitty. She never told me her real name, saying only that she hated it. Kitty suited her much better.

One rainy night she knocked on my door and when I saw her my heart ached with pity. My Kitty could barely stand on her own two feet. Her eyes were watering and face was pale. She had the flu.

Passing out, she fell straight into my arms. So needful of shelter and care, Kitty couldn't remain cautious anymore. She chose to trust me, entering my apartment for the first time. She was wordless. Her face had a strange expression of hopelessness and fear. I could do whatever I wished to her. And all I wished was for her to become my sister.

I bathed her and put her to bed. I offered her all the food I could round up. Then I ran down to the drug store and bought all the medicine I could afford. I was caring for Kitty as if she were my own child. Most of time she remained silent, but her look was becoming softer. The fear was melting in her eyes.

"Why are you doing it?" she asked. "Why are you helping me?"

I couldn't really explain. Probably, I was just afraid of being lonely again.

In a couple of weeks Kitty got well, but didn't leave me. She always thought I was the most kind and generous person ever because I'd saved her. In reality, it was her who saved me from complete and utter loneliness. She became my only friend, somebody whom I could genuinely trust and care for. Although we're not related by blood, as far as I'm concerned, Kitty will always be my little sister.

She returns in the middle of the night. I can't see her face in darkness, but can tell she's been crying.

"Please, forgive me," she pleads, offering a warm hug. "I didn't mean what I said earlier."

"That's okay," I say, holding her. "Nothing to forgive, we just need some rest."

"I can be your sister anytime you please," Kitty adds. "I guess I could be whoever you want."

I'm too tired to figure out what that means at the moment. My head aches. I feel like I got run over by a truck. Truly, it's been a long day.

I close my eyes, but can't fall asleep. I remain fully awake almost till sunrise. Kitty is lying beside me, snuggled up close and dreaming peacefully. Her head is resting on my shoulder. I watch her sleep. Kitty seems even younger than she really is. Her small face seems so childish and untroubled. What will happen to her now? What will happen to us? Gloomy thoughts swirl in my head. I see nothing good coming in the future.

You have to protect Kitty, I say to myself. No matter what, don't let Elimination get to her. Even at the cost of your own life.

When I wake in the morning, Kitty's gone. I call her name, but she doesn't answer. Panicking, I search the entire house, checking every room. She's left me!

I run outside searching, and suddenly see her walking toward me. Kitty smiles and raises the bag she's carrying.

"What the heck?" I say. "Where did you go?"

"There's a little town twenty minutes away," she answers. "I got us some food."

Great. While I was going crazy not knowing what happened, Kitty was robbing a store.

"You can't do this," I say. "Somebody may recognize you."

"Oh, c'mon," Kitty answers. "I'm a strong breaker. Nobody remembered anything. It's just food, and yes, they did think I paid for it."

I look angrily into her beautiful yet shameless eyes and see nothing mean or malicious in them. Kitty doesn't fully realize the consequences of her actions.

I sigh. Anyway, we have to eat. Having no money, hypnosis is the only option left at the moment.

Kitty opens her sack and pulls out a hotdog, juicy and still warm. I feel a hungry spasm in my stomach. I eat greedily, with no guilt for consuming stolen food now. Then I drink the bottle of water that Kitty provides.

"I also have chips and some candy," she says. "Plus cookies and milk for later."

Kitty seems very proud of herself and happy to be useful.

After breakfast we finally agree to head south. It's the wildest part of our country, where practically no law exists. Mostly just farmers live there, who simply shoot or hang any thieves trying to rob their farms. Home to me, this is where I grew up. Hopefully, nobody's been watching the news too closely down there.

We pass through the woods coming to a torn up highway. Some people still use it for traveling. An occasional car passes by, but they're not paying any attention. We pick one out with a neutral color. Kitty closes her eyes, concentrating, and the vehicle stops. A driver steps out, his face calm and indifferent.

"He won't remember us," Kitty says, smiling.

"Doesn't it hurt your head?" I ask.

"No," she answers. "Why would it?"

That's weird. I thought all mind breakers suffer from agonizing pain, when hypnotizing. Apparently, this is just my own personal affliction.

"May I drive?" Kitty asks. "I mean...I don't wanna die in any fiery car crash you may cause."

"I'll drive slowly," I answer sheepishly, getting behind the wheel. Suddenly the realization of what she's just said strikes me. "Wait!" I exclaim. "When did you learn how to drive?"

"Well," Kitty says, averting her eyes. "I did practice lots of useful things while you weren't at home."

I fall into a stupor for a few moments, her words echoing in my ears. Of course. How could I be so blind, not noticing anything going on? That's also how she's capable of hypnotizing people so well. Now I understand. While I was so busy working, Kitty had an opportunity to do whatever she wanted during the day. She probably hypnotized regularly, perfecting her skills. I saw her dressed in her school uniform every morning, carrying an arm load of books, but where did she really go?

Bitter feelings of unease and disappointment overwhelm me. I thought she had changed her ways years ago. Apparently, my Kitty has some secrets.

I keep driving till late evening, holding the steering wheel with shaky hands. My right eye is still blurry from the accident. I have to squint to see the darkening road. Our car jerks and I'm scared to lose control. I'll have to stop soon else we may end up in a ditch.

Spending the night in another abandoned house probably isn't the best decision, with no electricity and the temperature near freezing. I don't want Kitty to catch cold. We need to find somewhere better to sleep.

Passing a small town, I see the askew sign of a cheap looking motel. Its walls are uneven and scratched. The layers of plastic and wood replace the glass in some broken windows. Just nasty enough to give it a try, I guess. People who dare to stay in this rat hole must be in trouble themselves. Hopefully, they won't report us.

We leave the car in an obscured parking lot and walk through the squeaking entrance door of the motel. I feel Kitty's hand squeezing my fingers in friendly support. She knows I hate hypnotizing people.

The air is grayish blue from cigarette smoke. There's a filthy bar in the hall where several drunks sit, backs turned to us. I see a tall skinny girl pouring whiskey behind the stained counter. She's in her early twenties with short spiked hair, wearing a biker's jacket above an indecently open dress. A bizarre pattern of numerous tattoos covers her chest and neck. The girl wears black lipstick and heavy makeup, looking as freakish as possible. Her pale blue eyes meet mine for a moment and she turns away indifferently.

We approach the sleepy clerk. Irritated, he raises his head and asks what we want. That same moment I concentrate hard, sending my suggestions into his brain. I've no idea how it works really. I just feel our minds connecting. Familiar pain engulfs my head. The guy resists slightly, but only for a second. Then his facial muscles relax, leaving him with a silly expression. I expel a quiet breath of relief. You never know when you may meet a resistant. Thankfully, this clerk isn't one of them. At the same time Kitty is hypnotizing others in the room, making sure they won't remember our faces.

I place a torn piece of paper on the desk. The clerk grabs it, thinking that this is cash, and hands me a key.

"Good job," Kitty whispers.

I wince, rejecting her compliment. Everything we're doing now contradicts my principles. I feel ashamed, taking advantage of my skills.

We proceed to our room. It's very small and it stinks. A fat brown cockroach crawls along the smeared wall, moving its long antennas.

"Well, looks like sleeping outside wouldn't be that much worse," Kitty says.

"C'mon, it's just for one night," I answer.

There's only one bed. Fully dressed, we crawl under a thin blanket and hold each other, trying to keep warm. Kitty's tiny arms wrap around my neck. She mumbles something unintelligible and drifts off. I remain sleepless, unable to relax. I have the feeling of sinking in quicksand. Whatever I do seems wrong and only winds up making everything worse. On the run from police, hypnotizing people and stealing cars. Just like a real criminal. Maybe Tim was right about all mind breakers being plain evil? No, I won't stay like this. At least I hope I'm different.

Being worn out and feverish, I force myself to calm down. I need to sleep, but my mind outlines countless scenarios of our future. I imagine officers in black uniforms surrounding the motel. I see guns and rifles pointed at us. So needful of rest, I can't make myself stop listening and watching.

Around a midnight someone knocks on the door. This could be trouble.

CHAPTER 4

The steady rhythm of knocking sends chills throughout my body. I sit up abruptly on the edge of the bed, waking Kitty.

"What's wrong?" she whispers.

I shush to keep her quiet and walk toward the door. I don't believe that Elimination or the police could have come for us this soon. No, they wouldn't be knocking. They would boot the door with guns at the ready. This must be someone else.

Holding my breath and keeping as silent as possible, I take a cautious look through the peephole. I see the girl from the bar who gave me an odd glance earlier. She must be a resistant as our hypnosis apparently didn't work on her. What does she want? I can't read anything on her face.

"Let me in," the girl says. "I recognized you." Her voice sounds calm as if nothing unusual is happening.

She knows who I am. I instantly open the door, grab the girl and drag her inside. The door shuts closed. I press the girl tightly against the wall.

"What do you want?" I ask, squeezing my hands on her shoulders. I don't know how I should behave with her.

"Easy, easy," she says. "I'm a breaker like you. I'm here to help."

"How can we know that?" I ask. "Maybe you're just resistant."

"Don't be stupid," she says. "Elimination would already be here if I were just a resistant."

Her words make sense and strike a chord of truth within me. I lessen my grip.

"Rex, let her go," I hear Kitty's thin voice. "Can't you see? She's one of us!"

"Looks like your girlfriend has more brains than you," the girl says. The stranger remains absolutely calm as if she's in complete control of the situation.

After a brief hesitation I let her go.

"This is my sister," I say. "Not girlfriend."

"Whatever," the girl says. "It's none of my business. I don't care who you are or what you did. I came to offer my help, not hear to your relationship status. It's dangerous for you to stay here. Somebody else could have recognized you. I saw what you did in the hall. It was pretty impressive, but as you already know some people are resistant."

She speaks without emotion, nor changing the cold expression on her face. It reminds me somehow of a mask. Her black lips and heavy layers of makeup must be part of her disguise, I guess. If she were to ever wash her face, she'd be unrecognizable.

"If you wish, you can spend the night at my place," she offers. "I live thirty minutes from here."

"Why should we trust you?" I ask, still suspicious.

"I don't really care if you trust me or not," the girl answers. "You just don't have any other place to go that I'm aware of."

She's right. Remaining here is too risky. It was a bad idea to come to this motel. What was I thinking?

"Rex, please," Kitty pleads. "Let's go with her."

She must be excited to meet another breaker.

"All right," I agree. I'm probably becoming overly paranoid, seeing an enemy in every person I meet. Although in our current situation doing so may be the only way to stay alive.

Her apartment is large and empty for the most part. I only see a cheap mattress on the floor of the living room, several books and a TV set. No other furniture.

"It's easier to move this way," the girl explains. Looks like she lives in a constant readiness to run for her life, whenever needed. No photographs lying around. Nothing that might give a lead to a pursuer. Smart girl. She obviously knows what she's doing.

"You can take showers," she advises. "I can also provide a change of clothes for each of you."

She brings a dress for Kitty, which I think will be too large, and men's shirt and jeans for me.

"My ex left them," she comments, handing me the clothes. "And don't worry, he doesn't remember them anymore."

"Did you wipe his memory?" I ask. "You mean he wasn't a breaker?"

"He was," she answers. "Just a considerably weaker breaker than me."

This is surprising. I didn't know that breakers could manipulate each other.

Kitty goes into the bathroom. I remain alone with the girl, sitting on the stained carpet and feeling somewhat awkward. I'm not used to being a house guest. The girl doesn't pay me any attention, lost in a book picked from a stack on the floor.

"Thanks for taking us in," I say to break the silence.

"Don't feel too welcome," she answers. "You'll be leaving in the morning."

"Sure," I say. Her rudeness doesn't offend me. She is already risking her life, letting us stay here tonight. Expecting warmth and hospitality would probably be asking too much.

"What's your name?" I ask curiously.

"Why do you freaking care?" she says with an irritated look.

"Well, you know my name," I explain. "I thought it'd be only fair if I knew yours."

"Your name isn't real anyway, is it?" she asks.

"No," I admit.

Her black lips curl into an understanding smirk.

"Of course. We all have fake names," she says. "Anyway, why did you take such a stupid name? Rex Hunter. Sounds terrible."

"I was eight when I took it," I explain. "What would you expect from a child?" I smile, remembering my struggle with choosing a name. "Rex was borrowed from the Tyrannosaurus Rex. I used to like dinosaurs."

She rolls her eyes.

"Why are you telling all this to me?" she says, wincing. "I really don't want to know. The less you tell people about yourself, the safer you are. Learn to keep your mouth shut, stupid."

Don't take her rudeness personally, I remind myself. Rudeness is just a defense mechanism for her. We all build walls to keep our secrets safe. In a mind breaker's world you can't allow many close relationships.

After showering, our hostess warms up a large frozen pizza for our supper. We eat it, sitting on the floor and watching the news. My face is on every channel.

They use the photograph from my bank ID, which looks like a mug shot. I've never been photogenic, but watchers may easily come to some wrong conclusions after seeing this. This pic is exactly how Elimination wishes a mind breaker to appear.

Shockingly, police accuse me of a bank robbery attempt and homicide. I supposedly killed the security guard. I additionally shot Mr. Thompson and beat the hell out of Mandy and Tim. No word about the actual criminals. Strange.

I see Lola, the most popular journalist in the country, whose specialty happens to be mind breakers. She is overly thin, almost on the verge of anorexia. Her actual age is a mystery, but I'm guessing she's past fifty. Countless plastic surgeries have distorted the natural features of her face, leaving her skin too strained, lips too big and cheekbones too high. She wears a red mini dress which seems a bit obscene for her age, along with a blond wig and tons of makeup.

Today, Lola is interviewing Captain Wheeler from the Elimination force. He's a middle aged man with perfect posture and friendly face.

"This is an extremely dangerous case," Wheeler says. "This young man is unstable and psychotic. He can definitely kill again."

"Why do you think he committed these heinous crimes?" Lola asks.

"There's one primary reason," the captain answers. "He's a mind breaker. That's what all of them wind up doing sooner or later. Killing innocent people."

Wow, what a bummer. I'm being tried and convicted right here on national TV.

"Let's watch the video feed of these violent crimes," Lola suggests.

They show video taken from the cameras in the bank. Of course this is not the full version of what happened. On the first short video I kneel down over the breathless body of Mr. Thompson. I have a vicious looking snarl on my blood smeared face. Another video clip shows me hypnotizing the SWAT team. I'm holding a gun in my hand.

It's outrageous. They're making a real monster out of me.

"I didn't do it," I say to nobody in particular.

"Nobody freaking cares if you did it or not," the girl says. "You're a breaker. That's all they need."

I hear Kitty sobbing.

"How dare they?" she says with anger. "They don't know you. You're the nicest guy in the world."

I give her a hug, trying to calm her down. Our hostess watches us with a strange knowing expression. Likely, she doesn't believe that Kitty is only my sister.

"Anybody who sees this escapee needs to contact us immediately," the Elimination captain says. "Do not try to apprehend him alone or even approach him. Do not look into his eyes. He's an extremely dangerous and ruthless killer on the run."

Lola the journalist opens her mouth widely, imitating total shock.

After the interview with the captain they bring in witnesses. First, I see Tim's bruised face.

"I was fighting him," he says. "But the creature hypnotized me and then beat the heck out of me."

I must be becoming less sensitive to these attacks, because I feel nothing but emptiness watching Tim's betrayal. Someone probably paid him to witness against me.

Now comes Mandy. She has really dressed up for the interview and is smiling like a super model.

"I refused when he asked me out earlier in the day," she says. "That could be why he targeted me during his attack."

"How do you feel now?" Lola asks.

"I'm so scared," Mandy answers. "He almost took advantage of my helplessness."

I choke on a piece of pizza. Maybe I was wrong in saving Mandy?

"That's enough," Kitty growls. "Did you really ask her out?"

"No way," I answer. "She's just a silly desperate girl seeking attention."

"I'm sick of this!" Kitty says, turning off the TV.

We remain silent for several gloomy minutes. I have no appetite left, but force myself to take another bite. Never know when we may get a chance to eat again.

"So," the girl says. "Do you have a place in mind to go?"

"Not really," I answer.

"I've heard rumors about a group of breakers who help guys like you," she states. "It's said those breakers hide out somewhere down in the south. I don't know if it's true or not, but you may want to try to find them."

Good, I think, we're heading south anyway. It'd be great if somebody could help provide shelter and security.

"How can we find them?" I ask.

"How would I know?" our hostess answers. "Use your telepathic skills I guess, if you have that ability."

"Very funny," I answer, rolling my eyes.

"I'm not joking, idiot," the girl says. "You really don't know anything?" she asks. "Hypnosis isn't the only ability many of us have. Some are telepaths as well and others can even read memories."

"That's just a silly myth," I say.

"Whatever," she sighs, turning away and chewing on another slice of pizza. I think on her words, confused now. Maybe she's right. I don't know everything about our kind. She and Kitty are the only two breakers I've ever met.

The apartment has only one bedroom. Kitty and I lie on the floor, covering ourselves with a thin blanket that our hostess provided. My headache lessens and I drop into a deep slumber.

I see an odd place in my dream. A surgery room with white sterile walls and no windows. The sharp smell of disinfectant makes me gasp. I notice a small sad girl sitting on a gurney. She is about eight years old. Scary-looking electrodes stick out of her shaved head like so many octopus tentacles. She holds my picture in her tiny fingers, crying. Everything is so vivid that it seems real. At the same time I realize it's only a dream.

"Find him," an unrecognizable voice commands.

The girl gazes at me. Her oriental eyes are puffy from tears. I know she can't see me, but somehow feels my presence. Lena. Her name is Lena, I suddenly realize.

"What is this place?" I ask. My voice sounds muffled. She can't hear me.

I notice a man wearing a black uniform standing behind her, the same Captain Wheeler whom I recognize from the news. He raises his hand slowly and then slaps the girl. She screams helplessly, falling down.

"I said find him!" he yells.

"Stop!" I shout. "Don't touch her!"

They can't hear me. I want to run forward and protect the poor child, but remain at the same place. No matter how hard I try, I can't move an inch. Some wild inexplicable horror overcomes me and I yell, straining my throat. I sense everything that the little girl feels. Her pain, her fear, her despair. I can't tell who I am anymore and can only scream, helpless and lost.

I wake up, sweating and repeating her name. Lena. Where did it come from? I've never known anybody by that name. Instinctively, I squeeze

Kitty tightly in my arms, making sure she's here and safe. She complains and pushes me away in her sleep. I get the feeling this nightmare is somehow real and something awful is going to happen.

Unable to sleep, I get up and walk toward the window to take a look outside. The street is empty. Nobody's waiting to capture us, but I don't believe we're safe for a minute. Elimination knows how to track their victims.

I notice my teeth clattering and make myself relax. This strange dream has really knocked me off balance. I've never experienced anything like this before in a dream.

"Hey, what are you doing?" I hear a voice behind me.

I turn back quickly. Our hostess looks at me with raised eyebrows, awaiting my response.

"Boy, you are really jumpy, aren't you?" she adds with a grin.

"I can't sleep," I whisper.

The girl glances at Kitty and then gestures for me to go with her. I won't be sleeping again this night anyway, so I follow. We walk into the living room. I see a bottle of whiskey on the floor and a half-empty glass. Looks like I'm not only one having trouble sleeping.

"I'd offer you some, but it's better to remain sober in your situation," she says, taking a sip. She downs the whiskey like it was water, no problem.

"That's okay, I don't drink," I answer.

Breakers normally don't consume alcohol. It's impossible to hypnotize when you're drunk. This girl doesn't seem to care.

We sit together on her mattress in silence. She's drinking and I'm thinking of my nightmare. The girl probably notices that something is off with me.

"You know you can't freaking break down right now," she says.

"I'm all right," I lie.

"You look like death warmed over," she says. "You have to stay strong for Kitty."

"What?" I exclaim. "Do you really think I can't protect her?"

"I doubt you can even protect yourself," she answers.

"How can you think that?" I say. "You don't even know me."

"I've seen enough," she answers. "You are the most wanted criminal in the country right now. Every dog in the city is looking for you. Do you realize that you are dragging Kitty down? You have to split, otherwise Elimination will catch both of you."

There's some sense in her words, but I can't imagine leaving my Kitty. "No," I say. "She needs me."

"Don't be so selfish," the girl says. "You're a dead man already. You can't outsmart Elimination, they're pros. You know this. But Kitty may still have a slight chance. You have to let her go. "

She may be right. Together we're a vulnerable target, although some part of me doesn't want to admit it. Kitty is everything to me. The only person in this world who really cares about me. We're undividable in my mind. I can't leave her and become lonely again. I've already been a loner for too many long years.

"She isn't your sister anyway, is she?" the girl suggests.

I see the accusation in her eyes and realize that she must have the wrong idea about my relationship with Kitty. It makes me really angry. I've already been accused of every other crime possible. That's enough. I stand up abruptly.

"I'm tired," I say. "I'd better get some sleep."

"Sit back down, idiot," she hisses. "I'm only trying to help."

"I didn't ask for this," I answer roughly, walking out of the room.

No matter how angry I am, I realize the truth in what the girl was saying. Sooner or later Elimination will track me down. Kitty too, if she's with me. I endanger Kitty in keeping her close. Perhaps I should leave right now while she's sleeping, because Kitty will never let me go being awake.

I feel guilty thinking this way. Kitty trusts me. How can I betray her?

I walk into the bedroom and see her smiling in her sleep. She seems so tiny and fragile that I can't think of leaving anymore. No, I won't go away. I need Kitty too much.

Troubled, I lie down beside her. I stay awake till sunrise again, lost in worries and doubts.

In the morning our hostess hands me a sack filled with sandwiches and then offers her handgun.

"No, thank you," I say. "I'm not gonna shoot anybody."

"Don't fool yourself," the girl says. "When Elimination comes, you'll have to shoot or be shot. Take it. It's a gift."

Reluctantly, I take the gun and tuck it away under my sweatshirt.

"Don't steal any cars," the girl instructs. "It's too risky. Better to catch a train. Only a few people ride the rails nowadays, so you shouldn't attract too much attention." She pauses, giving a piercing look. "And think on what we talked about last night," she adds.

I nod, appreciating the advice. I thank her for everything and we leave. Kitty looks excited. Holding my hand, she walks with her head held high. Her eyes are full of wonder and curiosity. It's the first time she's ventured outside of the city.

"I've always wanted to travel," she says with a sigh.

"This is no vacation, Kitty," I say.

"We're together and traveling," she answers. "Feels like a vacation to me so far."

Nothing ever seems to change with Kitty. Her fresh well rested face shows no strain from the previous two hellish days of running from the police. Kitty is carefree and happy. I feel like somebody chewed me up and spit me out, unrested and stressed out to the max.

"Did you like Jessie?" Kitty asks. "She seemed cool. I liked her tattoos and all that piercing. It would be fun to be like her."

"Jessie? Is that her name?" I ask in surprise.

"Yeah," Kitty answers. "She said it's her real one. She's fed up with aliases and fake IDs. You know, Jessie is from the south just like you."

I'm aware of Kitty's ability to trigger sincerity in the unsuspecting. Looking so innocent and sweet, my little sister can manipulate even without using her breaker abilities.

Following Jessie's instructions we walk toward the train station. It's still early, so we don't run into too many people. Seeing someone approach, I turn away and pull my hood down low.

"Quit that," Kitty whispers. "You're acting suspiciously."

A long passenger train arrives within a couple of hours. This is an old noisy monster, ready to be retired soon. Kitty stares opened mouthed at the train. She's never ridden one before.

Most cars are empty just as Jessie suggested. We choose seats closest to the exit. It seems safer somehow although I'm not sure you can open the doors by yourself. Looks as if they're set to open and close automatically. Should Elimination arrive and order all exits blocked, we'd be trapped. I shiver from the thought and pull my hood back down, shielding my identity from a few nearby passengers.

Nobody seems to pay us any attention. When a conductor comes around, Kitty closes her eyes, concentrating. He walks away, being slightly drowsy and thinking that we both have the tickets.

I lie down across two empty seats, listening to the steady rhythm of the train's movements. The sounds are calming. Reminds me of a train ride I took years ago. I traveled the same way, only in the opposite direction from south to north. The south is where I grew up and belong. I remember endless meadows filled with colorful flowers and warm sunshine, the smell of honeysuckles and a hot humid breeze on my face. I wonder if our old farm is still there or not. That was the one place where I almost felt happy. At least until I was forced to leave.

Thinking of my past, I'm able to relax for the first time since the bank robbery. My body is extremely sore, but now the headache is gone. Exhausted, I fall asleep.

When I wake, the train is creeping slowly through a devastated part of the country, where people used to live before the Eruption. I can see nothing but the ruins of old cities and broken roads. A thick layer of grayish ash covers every inch of crumbled buildings and scorched streets, giving the place an unearthly appearance. Thousands died in here, their remains still buried beneath the ash.

A feeling of hopelessness creeps over me watching the gloomy scenery. Everything appears to be dead or ruined.

Kitty is glued to the window.

"Looks like another planet," she says in astonishment.

We stare at the ruins for a while, then eat a couple of sandwiches Jessie packed for us. They taste good and have a calming effect. Being rested and no longer hungry, Kitty's enthusiasm is starting to catch on. We've evaded capture for almost three days now. Not too shabby when you're dealing with Elimination. Apparently, they still don't know where we're at. Freedom is intoxicating, giving me hope for our future. In a few hours we'll be home free in the south. There should be many good places to hide out. Maybe we'll actually make it and keep our freedom after all. For the first time I truly start to believe.

I close my eyes again. I need as much rest as I can get because everything could change any second.

It's getting dark now. Kitty lies across the seat, using my lap as a pillow. I remain in a sitting position, dozing on and off. Fully relaxed and about to drift off, my pulse suddenly skyrockets. I feel suffocated and anxious. The inexplicable terror consumes me, forcing to open my eyes and look around. Nothing, there's no reason to be scared. A few passengers are sleeping, paying us no mind. Kitty is dreaming peacefully. I'm still tensed and full of adrenaline. This is weird. What's wrong with me?

"They're coming," I hear a childish voice whisper.

Instinctively, I turn my head toward the sound. Nobody there. Am I hallucinating?

"I'm so sorry," I hear the same voice again.

Everything fades. I fall into the darkness. I see the surgical room from my nightmare. The girl with electrodes in her head stands in front of me. Her face is red and swollen from tears. Her eyes look troubled and sad. She is in a hospital gown and wears a strange metal collar around her neck. Her scrawny little arms have dark bruises and multiple red marks. She seems so real. I feel like I can extend my hand and touch her. I know she's frightened. I sense something really nasty has recently happened to her.

"Lena," I whisper.

The girl glances at me in surprise.

"Can you see me?" she asks.

"Who are you?" I wonder. "What is this place?"

She doesn't bother to answer my questions. Large tears spill from her eyes and she covers her face.

"I'm sorry," she says, sobbing. "They made me do it. You have to run. I had to tell them where you are."

A strong feeling of guilt pierces me. This must be how she feels. Somehow we're connected. How did I know her name? I still can't understand if this is a dream or reality. I hear the sound of wheels pounding the tracks, and know I'm back inside the train. I'm still holding Kitty in my arms. At the same time this dream room and Lena seem so realistic.

"Run!" she screams.

Her frightened voice snaps me out of my bizarre hallucination. I touch the hard surface of the seat to make sure it's real. My heart is racing and my ears ring from Lena's desperate wail. Am I going insane?

Kitty wakes, staring up at me in confusion.

"Did you say something?" she asks.

"No," I answer.

"You were talking in your sleep," Kitty says. "Why did you call me Lena?"

I look around, feeling uneasy. Somehow I know that Lena is real and spoke the truth. Elimination has located us. They're coming. Right now. No time to hide.

"Rex! Are you okay?" Kitty asks, worrying.

"We have to go," I say. "Elimination has found us."

"What are you talking about?"

Abruptly, the train slows its speed. The momentum yanks us forward. Kitty grabs my arm for balance.

There's no reason for the train to stop here. We're in the middle of nowhere. I rush to the window to check what's going on outside. Several military helicopters are descending from the dark night sky.

CHAPTER 5

My first impulse is to grab Kitty and run. But I can't be panicking now. I need to stay calm and figure out our best option.

The sudden stop awakens the other passengers. I pull my hood down in a feeble attempt to hide my face. Should somebody recognize me and call out, Elimination would be on us in seconds.

I grab Kitty's arm as we slowly head toward the exit, trying to act unconcerned. Passengers should believe we're just taking a curious look around as to why the train stopped.

We step into the space between two cars and I try the door. No matter how hard I push, it remains closed. They must have closed down all exits on the train. Kitty glances at me worriedly, her face pale as snow. She knows we can't hypnotize Elimination. Our mind breaker abilities are useless against the resistant.

I hear noises coming from the car we've just left. Taking a quick glance back, I see several officers in black uniforms walking down the aisle, searching for me.

"This is Elimination. Remain in your seats," a loud command follows.

The officers check each passenger, shining a flashlight. Obviously, they won't stop till they find us.

"What do we do?" Kitty whispers. A finger to my lips signals her to keep quiet. I've no idea how we can escape from this train. It's impossible to break down the thick metal doors. No place to hide. The Elimination officers are methodically moving closer.

I take Kitty's hand and we head in the opposite direction, walking through numerous cars. It probably won't save us, but at least should buy a few moments to think. My mind races, searching for a solution. I see no easy answer. Surprisingly, I feel very calm and determined. My hand finds the gun tucked under my shirt. I'm not giving up without a fight.

As we approach the doors of the last car, they suddenly open and several Elimination officers pour through. A blinding light shines in my eyes. I step back, but don't run. Running would be pointless now. Other officers are coming up from behind, searching for us. We're completely surrounded and trapped.

"That's the one! Take him!" someone commands. "Everybody on the floor!"

Everything happens so quickly. The passengers scream out in surprise and drop to the floor. I brandish my gun firing in the direction of the officer shining the flashlight. The bullet strikes the officer in the chest, knocking him off his feet. A huge Elimination cop jumps over his fallen fellow officer, charging at me. I shoot again, but my vision blurs and I miss. The bullet only lightly grazes the sleeve of the big guy's jacket and hits the wall. The officer body slams me to the floor. My gun flies free. I punch and elbow the guy, but he doesn't lessen his grip. Within a moment several other officers dogpile on, grasping my arms and pressing my head down. I hear Kitty screaming my name. Instinctively, I concentrate, trying some hypnosis. Let me go, I project, back off! Someone pins my arms behind my back and presses a knee down hard on the back of my neck. My hypnosis doesn't work.

When the officers are about to place me in handcuffs, a sudden thought strikes my mind. The passengers aren't resistant, perhaps I can still manipulate them.

"Fire!" I yell. "Get out! The train is burning."

I imagine hot flames, burning walls and seats. I concentrate hard to transmit the acrid smell of suffocating smoke.

"Knock that off!" one officer yells, punching me in the back of my head.

"Fire!" Kitty screams. She's caught on and helps panic the passengers.

People jump from their seats and rush for the exits, pushing and climbing over each other. Desperate to find an open door, they crash into and over the officers, stomping me in the process. I feel a jolt of pain and hope I haven't broken anything.

"Rex!" Kitty yells, grabbing my shoulder. "Get up, hurry!"

Her desperate voice helps me regain my senses. I scramble up, noticing the dazed officers are getting back on their feet as well. In seconds they'll attack again. We have to get out of here!

I pick up the gun and shoot several rounds into a large window. A spider web of cracks grows across its surface. I grab Kitty's wrist, running toward the damaged window. The glass shatters as I slam into it full speed. We both hit the ground hard, Kitty falling beside me.

I hear a few shots and then an angry voice, "Hold your fire! We need them alive!"

That's something, at least they don't want to kill us. Grimacing from pain, I get up quickly. Kitty is already back on her feet, ready to run.

We sprint toward the ruins, sinking in ankle deep ash and leaping over train tracks along the way. I spot the beam from a search light slicing through the darkness. A large helicopter rises up from the ground, raising swirling clouds of ashes. We change direction several times, zigzagging to avoid its spotlight. My lungs burn and legs become heavy. Needing distance foremost, we must continue running as long as we can. Kitty is gasping, but following closely behind.

At last we reach the ruins. There are only a few walls left from the building. It's a bad place to hide, but we need a break. I can't run anymore. Kitty seems exhausted as well. We collapse on the ground behind one of the walls.

"What do we do?" Kitty asks.

"I don't know yet," I whisper as I peer around the wall, taking a careful look.

I hear a different freight train slowly approaching in the distance. If we could only crawl unnoticed inside one of its cars...Then I pick up something else, muffled voices. We won't be catching this train. Elimination officers have cut off our way to the railroad and are walking along the tracks. They search the ruins, coming closer with each step. The helicopter flies in large swooping circles. We're surrounded again. No escaping now. We need a distraction.

I know what I have to do.

I have to stop being selfish for one thing. This must be what Jessie was talking about back in her room. We can't run from Elimination together. On her own, Kitty may have a chance. I have to let her go.

I grab Kitty's arm firmly, pulling her close.

"Kitty, listen carefully," I whisper. "I'll draw their attention while you sneak off and catch this coming train. Stay low in the ash and when you reach the train, keep hidden inside one of the cars until you're well away."

Her expression changes to near panic.

"I'll follow you shortly after," I lie, knowing that she won't agree to leave me otherwise.

"No, you won't," she says, seeing through me immediately. "We belong together, please don't ask me to do this."

She cries in silence. My heart aches. If I go, I may never see her again. But it's the only way to keep Kitty free.

"We have to separate," I say. "You know we're surrounded and won't make it together. I'll keep them distracted. Get as far south as you can. Try to find those breakers Jessie spoke about."

"No, please," Kitty repeats, sobbing. "Don't leave me. I love you. I can't survive without you."

Her fingers clutch my shirt tightly. I push her away. I have to do this right now or I'll change my mind.

"Don't let them catch you," I say, taking a last long glance at my Kitty, and run out from behind the wall.

I head away from the railroad, shooting into the air, yelling and causing as much commotion as I can to attract the officer's attention. They must all come for me for this to work. The officers react instantly, giving chase.

Hopefully, Kitty will take advantage of any opening to get away as it may be her only chance. I can never be sure with Kitty. She's so stubborn.

Please, do as I said, I repeat over and over in my head as I run. Don't let them catch you.

One officer steps from the darkness in front of me. Taser gun! No time to react. Two needles attached to wire slam into my chest. An excruciating pain explodes throughout my body. I fall to the ground, moaning and twitching. When the shock subsides, I'm unable to move. The officer puts a knee on my back and handcuffs me. I squirm weakly, trying to free myself.

"Stop resisting or I'll tase you again," he says forcefully.

Other officers approach. I recognize Captain Wheeler from the television show.

"Great job, Chase," he says.

"Thank you, sir," the officer answers. He jerks me up to my feet.

Captain Wheeler stands before me, smiling. He looks exactly like he did during his interview, friendly and kind.

"Let me introduce myself," he says softly, slamming the butt of his rifle into my skull.

Darkness.

When I regain consciousness, I'm inside a large room with no windows. A huge flawless mirror takes up almost half of one wall. An interrogation room, I realize. Sparsely furnished with only a desk and a few chairs. A short old man with gray hair sits behind the desk, studying a thick folder overstuffed with papers. His face is wrinkled and has large brown eyes that hold a contemptuous expression. He wears an old fashioned suit and thick gold colored glasses that make his eyes look unnaturally big. A fish comes to my mind.

I sit in the middle of the room, arms and legs chained to a metal chair. I feel a tight heavy collar around my neck. My head still aches, but the bleeding seems to have stopped. Possibly, I'm in a police station or a prison.

Kitty, I think, what happened to her? Did she get away? Conscious or unconscious, thoughts of Kitty are constantly swirling in my head.

The door opens and Captain Wheeler appears. I recognize him immediately because it's hard to forget our last meeting. Officer Chase follows behind, carrying a rifle.

I'm too sick and exhausted to feel frightened. Watching them closely, I take in a long deep breath, preparing for the worst.

"Has he finally woken up?" Wheeler asks impatiently.

"Not really," an old man in suit answers. "He fades in and out, may pass out again at any moment. You hit him too darn hard."

"I should've hit him harder," Wheeler says calmly. "So we wouldn't have to waste our time here any further."

"Let me study the report first," the elderly man says and continues reading the documents.

Wheeler takes a bottle of water from the table, approaches me and slaps my face.

"Time to wake up, breaker," he says.

The room is spinning. I can do nothing. The shackles on my arms and legs keep me nearly motionless.

"Are you thirsty?" Wheeler asks, showing the bottle of water. "How about a drink, breaker?"

My mouth and throat are dry like sand. I involuntarily swallow. Noticing this, Wheeler flashes a sadistic grin and pours the water over my head.

"How do you like that, breaker?" he asks, smacking the bottle across my face. Then he grabs my hair and yanks my head back. His grin changes into a sneer. "I see you don't like being here," he says. "Guess what? I hate being in this place as well. I hate every minute I spend near you, stinking breaker. You disgust me. Look at you! You're just a freakish mistake in evolution. You're not even human. You're a lower life form than a miserable flea-bitten dog."

He speaks very slowly, relishing each word. I peer into his pale, hateful eyes and then look away as if I'm bored.

"You're mine now, breaker," Wheeler sneers. "Your days are numbered. Very soon you'll regret the day you were born. You know what Elimination can do to breakers, don't you swine?"

He jerks my head back and smiles, waiting for my reaction. I only gaze at him, keeping silent. I won't give him the pleasure of seeing me intimidated. I won't beg for mercy. Even If I have to die, I intend to keep some dignity.

"Wheeler, if you don't hurry, we'll miss lunch," the old man says with irritation. "Ask your questions and let's be done with him."

"If I want your opinion, I'll give it to you," Wheeler replies.

"Sir, he's right," Officer Chase says. "We do need to hurry. All those journalists are waiting."

Wheeler sighs in disappointment.

"Darn journalists," he says. "Well, breaker, I'll be very brief then. I'll ask you one simple question and you'd better answer truthfully, if you want to live."

He slams his fist into my head. My ears are ringing. I feel like my skull is about to crack.

"Where's your freaking breaker girlfriend?" Wheeler asks in an absolutely calm voice. "Come on, breaker. Where is she?"

My heart beats faster. I now understand they haven't found her. Kitty is free. In spite of all the pain and nausea, I feel happy.

"Answer me, you stinking freak," Wheeler says, striking me again. Drops of my blood splatter the floor. Wheeler rubs his fist.

Remain silent, I tell myself. Don't say a word. You have to save Kitty.

"Where's the girl?" Wheeler repeats, becoming more agitated. "I'll break every bone in your body, if you don't answer."

He punches me hard in the stomach. I lose my breath. Wheeler smiles, enjoying the process. He'll kill me, I suddenly realize. The thought of dying doesn't frighten me. I feel surprisingly calm as if anything that happens doesn't matter anymore. Kitty has escaped and that matters most.

"You'll answer me sooner or later," Wheeler says. "I know how to break breakers."

His face is only in a couple of inches from mine. He must be certain that I've given up and won't resist further. I return his smile and head-butt him squarely in the face, smashing his nose as hard as I can. Wheeler back-pedals, swaying. He growls in pain and covers his bleeding nose. I must have broken it. I smile wider and close my eyes, already aware of what Wheeler will do. It was well worth it, though.

Furious, Wheeler punches my head again and again.

"I'll kill you, freak," he yells, losing his temper.

Chase comes from behind, grabbing Wheeler with both arms and pulling him off me.

"Sir, you can't kill him," Chase suggests. "We may need him."

Wheeler pushes him away.

"Back off, idiot," he roars. "I can do whatever I like. And I'd like to shoot this freak."

He brandishes a 9 mm.

"Sir, please," Chase says, keeping his voice calm. "We really need to have him tested first."

"Actually, we don't," the old man interjects, closing his folder. "I've studied the reports and see no need for additional testing. He's an abso-lutely useless level one breaker."

"Level one?" Chase asks in surprise. "He hypnotized everyone on the train!"

"That doesn't impress me much," the old man answers with a grin. "We have plenty of breakers who could do that. His skillset is not what we're looking for," he glances toward Wheeler and adds, "You may waste him."

"That's the best news I've heard all day," Wheeler says, smiling.

The cold steel of the gun barrel presses onto my temple. This is it, I think. I'm about to die.

CHAPTER 6

As I wait for Wheeler to blow my brains out, the door opens and a tall young man walks into the room. He's so scrawny that all his clothes seem oversized and baggy. He wears a ridiculously bright shirt with a palm trees print and dark slacks. His long thin nose and neck resemble a bird. He glances at Wheeler holding the gun to my head, and his expression changes to astonishment.

"This is wholly unacceptable!" he exclaims. "Stop this madness at once!"

Wheeler instantly lowers his gun, sighing in disappointment.

"Oh, great," he growls. "Psycho has arrived."

The old man rolls his eyes. He doesn't seem pleased to see the new guy either.

"Mr. Wheeler, how dare you interact with the subject in this way prior to my arrival?" the bird guy admonishes.

"I'm in control here!" Wheeler shouts. "I don't answer to you, psycho."

"You will, Mr. Wheeler, otherwise everything that's occurred here will be reported to Mr. Browning," the bird guy says, stepping closer toward Wheeler. "Is that what you wish?"

For a moment they stare one another down. Disliking the obvious threat, Wheeler squeezes his fists tightly closed and bares his teeth in a vicious snarl. I expect him to punch the bird man, who looks like a nerd

stomed to fighting. A single punch would surely knock him
theless, he doesn't seem intimidated by Wheeler.

"You know I can ruin your career," the young man says in an official
e of voice.

Cussing quietly, Wheeler holsters his gun and backs off. I can't
believe it.

"Why are you here, Holtzmann?" the irritated old man asks. "What
do you want?"

"I've arrived to test the subject and make sure everything goes according to protocol," the bird man, apparently named Holtzmann, answers.

"We don't need additional tests," Wheeler growls. "Dr. Carrel has
examined the reports. He's just a level one breaker."

"That's right," Dr. Carrel adds, nodding his gray head in agreement.
"We have plenty of level one breakers. There's diminishing utility in keeping another one around."

Holtzmann raises his eyebrows and opens his mouth in deep indigna-
tion. Looks like he can't find the right words to express himself. I notice his
left eye twitching and both hands starting to shake.

"Excuse me!" Holtzmann exclaims, voice cracking. "I'm the lead
scientist on this project and the only one authorized to make that decision. Merely studying the reports is not sufficient to determine the level of
his abilities."

"Quit wasting our time," Carrel says with exhaustion. "I was testing
breakers since before you were born. There's no value in this one."

"Exactly," Wheeler agrees. "Let's just shoot this stinking rat and go to
lunch. I'm starving."

"Mr. Wheeler," Holtzmann says quietly. "If you shoot this breaker
without my authorization, your career will be finished. And I do mean
what I say."

It's a very strange feeling to watch them arguing over my fate. They
act as if I'm nonexistent and can't hear a word they're saying. I close my
eyes for a few moments, resting. Too much has happened over the last
three days. Too many times balancing between life and death. I'm numb

and can't feel overly worried or startled anymore. My head throbs, sending shock waves of pain with each movement. I need this process to be finished. Unfortunately, I don't believe they will let me out of this room anytime soon.

"Fine," Wheeler concedes. "Do whatever you want with him."

"Good afternoon, Mr. Hunter," Holtzmann begins. "My name is Egbert Holtzmann. You can just call me Professor Holtzmann. I'm the lead scientist for Elimination, charged with studying breakers. I will need to perform several simple tests to determine the level of your abilities. Please, choose to be as cooperative as is possible. It's a requirement in making an accurate determination and would be in your best interest.

I glance at him, guessing at what game he may be playing. His cool politeness and soft voice can't fool me. I'm fairly convinced he's got the same boss as Wheeler or Chase. Anybody working for Elimination is my worst enemy.

"Buzz off, egghead," I answer curtly.

My insult doesn't appear to have any effect. Perhaps Holtzmann expected me to say something offhand.

"If you don't fully cooperate, Mr. Wheeler will be more than happy to shoot you," he says without emotion. "You have to let me help you."

I sense him trying to manipulate the situation. Maybe Wheeler and Holtzmann are playing good cop, bad cop? Anything is possible. I keep silent, watching his left eye twitch several times.

"I saw the video recording," Holtzmann says slowly. "That is the uncut, original version of what happened at the bank."

I feel adrenaline shooting through my body.

"What?" I exclaim. "You know I'm innocent?"

"You are not innocent," he answers. "You're guilty of being a breaker. Which happens to be a very serious crime in our society. But I do realize this is likely the only crime you're connected to."

I look at him attentively, trying to calculate his true motives. Is he really willing and able to help? Everybody in Elimination must have seen actual footage from the bank cameras. They don't care if I'm innocent or not. I'm a rogue breaker, a threat to society. More than enough justification to kill me.

"I can conceivably take you out of here," Holtzmann says. "Just perform the tests to the best of your abilities."

As usual, looks like I have no choice in the matter. At least I can buy some time.

"All right," I agree.

Holtzmann seems very pleased. He turns to Wheeler and Carrel, flashing a toothy grin and stating proudly, "That's how you deal with a breaker, gentlemen."

Carrel snorts in anger, glaring at him with outright hatred.

"Have those idiots bring in the equipment," Wheeler orders Chase.

"And something to eat," Carrel adds. "We're gonna miss lunch for sure now."

Chase nods and walks out. I don't know what to expect. I heard rumors about Elimination torturing and beating breakers to death. I've never heard they perform some kind of tests on us. What are they going to do to me?

I study Holtzmann's face, trying to read the man. There's something off with this guy. He resembles one of those mentally ill, homeless people I occasionally meet in streets. His lips move, although he's not speaking. His sparkling eyes are fixated on something only he can see, long pale fingers moving constantly.

"Yes," he says quietly. "I'm certain."

Perfect. Now he's talking to himself. Looks like Wheeler was spot on calling him a psycho. And now this nutcase is about to perform some mysterious tests on me. Is he going to open my head and study my brain? Suddenly, an image of the little girl with oriental eyes and shaved head pops up in my memory. I remember the electrodes implanted into her skull. This time the vision doesn't seem so much like a dream.

Chase, along with several ordinary policemen, reenter the room, carrying laptops and metal boxes with protruding cables. The police officers glimpse at me with suspicion. One covers his eyes.

"Nothing to worry about here, gentlemen," Holtzmann soothes. "He's wearing a blocking collar and can't hypnotize anyone."

I've never heard of blocking collars before. Instinctively I concentrate, projecting my thoughts onto the cops. My head hurts intensely, but nothing happens to them. I can't break their wills. All my life I've resisted being a breaker, but now not being able to use my abilities puts me in a hopeless situation. So that's what the heavy collar on my neck must be for.

Holtzmann instructs the officers to place the metal boxes on the floor and connect cables.

"Bring in one of the inmates," Wheeler commands.

The officers walk away, returning several minutes later with a middle aged woman in handcuffs and prison issue clothing.

"Please, officers," she begs, dripping tears. "Don't make me do this."

An officer shoves her toward Wheeler and goes quickly away. Wheeler roughly grabs the woman and forces her onto the chair in front of me. She obeys, crying.

Holtzmann places electrodes on my forehead and temples.

"Mr. Wheeler, how many times have I asked you not to split their heads before testing?" Holtzmann asks.

Wheeler laughs and continues eating his lunch.

Chase has a rifle trained at my head, while Holtzmann removes the collar from my neck.

"It's not necessary to point that rifle at the subject," Holtzmann says.

"You can never be too safe with a breaker around," Chase answers.

Holtzmann rolls his eyes.

"Let's begin," he says to me. "I want you to hypnotize this lady. You may make her do anything you want within reason. Only do your best, please."

Holtzmann walks back over to the desk and sits down beside Dr. Carrel, looking at the laptops placed in front of him. Carrel seems bored, eating and hardly checking the monitors.

I don't want to hypnotize the lady, but what choice do I really have? A thought crosses my mind. What if I make her attack my captors? No, that's a stupid idea. She's not physically strong and can do little harm. It wouldn't work, especially with Chase holding the rifle on me. I'm sure he'd pull the trigger without hesitation if anything goes wrong. He may even want me to give him a reason.

Just wait for a better opportunity, I tell myself. Right now it'd be useless to do anything too provocative.

Concentrating, I make the lady get up from the chair and then roll on the floor. She does everything with a vacant expression, no longer sobbing. It's easy. My aching head becomes slightly heavier, but the hypnosis doesn't cause so much pain this time. Interesting. Perhaps I'm getting used to doing this just like Kitty.

"Thank you, Mr. Hunter," Holtzmann says. "Very well done. That will be sufficient."

I stop hypnotizing the poor lady. She lies on the floor motionless, recovering. Sometimes after hypnosis people have trouble in accurately perceiving reality for days.

"Let's try again with a resistant now," Holtzmann offers. "Chase, could you assist with this please?"

"What?" Chase exclaims in surprise. "No, you can't make me do this! Professor, I don't want a freaking breaker digging into my thoughts."

"Stop whining, Chase," Wheeler commands. "Just do as you're directed."

Reluctantly, Chase plops down on the chair before me. His face reveals unhidden resentment. I understand how he feels. Being hypnotized and manipulated must be a thoroughly unpleasant experience. However, if Chase is resistant as are the other officers in Elimination, why should he be worried?

"Mr. Hunter, could you hypnotize this subject, please?" Holtzmann says.

Chase winces, taking deep breath.

"Of course not," I answer. "He's resistant."

"Level two breakers can do it," Holtzmann says. "Please, try very hard. Your life may depend on the result we get."

I don't understand what he wants from me. Breakers can't twist the minds of resistant people, period. I've never heard of anybody capable of doing it.

"Mr. Hunter, we're waiting," Holtzmann says impatiently. He stares at the monitor with an anxious expression.

Expecting to fail, I still concentrate as hard as I possibly can. My head hurts from the formidable effort required. Listen to me, I project my thoughts into Chase's mind, listen to me. Useless. I can't breach the barriers to get inside his mind and twist his will. Being slightly tensed, Chase remains unfazed, his eyes clear and focused.

Dr. Carrel bursts out laughing.

"That's all we need to know," he says. "He's worthless."

Holtzmann shakes his head negatively.

"No, he's not," he exclaims. "We should check him for more advanced levels. Mr. Chase, please unchain Mr. Hunter."

Chase glances at his commander quizzically, waiting for his approval. After Wheeler nods, he approaches and frees my arms and legs. I stretch, feeling a tingling sensation in my numb muscles. I was stuck in the same position for too long. Now able to move, I have to fight a growing desire to attempt an escape. I watch Chase. If I can strike him quickly enough, I might get a chance to take his weapon. No, bad idea. Wheeler would shoot me in a blink of an eye. I have to wait for a better opportunity.

Chase notices my gaze fixated on his weapon.

"Don't even think about it," he says. "I'll break your neck if you try anything."

He backs slowly away, pointing the rifle at my head.

"Mr. Hunter, could you please read the memories of this lady?" Holtzmann says, gesturing to the unconscious woman on the floor.

I remember what Jessie told me about different breaker abilities. It must be true after all. But even if reading minds is possible, I have no idea how to do it. Being unsure how to proceed, I do nothing but stare at the woman.

"Mr. Hunter, you must try really hard," Holtzmann says. "Your life hangs in the balance."

"I don't know how," I answer sincerely.

"Just read her memory," Holtzmann says. "Don't think how. Don't doubt yourself. Just do it."

"I can't," I repeat.

Holtzmann sighs with exhaustion, thinking.

"Mr. Hunter, try reading her thoughts then," he requests.

I raise my eyebrows. It's getting ridiculous. What will he ask me to do next? To spread my wings and fly in circles above their heads?

"I can't read her thoughts," I say, losing my temper. "Shoot me if you wish, but let's just stop these stupid tests. I'm really tired."

"The first sane thing that I've heard from a breaker," Wheeler says. "I'm beginning to like this freak."

He draws his gun, ready to follow up on my suggestion.

"Read her mind!" Holtzmann commands. "If you don't I won't be able to help you."

"Come on, psycho, learn to lose," Wheeler says to him. "Let's finish it."

"Excuse me!" Holtzmann yells. "I am the lead scientist here!" He presses his hand to his chest. "We do what I say. And I say we remain in this room and test the subject until I get a conclusive result."

His eye twitches annoyingly.

"We'll finish the tests my way then," Wheeler says, approaching the woman and grabbing her shirt. "Wake up!" he shouts, slapping her face. She moans and opens her eyes, being still drowsy.

"Stop torturing the subjects, Wheeler!" Holtzmann orders. "That is unacceptable behavior!"

"Shut up, psycho," Wheeler growls.

He drags the woman closer to me and throws her at my feet. I hear the sound of her head hitting the hard floor. Something churns inside my stomach. I want to rush Wheeler, punching and smashing his face to a bloody pulp. That's what he expects, probably, smiling and holding the gun. I remind myself to be calm.

"Come on, breaker," Wheeler yells. "Let's see what you got."

He kicks the girl cruelly in the stomach. She cries out, rolling into a ball. Wheeler strikes her again, his heavy military boot slamming into her face.

I feel nauseated. Adrenaline fills my veins, burning like acid. I should do something but I don't know what.

"Cease and desist, Wheeler!" Holtzmann shouts.

"Just watch your monitor," Wheeler commands and kicks the poor woman in the head. Blood flows freely from her nose and mouth. She moans louder, gripping my leg.

"Help me, please," the woman begs.

Being so frightened of Wheeler, she doesn't seem to care that I'm a breaker any longer.

I feel disoriented, having the sensation of going down in an elevator.

Wheeler kicks the woman into the ribs. The same moment I gasp from a jolt of pain in my side.

"Do you feel it?" Wheeler asks.

I glance at him in confusion, not able to say anything. The woman coughs on the floor, having trouble breathing. I feel suffocated as well.

"I see some response," Holtzmann says, staring at the monitor.

"He's faking it," Carrel disagrees.

"Let's check," Wheeler says, grabbing the woman under her arms as he forces her up. She obeys, being completely submissive. I watch Wheeler lead her away from the room. The door shuts, but I'm still consumed by her despair and horror. The walls and the floor begin to swirl. I grasp the chair tightly with both hands not to fall. I have a strange sensation in my arm, as if somebody pulling me.

"Please, officer, please let me go," I hear her voice in my head.

My eyes are wide open, but the room fades for a moment. I see Wheeler standing in front of me. The next instant he puts the gun to my head and shoots. The bullet slams into my skull. I cry out and collapse onto the floor, wreathing in pain. I know he shot the poor woman. I can feel it.

"He's level four confirmed," Holtzmann says. "That's it. I claim this subject."

"He's just faking it," Carrel repeats.

Their voices sound distant. I can't understand where I am, or for the moment even who I am. Was I shot? Shakily, I tear the electrodes from my head. I can still feel the bullet, splitting my head and piercing my brain. It seemed so realistic.

Smiling, Wheeler reenters the room. An officer follows him, yelling, "Are you crazy?! You can't kill our inmates!"

"Shut your hole," Wheeler says. "Elimination has authorization to do whatever is deemed necessary."

I close my eyes, shuddering. I feel blood oozing from a nonexistent wound in my forehead.

"Hold on," I hear a soft voice. "It's all over now. You're all right."

As I look up, I see Chase crouching beside me and patting my shoulder. His face shows unexpected sympathy.

"Have I been shot?" I ask.

"No, you're just a telepath," he answers.

He locks the collar back in place on my neck as I black out.

When I awaken, I find myself in a small dark cell. It's windowless and has only a sink and toilet. I lie on the floor, dressed in bright orange jail issue clothing. My body aches, but the headache is finally gone. I touch my temple tentatively and feel stitches from where Wheeler hit me.

For a long time nobody comes in. I nap, enjoying the temporary reprieve. Kitty, I think. Where is she? I've no idea. Hopefully, she's gotten far away and is lying low. Never know what to expect from my little rebel always itching to use her skills.

A policeman brings in a sandwich and water. I eat greedily, biting off huge pieces. A good appetite means I must be recovering.

Finally the door opens and a tall blond lady walks in, wearing a sparkling green dress and high heeled shoes. I recognize Lola from her show. Her face isn't so flawless in person. I notice dark circles under her eyes. Wheeler, Chase and her crew team follow her into the now overcrowded cell.

"There he is!" Lola says loudly.

I sit up, glancing at her suspiciously. What is she doing here?

Chase and Wheeler pull me up to my feet and handcuff me.

"Oh my God," Lola says in shock. "You boys messed him up! He looks like a victim! Oh, no!"

A huge drama queen, she grabs her head in deep frustration. That's exactly how she acts in her show. Over emotional and extremely loud.

"Honey, you look like a victim for God's sake!" she says to me. "People will feel sorry for you. What a catastrophe! My show needs a vicious killer, not a victim. Make up won't help with the stitches."

"We can mask him," Wheeler suggests.

Lola drops her jaw.

"Honey! You're brilliant!" she exclaims. "Do it. And now let's go interview his lawyer."

I wasn't aware that I even had a lawyer.

Lola walks away happy and satisfied, accompanied by her crew and Wheeler.

"What the heck was that about?" I ask Chase.

"Today is the day of your trial," he answers. "Let's go, breaker."

He motions me toward the door. I don't resist, feeling weak. They must have drugged me. My thoughts tangle. A trial already? Everything is happening too quickly.

Chase leads me into a room with multiple camera monitors on the walls. He chains me to the only chair.

"Chase, what am I doing here?" I ask.

"You'll remain in this room during your trial," Chase answers. "It's too risky to allow you access to the actual courtroom, so you'll be only shown on screens there."

"Is this part of Lola's show?" I ask.

Chase nods. That is exactly what I was afraid of. They're gonna broadcast my trial and execution before the whole country.

Wheeler arrives with a mask and places it on my face. Usually it's reserved for the most dangerous prisoners to prevent bites. I must look really scary wearing this thing. Hopefully, they won't accuse me of being a cannibal as well.

As my captors leave, I stare down at the floor, trying to forget about the cameras. They make me really uncomfortable. Time moves slowly. Minute by minute. One hour after another. It seems endless. This is probably the worst thing they could do to me. Waiting in total ignorance of what's going on while Lola and the rest of the mob determine my future.

I look into the cameras. What if I try to explain everything? I know that ordinary people will vote, deciding my fate. If only they knew what really happened, maybe I'd have a chance to survive this mess.

No, that would be pointless. Lola would say that I'm lying. People would believe her, not an evil freak wearing an ugly mask. I'll just have to wait it out.

Holtzmann said he could help me. He was obviously looking for a breaker with special talents. Apparently I'm a telepath. It means they need me alive. I can't be sure. Many breakers have been sentenced to death over the last months. I hope Kitty isn't watching this fiasco.

When Wheeler opens the door, I flinch. The trial must be over. My pulse goes up and I notice my hands trembling.

"Congratulations, breaker," Wheeler says with a mocking smile. "You've been sentenced to death."

CHAPTER 7

I'm still in shock when guards come in to unchain me. My mind refuses to accept the fact that my life is over. They wouldn't really kill an innocent man, would they? This must be a mistake.

As guards lead me out of the room, I resist as much as possible, although I know it's completely useless. I'm tired of conforming. I want my freedom back and all this insanity to be over.

Being handcuffed and outnumbered, I have no chance to escape. The guards slam me against a wall and get a few additional licks in with their nightsticks. I fall, landing on my side. My ribs hurt and my head starts bleeding again. I concentrate, projecting calming thoughts onto the guards. It doesn't work. The collar around my neck blocks any ability to hypnotize.

"Let me go!" I yell desperately. Multiple pairs of strong hands grab hold, dragging me along the jail passageway. My feet barely touch the floor. Somebody places a smelly dark bag over my head, blinding me.

They throw me back into the same windowless cell, where I waited before the trial. I collapse onto the floor. When guards finally remove the bag from my head, I see an overly excited Lola and her team come in, escorted by Wheeler and Chase. I squint, turning away from cameras. Guards hold me tightly, making sure I can't move.

"You've been sentenced to death," Lola says joyfully. "Do you think you've gotten what you deserve?"

She holds the microphone close to my mouth, waiting. Everybody peers at me. I take a deep breath. This is my chance. I need to come up with something brilliant, something to change people's minds and prove my innocence. Nothing intelligent comes to my head.

"I didn't do anything," I blurt out.

"Surprise! Just what they all say!" Lola yells at the camera. "Instead of begging for forgiveness, he continues lying and feigning innocence. What a calculating, cold blooded murderer!"

Anger boils inside me. A death sentence isn't enough for them. Now I'm forced to be a part of this freak show, playing the role of a despised villain. This makes me sick! I'm not going to be their puppet.

Lola sticks her microphone to my face again. I remain silent, lips pressed tightly together, glaring at Lola. No matter what she does, I won't utter another word. Hope it drops her ratings.

After a few more failed attempts to get me to speak, Lola gives up and leaves. Guards remove my handcuffs and order me to stand facing the wall until they're gone.

Alone in the room I walk in circles, fighting a growing anxiety. I still can't believe all this is happening. It's like a bad dream, surreal and ridiculous. The more I think about it, the angrier I become. I'm not going to let them kill me so easily. This fight isn't over, maybe I'll find a way to survive yet.

Random thoughts cross my mind. If I could figure out how to fake a suicide, they might transport me to a hospital where escape would be more feasible. There's no easy way to go about it as guards made certain it's impossible for me to harm myself. I have no knife or rope. Of course I could slam my head against the wall, splitting my skull, but in that case I'd be done in for real. No, suicide isn't an option. I have to think of something else.

Discouraged, I sit on the floor holding my head.

Hypnosis. This is the only real advantage I have. Most of the guards aren't resistant. If I could only regain my abilities, I'd put them under and use them to clear a path to the exit.

I touch the collar on my neck. It's made of metal and securely locked. Smooth and seamless, I can't even find the place where it fits together. Agitated, I yank on it, wincing from the pain shooting through my neck.

"Nice try, breaker," I hear a mocking voice.

Officer Chase comes in, carrying a tray with sandwiches. I leave the collar alone, sitting motionless. Chase places the tray near me. He appears a bit arrogant, walking in here without other guards. He probably doesn't expect an attack. For a moment I consider my chances.

"Don't even think of doing something stupid," Chase says, smiling. "I'm used to dealing with far tougher breakers than you. There's no way you could surprise me."

He must have noticed my tension. Frustrated, I glance at sandwiches and push the tray away from me.

"Come on," Chase says. "You need to eat."

He's right. If I want to escape, I need to eat to become stronger. I take a bite out of a sandwich.

"When will I be transported to the prison?" I ask, hoping to gather some information.

"You'll wait for your execution day right here," Chase answers. "Actually it's against standard procedures, but we make an exception for breakers. You're supposed to be too dangerous to be transported."

This is really bad news. Being stuck in the same cell, I won't get many opportunities to escape. I force myself to look unconcerned, hiding my disappointment.

"See you later, breaker," Chase says, leaving. "Enjoy."

What a jerk! I should have smashed his head.

I really don't want to die in this place. Most likely I only have a few days or weeks. What can I come up with during such a short time?

The next several days I look desperately for any chance to escape. It never comes. They keep me locked away inside the same cell just as Chase promised. Three times a day he comes at the same time with the same sandwiches. I decide to give overpowering Chase a try. When he arrives like clockwork with the sandwiches, I'm waiting. I jump him, tackling Chase to the ground and reaching for his rifle. Chase reacts instantly, using his taser. I sprawl on the floor in shock and pain. I expect him to strike me, but Chase just leaves. The next day he returns at the same time with a tray, acting like nothing happened.

Other officers drop by to taunt me. They stand outside the door, yelling insults and laughing.

"You're gonna die soon, freak," one says, grinning. "A broken breaker."

I suppress my hatred and desire to punch one of them, because that's all they need to beat me. I won't let them manipulate me into giving them a reason to add injury to insult.

When I'm not plotting an escape, I spend my time worrying about Kitty. Not being with her hurts the most. My reckless little sister is on her own now. Hopefully, she did as I asked. But what if she didn't? Kitty is stubborn and arrogant enough to try rescuing me. It'd do about as much good as walking into a police station and asking to be locked up. Please Kitty, get away, I repeat over and over in my mind. Forget me and save your own life.

The cell seems smaller with each passing day. I feel suffocated and claustrophobic. They keep the lights on in the room 24/7. I can't tell the difference between day and night and have no idea how long I've been here. Distracting myself, I walk in circles and do pushups. Escape, I think, I need to escape.

One day Wheeler comes in with a squad of Elimination officers.

"Let's go, breaker," he says. "We're escorting you to death row. Tomorrow's your big day."

Looks like Wheeler truly enjoys delivering bad news. I wonder how many times he has spoken the same words to other breakers captured before. Smirking, he waits for my reaction. I remain calm, keeping my anger and frustration deeply inside. I'm not going to give him the pleasure of seeing me distraught or begging. I look hard into his eyes, saying nothing.

"Face the wall," Chase says, stepping toward me. "Hands behind your back."

I have to suppress the impulse to fight. There are too many of them. Resisting now won't do any good.

"Come on, breaker," Chase says with a smile. "You don't want to get tased again, do you?"

I have no choice but to do as he orders. Chase handcuffs me and leads to the door. Other officers watch, ready to tase and beat me at the first sign of disobedience.

"By this same time tomorrow you'll be dead," I hear Wheeler's voice. "And the world will be a better place."

Don't answer, I remind myself. Don't react. That's exactly what he's fishing for.

I lower my head and walk. Chase leads me through a lonely maze of passages. They probably evacuated the entire route ahead of time.

As we step out of the jail building, a crowd of journalists swarms us. The officers form a circle around me, pushing the story crazed cameramen out of the way. I'm overwhelmed by countless flashes, a cacophony of high pitched voices and hands with microphones jammed forward, reaching for me. I turn my face away and squint. I hate being the main attraction for their wicked show.

"No interviews!" Wheeler yells. "Out of the way!"

The officers shove away the more persistent journalists in our path ahead. Chase pushes me from behind and we move toward the sedans parked along the side of the road. Too bad I can't use my breaker abilities. It'd be the perfect opportunity to escape. I'd easily twist the journalists' minds, creating panic and confusion. A headache comes, but I can't project one single thought. Perhaps if I'm lucky, I'll get a chance to make a break for it during this trip.

I breathe in the fresh cold air greedily, taking a look around. I haven't been outside for so long. This may be the last time I see the sky, trees or feel the wind on my face. For the first time I truly realize how close I've come to death. I almost sense its shadow creeping up behind me.

The officers push me inside one of the vehicles. Wheeler and Chase sit on either side of me. Journalists crowd against the car, pounding the windows and shouting questions. Chase puts a bag over my head as the car lurches forward.

"Are you scared, freak?" Wheeler whispers. "You should be. We'll be killing you soon enough."

This guy is sadistic with zero compassion toward breakers. Wheeler's joyful laughter disgusts me. Chase and the driver remain silent, not showing any appreciation for Wheeler's mean spirited jokes.

The car moves slowly ahead, making several turns. We never stop. They're not taking any chances.

I calculate how much time I likely have. Probably less than twenty four hours. Not much to come up with a means of escape.

Don't lose hope, I tell myself. Don't let them break you. They want you to give up and play out the role as the fall guy. Public enemy number one.

I hold out hope that I can still find a way to deny them and survive.

There's a solemn atmosphere in the car during the last part of the trip. Everybody knows where we're going and precisely why. I suddenly realize that these men are soon to be my killers. They're all aware of my innocence. They all saw the actual video from the bank. Nobody cares.

As the car stops, I'm forced to get out and walk. I can't see anything. Chase and Wheeler grab my arms, pulling me forward. I hear heavy doors closing behind. A shiver runs down my spine. I've just stepped inside the place where I'm to die.

They remove the bag from my head and I squint from bright ceiling lights. I'm in a large room, surrounded by Elimination guards holding rifles. For a second I think they're about to shoot me right here, but it turns out it's just their way of welcoming breakers to death row.

An officer searches me for concealed weapons. That's funny that they're so worried about my committing suicide when their intent is to kill me. Suicide is not part of my plan. I want to escape and find Kitty.

The officers lead me to a separate room and order me to undress. Unwillingly, I strip off all my jail clothing. They leave the blocking collar on my neck. An officer brings a hose and knocks me off my feet with a forceful spray of cold water. The officers burst out laughing. Of course, letting me take a normal shower isn't their first option. Elimination has to find a more humiliating and violent method to wash their inmates. When the procedure is over, I get up, shivering and spitting water. Chase throws some fresh clothes at my feet. Apparently, he's the only one not amused at my predicament.

The officers lock me up in a large cell with the cameras mounted on the ceiling. They probably broadcast this video throughout the entire Republic. It hurts to think that my imprisonment and death are just part of the show. This is how they divert public attention from real problems into hatred for breakers. We're blamed for the high criminal rate in society, shortages of food and crumbling dilapidated housing. No matter what tragedy occurs, some poor breaker will have to be killed to satisfy the public bloodlust for revenge.

I lie down, resting and trying to think. All normal people can't hate us, can they? I heard there's a group of protesters. They don't do much, just walk with signs calling for freedom and equality for breakers. They haven't actually rescued anyone yet.

Time marches steadily on, each tick on the clock bringing me closer to the time of my execution. There are only a few hours left. I have to do something right now, before it's too late. I can't think of a damn thing.

My hands tremble and I close my eyes to calm down. If I have to die, I want to die like a man.

Being so frightened and desperate, I find my only peace in thinking of Kitty. She's still free and hopefully untraceable for Elimination. I haven't failed her after all. I did all right. I can accept dying for Kitty. It's much better than both of us being killed.

I can't help from smiling as I remember our first Christmas together. The only Christmas tree we could afford was a total disaster, one with broken branches and needles already falling off. Despite everything, Kitty was overjoyed. She never had a Christmas tree before. We decorated it with paper ornaments and then drank hot chocolate, another luxury we couldn't afford every day. I remember Kitty laughing and singing. Gosh, we were so happy together. Even being so different, we managed to become really close friends. Now I'm on my own, just as I was before I met her.

It's fine, I tell myself. You can handle it.

I've probably been doomed from the very beginning. Even as a child I was unwanted and even despised by my own mother. What other fate could I expect to have? Any memories of my mother are vague. She was younger than I am now, when I was born. I've never known my father. My mother often told he was a nasty man, a vicious breaker who took advantage of her. If she had enough money, she'd have gotten rid of me before it was too late.

In spite of everything, I loved her as any little child would love his mother. She always made sure to make me feel guilty for my very existence. She said I was the spitting image of my father. Even as a kid I hated myself for being a constant living reminder of what had happened to her. I remember her crying and throwing things, wishing that she was dead. Being upset and depressed most of time, she wasn't capable of taking proper care about my younger sister. That soon became my job. I fed, washed and then calmed her by making up bed time stories about a happier future. She had red curly hair and green eyes, just like my Kitty.

My mother first learned about my abilities to hypnotize when I turned eight. Afterward, she spent the whole night crying. When morning arrived she gave me a basket with food and asked me to leave.

"Go away and never come back," she said. "Forget your name. Never tell anybody about me or your sister."

I cried, pleading to stay. Nothing could change her mind. I don't think I can blame her now. Elimination would lock her up for concealing a breaker.

I left. Since that time, I've been on my own.

A door opening snaps me back from the grim memories. Chase comes in with a dull face.

"You have the right to one phone call," he says. "Do you have anybody you wish to call?"

I shake my head negatively. Presented as an act of humanity, a phone call is just one more method Elimination would use to track people I may know.

"Too bad," Chase sighs. "Well, breaker, then tell me what you want for your supper," he pauses and then adds. "Your last supper, I mean."

One more sadistic ritual, feeding an animal before sacrificing it.

"I'm not hungry," I answer, unwilling to play along their game.

"Come on, breaker," Chase exclaims. "Order something. You don't need to spend your last hours hungry."

"What do you care?" I ask. "You and your friends are gonna murder me anyway."

He averts his eyes.

"Listen, breaker," he says. "This is not personal, okay? I'm just doing my job."

"You know I haven't done anything to deserve this," I insist. "You saw the video from the bank, didn't you?"

Chase sighs.

"Just order your darn supper," he says. "I didn't come here to chit chat. Actually, I'm not allowed to talk to you outside of procedural matters."

"I'll take a huge juicy steak with mashed potatoes," I say. That was my favorite food when I lived on the farm. "Medium rare, with onions," I order. "And ice cream for dessert."

"Maybe you'd also like some freaking lobster tails with butter sauce?" Chase asks. "We're on a tight budget here."

"You got to be kidding," I laugh. "My last supper and you're on a budget."

Chase fidgets on his feet. I'm starting to have a bit of fun with him.

"I'll see what can be done," he says, leaving.

I lie down and become motionless, thinking. What can I do to escape? Probably nothing, although I refuse to believe it.

Kitty, just think of Kitty. Make the time you have left less miserable.

Chase comes back with a tray and places it in front of me. Looks like a tray straight out of a frozen TV dinner. It's only slightly warmed up.

"What the heck is this supposed to be?!" I exclaim.

"Sorry," Chase says. "That's all we had. At least it's steak."

"I'm not gonna eat this garbage," I say.

Chase rolls his eyes.

"You won't get any breakfast," he says, pushing the tray closer. "Just eat!" he orders.

Groaning, I take the plastic spoon and try some mashed potatoes. Chase watches me attentively. This is weird. What is he waiting for?

I manage to swallow only a few scoops before understanding what he was expecting to happen. My mind becomes hazy. The chamber swirls in front of my eyes and I lose balance, falling on my side. The floor seems to sway under me. They've poisoned the food!

I open my mouth to speak, but a heavy cloud of fatigue forces me to relax.

"That's a little gift from Holtzmann," I hear Chase's voice from above. "He didn't want you to remain awake and worry your entire last night. Don't worry, breaker. It's only sleep meds."

His silhouette dissolves into an overlapping darkness and I lose myself in a heavy dreamless sleep.

I wake up with only one thought, that I'm going to die today. Still being under the effect of whatever drug they spiked my last supper with, I don't panic or feel worried. I only regret of having wasted my last hours sleeping. I wanted to spend that time thinking of Kitty. I intended to be brave and die well, not meet death from a half drugged and senseless state.

Why did they do it? They probably chose to drug me to avoid resistance. They want everything to go smoothly for the benefit of the TV cameras.

Looks like they're succeeding. Being drowsy and disoriented I can't resist too much.

The officers come in, yawning and appearing bored. Killing a breaker is just an everyday monotonous task for these guys.

Lola follows behind, barking orders to her crew.

"He can't wear the mask on his face during the execution," she says. "We have to do something to make his face more presentable to our viewing audience."

"We could make him over as a drug addict," her cameraman suggests.

"Brilliant!" Lola exclaims happily.

I guess I do look like an addict right now. My eyes are unfocused and I stare into space, being in a semi catatonic state. Nevertheless, the officers grab me up by my arms and hold firmly, while Lola's crew works on my face.

"Put some make up on the bruises," Lola yells. "People may think that he was abused, possibly triggering some false sympathy."

I don't resist, oblivious to what they're doing. I just want to go back to sleep. They must have used a really strong sedative on me.

"Honey, would you do me a favor?" Lola asks me. "Could you please scream or threaten the witnesses during your execution? We wouldn't want your show to be boring."

If I wasn't so drugged, I might slap this lady. Instead, I just turn away, keeping silent.

"Please," Lola begs. "We really need to maintain higher ratings."

"One hour to injection time," I hear Wheeler's voice. "Bring him to the execution room for prepping."

The officers lead me out of the chamber. My legs are weak and I can hardly walk. They have to almost drag me. One hour, I think. They'll kill me in one hour.

Suddenly, I realize that I won't get a chance to escape. I can't run. I can't use hypnosis. This is it, I think. The end of the road. The sedative in my blood muffles all emotion and I feel nothing. Maybe being heavily medicated is for the best.

As I enter the execution room, my eyes glue to the gurney and the intravenous bag hung on a metal pole. This is where everything will happen. I had no idea what method they'd use to kill me, but it's obvious now. Lethal injection.

It's supposed to be painless, I guess. At least preferable to shuddering in agony in the gas chamber, fried in an electric chair, or being hung.

I see Holtzmann dressed in white laboratory clothing, checking the poisonous concoction in the bag. Is he the chosen one to perform everything?

The officers instruct me to lie down on the gurney and strap me down. They step quickly away, probably following protocol. Nobody speaks, each being focused on his role.

One wall has a large window looking out onto another room with several rows of chairs. I watch people coming in and taking seats. They're the witnesses to my execution. They look excited as if waiting anxiously for a spectacular performance at the theater. I notice Mandy smiling and chatting up other guests. There's Tim, looking at me with contempt and disgust. They've both come to enjoy watching my demise.

"Fifteen minutes," Wheeler announces.

I notice a phone on the wall. I hope for it to ring and somebody to postpone or better yet, cancel the execution. It doesn't happen.

"Five minutes," Wheeler's voice interrupts the silence.

"Do you have any last words?" an unknown man, possibly the warden of this prison, asks.

I shake my head no. I have nothing to say to my killers.

Wheeler nods and Holtzmann takes my arm, wiping across my skin with a wet cotton ball. This must be one of the most ridiculous things I've ever seen in my life. Even during the process of killing me, he's afraid of putting some germs into my system. I glance at him. Holtzmann catches my eye and then winks. It seems strange. Although, I can't really tell if he's winked or just suffered a nervous twitch.

"It's all right, Rex," Holtzmann whispers quietly. "You've received approval to become a subject in my study."

I don't have time to think of what that might mean. The needle pierces my skin, quickly finding the vein. I watch anxiously as the venomous liquid flows through the tube into my bloodstream. My body relaxes.

I feel very sedated. Then the poison paralyzes me to the point I can't even close my eyes.

Think of her, I repeat in my mind.

Kitty is my last thought before I lose consciousness.

PART 2

CHAPTER 8

A monotone humming noise hurts my ears. It's so irritating that I have to force my eyes open to try and find the source of my discomfort. My vision is blurry. I can spot some figures around me, but can't quite make out their faces.

What's happened? Am I alive or dead? I don't know for sure. But I do know I want the annoying noise to stop so I can go back to sleep.

I'm lying on some type of hard, cold metallic surface. I sense motion, but my body is still. Where am I? I raise my head to look around, but still can't focus. I manage to hold my head up only for an instant before it drops back onto the metal floor. I'm still too weak. Feels like every muscle in my body has been paralyzed and my bones turned into soft mush. I can't even feel my legs.

After a few more minutes pass, my senses begin awakening. I can now at least tell that I'm inside an aircraft. The disturbing noise is the sound of an engine. How did I end up here? I can't remember anything.

"Why the heck is he awake?" a nearby voice questions. I can recognize it even suffering from amnesia. Wheeler. Somebody I could never forget.

"I don't want to overdose him," a different voice answers. I guess this must be the psycho guy who performed tests on me.

"Put him back down," Wheeler commands.

"Any additional sedative could induce a coma. If he doesn't awaken, you'll be held accountable," the psycho guy says.

"More sedative or the butt of my rifle," Wheeler counters.

A needle pricks my skin, and the noises of engines and voices disappear.

When I come out of the dark abyss, I can see only the ceiling above. It's white and flawless. No other thoughts come to mind. I feel good and nothing bothers me. I stare into the perfect whiteness, being in some state of euphoria.

As my memory begins to return, I wonder about Kitty. Is she safe? Has Elimination captured her? Then I remember the execution. I'm supposed to be dead. So how in the world am I still breathing?

Unable to move, I feel the pressure of tight straps against my wrists and ankles. I'm strapped down on some sort of the gurney.

Overcoming my weakness, I turn my heavy head to the right. I see a large sterile looking area filled with empty gurneys and medical equipment. It resembles the operating room from my hallucinations about the girl with electrodes protruding out from her shaved head.

A gray-haired man with gold colored glasses sits in a chair close by. He's dressed like a doctor. I recognize him. His name is Carrel. He's the guy who kept insisting I was uselessness, even approving my death.

He notices my glance and smiles.

"Do you believe in life after death?" he asks. "If you do, you must be in hell."

Not one for warm greetings I guess. Watching him carefully, I remain silent.

"You remember me, don't you?" Carrel asks. "Do you understand what I'm saying?"

He reaches for me, grabbing my head and directing a small flashlight into my eyes. I squint, trying to resist. I'm still too weak. I've probably been heavily drugged.

Having checked my eyes and taken my blood pressure, Carrel leaves me for a few seconds. Then he returns with a needle.

"Let me help you wake up," he says, injecting something into my vein. "We've got little time."

The medicine kicks in almost instantly, increasing my pulse and sending a warm impulse throughout my body. I gasp, shuddering from the strange sensation.

"Better?" Carrel asks, grinning.

"What the heck is it?" I mumble. I still can't completely control my tongue and lips.

Carrel doesn't answer.

"Welcome to your hell, breaker," he says. "First, let me congratulate you on being alive. You've probably already understood that your execution was just a well-planned performance. We've spared your life, only sedating you deeply. But don't get too happy. Very soon you'll come to regret being alive. I personally guarantee it."

He pauses, watching my reaction. I just stare at him.

"Officially you're dead," Carrel continues. "Your empty casket was even buried a few days ago. What that means, breaker, is that now we can do whatever we wish with you. You officially no longer even exist."

"Isn't all that too much trouble?" I ask. "Why bother with a fake execution and funeral if you only plan to torture me anyway?"

"It's all been about ratings for the show," Carrel answers. "The public needs an enemy. We gave them you. Your execution was a big hit, received the highest ratings of the year."

He gives a highly satisfied laugh.

"Whatever," I say, turning away. It doesn't stop Carrel. He walks around the gurney, placing his face near mine.

"You're my lab rat now," he says. "You're lying in the Elimination primary research facility. Where at least you'll now be serving a scientific purpose. The moment we get what we need, you'll be put down for real. If you'd only be good enough to last till then, of course."

I'm disgusted. I can't help myself. I spit right into his arrogant, wrinkled face.

This angers Carrel. He slaps me, yelling and promising to make me regret it.

"I'll teach you some respect, breaker," Carrel says, still trembling from anger and pointing his finger. "Trust me, I know precisely how to deal with spiteful little pigs like you."

I don't worry about Carrel's threats. I've died once already. What else can they do to me?

The door suddenly slides open and Wheeler along with an unfamiliar middle aged man enter. The stranger wears a business suit and tie. Three guards follow closely behind, carrying rifles and gazing suspiciously at me. I recognize Chase as one.

"Good morning, Rex," the unknown man says. "I'm Warden Browning, in charge of this prison and acting director of the breaker rehabilitation program."

His voice sounds soft, but I perceive a hidden menace underneath.

"I believe that even the most evil of souls deserve an opportunity for redemption," Browning continues. "Here you'll get an opportunity to start fresh, serving the greater purposes of our country. If you're cooperative enough and manage to demonstrate some useful talents, you may possibly earn your pardon. You may even become a contributing member in a future society whereby mind breakers and normal humans live together harmoniously, and in peace."

Browning smiles, acting like the most righteous man in the Republic. I don't believe one single word he says.

"On the other hand, should you show any resistance or refuse to work with us in any way, you'll be sent straight to the Death Camp," he threatens. "This is the name for another prison housing only the most dangerous of breakers. Nobody has managed to last longer than two months there. If you want to live, you'll simply have to become very agreeable and respectful. I have great hopes for you. Don't disappoint me."

He glances at Wheeler.

"The subject is yours," Browning says, leaving. Chase and Wheeler remain in the room.

"Did you miss me, freak?" Wheeler asks.

Dr. Carrel smiles, ready to watch the fun. I decide to keep silent. Just like I did during my interrogation at the jail.

"Hit him," Wheeler commands.

Chase looks back in surprise.

"Are you deaf?" Wheeler growls. "I said hit him."

Chase approaches me and sways his rifle. I expect my face to be smashed, but he strikes very gingerly with the butt of his rifle.

"Come on, Chase," Wheeler groans. "Don't hit like a girl. I know you can do better than that."

Wincing, Chase strikes me again, this time a crunching blow to my head. The room blackens for a second as sharp pain shoots through my head. Wheeler smiles.

"That's better," he says, approaching. "A hearty welcoming is very important. Now I have a few questions, breaker. It's in your best interest to answer truthfully. What's your real name?"

I keep silent.

"In case you're wondering, cockroach, that was question one. What's your real name?" Wheeler repeats.

I turn my face away, determined not to let Wheeler intimidate me.

"Cat got your tongue, breaker?" he asks. "Let's see what we can do about that. Chase!"

Chase hits me again. Blood sprays from my nose. I've been through worse, I tell myself, remaining silent.

"I see," Wheeler says. "So you don't care if you live or die. Well, in this case I have a little surprise for you. Chase, bring her in."

I feel a jolt of panic. Have they captured Kitty? I dread this far more than my own death.

Chase leaves the room. We wait for several long torturous minutes.

Only not Kitty, please, I beg in my mind.

Chase returns, leading a skinny woman wearing an inmate jumpsuit, handcuffed and collared. Her face is swollen and bruised, covered in dried blood. This is not Kitty, I realize, breathing a sigh of relief.

"Are you surprised, breaker?" Wheeler asks. "Do you recognize your little friend?"

My friend? I don't have any friends besides Kitty. I take a closer look at the battered woman. Her features have been so distorted that it takes me a few seconds to realize who she is. They've captured Jessie, the girl who helped us hide. What can I do? All I can think of is to pretend Jessie is a complete stranger to me.

Wheeler and Chase strap Jessie into a metal chair. It's obvious that she's in great pain. Her head is drooping and her eyes unfocused. They've beaten her viciously.

Think of Kitty, I remind myself. Your main goal is to protect your sister. Don't fail her.

"What do you say now, breaker?" Wheeler asks. "What about this girl? I know she's your friend. But can you continue to keep silent while watching your friend being killed?"

My hands squeeze into fists. The straps on the gurney keep me from any action. They're too thick and hard to tear.

It pleases Wheeler immensely to see me squirm. He laughs and then suddenly snaps Jessie's jaw with a heavy punch. Jessie utters a small moan as her head lolls to the side and then drops down.

I can't stand it.

"Stop it," I demand. "There's no need in beating this poor girl. She's nobody to me. I've never even seen her before."

"Really?" Wheeler asks. "Then why are you so worried?"

He grabs Jessie's short hair and pulls her head back. Looking into her foggy eyes, he asks, "You know this guy, don't you darling?"

"Go to hell," she snarls through bloodied teeth.

Wheeler strikes her again, breaking her nose this time.

"Stop it, Wheeler, you freaking coward!" I yell.

Chase stands motionless on the other side of Jessie.

"You're the only one who can stop this, breaker," Wheeler says. "Just answer my questions. What's your real name? And where did your little girlfriend get away to?"

Although telling him my name can't really hurt me, it may be a way for Elimination to track down my blood relatives. As for Kitty's location, I have no idea where she went. My headstrong sister could have followed my instructions or done something entirely different.

"Answer, freak!" Wheeler commands. "Her blood will be on your hands if you make me kill her."

He backhands Jessie. I turn away, unable to watch.

"No, breaker," Wheeler growls. "Don't turn your head. You have to watch!"

He approaches and grabs my head.

"Look at her," he whispers. "Look what you've done to her. She's suffering. Are you really ready to just let her die? Are you so heartless?"

Wheeler turns my face toward Jessie. Blood drips from her nose, running down her lips and chin. She spits on the floor, groaning.

"Leave him be, you idiot," Jessie says in a surprisingly calm voice. "I've already told you, he's never seen me before."

Apparently, this is a message for me. She's letting me know we're on the same page.

"Chase, shut her up!" Wheeler commands.

Chase approaches Jessie and then hesitates. Seems like he can't decide what to do.

"Keep your mouth shut," he demands.

"What the hell was that, Chase?" Wheeler asks.

"With all due respect sir, I think we should stand down," Chase answers. "She's really messed up already. I doubt she can take much more."

"Do I have to do everything for myself, wimp?" Wheeler shouts. He steps toward Chase and shoves him away from Jessie. Chase looks perplexed as if he doesn't want any trouble with Wheeler, but continuing with the torture is too hard for him.

"Look, breaker," Wheeler says. "Everything that happens here is on you."

He punches Jessie again. She's very brave, keeping silent even as her eyes swell shut and her blood splatters everything around.

"She'll die if you don't answer my questions," Wheeler promises, breathing heavily. "How can you be so selfish? You still have a chance to save her!"

My arms strain at the straps so hard that it hurts. I don't know what to do. My thoughts alternate between saving Jessie and protecting Kitty. How can I protect both?

"Do you want her to die?" I hear Wheeler's angry voice.

He's no human, I think suddenly. Normal human beings can't torture and kill so easily, smiling and relishing in each minute of the victim's pain. He's a vicious monster who's going to kill us anyway. It means we're already doomed, having been captured. I believe Kitty still has her freedom and therefore still has a chance to survive. I must protect Kitty, whatever the cost.

"Why not just kill her already?" I answer. "She's nobody to me anyway."

Of course I'm bluffing. I just hope that Wheeler is bluffing too.

Wheeler stops his beating of Jessie, pausing to think. Seems like he didn't expect me to answer in that manner. Jessie glances at me for the first time and her swollen wounded lips move in some resemblance of a smile.

"You must think Elimination has no way to break you, don't you?" Wheeler asks. "Chase, bring Victor," he orders. "Let's see how our uncooperative little lab rat likes having someone in his head."

Looks like Jessie isn't the only surprise Wheeler has prepared for me.

Keep silent no matter what, I repeat in my thoughts. You can handle this.

"Wait, you can't use Victor," Carrel protests. "He's been doing some reading recently. I don't want to exhaust him."

"I don't care," Wheeler says. "And I can use Victor any time I want."

As Carrel mumbles something incoherent in disapproval, Wheeler gestures for Chase to go. I've no idea what to expect. Who's Victor? I've never known anybody by that name.

"You know how hard it is to acquire such a talented breaker," Carrel grumbles. "Victor is one of the most valuable subjects."

Wheeler rolls his eyes.

"If you damage Victor, where will we find another like him?" Carrel continues.

"I'll be bringing plenty of new breakers soon enough," Wheeler answers. "Just stop with all the bickering."

Chase comes in leading a short guy decked out in a similar style prison issue jumpsuit as Jessie. He has a youthful looking face, making it difficult to determine his age. Apparently, Victor is another inmate breaker. Seems odd he isn't wearing a blocking collar though.

"What do you need, boss?" Victor asks.

"Read her," Wheeler motions toward Jessie.

Victor glances at her, then at me and says, "You're kidding."

"Victor, we need you to give us information concerning this lady," Carrel says. "Please, do as Wheeler requests."

"Can't you guys get that on your own?" Victor asks. "It's your job to interrogate them. It takes a piece of me every time I have to do this."

"Victor, your willingness to read these breakers when required is the only thing separating you from them," Wheeler threatens.

"Come on, just beat this girl a little more," Victor suggests. "She'll eventually tell you everything she knows."

I watch them arguing. Seems strange to me that Wheeler hasn't smashed Victor's face, after putting up so much resistance. Wheeler looks agitated, but he's suppressing his anger for some reason. Victor must be very important for Elimination, I conclude.

"Stop whining and read her," Wheeler repeats calmly.

Victor groans.

"Okay," he says, searching his pockets. He finds a candy bar and eats it greedily, finishing it off with a few huge bites. Then, he wipes his mouth on his sleeve and approaches Jessie.

"Don't touch me, freak," she mumbles.

"I'm sorry, okay?" Victor says softly. "I'll try not to mess you up too badly."

"Get away from me!" Jessie demands, apparently being well aware of what he's about to do.

Victor takes a deep breath, closes his eyes and grabs Jessie by the neck, pressing his forehead into hers. She gasps and her legs and arms twitch in spasms. Not opening his eyes, Victor tightens his grip. Terrified, I watch Jessie's mouth foaming as convulsions shudder through her body. What in the world is he doing to her? I've never seen anything like this before. I hear Wheeler's mocking laughter.

"Are you enjoying the show, freak?" Wheeler asks.

"Stop!" I shout at Victor. "Leave her alone!"

He doesn't react, possibly not even hearing me. Concentrating and tensed, he winces from the effort. At the same time Jessie emits a muffled cry. Chase turns away as if the scene disgusts him. Dr. Carrel, on the other hand, seems very curious, watching attentively.

Jessie stops screaming, her eyes wild and widened with insanity. Victor releases her and collapses on the floor, holding his head. He mumbles something, trembling.

"Have you read her?" Wheeler asks.

Victor glances at him blankly, getting up. Exhausted, he loses his balance, hitting the floor again. Chase reaches to help, but Victor pushes him away.

"Wait!" he exclaims. "Don't touch me!"

Chase steps back. Victor shakes his head, seemingly disoriented.

"My name is Victor," he whispers. "I'm in the lab."

Looks like he's struggling to remember who he is. What the heck has just happened, I wonder. Have I just witnessed a memory reading? This can't be true. I thought it was only a fairy tale.

After Victor regains his strength and stands, Wheeler repeats the question, "What have you learned?"

"Her name is Jessica Pond," Victor answers. "She's twenty one, works for some trashy motel where Rex and his girlfriend stopped for a night. She did help them, even letting them stay in her apartment."

"Any relatives?" Wheeler asks.

"She has parents in the south," Victor answers. "They operate a farm. I've got their address. She grew up there, then ran away at sixteen. Being a breaker, she didn't want to endanger her parents. You should be able to use them. She loves her parents a lot."

Victor gazes at Jessie with unexpected guilt. Although Jessie's eyes are open, she doesn't seem to notice him. Only the chair straps prevent her body from falling to the floor.

"That's my boy," Carrel exclaims proudly.

Victor winces annoyingly and requests Carrel to shut up.

"Good job. Now read this freak," Wheeler says, pointing at me.

CHAPTER 9

"You truly want me to try to break two subjects in a row?" Victor asks as he spits on the floor.

"You'll survive," Wheeler answers. "Do as I said."

Victor groans. Perhaps he's being forced to cooperate with Elimination, I realize suddenly. He could be every bit as much a victim here as Jessie or myself. Nevertheless, I can't help but hate him. Seeing Jessie lost in oblivion with a blank and meaningless stare only makes me want to smash Victor's face. If I could only get out of these straps…Desperately, I flail my arms and legs. Nothing works, the effort only serving to rub off some skin on my wrists.

Letting out an exhausted sigh, Victor approaches. As he grabs my neck, I snarl and move my head away.

"Don't resist," Victor says. "The more you resist, the more it messes with your mind."

"Back off," I say through clinched teeth.

"Easy, easy," Victor says, getting a firm grip on my head and stopping me from further movement. Then he closes his eyes and presses his forehead against mine. The same instant, I can almost physically sense how some invisible force breaches my mind, breaking through it. I convulse as a jolt of incredible pain shoots through my head.

I can't let it happen. I must fight to resist Victor. No matter what, I have to block my memory somehow.

A nauseating feeling of weightlessness enfolds me as if I'm falling. Victor tightens his grip, making a low growling noise. The room blackens and I can't see anything.

Stay awake, I command myself. Don't let him knock you out. If I lose consciousness, I'm done and Kitty's vulnerable.

I begin to hyperventilate. My heart pounds heavily and large drops of sweat roll down my face. I feel like I'm losing my mind. For a few seconds I don't understand who or where I am. Reality fades, overlapped by images of Kitty flashing in my thoughts. This is Victor, I realize, he's inducing me to remember Kitty so that he can rip off my memories. It's outrageous! I can't let anybody do this to me. I have to protect Kitty!

Get out, I project. Get the hell out of my head.

I concentrate, projecting my intense desire to block him. I have to put all my strength into the effort.

Get out, I repeat in my mind relentlessly. You can't break me. Leave me alone.

I grab the edges of the gurney and clench my fingers so tightly that it hurts. I hear Victor's teeth scraping together. I have him struggling now. I have to concentrate even harder.

Leave me alone, I repeat. Get out of my head!

Suddenly, Victor shudders, groaning as if somebody punched him. The next moment his grip weakens and he collapses on the floor. My body relaxes and the headache disappears. My vision normalizes.

"What happened?" Carrel asks in confusion. "Did you read him?"

"I couldn't," Victor laughs.

"What do you mean you couldn't?" Carrel says in shock.

"He freaking blocked me!" Victor answers, still sitting on the floor.

"What are you talking about?" Wheeler asks.

"That's nonsense!" Carrel shakes his head. "Victor is just tired. I told you we can't make him read memories too often. He's run out of strength."

"Guys, are you stupid or what?" Victor asks. "It's not a problem with me. It's all him. He's a stronger breaker than I am, period."

For a few moments Carrel and Wheeler keep silent.

"That's impossible," Carrel says. "You can break anybody. You've never had a problem with reading anybody's mind."

"Well, you've never given me a subject like this, where it's virtually impossible to swipe memories," Victor answers.

"What the hell are you?" Carrel asks, approaching me. "How did you block my best breaker?"

I turn away.

"Answer!" Carrel shouts. "What are you?"

Watching him become so frustrated somehow makes me feel really good.

"You may think you got away with something, breaker," Wheeler says. "But I have other methods to gain the information I need."

No, you don't, I think. You can torture me, even kill me, but you will never make me give up Kitty.

Wheeler unholsters his gun and presses the hard barrel against my leg.

"This is gonna hurt really bad, breaker," he says, lips curling into a vicious smile. "You'd best start talking."

I hold my breath, preparing mentally for the pain to come.

"How dare you interact with my subject in this manner?!" a shrill angry voice pierces the air. I see a furious Holtzmann enter the room shaking his fists. Instantly, Wheeler holsters his gun. Carrel winces, stepping away from me.

"We're only speaking with the subject," Carrel says.

"Only speaking?" Holtzmann looks at Victor. "What is Victor doing here then?"

"Oh, don't worry, professor," Victor says. "I couldn't read your precious subject."

Holtzmann gives a disproving look and says, "I wouldn't expect you could. He's a level four breaker."

"Why don't you come back later," Wheeler says. "I need to finish my interrogation."

Holtzmann brushes past Carrel.

"Excuse me, but you have no business interacting with my subject at all," he says with a trembling voice. "And I hope you're aware there will be consequences should I find it necessary to report your ill-advised behavior."

I notice Wheeler's hand resting on the butt of his gun. For a moment I think that he'll shoot the mad professor. Holtzmann doesn't intimidate easily, his twitching eye glaring straight through the agitated officer. Wheeler sighs heavily, weighing his options. Finally, he steps away.

"Thank you, Mr. Wheeler," Holtzmann says curtly. "Officer Chase, please unstrap my subject."

Chase executes the request promptly. I sit up on the gurney, rubbing my numb wrists. I've been strapped in for so long that can't feel my fingers.

"Are you able to walk, Rex?" Holtzmann asks.

I nod. I'm ready to do anything to get out of this hellish room.

"Follow me, please," the professor requests, heading toward the door. I jump off the gurney and follow behind unsteadily, still being weak and dizzy from my encounter with Victor.

"Wait a minute, Holtzmann," Carrel protests. "You can't just take him like that."

"Of course I can," Holtzmann counters. "Chase, could you help the subject along, please?" he instructs, noticing my limp.

"Hold on a sec, breaker," Chase says, throwing my arm across his shoulder.

We leave the interrogation room, walking along dark windowless passages. I look around, trying to figure out the size of the building I'm in. It must be enormous. A few groups of Elimination officers appear along our way. Instinctively I slow down, feeling threatened and tense. But the officers only greet Holtzmann and pay little attention to me in passing by.

Holtzmann suddenly stops, pressing his back against the wall. Something must be wrong with him. He bends over, gulping air as he searches his pockets.

"Sir, are you all right?" Chase asks.

"I'll be fine," Holtzmann whispers.

He pulls out a plastic bottle of pills and swallows a few, choking them down. In a couple of minutes his breathing normalizes and we continue walking.

The idea of attempting an escape comes to mind. This may be the only chance I'll get. I doubt the professor could stop me. He probably doesn't even have a gun. Officer Chase, on the other hand, might prove more than I can handle right now. Especially in my weakened state. I need to recover a bit first, collect more information about this place and work out a plan.

Holtzmann slows down in front of a large metal door.

"Chase, you may leave us now," he says.

"I can't leave you alone with a breaker, sir," Chase protests. "You know that's against protocol."

"Nonsense," Holtzmann says. "Protocol wasn't exactly being followed back in the interrogation room, now was it? This subject is far too intelligent to attack the only man standing between him and Wheeler, besides this facility is quite secure."

Is it what he really thinks of me? That I'm scared of Wheeler? I can't help from smiling. His misjudging my cooperation may come in handy in the future. While I haven't committed the crimes I've been accused of, I'm in no way harmless to Holtzmann.

Chase seems surprised.

"Go, leave us!" Holtzmann orders, losing his patience.

"Be on your best behavior, breaker. This man just saved your life," Chase says walking away.

"That's better," Holtzmann smiles. "Please, Rex, come inside."

He swipes a plastic card, opening the door and we enter a large room. I walk slowly, looking carefully around.

I'm overcome by a sudden sense of deja vu, causing a cold shiver to run down my spine. I realize that this place is an exact replica of the interrogation room where I first woke, as well as the room from the dream with the girl. Windowless, with a sterile white ceiling and walls. Plenty of unidentifiable scientific equipment scattered around.

"This is the lab where I work," Holtzmann explains. "I suppose I could even call it my home away from home. This is where I spend the majority of my time, performing subject test and analyzing the data."

"Your life must really suck," I say.

Holtzmann doesn't respond. He plops down behind a big wooden desk cluttered with piles of papers, then gestures toward an empty chair. "Have a seat, Rex, there is much for us to discuss."

Accepting the invitation, I sit down. There are only a few feet separating us and no guards around. Should I attack right now, I have a good chance to knock him down and escape to…to where? Limping down the corridors, dodging guards?

I hesitate, assessing my strength. I'm weak and my mind is still foggy. I'll likely have only one chance, so I need to be healthy and better prepared.

"First, I apologize for everything that's happened today," Holtzmann says slowly. "I felt a little under the weather this morning and couldn't be there when you woke. Unfortunately, Dr. Carrel and Wheeler obviously took advantage of my absence to break protocol to do as they darn well pleased."

His voice is full of guilt, but I'm not buying it. There's nobody here I can trust. This may be another trick to get me to give up Kitty's whereabouts. Be nice and kind enough to make me wish to reciprocate and give something back. It won't work, although at the moment I need to play along.

"I've been through worse," I answer carefully. "Why am I here anyway?"

"I'll explain everything," Holtzmann promises. "But first let's make sure you're sound enough to hold such an important conversation."

He pulls out a blood pressure monitor and thermometer from a drawer and begins his examination.

"Not bad," he says, seeming satisfied. "Are you experiencing any nausea or fatigue?"

"Only a little," I lie. "What drug did you use on me?

"Nothing too serious," Holtzmann assures. "It was a tranquilizer designed to induce a comatose state during transportation. It's non-addictive and post side effects should dissipate within a couple of days," he pauses. "We should feed you soon," he decides. "Think you can eat?"

"I can definitely try," I say. I can't remember when I last ate. I guess it was my last meal just before my execution.

Holtzmann phones in a delivery from the kitchen.

"How long have I been here?" I ask.

"Five days," Holtzmann answers.

I've completely lost track of time.

"Why did you need to kill me back at the prison?" I wonder.

"The dead have no legal rights," he explains. "You're government property now. They can do with you whatever they want. Additionally, during tough times the society needs a distraction of sorts. A figurative enemy to hate, so to speak, helping divert people's attention from the misery of their daily lives. Unfortunately for you, mind breakers make the best enemy the government could possibly conceive," Holtzmann sighs. "They just don't realize what they're doing," he adds quietly.

"What exactly did Victor do to the girl?" I inquire, worrying for Jessie. "Is she gonna be all right?"

Holtzmann doesn't answer, lost in thought.

The door slides open and a tall young woman comes in, carrying a tray with food. She wears a gray business suit and black framed glasses, both serving to make her appear very serious despite her youthfulness. She's probably around twenty. Her dark smooth hair put up in a tight bun complete her business image.

Her appearance snaps Holtzmann out of his trance. His smile is unexpectedly gentle. The girl places the tray on top of his messy desk, avoiding my glance. She seems tensed, her movements a bit nervous and jerky.

"Thank you, Rebecca," Holtzmann says. "You may go."

She nods, but doesn't leave, looking at him with hesitation.

"Egbert, let me send guards," she pleads, her voice being full of worry.

"I don't need guards," Holtzmann answers. "And we've already discussed this."

"Please, it's not prudent for you to be alone with this breaker," Rebecca adds, throwing me a distressed look.

"For goodness sakes!" Holtzmann exclaims. "It's okay, just leave us, Rebecca."

She sighs and heads unsteadily toward the door.

"My apologies, Rex," Holtzmann says after she leaves. "My cousin has trust issues after going through a very traumatic experience with breakers."

I shrug, not being too interested in hearing their family history.

After Holtzmann passes me a plate with steaming mashed potatoes and a large juicy steak, my stomach growls in anticipation. I eat greedily, taking huge bites. Holtzmann watches me attentively, as if he's never seen anybody eating before. He has some salad on his plate that he doesn't even try, only tossing the leaves of lettuce with his fork. I wonder whether or not they've drugged my food, but am too hungry to worry about it too much.

Having finished my meal, I wait for any symptoms of being sedated. I feel nothing unusual. My food was clean.

"I'm guessing you've already figured out where you're at," Holtzmann says.

"Well, some sort of prison I suspect," I say, "certainly not a resort although the meal was first rate."

"Officially, this is a research facility," Holtzmann explains. "Technically, it's not much different from a prison. You must be well behaved and very cooperative if you hope to thrive and survive."

"I believe I've heard this spiel already," I answer.

"I'm not threatening you in any way," Holtzmann says. "But my power is limited. I'm the lead scientist here, but the fact is, I too have to follow set guidelines. A second fact of this place is that uncooperative breakers aren't allowed to live very long."

"I've already died once," I answer. "I guess I can do it again if needed."

"Unfortunately, the next time will be for real," Holtzmann says, his eye twitching. "You've only been spared initially because I've detected in you some extremely rare abilities. Dr. Carrel was overly arrogant and distracted by Wheeler during the initial assessment, thereby misjudging your level. Carrel is a proud man who doesn't like to be made a fool of, so he's a little bitter as you may have surmised. You see, each breaker here is assigned to a certain scientist. Dr. Carrel and I are allowed to choose our own subjects for studying. Naturally, Carrel would want to have such a singularly unique breaker to study himself. But it's too late," Holtzmann adds, smiling. "I've claimed you first."

Holtzmann looks like he's just won the lottery.

"Aside from my being a breaker, what's so unique about me?" I ask. "I'm not the strongest by a long shot."

"Oh, contraire Rex, you've just never developed your talents," Holtzmann answers. "Trust me, I've studied your kind in depth. I can tell a strong breaker from the weaker ones. You've shown obvious tendencies for telepathy. This in itself is an outstanding gift!"

I shake my head, trying to understand. I remember the pain and horror I experienced back with Wheeler, while he was torturing the inmate woman. Even being in a different room, I knew that he had shot her.

"What are you talking about?" I ask, disbelieving. "Telepathy isn't real."

"It is very real, Rex. Telepathy was actually the technique Elimination used to locate you," Holtzmann explains. "As it happens, Dr. Carrel has his own level four breaker, a strong telepath. She envisioned you on the train in her mind and even identified its exact location."

Lena. The little girl from my dream, I realize.

"What are these levels everybody keeps talking about?" I ask.

"I've created these classifications," Holtzmann says. "Each level roughly matches the skills that a breaker of that certain level demonstrates. The first level is the most common. It consists of the ability to hypnotize ordinary humans. We look for something more advanced, at level two, whereby breakers are able to hypnotize and control the minds of people resistant to level one abilities."

"What?" I exclaim. "You're telling me that some of us can control the resistant?"

"It's uncommon, but quite possible," Holtzmann confirms. "Carrel's subject Victor has this skill. Although he's forbidden to utilize it on Elimination employees. I doubt he would anyway, hoping to build a career here."

I've never considered a breaker may be willing to cooperate with Elimination. This Victor dude must really be some kind of rat.

"At level three, breakers are capable of reading memories along with the abilities of the first two levels," Holtzmann continues. "As you likely already surmised Victor is level three. That's his primary job function here, to scan the memories of captured breakers."

"And I'm level four?" I ask.

"You certainly are," Holtzmann nods. "Your additional gift is telepathy. Less than one percent of breakers possess this gift. Actually, you're only the second telepath we've managed to obtain."

The first one must be Lena, I realize.

"Officially, this system of classification is very informal," Holtzmann adds. "Mind breaker phenomena is far too complex. I'm fairly certain there are additional levels we haven't discovered at present. An excellent example would be the way you managed to block Victor from taking your memories. It doesn't fit into any classification currently documented."

I raise my eyebrows. Blocking Victor didn't feel like anything outstanding to me.

"Thanks for the very entertaining lecture, professor," I say. "But what do you want from me? What is this all about?"

"You see, in spite of the fact I'm an Elimination scientist, I do follow ethical principles and have never practiced a more violent approach of the sort Dr. Carrel employs," Holtzmann says. "Bottom line, Rex, I want you to agree to participate in my studies. But it must be your own decision. I believe this to be the only appropriate way to work with breakers and conduct the necessary research."

"You're pathetic, egghead," I say. "Sorry, but I truly don't give a damn about your experimental research. I don't care to be anybody's lab rat."

"Careful now," he warns. "If you don't agree to work with me, Carrel will surely take you. I won't be able to stop him."

"I'm not afraid of Carrel," I answer.

"You can't imagine what this monster can do to breakers," Holtzmann adds.

"I don't care," I answer. "I'd sooner die than work for Elimination."

"This isn't only about you," Holtzmann raises his voice suddenly. "This is about the survival of entire human race!"

My mouth falls open. "What?"

"Do you believe in fate, Rex?" Holtzmann asks.

"No, not really," I answer, trying to figure out where this conversation is leading. I get a creepy feeling I'm talking to a very sick guy.

"I do," he says. "Maybe it's strange for a scientist, but I do believe each person has his own purpose in the world. My purpose is to prevent the coming war."

This nutbag is also paranoid, I think.

"There's no war," I say. "And there's not even another country to go to a war with. We're the last country left on Earth."

"I'm referring to the coming war between ordinary humans and mind breakers," Holtzmann says confidently. "Perhaps the war hasn't started yet, but soon it will."

"There's not enough breakers to fight a war with humans," I argue.

"Our latest data confirms that in excess of thirty percent of the population possess breaker abilities," Holtzmann explains. "Furthermore, I hypothesize more breakers are coming soon. You are the latest dominate subspecies threatening to displace Homo sapiens as the highest rung on the food chain."

"Your facts are all twisted," I say, smiling. "Breakers aren't the reason this is the only country left in the world. We just want to live and let live, to coexist peacefully, and get nothing in return but hate for our efforts. Why do you think we have to displace your kind?"

"Because that's what usually happens when a new species appears," he answers. "Can't you see what's happening? The Yellowstone Eruption triggered a type of punctuated equilibrium, a sudden, rapid change in mankind after a long period of stasis. You see, for thousands of years the human race remained relatively unchanged. Sudden and extreme alterations in environmental conditions forced humans to adapt more quickly. Your species is the result of that sudden change, being more advanced and ultimately supreme. You don't require weapons to hunt or protect yourself from enemies. The only weapon you need is your mind. Ordinary humans are like cavemen or even dinosaurs in comparison to you. Do you know what happened to the dinosaurs? Total extinction! I fear a similar fate is awaiting what remains of the human race. Our government has recognized this threat, and that's why mind breakers are being hunted and killed. It's a basic survival instinct. This research center provides a means for studying our enemy." He pauses, catching his breath. "Do you see what kind of conflict we have? Both species, humans and breakers, want to survive. A war is ultimately unavoidable. Unfortunately, with our current population issues, it's a war we can't afford. I believe once the real fighting and killing starts, both species will end up being exterminated."

I listen quietly. No point in arguing with a delusional madman.

"Humans and mind breakers must quickly learn how to coexist," Holtzmann concludes. "It's the only way for us to survive. Finding a means for peaceful coexistence between the subspecies is my life's work and purpose."

"Good luck with saving humanity and all that," I say, "but count me out. I have my own troubles to deal with."

"You don't believe me, do you, Rex?" Holtzmann asks sadly.

"Sorry professor, but it's too late," I answer. "Nobody has exactly tried to peacefully coexist with me lately and now I just don't care."

"Well, I'll give you time to sleep on it," Holtzmann decides. "We'll meet in the morning to determine what happens next."

He calls for the guards. As they lead me away, Holtzmann suddenly stands up and approaches.

"Just know I'm not your enemy," he says. "I'm fascinated by your kind and want you to survive. I really do believe that there's enough room in the world for all of us."

I don't answer. Saving the world isn't my main priority right now. I need to think of escape, and then to find Kitty.

Locked away inside a small cell, I lie down on the floor. Apparently, this is some type of high security facility. I can't rely on my breaker skills as long as this blocking collar is around my neck. There are plenty of well-armed guards, ready to put down any signs of trouble. So I can't fight my way out. How can I even stop them from attacking me?

I can see only one possible option. To use Holtzmann as a human shield. Tomorrow after the guards deliver me to him, I would need to over-power only one officer and get his weapon. Then press the barrel against Holtzmann's head and hope any guards along the way out don't shoot us both. The professor is obviously a very important scientist around here. I just might get a chance to escape.

I've never had to contemplate such an outrageous idea before, always being a law abiding citizen. It's crazy how much I've changed within the last few weeks. I've adapted quickly, accepting the new rules and conditions of life. Except for all this business of being locked up anyway. Now the idea of using Holtzmann as a human shield doesn't seem too farfetched. I'm determined to regain my freedom, no matter what.

Jessie, I think suddenly, I must help her somehow. She's in this mess because of me. First I endangered Kitty, now Jessie is imprisoned. Seems like I'm a bad person to be around these days.

I close my eyes, resting. Tomorrow's going to be a big day.

CHAPTER 10

I'm fully awake in the morning when guards arrive. They check the blocking collar on my neck, holding their rifles ready.

"Face the wall," one commands. "Hands behind your back."

They're going to handcuff me. I feel anxious, realizing that my plan is already falling apart. If I'm handcuffed, I'll have no way to fight.

"Now breaker, face the wall!" a guard commands, slamming the butt of his rifle into my stomach.

I groan, turning to the wall. There are five of them, each watching closely for any sign of resistance. Now is obviously not the time for heroics, so I put my hands behind my back and let the guards handcuff me.

That's all right, I think. Holtzmann likely will order to have handcuffs removed as he seems to prefer softer methods. I may still get a chance to carry out my plan.

As the guards lead me through numerous corridors, I see Officer Chase walking toward us.

"Hey! What's going on here?" he asks. "Where the heck are you taking him?"

"That information's on a need to know basis, and you don't need to know," one guard answers. "Out of our way."

Chase doesn't move an inch.

"Holtzmann is waiting for him," he says.

"We have other instructions," the guard answers arrogantly.

Chase frowns, thinking.

"I'll have to report this to my commander," he warns.

"To Wheeler? He already knows," the guard says, grinning. "It's his order we're executing."

Chase steps away, seemingly confused, as the guards proceed forward.

Something is wrong. Where are we going? I can only guess.

Finally, the guards open a large metal door and push me inside a spacious room. The sharp smell of disinfectant makes me gag. One quick glimpse around and I understand exactly where I am. This is the same room I awoke in yesterday from a coma.

Dr. Carrel rises from his desk, smiling.

"Welcome back, breaker," he greets.

I don't look at Carrel. My attention focuses on a little sad girl with puffy, oriental eyes, sitting on a gurney. I stare at her shaved head with protruding electrodes. Lena. The same child from my vision.

"What have you done to her?" I shout at Carrel. "You sick monster!"

Dr. Carrel laughs, seeming very pleased with my reaction.

"Do you like my little star breaker?" he asks. "This is whom you need to thank for being here. She located you for us."

He probably wants to shock me, but I already know everything. I don't blame Lena for directing Elimination. She was probably forced to do this in order to save her own life. Moreover, Lena tried to warn me, communicating through visions. Only it was too late.

"I'm so sorry," Lena says.

"You'll pay for this!" I threaten Carrel.

"My dear silly breaker," Carrel says with condescension. "You must have no clue as to your predicament to even make such statements." He pauses and then commands loudly, "Strap the subject in the chair."

Guards follow his order willingly, dragging me across the room. I wind up being strapped to some kind of a recliner, like a dentist chair. Lena sobs, wiping tears with her shirt.

"You'd better let me out of here or I'll miss my meeting with Professor Holtzmann," I say. "We have an agreement and I'm working for him now," I lie.

Dr. Carrel rolls his eyes.

"You're even more stupid than I originally thought," he sighs. "You picked the wrong person to be working with. What did you call him? Professor Holtzmann? He's no professor! He doesn't even have a university degree. Your Holtzmann is only an ignorant epileptic wannabe who lives locked away in a fantasy world of perverted dreams."

He pauses, looking down on me.

"Holtzmann has no real power in this place," he continues. "He's just a pawn. I'm the only real scientist here. You do have a choice, breaker. You can choose to work for me, or you can die."

"Then you can shoot me right now, moron," I answer. Somehow I know he won't kill me. Carrel needs me alive.

"I may consider shooting you," Carrel says. "First I want to see what abilities you've got. If I find you worthy, I may use you for my work. Believe me, even less agreeable breakers than yourself have ended up working for me."

I wonder if Carrel is referring to Victor.

"I'm sure that psychopath has already told you all about his apocalyptic prophecy," Carrel says. "But were you silly enough to actually believe his yarn? He tells the same fairy tale to every breaker he can, the spiel about humans and breakers living in peace."

Carrel removes his glasses to clean the lenses. I remain silent.

"Anyway, let's see what you can do," Carrel says. "Lena, come here please."

Lena shivers upon hearing her name. Obediently, she slides down from the gurney and walks toward Carrel. I notice her limp.

"This is my number one breaker," Carrel says, pushing Lena closer to me. "She's a telepath. You're slotted to be a telepath as well. So, prove it, connect with her mind."

Not again. I vividly remember seeing the world through the eyes of the inmate lady at the jail followed by the sensation of a bullet crushing my skull.

"Do it, breaker!" Carrel raises his voice.

Lena closes her eyes, concentrating.

"Please, work with me," she begs. "Just do what he says, otherwise they'll beat us both."

Her arms are covered by varying shades of bruises.

"I don't know how," I say.

"It's easy," Lena answers. "Just think of me."

Carrel orders Lena moved into another room.

"Hey!" I shout at guards. "Don't hurt her!"

"Don't worry," Carrel says as he places electrodes on my forehead and temples. "We're not going to kill our best breaker. She'll be fine."

Desperately, I shake my head, trying to knock off the electrodes. Nothing works.

"Calm down," Carrel commands. "You're only screwing up my data."

He stares at the monitors on his desk.

"Concentrate on her," he orders.

Something burns my left hand. I flinch from the immense pain. Carrel glues to the monitor, watching. Then he looks at me.

"You felt that, didn't you?" he asks, smiling.

"What are they doing to her?" I shout, worrying for Lena.

"You really are a strong telepath," Carrel admits. "Possibly, even stronger than Lena I think."

He calls for the guards to bring Lena back in. I feel relieved seeing her, at least she is alive. I notice a fresh red burn blistering on her left hand. The guards must have burned her for the test, sadistic jerks.

"Are you all right?" I ask.

Shivering, Lena nods. Watching her being in so much pain and fear makes me sick. If I had a gun and my hands were free, I'd kill Carrel and the guards without hesitation. Such monsters don't deserve to live.

"Very well. Now let's check if you can read memories," Carrel says, rubbing his hands. "Bring Victor and Jimmy," he commands as he takes a key from the desk and removes the blocking collar from my neck.

I watch him attentively. If I'm ever to escape, I'll have to take care of the blocking collar somehow.

"Don't get too overexcited by temporarily regaining your ability to hypnotize, breaker," Carrel says. "All Elimination employees are resistant."

I need to think. What did Holtzmann say about the different breaker levels? Each higher level has all the abilities of the lower ones. Level four not only means telepathy and reading memories, but I should be able to hypnotize even the resistant. I focus, projecting my thoughts toward Carrel. Nothing. I don't know how to hypnotize the resistant, at least not yet.

The guards return, leading a scared teenaged boy wearing a blocking collar. This must be Jimmy, another breaker. I'm guessing he's between twelve and fourteen. Hard to tell, because he's short and skinny, with a round freckled face. He reminds me of Kitty somehow. My sister has the same type build, narrow shouldered, childlike and seemingly fragile.

Swaying, Victor follows the guards with unsteady steps. He looks drowsy, his eyes cloudy and unclear. The sight of him repulses me. I won't be forgetting what he did to Jessie.

"Why did it take you so long?" Carrel demands.

"Sir, we had some trouble with Victor," a guard reports. "This idiot is high."

Victor smiles and waves to Carrel.

"Goodness!" Dr. Carrel exclaims. "Victor, you knew not to use anything today!"

"Relax, doc," Victor answers. "I'm in a great shape. Can swipe any memories you wish," he stares at me, "except the memories of this dude, I guess."

"Just sit down somewhere," Carrel says.

Stumbling, Victor approaches one of the gurneys and hops up awkwardly. He obviously has problems with coordination at the moment. I watch him with despise. Dr. Carrel may be providing drugs to Victor to keep him under Elimination's control. It'd explain a lot.

"Come here, Jimmy," Carrel says.

Indecisively, Jimmy approaches him.

"Am I in trouble, sir?" he asks. "I haven't done anything wrong."

"Don't worry, my boy," Carrel answers. "I just want you to participate in a simple scientific experiment, allowing our friend Rex here to read your memories."

Jimmy steps back, clamping his mouth with a trembling hand. He remains quite for a few moments. Then he shakes his head.

"No, please," Jimmy begs. "Don't do this to me again, sir."

Guards push him toward me.

Jimmy sobs, covering his face. He doesn't even try to resist. I notice dark purple bruises on his neck and wrists.

"I won't read his memories," I state.

"Of course you will," Carrel answers, nodding toward the guards. They react instantly, punching Jimmy hard in his temple. The boy expels a muffled cry, collapsing onto the floor.

"Stop it!" I yell, pulling at the straps binding me. "I have no idea how to read memories."

"I'll help you," Victor says calmly, approaching. "It's not that hard."

"Back off, junkie," I growl.

Victor doesn't seem offended. He smiles widely and says, "Look, breaker. I can respect your desire to resist these fools," gesturing toward Carrel and the guards. "I despise them too. Once upon a time, I was pathetically naive and carried some of the same stupid principles as you. Trust me, you're gonna need to change that if you hope to survive here."

Surprisingly, Victor doesn't seem too drugged anymore. The effects must have worn off as even his eyes have cleared.

"Reading memories is child's play," he continues. "You just focus in on your subject of interest, imagine that you're him and then," he snaps his fingers, "you break the subject's mind. You're a breaker, aren't you? It's in your genes. That's what you were born to do." Victor pauses, thinking. "Only don't forget yourself," he warns. "Things can get a little confusing."

"I don't want to hurt this boy," I say. "He's done nothing to me."

"Don't worry about him," Victor says. "It may look rough, but eventually the subjects always recover. You're at a higher risk of being damaged in the process."

I don't understand what he means. It was Jessie who seemed completely messed up after Victor's memory reading. Although, I can remember Victor repeating his own name as if he was trying not to forget who he was. Weird stuff.

A guard pulls Jimmy up from the floor and presses a rifle to his head.

"This boy is only a level one breaker," Carrel explains. "About as common as dirt. I'll order him shot, should you choose to remain noncompliant. I have dozens of level ones, and am more than willing to have them all killed if that's what it takes to make you more agreeable."

I taste bitterness in my mouth. Jimmy closes his eyes, waiting for a bullet. Somehow I don't doubt Carrel's threats this time. If Jimmy dies here, it's going to be on me.

"All right," I say. "I'll try."

The guard shoves Jimmy forward, forcing his head only a few inches from mine.

"Concentrate," Victor instructs. "He'll instinctively try to block you to protect his memories. You have to break through any mental barriers he builds."

I close my eyes, concentrating on Jimmy. I still have no clue what to do.

"Read his memories!" Carrel demands.

Memories, I repeat in my mind, concentrating. I hear Jimmy sobbing. Help me here Jimmy, I project. Tell me something.

The first few moments nothing happens. I just lie back in the chair, eyes closed. A splitting headache suddenly explodes in my head. I feel nauseated. A momentary sensation of falling down. I open my eyes as the room, the guards, Carrel…everything disappears. Some invisible force carries me far away from reality. No sound. No time. Complete nothingness.

Then random images flash in my mind.

I see a woman sprawled on the concrete in a large puddle of blood. This is my mother, I understand suddenly. Elimination has killed her!

I get on my knees beside her, crying in despair. Officers wearing black uniforms surround me, aiming their rifles.

Now, I'm inside a cell in the prison. My life is over. My both parents are dead. It's my fault because I revealed my breaker abilities. What a fool I am! How could I have ever done this? Everything I do turns out wrong. I'd be better off dead.

Images are flashing across my mind so fast that I can't comprehend everything. Somebody beats me. I beg them to stop. I cry alone in the cell. I think of death. Feels like I'm losing my mind.

Then everything abruptly stops.

I open my eyes and realize that I'm still in Carrel's lab. Jimmy lies on the floor unconscious. I see his mouth foaming. Lena cries somewhere nearby.

"What's your name, breaker?" Victor asks.

He approaches and slaps my face.

"What's you freaking name? Answer!" he repeats.

"Jimmy," I say.

"Darn," Victor groans. "Come on now. You have to remember who you are. I know it's hard sometimes. Who are you?"

I don't understand what Victor wants from me. I've just told him my name.

Wait. That's not true. Jimmy isn't my name. Elimination didn't kill my parents. Those memories aren't mine.

"Rex," I answer. "My name is Rex."

"There you go, breaker. Never forget to come back," Victor smiles.

Dr. Carrel claps his hands.

"Great!" he says. "You're even stronger than Victor. I've never witnessed such a fast memory reading. Now I need to see what's happening in your brain."

Guards carry away the still unconscious Jimmy. Glancing at him, I feel deeply sorry. Hopefully, he'll be okay. Victor did say that all subjects of a memory reading recover sooner or later.

One guard presses my head back against the chair, placing straps across my forehead. Dr. Carrel approaches me with an electric razor in his hand.

"What the heck?" I exclaim.

"There's a little problem, breaker," Carrel says, shaving my head. "Placing monitors only on your scalp doesn't provide complete data. And I really need to understand fully what's happening inside your head."

The realization of his intentions strikes me. He intends to attach the electrodes directly into my brain, as he previously did with Lena. I growl, yanking my arms and legs in a desperate attempt to free myself.

"Calm down," Carrel says. "You'll hardly feel a thing. I'm giving you a strong anesthetic."

He wipes my shaved head with a cotton ball. I notice a drill on the table and understand that in a few moments Carrel will be drilling holes in my skull. I strain against the straps so hard that the lock on my left wrist snaps, breaking. I punch Carrel in the face. He cries out, backpedaling. Instantly, I cover to block a strike from the guard. He grabs my wrist, twisting and pressing it back down onto the chair.

"I've got him," he says, holding my wrist firmly.

"I've changed my mind," Carrel says. "I'm not using anesthetic this time."

He approaches, wielding a scalpel in his hand. I feel the sharp blade slicing through my skin.

CHAPTER 11

"Stop!" I shout, focusing my thought on Carrel. "Drop the knife!"

Carrel's hand freezes. The scalpel falls onto the floor, having left only a slight incision on my forehead. Having lost the collar, I can break resistant minds as well. Carrel follows my directions. I concentrate harder. My nose bleeds from the effort.

"Back off!" I command.

Carrel takes a step back. His eyes are wide open, but I don't think he can see anything.

"What the hell?" one guard exclaims. Others only stare in shock. They still haven't realized what's happening. I have to hurry.

"Don't move!" I shout, directing my thoughts toward the guards.

The guards stand motionless. I feel their minds trying to resist, but my will is much stronger at the moment. Nevertheless, I doubt I can hold them under hypnosis much longer. I'm already exhausted and running out of strength.

"You! Unstrap me!" I command the nearest guard.

Unsteadily, he takes one step toward me and stops, hesitating. He's really strong. My head spins. The guard winces, but takes another step.

"Unstrap me!" I repeat. "Now!"

Moving torturously slowly, he frees my arms and legs. I grab his rifle and swing it around hard, slamming into his head. There's a crunching sound as it connects with his skull. The guard collapses. One less to hypnotize. Next, I strike Carrel's indifferent face with the butt of the rifle. He expels a muffled cry, slumping to the floor.

Lena screams. I've almost forgot her. I can't leave her behind. I have to get her out of here.

Holding the rifle on the guards, I jump off the gurney and approach Lena. I stumble, being slightly unbalanced.

"Wow!" Victor exclaims. "You're really good!"

I point the barrel at him. Victor rolls his eyes.

"Oh please, breaker!" he groans. "As if I don't already have enough problems with these Elimination fools pointing guns at me all the time. Besides, I'm in no mood for fighting today." He approaches the cabinets with medicine supplies. "Go on, shoot these jokers. I couldn't care less."

Victor grabs several bottles of pills, stuffing them in his pockets. Apparently, I can't hypnotize him. I turn back to the guards. As long as Victor doesn't try to interfere, I don't have to worry about him.

Holding the rifle on the guards, I grab Lena up with one arm. She trusts me instantly, wrapping her tiny arms around my neck. Slowly, we head toward the exit. The guards reach for their rifles. I'm too weak. Can't break their wills any longer.

"Stand down!" I shout, trying anyway.

A guard raises his rifle. I pull the trigger. The guard groans, falling. Lena screams, squeezing my neck tighter.

"Nice shot," Victor says.

The other guards turn their heads, looking for the shooter as their minds begin to clear. The sliding door to the outside is closed. I anxiously fire several rounds into the locking mechanism on the door until something finally clicks inside the lock and the door slides partly open. I run out, holding Lena.

"Shake it off and get after him!" Carrel's voice thunders from behind. "I want him taken alive!"

It's a very long straight hallway before coming to any corridors we could turn down. The guards pursue, firing shots above our heads. I stoop as much as possible to keep Lena out of the line of fire. We're too slow with me carrying her and I've no idea where to go anyway. I aimlessly return fire until the rifle is empty. I keep the weapon although it's now no better than a club.

More officers pour from a corridor into the hall in front of us. I stop abruptly, looking around.

"Can you help, Lena?" I ask.

"I'm trying, but haven't learned hypnosis yet," she answers.

"Drop your weapon!" a guard commands, shooting into the wall beside us. I step back. Lena cries, pressing her face against my shoulder.

"Don't kill them!" Carrel yells. "I need those two alive!"

The guard fires again and a bullet slams into my arm. I drop the rifle, shuddering from pain. The floor begins to sway as I'm overcome by dizziness. Still holding Lena, I press my back to the wall to regain my balance.

The guards are on us in an instant. They rip Lena from my arms and throw me to the ground. Somebody punches me in the head on the way down. I hear Lena scream.

"Don't injure the girl!" Carrel shouts, wiping blood from his face. "I need them both alive."

I elbow a guard as they struggle to get my arms behind my back. Someone slams my face back into the floor for my effort.

"Stop!" a loud voice commands as a gunshot slices the air above.

The guards back slowly away. I see Holtzmann walking toward us. Chase follows him. At first I think Chase is aiming his rifle at me. Then I realize he's targeting the guards.

"Carrel! You shameless thief!" Holtzmann shouts in a high pitched voice. "How dare you attempt to commandeer my subject?!"

He pushes the guards away. They keep their weapons at the ready, but step back.

"Oh God!" Holtzmann exclaims, seeing the blood oozing from my wound. "What have they done to you? Good Lord!" he repeats in shock.

"I have authority to examine any breakers I wish," Carrel protests. "You're interrupting my work."

"Enough!" Holtzmann counters. "You've crossed the line! I'll have to report these violations to Browning."

I expect Carrel to continue arguing, but he only sighs. Holtzmann and Chase help me up. I can hardly stand on my own, but manage to reach out and snatch Lena from the guard.

"Let's go," Holtzmann commands, turning to leave.

"Wait!" Carrel stops him. "Lena is my subject! You can't take her."

He approaches me. Purposely, I step away, drawing Lena closer.

"No!" I growl. "Lena goes with me."

"She's mine," Carrel says. "Take the girl," he orders, but the guards don't move to follow his command.

Holtzmann looks at me and Lena quizzically, but seems to understand that I won't let them take her without a fight.

"Your subject will be returned later," Holtzmann promises as we leave.

Chase walks behind, holding his rifle on me. It was likely Chase who brought Holtzmann to Carrel's lab, which means he possibly just saved my life. I still don't trust him although I'm somewhat grateful. He didn't have to save me, but he did.

My injured arm is still bleeding. No idea how much blood I've lost. I'm afraid of passing out. Should that happen, they'll likely take Lena away. I grip her tighter. She wraps her arms around my neck and has quit crying. Seems like I've known her for a long time. Somehow we're linked together, more so than just being in the same predicament.

We walk into a large office. There's a soft carpet on the floor and plants occupying the corners. A sharply dressed lady in a business suit rises from behind the desk. She seems astonished.

"What's this?" the lady exclaims. "What is he doing here?" She stares at me.

Holtzmann heads toward the huge door leading to a separate office.

"I need to see Browning," Holtzmann states. "Immediately!"

"That's not possible, sorry," the lady shakes her head. "He's in a meeting. You'll have to wait."

Unconvinced, Holtzmann yanks the door open. The lady steps aside, letting us in. We enter Warden Browning's office.

It's a brightly lit and spacious room. I see Browning sitting behind a large desk. Elimination officers sit in chairs on the other side of the desk, all dressed in black uniforms. I recognize Wheeler. He looks angry, but says nothing. A young man wearing civilian clothing stands next to Browning. His face seems familiar, but I can't place him. He looks at me with curiosity.

"Holtzmann!" Browning exclaims. "What are you doing barging in here? I'm having an important meeting and…"

"I don't care!" Holtzmann cuts in. "If you want me to continue working for this project you'll have to listen to what I have to say. Otherwise, I'm quitting."

Browning raises his eyebrows.

"Go on," he says, leaning back in his chair. "I'm listening."

"I can't work efficiently with somebody continually confiscating my subjects," Holtzmann shouts. "This breaker is assigned to me," he adds, pointing a trembling finger. "Nobody can touch him without my say so. Today, Dr. Carrel has taken him, tested him, and managed to get him shot. This is an outrage and is completely unacceptable!"

His voice cracks as he begins to hyperventilate.

Browning seems bored. The man in civilian garb just smiles, watching the scene unfold.

With no blocking collar on, I decide to test my ability to hypnotize, projecting my thoughts. Useless. Nobody even notices my attempt. Looks like only when being on the verge of death can I manipulate the minds of the resistant.

"I haven't the time to concern myself with your little misunderstanding with Dr. Carrel," Browning says.

"I understand you're a very busy man, Mr. Browning," Holtzmann says, "but please listen very carefully. If in the future you should authorize anybody to access my subjects without my approval, you'll be receiving my resignation letter. I'm certain you realize I'm your top scientist here, as well as best hope for the success of this project. So please do take the necessary time to help keep my work environment productive, else you'll be spending even more time, cleaning up the messes Carrel leaves behind."

"You can't leave the project," Browning answers. "We simply won't allow it. You know that."

"Forced to work in such an environment, I regret escape would become necessary," Holtzmann says. "The manner of escape only being limited by my own imagination. Self-termination is of course always an additional option. You've previously documented my instability on more than one occasion. And you know that."

Having spoken, Holtzmann turns and quickly leaves the office. Chase nudges me with his rifle and I follow.

"Wait!" I hear Browning shout. Holtzmann doesn't slow down or even look back. I wonder if he was really threatening to kill himself with all that talk about self-termination. He's one crazy scientist for sure and I've no clue what's going on in his mind.

As we walk down a long passage, Holtzmann stops abruptly, gasping and pressing a hand to his chest.

"Sir, are you all right?" Chase asks.

Holtzmann gestures for us to stay away. His legs suddenly give and he sits down hard on the floor, gulping for air. His breathing is short and fast.

"What's wrong with him?" I ask Chase. I've never seen anything like this. Holtzmann's face becomes red. He's suffocating.

"I don't know," Chase answers. "He's sick."

Holtzmann sprawls on the floor, choking. I feel like I need to help, but what can I do? I'm not even sure what's wrong.

"Oh my goodness! Egbert!" I hear a worried woman's voice.

It's Rebecca, Holtzmann's cousin. She runs along the passage and kneels beside Holtzmann, checking his pockets. Finally, she finds a bottle of medicine and makes him swallow a few pills.

"Just breathe," she says softly, rubbing his back.

Holtzmann manages a deep breath, normal color returning to his face. He smiles.

"I'm fine, really, Rebecca," he says weakly. "Please, don't be concerned."

"This is happening far too often," Rebecca says. "You need to avoid stressful situations. Why must you endanger your own health over a test subject? It's not worth it!"

"Stop worrying over me like a mama bird. I'm not the one seriously injured here," Holtzmann answers, getting onto his feet. Chase takes his arm, helping.

"Just let Carrel have him," Rebecca suggests.

"Rebecca!" Holtzmann says. "I won't allow Carrel and Wheeler to torture another innocent man, especially when the subject is assigned to me."

"He's not innocent! He's not even a human, he's a breaker!" she cries. "They're all monsters. You really need to quit protecting them."

"You should know by now that I'm a man of principle," Holtzmann answers, walking away. Chase gives a push from behind, willing me to follow. Rebecca covers her face in attempt to hide her tears.

Suddenly, I feel ashamed. Here I am, planning to use Holtzmann as my hostage. And he's just a nice guy, although sickly and more than a little crazy. I can't do a person like that any harm. It's possible he's even being forced to work with Elimination against his will.

We finally arrive back at the small room filled with gurneys and medical equipment. I look around cautiously.

A man in hospital scrubs glances at me through sleepy eyes.

"He is in need of immediate medical attention," Holtzmann says, gesturing toward me.

Hesitantly, the doctor approaches. Chase extends his arms to take Lena from me.

"No!" I protest, stepping away.

"You can't hold her during surgery," Holtzmann says. "I'll take Lena to my lab. Carrel won't get to her there. You have my word."

I search his eyes for signs of truth. I can't tell.

"Please," Holtzmann pleads.

"No, I want to stay with you!" Lena cries, grabbing my neck.

Chase grabs hold of Lena, pulling her away. Something pricks my shoulder. I turn my head and see the doctor injecting a needle. The room fades and all sounds become distant. I let Chase take Lena from me, too weak to resist.

"It's okay," I hear his voice.

My legs weaken. Falling, I grab something, trying to regain balance. Everything fades to darkness. I sleep.

I awaken on a gurney, covered by a thin blanket. Groaning, I sit up. I'm still wearing my clothes, but the shirt is missing one sleeve. They must have cut it off to treat my arm. Momentarily, I remember everything and stare at the bloody bandages on my wound. I carefully move my fingers. It hurts, but my hand seems to work fine.

Lena! What's happened to her?

Worried, I attempt to get off the gurney. A chain quickly stops my progress. It extends from the collar on my neck to a metal ring attached to the floor. I pull the chain, checking. Too strong. I can't break it.

"Relax," I hear a calm voice. "You're still too weak to be going anywhere."

I see Chase sitting in a chair by the door, his rifle across his lap.

"Where's Lena?" I ask.

"Don't worry, breaker," Chase answers. "Holtzmann's keeping her in his lab as promised. Carrel is really furious, but can do nothing about it."

"Holtzmann wouldn't hurt her, would he?" I worry.

"No, that guy is entirely too nice to breakers," Chase assures. "No hatred in him."

I breathe a sigh of relief, lying back down. Somehow I'm beginning to trust Holtzmann more now. He seems just weird enough to be a friend to breakers.

"Thanks for rescuing me," I say. "That was you who brought Holtzmann, right?"

"Right," Chase answers. "But thanks isn't necessary. I really wish I hadn't done that. Wheeler is disappointed and angry with me now."

"The guard I shot," I say, "is he all right?"

"Critical, but still alive," Chase answers.

I don't really care about that guard. I just don't want to be a killer, if I'm not one already.

They keep me chained up in the prison infirmary for several more days. I sleep most of the time being under sedation. Chase occasionally nods off in his chair, holding his rifle. A doctor comes every morning to check my arm and take my temperature. I'm feverish, but my wound slowly starts to heal. Luckily, the bullet missed the bone. I'll be fine in a week or so.

Sleeping, I often see Kitty in my dreams. She's wearing a military uniform, holding a gun and shooting at some distant target. I can smell gunpowder.

When I wake, my head is aching and heart pounding. God, I miss my Kitty so much. Where's she now? I worry for my little sister. She must think I'm dead. She could have even watched my execution on TV somewhere. I sure hope Kitty doesn't do anything stupid.

I'm also concerned for Lena and Jessie, and wonder whether little Jimmy is okay or not. How on earth can I help everybody? Jessie was right, I can't even help myself.

Rebecca brings me food three times a day like clockwork. She's always silent and looks at me through unhidden resentment.

"Who's the girl?" I ask Chase.

"Holtzmann's cousin and personal assistant," he explains. "Still being new, Rebecca hasn't yet received enough knowledge or training to really participate in his work. But she's smart, and most importantly, resistant. Being resistant is the primary requirement for Elimination employment. It was Holtzmann who brought her here. Although Rebecca is given a few minor tasks, her primarily role is to take care of her crazy relative for the most part. She makes sure Holtzmann eats every day and takes his medicine."

"Looks like she hates me," I say. "Must be my incurable charm."

"To be sure, Rebecca hates all breakers," Chase answers. "You don't need to be worrying about her. She's really messed up. One of you breakers killed her entire family. She only managed to survive because he couldn't hypnotize her."

"Well, at least now I understand," I say. "I'd hate breakers too if I were in Rebecca's shoes."

"That idea really conjures up a bad image, Rex. You should probably keep your big feet out of Rebecca's shoes," Chase comments with a laugh.

Holtzmann returns with Lena in tow. The little girl smiles broadly and jumps up on my gurney. I give her a hug, feeling delighted. Lena looks much better. The dark circles under her eyes have faded. She has a little more color to her cheeks.

"I still don't have your formal agreement to participate in my studies, Rex," Holtzmann says. "Have you made a decision?"

"I'm not working for Elimination," I answer.

"Our work will save countless lives," Holtzmann persists. "And in doing so, we'll perform the singularly greatest achievement for mankind in our generation. Carrel and Browning intend to strictly use breakers for military purposes, behind some unknown hidden agenda. I view the future quite differently. I envision breakers utilizing hypnosis to treat all manner of bad habits, addictions and even some certain mental disorders. I foresee breakers with telepathic abilities locating missing persons, recapturing escaped convicts, and to help recover survivors of natural disasters. There are multiple possibilities to use such abilities in a peaceful and productive way. We just need to learn how to trust each other and work together. Mutual trust is the only way we can coexist in peace."

I shake my head in disagreement. Perhaps Carrel was partly right about Holtzmann, concerning certain things. Holtzmann is an idealist living in a dream world. He doesn't realize that normal people will always fear and hate my kind, forever seeking new ways to exterminate us. And some breakers will always misuse their abilities to commit crimes. We can't coexist peacefully. It's ingrained in our nature, to hate and kill one another.

"I need to show you something," Holtzmann says. "Chase, please unchain my subject."

Chase hesitates only for a moment. Then he sighs and removes the shackles. I glance at his rifle, but don't attempt anything. Chase is too tough and attentive to be taken by surprise.

Holtzmann leads me to his lab and requests I watch something on his laptop. I stare into the monitor. Chase stands behind, keeping his weapon at the ready.

It's a news feed video. An over jubilant Lola is reporting on a story about an attack on the county jail by a group of breakers. They hypnotized police officers who in turn killed several Elimination guards and freed two captured breakers. The video cuts to a live camera feed of the crime scene. I can't believe my eyes, when I see my photograph plastered on a wall. Printed in black and white above the photograph is some type of slogan or call to action, saying, "Freedom and Justice for Breakers."

"What the heck is this?" I exclaim.

"This is the beginning of the war," Holtzmann answers. "And it appears you're the poster boy."

CHAPTER 12

After the video clip finishes, Holtzmann turns off his laptop. I'm so stunned that I continue staring at the dark screen.

"Why did they use my picture?" I ask.

"Vengeance," Holtzmann answers. "The first assault happened the day following your execution. You've been martyred now, and your death is being used as a rallying point for the renewed breaker revolt."

"Wait, this isn't the only attack? There have been others?"

Holtzmann nods. I think for a minute. I've got nothing to do with those breakers, but the inclusion of my picture somehow makes me a partner in crime. At least in people's minds. I don't like this. I've already been involved in too much and falsely accused too often. Besides, I've never asked to become anybody's martyr.

"Why have they chosen me?" I wonder. "Plenty of other breakers are being executed every week. What's so freaking special about me?"

"That's a very intriguing question," Holtzmann admits, "one I hoped you could help me come to a suitable conclusion about."

"You must be kidding, egghead," I laugh. "How would I know? I've been locked up or drugged out of my mind the last few weeks. I wasn't aware of the poster or the attacks. I know less than you."

Holtzmann looks at me quizzically.

"Are you telling the truth?" he asks.

At first I don't understand why he doubts my words. Then I realize what Holtzmann hopes to hear. He must think that I knew those breakers somehow.

"Yes, I'm telling the truth, and I don't know them," I answer. "I've no idea why they used my picture."

Holtzmann glances at me with hesitation.

"I do believe you, Rex," he says finally. "I only hoped you knew a way to stop them."

"Why would I want to stop them?" I ask. "I'm a breaker. I see nothing wrong with what they're doing. I only wish somebody would have come to break me out of jail while I was still there."

"As I previously stated, it's not the only attack," Holtzmann answers. "There have been at least two others. Similar tactics were used in each instance, although there was an increased level of violence in the second attack. We were watching the video feed from the third assault. A group of breakers had burned the police station and freed a few inmates. The second attack was much more serious. They burned a school to the ground with students and teachers locked inside."

"What? You mean for real? This isn't another Elimination ploy to make monsters out of breakers?"

"I wish it were," Holtzmann answers. "Unfortunately, it was a worst case act of terror."

"There's no point in killing innocent people," I protest. "It won't help anybody. Why would they do that?"

"In retaliation for Elimination's continued atrocities against breakers," Holtzmann says. "And to demonstrate that breakers aren't willing to idly stand by while the government hunts down and kills their families and friends."

"But those students and teachers weren't part of Elimination!" I exclaim. "Why target them for goodness sakes?"

"Because those teachers and students weren't breakers," Holtzmann explains. "And they wanted to make a statement. The world has split, breakers on one side and ordinary people on the other. These attacks are the first shots in the brutal war that is beginning."

"Why does it have to lead to all-out war?" I ask. "This is obviously the work of only a single group of revenge crazed criminals. They don't represent all breakers nor could they really do anything against the hundreds of trained killers from Elimination."

"Well, nobody knows the actual strength of the outlaw group," Holtzmann answers. "I think there may be more than we expect. I'm also worried that additional breakers may subsequently follow their bad example. Elimination and the government will retaliate by torturing and killing every breaker caught. It will become a genocide of epic proportions, especially after the school massacre. Fighting for survival of their kind, breakers will be killing humans whether soldier or civilian, and they've already started. Oh, this is going to be a terrible war! The last one, I believe. Neither race will survive a war like this."

Holtzmann's mind seems to wander while he's speaking. I listen patiently. Nothing I could say would change his mind. Holtzmann is completely obsessed with the idea of a coming apocalypse.

"We have to stop this," he says. "If we don't learn how to peacefully coexist or at least tolerate each other, we're all doomed."

I remain unconvinced but feel some sympathy for the professor.

"Okay, okay, I believe you," I assure him. "We're at the edge of the war of wars. What now?"

"We have to work together to prevent this catastrophe," he states. "You have to agree to offer your full cooperation and work with me."

"Why me?" I ask. "You have an entire prison filled with breakers."

"I believe you're the strongest. I've never met a breaker with your level of abilities. You're quite unique."

I'm surprised at hearing there's anything special about me, but don't disagree.

"Additionally, the majority of breakers here are truly guilty, not falsely accused as you have been," Holtzmann adds. "We have thieves, rapists and murderers. I'm not willing to work with them."

"I appreciate your high opinion of me professor, but I won't work for Elimination," I answer.

Holtzmann stares at me for a long time. Probably waiting for me to say something more, but I keep silent. Finally, he sighs, saying that I may take more time to think. Then he calls for guards.

"By the way, was it true what you said to Browning?" I wonder before leaving. "I mean…all this talking about killing yourself?"

"No, I don't think so," Holtzmann answers. "My role is too important for the cause. I just wanted to make certain that Carrel won't be bothering you again."

Chase and two other guards lead me away. After passing a maze of corridors and stairs, we walk into a spacious three story cell block. That's where they must keep most of the population. Looks like my solitary confinement is over.

My cell is only slightly different from the last one. It does have bed though. I lie down, trying to concentrate. How can I escape? There are plenty of cameras on the walls. The doors must be remotely controlled. Watchful officers walk along the rows of cages, armed with nightsticks and handguns. Won't be an easy place to escape, but I can't afford to lose hope.

The following morning after a meager breakfast, I'm allowed to join other inmates in the yard. It's a small area, surrounded on all sides by a tall fence topped with coils of razor wire. I feel odd, being around so many breakers, everyone wearing a collar. Most of them seem resigned, walking or sitting on the ground alone as if in some kind of trance. I notice several spot dark bruises on their faces and arms. Some have electrodes attached to their heads. A shiver runs down my spine seeing this image of my possible fate.

I notice Jimmy sitting alone on the ground. As I approach, the boy gets up, seemingly frightened. Looks like he can't decide if he needs to flee or stay. Being much taller and older, I must appear intimidating to him.

"Are you all right?" I ask.

Realizing that I'm not going to hurt him, Jimmy smiles.

"Yeah, I'm fine," he answers. "That wasn't the first time I had to go through a memory swipe. Victor read my memory when they first brought me here. It was much worse. I totally forgot myself for two days!"

"I'm really sorry," I say. "I wish I didn't have to do that."

"You'll have to do it again."

"What do you mean?"

"Well, they use breakers like you to scan memories of other inmates all the time. Didn't you know? It makes things easy for Elimination. Sometimes they even bring ordinary people for scanning."

"I didn't know," I say.

No way am I reading somebody's memories again. Too painful. Too disgusting. I'm revolted even thinking about my last experience.

"There's nothing you can do about it," Jimmy says. "They use pain or some weakness you may have to force you to do it. Just one problem. If you read memories too often, you can lose your mind. Why do you think Victor got hooked on drugs in here? To get some relief from the pain. Carrel makes him read minds all the time."

"I thought Victor does that of his own free will," I say. "Looks like they don't even keep him in a cell."

"Some of the more useful breakers get privileges," Jimmy explains. "Too bad I'm not one of them. I'm only a level one breaker." He sighs sadly and then glances at me with curiosity. "Did you see the dogs?"

"What dogs?"

"Well, my parents had five dogs," Jimmy explains. "I thought you would see them while reading my memories," he smiles. "I used to hate those tiny mean spirited dogs. Barked at me all the time! But now," his smile fades, "now I can't stop thinking what may have happened to those stupid dogs. There's nobody left to care for them. I'm stuck in here and my parents are dead."

Jimmy wipes his eyes with a sleeve. I did see Elimination kill his parents.

"I'm so sorry," I say quietly.

"They died because of me. Because I'm a breaker. My mom always told me to keep it secret. But some neighbor kids stole my bicycle. I just wanted it back. I didn't hurt anybody really. Somebody saw me hypnotizing those guys. When Elimination came, my parents tried to protect me. My dad even threatened them with a gun. They shot him down. And then they shot my mom too."

I don't know what to say. I just stand beside silently.

"Do you have any relatives?" Jimmy asks.

"No," I lie. I can't tell anyone about Kitty.

"So, you're in the same boat as me?" he asks. "I have no family at all."

"Sounds like," I say.

Unfortunately, it might be true now. I've no idea what happened to my Kitty.

A new group of inmates enters the yard, tall muscular guys in their early twenties. Most have tattoos. None of them wear blocking collars. I see other inmates moving out of their way. The biggest guy gives me a long hard stare. I don't want any trouble, so I pretend not to notice. Not getting any reaction, he turns away.

"Who the heck was that?" I ask.

"Oh, the big guy is Bulldog," Jimmy whispers. "Nobody knows his real name. They say he's a hardened criminal."

"Why no collars?" I wonder.

"Bulldog and his gang work for Browning," Jimmy answers. "You'd best not mess with those guys. They could kill us, and nobody would do so much as punish them. Oh, they beat me really bad when I first came here."

"For what?" I ask.

"Just for fun," Jimmy says curtly.

I glance at Bulldog. What a jerk! Somehow I'm sure that sooner or later our paths will cross. Especially if he bothers Jimmy again. I won't be able to stand aside. I'll have to stop him somehow, although Bulldog appears stronger and more seasoned than me.

The rest of that day I spend locked away inside the chamber. The metal door is solid. No way to communicate with other inmates. I lie in bed, pondering my dream from the night before about Kitty. When I see her, I always get the sensation that my sister is in harm's way, playing with death. It all seems so real. What if I actually have some sort of telepathic link with her? It wouldn't be surprising. We're so close. And I miss Kitty so much. Holtzmann says I'm level four. Can I connect with her telepathically? Well, a few weeks ago this idea would seem crazy. Now I think it's quite possible.

Worrying for Kitty, I try to fall asleep so I can find her again. This time I must remember to get a good glimpse at her surroundings.

Sleep doesn't come. I stay fully awake, being too worried. I'm not sure how to induce telepathic connections. It's only happened spontaneously so far, never by my own will.

Holtzmann might know how to manipulate my abilities this way, but unfortunately I can't ask him. Nobody can know about Kitty.

Being restless, I toss and turn in bed all night long. I close my eyes and try to relax my mind. I imagine Kitty standing in front of me. Come on, I think, tell me something. Give me a clue. Where are you?

Nothing. I can't contact her.

The sound of the door opening wakes me. I sit up, alert and ready for anything. Chase and two other officers enter the cell.

"Relax, breaker," Chase says. "We aren't gonna kill you this time. Browning wants to see you."

What the heck? What does Browning need from me? I expect nothing good coming from this visit.

I follow the guards. They haven't handcuffed me this time, probably thinking that I've given up any plot to escape. Should I attempt anything? The odds are against me, three against one. And my wounded arm is still hurting.

The guards lead me into Browning's office. He pays no attention to me, continuing to read some documents at his enormous desk. Guards push me toward an empty chair, gesturing to sit down. I sit, waiting for Browning to speak. The guards stand behind, holding their weapons on me.

"My congratulations, Rex," Browning finally says, putting the documents away. "Today you'll get an excellent opportunity to prove your loyalty to Elimination."

My loyalty to Elimination?

"Professor Holtzmann has reported about your willingness to work for us," Browning continues. "I appreciate this and am glad to see such rapid improvements in your behavior. After all, that's exactly what this project has been made for. To rehabilitate criminal breakers into safe, productive members of our society."

"Why am I here?" I ask.

"You've been chosen for a special project," Browning answers. "We've been looking for somebody like you, trustworthy and strong. Only a level four breaker would be acceptable for this role."

"What project?" I ask. Holtzmann must have told him something completely false about me.

"I guess you're aware of the recent terrorist attacks," Browning says. "Elimination has to stop them. So, I've made a decision to create a special team of breakers, who will help Elimination catch those terrorists. You've been chosen to be the leader of this highly specialized team."

"Really?" I grin. "And you think I want this? I'm a breaker. Why would I help you capture other breakers?"

"They kill innocent people," Browning says.

"So do you," I answer honestly.

The news about burnt kids and teachers chilled me to the bone. It was the most stupid and disgusting thing I've ever seen. Nevertheless, I'm not willing to help Elimination.

"Think about it, Rex," Browning says. "Elimination can be very forgiving when breakers are willing to change their ways and cooperate."

"Forgive me for what, warden?" I ask. "We both know I haven't committed those crimes that I've been accused of. I shouldn't be here. Elimination has ruined my life. You've even killed me at one point. Why should I trust you after everything you've done? No way in God's green earth am I working for you."

"Is this your final decision?" Browning asks calmly.

"Final as it gets."

"Well, I'm extremely disappointed, Rex."

Guards lead me away.

"You're a total idiot," Chase says, walking beside me. "Holtzmann is gonna freak out and probably throw another tizzy!"

When we enter Holtzmann's lab, he meets us at the door. His eye is twitching.

"Sorry, professor," I say. "I've turned Browning's offer down."

Holtzmann closes his eyes, groaning, "Oh, no!"

"Why did you tell him that I'm willing to work for Elimination?" I ask. "What's that all about?"

"I was trying to save your life," Holtzmann answers. "You have to agree to become a contributing member of that project to be considered useful. You can't imagine how important this project really is. It's not only about your life. It's about the lives of thousands. This may be the only way to prevent war!"

"How's that?" I wonder.

"This particular project was my idea," Holtzmann says. "Browning and Wheeler have come up with a completely different plan. They want to implement a total scanning process of the entire human population, imprisoning all breakers. Of course, you wouldn't know about that. Dr. Carrel is currently developing a special scanner that can instantly identify breakers. Once online, Elimination intends to subject everyone to this special test. It will further divide the population and bring chaos. The breakers will fight back. And payback won't be coming as a single act of terror. Breakers will organize their efforts and join forces to survive. They'll fight back together as an army with nothing to lose." He pauses, catching his breath.

His face becomes red and I'm worried he might have another panic attack.

"My project may represent the only methodology to stop all this madness," he says passionately. "If successful, it will demonstrate how ordinary people and breakers can work together and coexist peacefully. This project will disprove Carrel's theory that all breakers are inherently evil. This is our only option for growing mutual tolerance and trust. Can't you understand? The future of humanity is in our hands. We have to stop this war."

I frown, thinking on his words. I still don't believe him, but the possibility of Carrel's scanning machine is terrifying. If Elimination develops such a thing, breakers will have nowhere to hide.

"You sure that scanning machine can really be produced?" I ask.

"Of course I'm sure!" Holtzmann exclaims. "Elimination already has the technology and I have the know-how. I just don't want to use my knowledge to help them. Hopefully, it'll take Carrel longer to produce the scanner than it'd take me."

"In any case, professor, I won't work for Elimination."

"I'll be the manager of the project. You and I could handpick members of our team together."

"You've picked the wrong breaker," I answer.

"No, I'm certain you're the right choice," Holtzmann says. "I need someone other than a hardened criminal with your skills to lead this project."

"You don't really know me," I answer. "How can you be so sure?"

"I've met enough of the bad ones to know the difference," he says.

For a few moments we remain silent.

"All right then," Holtzmann says. "Hopefully you'll come around. Just be careful. Browning doesn't accept refusals easily."

His words sound somewhat ominous.

Chase leads me back to my cell.

"Some breakers would kill for such an opportunity," he says. "Why don't you want to cooperate with us?"

"Would the fact that Elimination has been chasing, torturing or threatening to kill me as long as I can remember be reason enough?" I answer.

"C'mon, breaker," Chase sighs. "It's not personal, you know. We're just doing our job."

I don't argue. Being completely brainwashed, Chase is sure that he's doing good, protecting society from vicious breaker monstrosities. Nothing I could say would change his mind.

In the chamber I try again to contact Kitty. I'm lying in bed with my eyes closed, concentrating hard. I see nothing, but the dark.

In the evening I meet Jimmy out in the yard. Seeing me, he smiles and talks about his dogs, school and past freedoms lost. I'm not in the mood for conversation, thinking of Holtzmann's predictions of war, and Kitty being in danger, but Jimmy doesn't seem to care. He's the most talkative breaker I've met so far.

Bulldog and his gang look our way and begin walking toward us. I remember what Jimmy told me yesterday about these guys. They work for Browning. And Holtzmann warned me to be careful because Browning doesn't accept refusals. I get a bad feeling in my gut.

Jimmy stops speaking, staring at the gang.

"What do they want from us?" he whispers.

Bulldog points a finger my direction and makes a slicing motion across his neck.

"Get out of here," I whisper to Jimmy.

CHAPTER 13

Jimmy flees as I watch the gang walk closer. Seven against one. I still have time to run, but am just too tired with running and hiding. Bulldog's gang is likely under Browning's orders to teach me a lesson. They won't stop till they find me, so why put it off?

It's not the first time I've been outnumbered. Fights were pretty common around the area where I grew up. To combat boredom, guys from different farm sections would meet at some agreed upon spot to fight just to see who was the toughest.

Approaching, Bulldog spits near my feet and proclaims, "Hey! You can't stand in that spot."

I sigh, already knowing exactly what he intends to do.

"That happens to be my spot," Bulldog continues.

"Really?" I ask, smiling. "And what spot in this yard isn't yours?"

"Oh, so you want to be a smart one," Bulldog laughs. "Do you know what we do with smart boys like you?"

Other gang members laugh as well, forming a circle around me. I watch them carefully, preparing for the coming attack.

"Ray, teach this moron some manners," Bulldog commands. All this time he keeps his voice low. Good self-control, I have to admit.

A huge, tough-looking guy steps toward me. He is a full head taller than me, almost as big as Bulldog.

"You're gonna swallow your own teeth now, punk," he promises.

Other gang members step back, clearing some space for fighting and smirking in anticipation.

I realize Ray could probably knock me out with a single blow.

Calming myself, I wait patiently for him to make his move. Ray throws a haymaker at my head as I move to the side, slipping his punch and sending a hard kick to his kneecap in the same instant. There's a loud snapping noise, his leg now bent in an unnatural way as Ray collapses onto the ground. As the big guy grabs his wounded knee in pain, I slam a foot straight into his face. Ray is out, but six to one is still not much better odds.

"Who's got next?" I ask.

"Damn," one of them utters.

"We'll kill you," Bulldog states.

The gang isn't going to come at me one at a time after watching Ray. They attack together this time, like a pack of wolves and raining a hail of punches and kicks as they move in. I manage to slip the first punch, throwing a jab into the nose of the closest. Suddenly, they're all on me and I'm knocked to the ground. I'm only half conscious after the first few solid kicks and punches land, my face and body already numb from the beating and not really feeling any more pain.

Somebody fires a round.

"Back off, freaks!" a sharp command follows. "Get off him! Now!"

Bulldog and his gang back slowly away, leaving me bleeding on the ground.

"Return to your cells!" I hear another command. The voice sounds muffled.

I can't understand what's happening, balancing on the edge of consciousness, and I don't really care too much. The beating has stopped and that's all that matters for the moment.

"Rex! Can you hear me?" somebody speaks. "Can you get up?"

Somebody shakes me. I open my eyes and see Chase.

"Whoa!" he exclaims. "You're messed up pretty bad. Hold on, I'll get help."

"That's all right," I say, not recognizing my own voice. "I can walk."

Chase helps me onto my feet and grimaces. "You sure you can walk?"

"Yeah," I answer. "I've been through worse. It's okay."

I spit blood through split lips. No idea what other injures I've sustained. My entire body is hurting. Looking around, I notice a few guards dragging the still unconscious Ray away. No sign of Bulldog and his gang. Jimmy stands far off, watching. He's probably the one who notified Chase.

"Thanks," I say.

"For what?" Chase asks.

"I said thanks for saving me again," I answer.

"Just shut up!" Chase growls. "Know what? You're the worst breaker I've ever met. You're nothing but trouble. Why is something always happening to you? Why can't you just be an orderly inmate?"

I attempt a smile, but my lips hurt too much.

"I like you too, Chase," I say sarcastically.

"Shut your trap!" he repeats, helping me walk. I'm limping. Blood seeps from my head. "Damn you, Rex," Chase mumbles. "Never seen anybody who could be punched and kicked into the head so many times and survive. You must be brainless, otherwise you'd be in coma."

I begin coughing.

"A brainless idiot," Chase says. "Holtzmann advised you to agree with Browning. I've warned you as well. Why do you insist on being so stubborn?"

Looks like Chase knows all too well why Bulldog's gang targeted me.

We finally make it to the prison hospital. At first the doctor refuses to treat me, saying that he hasn't received any approval for this. Chase raises his rifle, saying, "Is this approval enough, doc? Treat the breaker."

Reluctantly, the doctor examines my head, then injects something into my arm and stitches my wound. I have a broken nose, fractured skull and bruised ribs. It could be worse, I guess.

"They will be looking to try it again," Chase says. "I mean Bulldog's gang. They'll want revenge for Ray."

"I don't care," I answer.

Chase sighs tiredly and says, "Listen, breaker. Holtzmann really thinks that…"

Chase doesn't finish his sentence, because the door slams open and a furious Wheeler enters the doctor's office.

"Who ordered him brought here?" he demands.

"I brought him, sir," Chase answers. "He was bleeding and…"

"Can't you hear?" Wheeler cuts him off. "I asked who gave you the directive to bring breaker here."

"There was no direct order, sir, there was just no other choice."

"He's started a fight with other inmates. He's aggressive and unpredictable. So, I ask again, what's he doing here in the infirmary? Protocol calls for troublesome breakers to be restricted to their cells. Did you flagrantly break protocol or conveniently forget? I expect better from you, Chase."

Chase opens his mouth to speak, but Wheeler doesn't give him a chance.

"Follow me," Wheeler commands. "And bring the freak along with you."

Chase raises up his weapon, motioning me to walk. Limping, I stagger out of the room.

"Move!" Chase commands, poking my back with the barrel.

I wind up in another interrogation room, surrounded by officers and facing Wheeler. They don't even bother to handcuff me, being confident in my inability to resist. I look around, examining my surroundings. A windowless room with a low ceiling and smudged walls along with several spots of blood coagulated on the floor. Several metal chairs with straps and a long table with numerous instruments for torturing. God only knows what they've been doing to prisoners in this chamber.

"Do you like it in here?" Wheeler asks, smiling. "What's wrong, breaker? Don't want to fight anymore?"

He approaches, while two other officers hold my arms tightly. Chase stands quietly aside.

"Why have you attacked other inmates?" Wheeler questions, smiling. I'm sure he knows exactly what happened. He must be under orders from Browning to torture me in case Bulldog's assault failed.

"Notify Holtzmann," I request.

"Shut your hole," Wheeler growls and one of the officers smashes the butt of his weapon into my face. The room spins and I go down. Two officers catch me, not letting my body completely collapse to the floor.

"Nobody will bail you out this time, freak," Wheeler says. "You're all mine now. I've been waiting for this too long. Now you're gonna beg like a whipped dog."

He punches me hard into the stomach. I gasp, coughing. I'm thankful for the anesthetic administered in the infirmary. It's still working, helping numb my nerves.

"We have no tolerance for aggressive breakers here," Wheeler says.

He's still playing his game, blaming me for the fight.

"Well now, what to do with you?" Wheeler asks. "Shall we cut your fingers off? Or rather begin by ripping off your finger nails and pulling your teeth?" he looks into my eyes, smiling. "Would you prefer to choose your own fate, breaker? Or rather leave it to my discretion? Choose."

How can he smile and remain calm, saying this? Suddenly, I realize that his hate has little to do with my being a breaker. This is just Wheeler's nature. He's a worst case sadist craving to pour out his violence on the innocent. If there were no breakers around, Wheeler would probably wind up in prison himself for kidnapping, torturing, and killing innocent people. Unfortunately, he has plenty of legal targets for satisfying his sadistic needs. In our warped society, Wheeler is a respected professional getting paid a salary to commit his crimes.

"It's so disrespectful of you to ignore my question," he says, smiling.

He pistol whips my head. This time I fall onto the floor.

"Stinking rat," Wheeler spits. "You're disgusting." His heavy boot strikes my rib cage.

"Sir, I think this breaker has had enough," I hear Chase speaking. "He's already been beaten. We don't really need to kill him."

"I didn't ask you for your opinion, Chase," Wheeler chides, kicking me again.

"Bring Holtzmann here," I repeat sluggishly.

Chase hesitates for a few moments and walks toward the exit.

"Halt!" Wheeler commands. "What the hell are you doing? I didn't dismiss you."

Chase freezes, moving his eyes from me to his commander.

"We shouldn't kill him, sir," he says. "He's needed for project work."

"Let me give you some advice, Chase," Wheeler answers. "We've got plenty of young resistant officers, ready and willing to take your place. If you walk out of this room against my orders, you'll be walking out of Elimination forever. I brought you here, Chase. You can be sure, I could just as easily boot you out. Decide."

Chase lowers his face in complete submission. "Yes, sir."

I'm done, I realize. They don't intend to let me out of here alive. And nobody will come to my rescue this time. I'm on my own.

I concentrate, projecting my thoughts toward Wheeler and other officers. Let me free. Let me out. It doesn't work. The blocking collar makes my attempts useless.

"Now where were we, breaker?" Wheeler says, looking at me with the kindest smile you can imagine. "I've decided what we're gonna do first. We're gonna teach you how to swim."

He grabs me under the chin, jerking my head to the side and drags me toward a big rusted barrel in the corner of the room. The officers follow, weapons at the ready should I decide to resist. Chase stands aside wearing a gloomy expression.

"I hope you like water," Wheeler says enthusiastically, forcing my head into the barrel filled with reeking liquid. I hold my breath, grabbing the edges of the barrel and pushing. A pair of hands hold me tightly, keeping my head pressed down. It seems to last forever. My lungs burn, but I know I can't take a breath. Drowning.

Wheeler finally pulls me up. I gulp air greedily, coughing and spitting the noxious water. The room is hazy. I hear laughter.

"Do you like the taste of mop water, jerk?" Wheeler asks.

"Call for Holtzmann," I try to say again, but can't quite manage.

"Drink, breaker, drink," Wheeler growls, dipping my head once again into the blackened liquid.

I have to do something or he'll drown me. It won't matter if Wheeler lets my head out of water this time or not, eventually I'll wind up dead.

I push back against the barrel and resist at first, then relax, sagging as if passed out. I fight back my panic to try to get air. My entire body aches and I'm risking a blackout for real.

Seconds pass slowly. I'm about to give up, when Wheeler suddenly pulls me up. The officers must believe I'm unconscious, because they don't secure my arms. Wheeler is the only one holding me at the moment. I swing my arm around violently, smashing an elbow into Wheeler's face. It catches him by surprise. He doesn't have time to move away or block my strike. Groaning, he steps back, swaying and letting me go momentarily. The same instant I snatch his gun and press the barrel against Wheeler's head. The officers, including Chase, point their rifles at me.

"Drop your weapons!" I command.

"I'll kill you!" Wheeler growls.

"Quiet," I calmly answer as I thumb back the hammer.

"Easy there, breaker, easy," Chase says.

"Anybody moves, I kill him," I warn as I walk toward the exit, half dragging Wheeler. "Chase, open the door. Now!" I command.

"No way, breaker," Chase answers.

"For God's sake, Chase!" Wheeler groans. "Just do as he says!"

Chase hesitates, then opens the door.

"Don't follow me unless you want to scrape Wheeler's brains off the walls," I suggest as we're backing out of the doorway.

I don't really expect the officers to comply with my commands, but they do. My actions must have taken everybody by surprise. Hopefully, at a minimum I have bought some time before they recover and hunt me down. Now, having Wheeler as a hostage, I may finally get a chance to escape. This is the opportunity I've been waiting for.

"You can't get out," Wheeler says. "No breaker leaves here alive."

"I said keep quiet," I say, smashing a handgun into the side of Wheeler's head. Wheeler drops to a knee, bleeding. I point the barrel at him, hesitating. Calm down, I tell myself, you need a hostage to escape. Until I escape, Wheeler will be useless to me dead.

"Damn you, freak," Wheeler hisses.

"Get up," I command. Slowly, he obeys, looking hatefully into his own handgun aimed between his eyes. I nudge Wheeler with the gun to keep moving, making him walk ahead, so if needed I can use him as a human shield. Hopefully, the officers won't blast their own commander. I can't be sure though. These Elimination killers are brutal and unpredictable.

Each set of doors that could lead outside are locked. They must be externally controlled. How do I open them? There must be an operating center somewhere. That's where I need to go, I decide.

"Listen closely, you pig," I begin. "You get exactly one chance to be spared. Lead me straight to the security center. And don't even think about messing around with me, Wheeler. You can be sure, I'm completely convinced the world would be much better off without the likes of you."

Wheeler exhales deeply and turns down a side corridor. We walk slowly. I hear footsteps coming up from behind and look back. Chase and several officers follow at a distance.

"I'll kill him if you get any closer," I warn.

They stop, but I doubt I can keep them away forever. I need to hurry.

We proceed through several long passages. I have no idea if Wheeler is leading me in the right direction or into a trap.

A few guards appear along our way, but let us pass.

"You can't escape, breaker," Wheeler growls. "You're already a dead man and just don't know it."

"As you are," I answer, keeping my voice low. "Your life depends on my escape, Wheeler."

We enter a small room where several officers sit staring at screens. There are multiple panels loaded with buttons and switches. This must be the operating center.

"Open all the doors," I command. The guards suddenly turn, hands reaching for their holsters.

"Not happening," one of them answers.

I fire the gun at the guard, hitting him in the shoulder and immediately press the barrel back against Wheeler's head. Others raise their weapons.

"Stop," I command. "Lower your guns and open the doors, or Wheeler dies. Now!"

"Take it easy, inmate," a guard near a panel states. "Nobody else needs to get hurt here."

They lower their weapons and one presses a couple of buttons on the control panel. I watch the doors of multiple chambers open on the screens. Some inmates walk out of their cells. The doors to the outer world remain closed.

"You can't get out of this prison," the guard says. "The main doors aren't automatic. We can't open them from here."

"I believe you can," I say.

"He's right," Wheeler says. "It was designed this way to prevent escape. The outer doors can't be accessed from the control room."

Something tells me he's not lying, but I can't give up. They'll shoot me if I do. I have to keep going.

"On the floor!" I command. When the guards are prone on the floor, I fire several shots into the panel they utilized to open the cell doors. Then I slowly back out of the room.

"Make it easy on yourself and surrender," Wheeler says. "You can't get out, so just what do you intend to do?"

"Haven't made up my mind yet," I answer. "At the moment, I'm considering whether or not to put a bullet into your head."

"That won't help your cause," Wheeler says. "I have orders. Carrying them out is my job. I don't necessarily always like it."

"I think you must," I say.

As we turn a corner from a control area, several officers leap out, pulling Wheeler away as one reaches for my gun. I put a bullet into the offending arm and take off running. Sprinting down the aisle, I hear the officers collapsing on top of Wheeler to protect him from further gunfire.

"Get off me!" Wheeler yells furiously. "Get that freak!"

I manage to make another turn before the shooting begins. I don't stop. I scramble up the stairs through a long corridor, passing several empty cells. I've no idea where to go next. Officers are in pursuit from behind. I fire the gun their general direction, emptying the clip.

Running hard, I come upon a group of inmates. Some of them have rifles, taken from other officers. The prisoners pay little attention to me, being busy shooting into my followers. I keep running, leaving everybody behind.

An alarm sounds, a shrill and deafening noise, as all the lights shut off. I can see nothing now, just total darkness. Unsteadily, I press on, hoping for my eyes to adjust. I have to slow to a fast walk, placing a hand on the wall for guidance. Soon I hear the gunfire coming from the area I've just left and realize I've started a prison riot. Freshly released prisoners are viciously attacking guards, fighting to the death for their freedom. I don't mind. Maybe I can somehow slip away unnoticed in all the confusion.

Somebody charges into me from the side, narrowly missing with a hard elbow. I slam him into the temple with my gun. He grabs me as he falls, pulling me down on top of him. I smash his head into the floor until he stops moving. Then I pick up the flashlight my attacker dropped and shine a beam of light at him. The clothes he's wearing are inmate issue. I'm confused. Why attack me, if he's another breaker? Then I realize that I must be in the section housing the hardcore prisoners. Most breakers in here are legitimate bad guys and criminals.

Carefully, I pick my way along the pitch black passage.

I hear a woman's desperate call for help. The voice sounds vaguely familiar.

CHAPTER 14

I proceed closer toward the voice, winding up in a long corridor only slightly illuminated by emergency lighting. Up ahead, I can barely make out two figures struggling. As I approach, I realize there's no real fight between them at all. A tall guy in a prison jumpsuit is dragging a girl by the hair. I recognize him as being one of Bulldog's gang members. The girl is screaming, flailing her arms and kicking out into the empty air. She's too weak and small to fight this guy. I've met the girl before although I can't place her at the moment. She wears a business suit and slacks. Her blouse is torn from scuffling. Rebecca, I finally realize, Holtzmann's cousin.

The guy shines his flashlight into my face. I squint into the blinding light, keeping a distance.

"Who's there?" he asks. "Ah, it's you. Get the hell on out of here."

Seems like he doesn't care about our confrontation just a few hours earlier. Nobody keeps grudges in this place, I remind myself. He was likely only following Browning's orders. Now he has nothing against me.

"Help!" Rebecca cries out again.

"Quiet," the inmate growls, slapping her face hard.

I should leave. It's really none of my business what's happening here. I need to save time, and distance myself from those still in pursuit.

Rebecca sobs, giving me a look of desperation. Kitty had the same expression when we first met. And suddenly I know I can't allow what's about to happen and just let it slide. I have to do something.

"Get moving," the inmate commands, brandishing a gun. "Now!"

I'm still holding a gun in my hand, but it's not loaded. I can't tell if the guy has bullets in his weapon or not, and I really don't want to find out the hard way.

I smile broadly, staring at Rebecca. There are about eight feet separating us. Hopefully I can fool this guy.

"Let me have a turn with that little screamer," I say, walking closer. The gun is still pointed at my chest. The inmate looks me over with suspicion. "C'mon," I say, continuing to smile. "I've been locked away in here for weeks, don't be so selfish."

He obviously doesn't trust me, but appears to at least ponder what I've said.

I take another step. It's now or never.

I bum rush the guy, grabbing his gun hand as he pulls the trigger. The bullet whizzes past my ear. I strike the guy squarely in the face. My punch doesn't seem to have a great effect. He steps in, swinging his free arm around to smash my ribs. I groan, doubling over, but keeping my grip and pulling him down. We fall to the floor, the inmate landing on top of me and throwing bombs. He's too big and strong. I'm losing down here. Blood sprays from my nose as he slams an elbow into my face. Tasting my own blood, I cover up, partially blocking another hard punch he delivers. The impact smashes my own arm into my face. He's gonna kill me, I realize, if I don't do something soon. I'm close to passing out. Unconscious, I'll be good as dead.

As the criminal reaches for my throat, I stick my thumb into his eye as hard as I possibly can. He cries out and weakens his grip on my neck. I shove him off, scrambling up to my feet. I punch him in the throat, then ribs, finishing with a kick into his knee as I work my way down. He staggers, grabbing his knee as I land a round kick flush to the side of his head, putting him down.

I kneel down for a moment to catch my breath and clean the blood off my face.

Rebecca stands sobbing in front of me, leaning up against a wall. She's watching the unconscious guy on the floor. I notice his gun lying at her feet.

"Why didn't you shoot him?" I ask.

Rebecca shivers from the sound of my voice. "I don't know how. I've never fired a gun before."

I can't believe that there are still people in the world who have never fired a gun.

"That's all right," I say, getting up.

Rebecca sobs as I move closer.

"Come on, don't do that," I say, picking up the gun and checking the clip. It's still got ammo. I tuck it into my pants behind.

"You won't hurt me, will you?" Rebecca asks.

I take a deep breath, "I've just saved you, haven't I?"

"I still can't trust you, you're a breaker."

I snort in anger, being sick with hearing nonsense about evil breakers. Then I remember what Chase told me. A breaker killed Rebecca's family and she survived only because she's resistant.

"I just want to get out of this place," I say. "Can you help?"

Rebecca shakes her head. "I can't."

"Come on, you work here. You must know how to exit the main doors."

"I don't," Rebecca sobs. "I only know that they lock automatically in an emergency. You have to input a special code."

"What code?"

"I have no idea. I'm not with security. I'm only Holtzmann's assistant."

I direct a beam of light into her face.

"Rebecca, are you lying to me?" I ask.

"I'm not lying," she cries. "Please, don't hurt me. I really don't know anything."

"It's okay," I say. "I believe you."

"Thank you," Rebecca whispers.

She appears afraid to move or even to speak too loudly.

"It's not safe for me to stick around any longer," I say. "And you'd best get going as well. You wanna be clear of here when this jerk wakes up."

Rebecca remains motionless.

"Where can I go?" she asks. "The inmates are all over the place. You can't leave me alone."

"What?" I say in surprise. Just a moment ago she thought I was gonna kill her.

"Please," she begs. "I'm more afraid of these breakers."

"Lest you forget, I'm a breaker last I checked."

Rebecca grips my arm, "Please."

"All right," I concede. "It's dangerous, but you can tag along for a while. Now let's get moving away from here."

I take her hand and we walk down a dark passage, illuminating the way with a flashlight.

"We need to rescue Egbert," Rebecca whispers. "Bulldog and his gang attacked the lab. Egbert is still in there. They all hate him and will definitely want to hurt or even kill him."

"He's one of my captors, why should I help rescue him?"

"He's my cousin," she answers defiantly.

"That's a really nice thought," I say. "But I'm not willing to risk my life, attempting to save an Elimination scientist hoping to use me in some stinking experiment."

She keeps silent for a few moments and then says, "Egbert is a good man. You can't be so heartless."

"Sorry, but I can," I answer.

"Those breakers will kill him. Egbert is sick and isn't capable of defending himself."

"I don't care one iota."

Rebecca sobs again. She must really love her cousin. I owe my life to Holtzmann. He didn't let Wheeler shoot me and cared for Lena while I was in the infirmary. Holtzmann is part of Elimination, but I can't hate him. And I don't wish him dead.

"Please, Rex," Rebecca begs.

I didn't expect Rebecca to remember my name.

"Fine," I say. "I'll help you, just stop with all the crying. Although I've got no idea how we can go about rescuing your cousin from Bulldog's gang. They probably have guns. And even if they don't, they still outnumber us."

"Maybe we can find some guards to help?"

"Rebecca, I'm an inmate and a breaker. Guards will probably just shoot me on sight."

I hear gunfire and the sound of heavy footsteps somewhere nearby. We slow down, listening carefully. Rebecca shivers, clamping her mouth to suppress a scream. I hold my gun ready. A group of people are moving toward us. No telling if they're guards or prisoners. In either case, we won't wait to find out.

"Let's go," I whisper.

We change direction several times, jogging our way down multiple passages and climbing up stairs. I'm completely lost, but Rebecca must know the place well enough to remain oriented even in the dark. She tells me where to turn and in which direction to go. We pass several empty cells and I notice somebody hiding in a chamber. I shine the flashlight into the dark room. It's Jimmy, crouching in the corner. He covers his head and mumbles something incoherent.

"Hey, take it easy," I say. "This is just me, Rex. What are you doing here?"

He stares through me, wide eyed and panicked.

"Come with us," I say.

"No!" he exclaims. "I don't want any more trouble."

"It's not safe here," I persist, walking into the cell and dragging Jimmy out of his corner. He complains, but doesn't resist. "You can't remain here. All the inmates are on the loose. Bulldog's gang may beat or kill you. Guards may shoot you."

"No, I'll be in more trouble if I leave," Jimmy answers. "I'm not trying to escape."

"Nobody is trying to escape at the moment," I say. "We're going to rescue Holtzmann first."

Confused, Jimmy stops talking.

"It's okay," Rebecca says in a calming voice. "Rex will protect us."

At least she's consistent in her having a wrong impression of me.

"Freeze!" a loud voice orders. "Don't move, freak!"

I turn to the sound of voice, gun raised. I see Chase holding an automatic weapon, ready to shoot.

"Let's not try it, Chase," I sigh. "I don't want to have to kill you."

"Let the girl go," he commands.

"Chase! Thank God you've found us!" Rebecca exclaims. "We need your help. We're going to rescue Egbert."

"What?" Chase asks, looking at her and then at me in surprise. The barrel of his weapon is still pointed at my chest and Chase's finger is on the trigger. I can't quite make up my mind whether I should use this moment of hesitation to shoot first.

"Please, Chase, help us," Rebecca begs. "Bulldog has attacked our lab and taken Egbert hostage. Bulldog's gang was trying to harm me as well, but Rex interceded and saved me. Now we need to save Egbert."

"You can't be serious, this freak is who started the riot," Chase says, motioning into my direction.

"Is that true?" Rebecca asks.

"It's true I let them loose," I answer. "But it was done in self-defense."

A long pause follows, while everybody is thinking.

"Chase, please," Rebecca says softly.

Chase lowers his weapon. Rebecca definitely knows how to sway a man's opinion. I relax a little and lower my gun as well.

"Okay, breaker," Chase says. "Help us rescue the professor then, but you'll have to give up your gun. Just don't try anything stupid. I swear to God I'll shoot you dead should you try anything."

"All right, I guess I can agree to that," I say, handing over my gun. I didn't think it'd be so easy to convince Chase of my good intentions.

Rebecca leads us toward the lab. I follow her with Chase bringing up the rear. I can almost physically sense the cold steel barrel of his weapon pointed at my back. Even though we may be temporarily on the same side, Chase and I still don't trust each other very far. Everything could change at a moment's notice and we wind up killing each other.

Jimmy walks somberly beside me, occasionally sobbing. I shush him to keep quiet.

We have to stop a few times along the way, ducking into shadows, as groups of prisoners pass by. Chase stands ready, watching as the inmates walk by. Should they notice us, he'll be targeted first while I may be considered just a captured inmate. Rebecca remains silent, showing no signs of panic or hysteria. I have to admit she's holding up pretty well.

As we proceed carefully Chase whispers, "How many breakers are holding the lab?"

"No idea. How many guys are in Bulldog's gang?"

"Eight."

"Possibly six. I knocked out one who attacked Rebecca. Hopefully, Ray hasn't recovered from our fight this morning."

"They probably have weapons," Chase warns. "Swarms of inmates have attacked and overwhelmed guards, gaining possession of guns and rifles. I believe Bulldog and his gang have done so as well."

"Why would they attack Holtzmann if they're working for Browning?"

"Because they also associate with Carrel. Carrel hates Holtzmann and wants to take his place as lead scientist."

"This place is really messed up," I say. "Anyway what's the plan?"

"I haven't figured one out yet. What about you, any ideas?"

I don't answer. We'll have to plan as we go.

I consider our predicament as we walk. We obviously need to avoid a gunfight. Bulldog and his gang are trapped inside just like me. After all this mess is over, Elimination will count its losses and the guilty breakers will be punished. Browning won't be happy if his lead scientist is dead. Bulldog should know that. Maybe he won't kill Holtzmann, but I can't be certain.

As we arrive at the lab's entrance, Chase stops and looks at me quizzically.

"We just have to march in there and take them by surprise," he says. "We have two weapons. Can I trust you, Rex?"

"You don't really have much of a choice," I say. "You shouldn't go there alone, but if you'd rather take Jimmy or Rebecca…"

Chase hesitates, then hands back my gun.

Leaving Jimmy and Rebecca concealed as best as we can near the entrance, we enter Holtzmann's lab. We estimated their strength correctly. There are six of them, two armed with Elimination guard rifles. Bulldog is sitting behind Holtzmann's desk, playing with a knife. The other three are rummaging through shelves stocked with medicine. They've tossed the room. Holtzmann is lying motionless on the floor, unconscious or dead. His face is bloody and mouth is foaming. Looks like he's suffered a seizure.

"Don't move!" Chase commands, aiming his weapon at Bulldog. I stand aside, holding my gun ready. The two with rifles square around to face us. Bulldog looks up slowly.

"Why should we follow your orders, Officer Chase?" he asks, grinning. "We're in the middle of a riot here."

"We're just here for Holtzmann," I say. "Take your guys and walk away. If you've killed Holtzmann, Browning will kill you."

"Look who's talking now," Bulldog says. "Are you working for Elimination now? What side are you on, boy?"

"It doesn't matter," I answer. "What really matters is that I'll be putting my first bullet right between your eyes. Don't try me. Just take your guys and go."

"Other guards are already covering the front of the lab," Chase warns. "And more will be arriving soon, then it will be too late to leave by the back exit."

Bulldog thinks, while his gang waits patiently. I expect shooting to begin at any moment. Nobody backs down.

"You can have the scientist," Bulldog says. "We'll pick up another hostage along the way. We didn't intend to kill this psycho anyway, he just flipped out and started foaming at the mouth."

"Stand down and leave," Chase commands.

I breathe out, watching Bulldog and his guys backing toward the rear exit. Bulldog gives me a lingering look.

"I should've killed you," he says.

I grin slightly. Everybody wishes me dead today.

After the gang clears the area, I go to retrieve Rebecca and Jimmy. Being too tired to continue with my own escape plan, I follow them back into the lab. Chase slams the entrance and exit doors shut and barricades them with chairs. Jimmy eagerly assists. Rebecca rushes to her cousin and falls on her knees beside his body. She checks his pockets and finds the plastic bottle with pills. Then she looks at him helplessly. Being unconscious, Holtzmann can't take his medicine.

I approach them and help her pull Holtzmann up and put him in the chair. His body sags, head lolling to one side. Rebecca wipes foam and blood away with her hand. His nose may be broken.

"Wake up, Egbert," Rebecca cries. "Please, don't die."

"Nobody dies from a broken nose," I say. "Mine is broken as well."

Holtzmann moves his head, coughing. He opens his hazy eyes for a moment, muttering something, and passes out again.

"He'll be all right," I say. "Don't worry."

Then we wait, sitting on the floor in silence. It's too dangerous to walk out of this room. I can hear sounds of shooting and fighting in the distance.

"What if the inmates gain control?" I ask Chase.

"Negative. We have more guards here than prisoners. Also some breakers aren't hardened criminals. They won't be as willing to fight."

"I don't wanna fight," Jimmy says quietly.

Rebecca's hand finds mine and she says, "Thank you."

"For what?" I ask.

"For saving Egbert and I."

"That's about right, Rebecca, give all thanks to the breaker," Chase says. "What about me? I was risking my life too by the way."

"I'm grateful to you as well, but that's your job, Chase," Rebecca answers unsympathetically.

"I hate my job," Chase groans. "And hate breakers even more."

I close my eyes, resting. I think of Kitty. I'm really happy she's away from all this trouble. I wonder what will happen after the officers get the inmates subdued. I am the one who began this mess.

"Rex! Where the hell are you?" a harsh woman's voice comes from outside the room.

Chase scrambles onto his feet, taking up his weapon.

"Who are you?" I ask.

"Damn you! Just let me in, stupid!"

I recognize Jessie's voice.

"It's okay, let her in," I say. Chase doesn't protest. Together we move the chairs from the door and open it.

Jessie comes in, carrying an officer's rifle. She looks much better, although her face is still bruised. Lena enters the room behind her, sees me and smiles broadly.

"I knew you were here," she says. "I saw you."

Lena's a telepath, I remind myself.

"What are you two doing here?" I ask Jessie.

"Looking for you, idiot. I ran into Lena at the beginning of all this craziness. Lena suggested that you'd started it and was looking for a way to escape. She wanted to help."

"Sorry," I answer. "We can't escape. The main exits are locked down."

Lena sighs, "That's all right."

She doesn't sound like a child.

"Hey, I can hear you plotting," Chase says angrily. "I'm still an Elimination officer. Stop talking all this escape nonsense."

Lena looks at him seriously.

"You won't hurt us, Chase," she says. "I can see things about you too. You're a good guy."

Chase frowns, seeming confused by the compliment.

"Are you all right?" I ask Jessie. "I'm really sorry for all what you've gone through."

"Forget it," she answers. "I knew what I was doing." She keeps silent for a moment and then says with unease, "They've got my parents."

I understand what Jessie is talking about. Victor read her mind and told Elimination how to find her relatives. Now Elimination can use her parents to manipulate Jessie. I can't find words to say.

"May I kill this freak?" Jessie asks, pointing her rifle at Holtzmann.

"No, don't," I answer. "He's got nothing to do with it. He doesn't want to hurt anybody. He's just a very sick guy."

Chase holds his weapon on Jessie, waiting.

"Whatever," she concedes as she sits tiredly down on the floor.

Time passes slowly. I'm drained and my entire body is hurting. I have no strength left to fight or run. It's useless anyway. No matter what we try, we won't be able to escape from this place. Maybe it's time to give up. Maybe I'll change my mind later, but right now I just want to forget about everything and sleep.

It's several hours later before guards break into the lab. I don't resist.

CHAPTER 15

"I'm very disappointed with your behavior," Browning says. "I'm afraid you haven't left me any choice, but to transfer you to our top security prison."

Browning stands several feet away, perched in a doorway, accompanied by two armed guards. I remain in a sitting position on the floor, paying little attention to Browning's words. I'm completely worn out.

After Elimination subdued the outbreak, I was thrown into solitary. I haven't received any medical attention. Nobody has brought food and water. I'd been waiting for hours to learn my fate. Finally, the warden has arrived to announce my punishment.

"Maybe you think you're in prison right now," Browning continues. "You would be mistaken. This facility is merely a secured reorientation and rehabilitation center for breakers. We don't blame you for being what you are here. Here we all have optimism for correcting a breaker's wayward nature. We give breakers an opportunity to become a useful part of society again. You have wasted your opportunity, Rex. I offered you important work. Many breakers would kill to get such an offer, but you unfortunately rejected it. Additionally, you've endangered everybody's life by initiating a riot. It's very frustrating for me. I truly regret that everything has to end this way. You're to be sent to our maximum security prison for breakers, which the residents there refer to as the Death Camp."

I feel somewhat amused, listening to Browning. He sounds pathetic. Even now he continues wearing a mask of goodness and virtue.

"Whatever," I answer.

I don't really care what fate they decide. I'm good as dead already. I'm only a little surprised by Browning's decision to transport me to another prison. Wouldn't it be easier just to kill me here? Well, maybe he wants me to die a little more slowly to maximize my suffering.

"Such a waste," Browning says, leaving. The guards close the cell door.

Left alone, I think of Kitty. Where is she now? I hope she's far away and somewhere safe. No matter what happens to me, I'm comforted in knowing that she escaped, and in keeping the belief that she remains alive and well.

In an hour or so, the door opens and in walks Chase. At first I think he's come to transfer me into the higher security prison. But he just stands in front of me, looking concerned, then asks, "Are you all right?"

I realize he's just visiting.

"Do I look all right to you?" I answer.

"I assume Browning has informed you about your imminent transfer to the Death Camp."

"What's the big deal? I don't care whether they keep me locked away in this prison or another one. I don't have freedom in either place."

"That's because you've no freaking idea what the Death Camp is. That place is a real hellhole for breakers."

"We have Wheeler, Carrel, Browning, and are caged like animals right here. How can it get much worse?"

"Don't be stupid, Rex. You can't imagine how bad it can actually become. Do you want to know why we call it the Death Camp? Because no breaker ever comes back alive from there. It's not so much of a prison as a slaughter house for breakers. That facility was designed to terminate breakers. They shoot hundreds of inmates each month and burn the bodies. Do you fully understand where you're about to be sent?"

I shrug.

"What? You don't care?" Chase asks.

"I wonder why you care."

"Cause I know you haven't committed the crimes you've been accused of. Everybody here is aware of that."

"So what's your point?"

Chase doesn't answer. He only gives me a hard look, thinking. "In any case, the current situation is only your own doing," he says. "You should have agreed to work with us. It was your opportunity to disprove Carrel, earn some respect as well as the privileges that come along with that."

I laugh.

"What's so funny?" Chase asks.

"Nothing. You sound just like Browning."

Chase frowns.

"Anyway, how's Holtzmann?" I ask.

"No worse from the wear," Chase answers.

"And his cousin?"

"Rebecca will be okay. She's worried out of her mind about you."

I smile. At least I saved Kitty, and Rebecca from Bulldog's gang. I won't be dying for nothing.

"Gotta go, breaker," Chase says. "We'll transport you tomorrow. Try to enjoy your last night here."

After he leaves, I lie down on the stone floor and think of Kitty. I always think of her when I'm at my limit. Her image brings calmness and peace. I remember how we spent time together, planning for the future. When we'd have saved enough money, we'd leave the city and buy a house out in the country. Lots of land, a ranch with plenty of animals. Well, perhaps it was only my dream to have horses and live far away from the mainstream. Kitty dreamt of a villa close to the ocean, surrounded by palm trees. She'd never seen a real palm tree, but she always associated them with the lifestyle she hoped for. I smile, remembering her excitement as Kitty spoke about our future.

Falling asleep, I see an odd dream. Kitty is standing in front of a tall, tough looking guy. He's in his mid-thirties and wearing military style clothing. His face is lacking expression. Drake, I understand. His name is

Drake. Another man stands beside Kitty. He wears the same uniform and is holding a shotgun. His face is disfigured with ugly burn scars. Somehow I understand that he dislikes Kitty and wishes her harm. He only tolerates her because of Drake.

"They have to pay for his death," Kitty says.

Drake nods.

"Retaliation will make them pay for everything they've done," Drake says. "Our time is now."

My vision fades and I see Wheeler pressing a gun barrel to my head. He pulls the trigger and the bullet blows a large hole out the back of my skull. I cry out, waking me from my sleep. I have to touch the back of my head to check if I was really shot or it was just a dream.

I'm not used to being a telepath and seeing visions. I need to learn how to determine dreams from actual visions happening in real time. I must be telepathically connected to Kitty. I don't know how and why. Maybe because we spent so much time together or maybe it's just because I thought of her before falling asleep. It doesn't matter right now. What truly matters is that my Kitty is in serious danger.

I hear the sound of footsteps and voices coming toward my cell.

"Five minutes! No longer! They can discharge me for doing this," I hear Chase's voice.

"Thank you so much, Chase," a woman's soft voice answers.

I'm getting on my feet, as Rebecca enters the room. I'm surprised at seeing her. Moreover I'm amazed that Chase even let her in. She's alone with no guards for protection. It must be against all their rules.

Rebecca wears a simple black dress and a business style jacket. Her face has bruise marks from the night before, but she still looks beautiful. Her pitch black eyes carefully study me and are filled with worry.

"Hi," Rebecca says shakily.

"Rebecca, what are you doing here?"

"I've come to thank you once again for saving my life and the life of my cousin."

"It was coincidental," I say. "I wasn't exactly planning on saving anybody. I just wanted to escape."

"Nevertheless, you've saved us and I now feel very awkward. I really don't even know what to say. After the death of my parents, I thought I'd never be obliged to a breaker. I used to hate all of you," she sighs. "Now I think that my cousin may be correct believing that some breakers are actually good."

I listen in silence, still not understanding why she came to see me. Just to thank me? There must be something else.

"I'm aware that Browning is sending you to the Death Camp," Rebecca says. "Egbert protested as much as he could, but his power is limited. We all have to do what we're told. We couldn't help you in this matter."

"It's all right," I answer. "I don't expect any help."

"No, it's not all right," Rebecca says. "Many wrong things happen in this place. I don't want them to kill you. Once you enter the Death Camp, you won't come out alive."

"So I've heard."

"Listen carefully. Tomorrow, Wheeler and several guards will be transporting you. The Death Camp is far away and they'll have to stop for the night somewhere. It's likely they'll keep you in a cell within a police station where the officers are nonresistant. You understand?"

"Not really."

"If you hypnotized those people, you might have a chance to escape."

"I have a blocking collar on," I remind.

"I can break it," Rebecca answers.

"What? I mean for real?"

She nods.

"I can't take this collar off you because I don't have the key. But I do know how to mess it up. This isn't rocket science. I've worked for Egbert longer than a year and learned a few tricks."

Rebecca approaches cautiously, as if I may bite. She removes a small metallic object from her pocket and presses it against the collar around my neck. Her face is only a few inches from mine and I can feel her warm breath.

"It's a very strong magnet," she says. "It should mess this thing up." Then Rebecca looks me straight in the eye, saying, "I sincerely hope I never see you again, Rex."

She kisses me lightly on the cheek and leaves. I stand for several minutes, stunned and not believing what just happened. I touch the collar on my neck, checking for anything different. I still don't know if the collar has been deactivated and if I can hypnotize people or not. I'm not sure I can trust Rebecca. But for the first time I do realize I might get a real chance to escape. And maybe even see Kitty again.

The next day Chase arrives with three other guards and says, "Time to go, breaker." He handcuffs me and leads the transport group out of the chamber toward the shower area.

The officers give me the Elimination version of a shower, spraying me with a strong blast of cold water from a high pressure hose. Afterward, I get fresh inmate clothing, an orange jumpsuit free from stains of blood. I change, thinking about what may be coming next. I'm determined to escape, no matter how hard it proves to be.

When we cross in front of Wheeler, he gives me a hateful look. I expect him to attack me or at least make some vicious comment, but it doesn't happen. He only glares, remaining silent. Holtzmann is following closely behind Wheeler, shaking his head and arguing about something. Wheeler directs Holtzmann to shut his mouth, but the professor continues arguing.

As they lead me outside, my heart races. I haven't seen daylight for ages, it seems. Finally, I'm about to find out where I am. I've got no idea if the prison is in the city or somewhere in a less populated area.

Chase suddenly places a blinding hood over my head and all I can see is darkness again. Officers grab an arm on each side and pull me along.

"He's still my subject!" I hear Holtzmann object. "I insist on escorting him myself. I have Browning's permission."

"No way psycho," Wheeler counters. "You're staying right here. We've got enough problems without you."

"I'm responsible for securing all subjects and making sure nothing happens to them during transportation," Holtzmann says. It doesn't sound like a realistic explanation. Something is a little fishy about Holtzmann today.

He argues for a good ten minutes longer when finally Wheeler gives in, "Fine! You can come, just don't have a seizure. If you do, I'm not responsible."

"Thank you, sir," Holtzmann answers in his usual polite manner.

Outside the prison, I feel a chilling wind and can smell freshness in the air. I still can't see where we are.

They lead me inside a transport vehicle. It must be a bus, because I have to climb up two steps. Then guards shove me into a seat and chain my arms and legs. I'm blinded and trapped. I hear heavy footsteps. More people are ushered inside. I realize I'm not the only convict being transported.

"You freaks sit tight now," Wheeler says. "If anybody tries to get up or so much as even move, I'll blow his head off. Simple as that, I won't warn you twice."

He barks a command to the driver and the bus lurches forward. I think of my options. Can I really be sure that my blocking collar is now ineffective? I don't know. I choose to trust Rebecca because she seems to be a sincere and honest person. As soon as we stop and I'm left unshackled near nonresistant officers, I'll try hypnosis. Hopefully, I can make them do whatever I want. Then I'll need to put as much distance between myself and Elimination as possible. Getting rid of this orange inmate clothing will be the first order of business. Then find a good place to hide and wait. Maybe later try to look for Kitty. Something else nags at me. Why would Elimination stop for a night and leave me inside a police station? What if they keep driving all night long? Hopefully it won't happen and…

"Stop here," Wheeler commands.

The bus slows down and comes to a complete stop. Have we arrived? I don't think so.

"Take this freak out," Wheeler commands and many arms grab hold, pulling me up and leading me outside.

"Wheeler, what are you doing?" Holtzmann protests.

"Sir, we're not supposed to stop here," Chase says.

"I'm authorizing this stop," Wheeler answers.

Something is wrong.

Wheeler pulls the bag off my head. I squint into the sudden burst of sunshine. I find myself standing beside the large orange bus, surrounded by officers. I see two Elimination sedans, stopped behind. Wheeler stands before me, smiling.

"Enjoy your last minutes, breaker," he says.

"Sir, this is against protocol," Chase warns.

Wheeler pays no attention. "Unchain this freak," he commands and an officer frees my arms and legs.

"You can't do this!" Holtzmann protests. "You have no authorization. I'll report everything to Browning."

Wheeler doesn't care.

"I see no reason to transfer you into another prison, breaker," he says. "Things should be simplified when dealing with such outlaw breakers. You want your freedom, so take it. Now run."

He pulls his gun and switches off the safety. I realize that if I run he'll shoot me in the back.

"Let's go, breaker," Wheeler says. "Move it!"

I stand still. A squad of Elimination officers hold their rifles on me. I look around. We're on a deserted road in the middle of nowhere.

"Sir, they're expecting him to arrive alive," Chase protests.

"Wheeler! Stop this insanity!" Holtzmann shouts, coughing.

"You don't want to escape?" Wheeler smiles. "Run, or I'll shoot you where you stand."

"Stop this!" Holtzmann yells. "You can't shoot my subject!"

Wheeler shoves him away and presses his gun barrel against my forehead. I close my eyes and concentrate as hard as I can, projecting my thoughts. I have to hypnotize the officers now or be killed. The excruciating headache hits me. They say I'm a level four breaker. I've done it once, let's see if I can do it again.

My hypnosis doesn't work on the officers, but the bus driver steps out wearing a blank expression. His eyes are fixated on me. Attack the officers, I project. Attack them. They're trying to kill you!

The driver approaches one officer and suddenly grabs his rifle. The officer accidently fires his weapon as he reacts. The bullet strikes Wheeler in the shoulder, causing him to drop his handgun. Guards swarm the bus driver as Wheeler reaches for his weapon. I quickly dive down, knocking Wheeler back, then pick up the gun.

As the guards begin to swing their rifles back around on me, Holtzmann leaps into the line of fire, waving his arms like a madman and yelling for them to stand down.

Spontaneously, I point my gun at Holtzmann. He stares at me in shock, but doesn't say anything.

"I'll shoot him," I yell. "Drop your weapons if you want Holtzmann to live."

The officers don't move.

"Kill this breaker!" Wheeler snarls, holding pressure on his injured shoulder while glaring at me.

"I'm not joking," I repeat. "He'll be dead along with a couple of you if you don't do as I've asked."

"You don't have to do this, Rex," Chase says with a calming voice. "We can still work things out."

"Shut up, Chase," I command. "Now drop your weapons!"

A long pause follows. Everybody's waiting. Holtzmann mumbles something incoherent. Wheeler must realize that the officers won't shoot as long as I hold the professor hostage because he finally orders the officers to place their rifles on the ground. Holtzmann must be very important for their project.

"Back away slowly," I command. The officers hesitate, then step back. "Now everybody get back inside the bus. Not you, Holtzmann," I say as he begins to follow the group.

As Chase boards the bus, he glances back at me with a long hateful stare.

"Move," I command. I shoot out a bus tire and order Holtzmann to gather up the weapons on the ground. I stay close by the professor as I keep an eye on the windows of the bus. Once Holtzmann has an armload of rifles, we walk slowly toward the cars.

"Remain inside the bus!" I yell. "If anybody follows, I'll shoot the professor!"

Hopefully, it will keep them off of us long enough to get away.

I shoot out two tires of the sedan without keys and command Holtzmann to sit in the front seat of the second vehicle where keys are left dangling. He drops the rifles into the back seat and takes a place up front. Hurriedly, I slide in behind the wheel and drive away.

CHAPTER 16

As soon as I get the hang of it, I press the pedal to the floor to put as much distance between us and Elimination as possible.

Holtzmann is half lying in his seat, grabbing the seatbelt tightly. In shock, he talks to himself. I wish he would stop because I really need to watch the road and his mumbling is distracting.

"Shut the hell up, Holtzmann!" I growl. I don't mean to scare him, but my harsh voice has an undesired effect. Holtzmann gulps for air as if he's suffocating. He begins to have a seizure right there in the front seat, hands trembling and body shaking.

"Damn it," I say, pulling over. I've no idea what's happening to Holtzmann and how I can help. I've never had to deal with an epileptic. What if he dies?

"Calm down," I say, dragging Holtzmann out of the vehicle and placing him on the ground. Hopefully, some fresh air will help. I look around anxiously for any signs of pursuit. The road is empty.

I turn back to see a red faced Holtzmann struggling to breathe. He opens his mouth widely, sucking in air. This guy is completely messed up. I kneel down beside him, saying, "I won't hurt you. Just calm down." I don't know whether he can actually hear me or not.

I search his pockets and find two bottles of pills. It may be risky to give him these, but I have to do something.

"Listen to me," I say calmly. "I'm gonna give you a pill from each bottle and I want you to swallow."

I tilt back his head and drop the pills into his mouth. Holtzmann groans, but seems to swallow them. His body is still twitching.

"Now try and take a deep breath," I command. Holtzmann inhales the air greedily. "Take it easy! Now, breathe out. All right. Just breathe."

His breathing normalizes. I laugh nervously.

"Damn you," I say. "You really freaked me out. What's wrong with you, dude?"

I sit down on the ground, relaxing. There's no time for rest, but I can't help it. I wipe Holtzmann's foam off my shaky hands. Holtzmann is lying still, recovering.

"We've got to go," I say calmly. "Elimination must be after us by now. Can you get up?"

Holtzmann makes a weak attempt to sit up, but fails. I have to help him. Dragging him back inside the car, I say, "I won't hurt you, all right? You don't need to go crazy. We've got no time for that."

As I drive off, Holtzmann asks, "You won't kill me, will you?"

Just like his cousin Rebecca.

"Why would I kill you?" I say. "Think about it. I saved your life the other night. And you know I'm not a killer. So, why would I?"

"I'm just verifying your intentions," Holtzmann answers quietly.

"Listen, I'm really sorry I had to use you as a hostage. I felt I had no choice."

"Whatever you say," Holtzmann answers.

"Come on, quit acting like a hostage. I'm gonna cut you loose."

"Won't you keep me?"

"No."

Holtzmann thinks for a few moments.

"It's not logical," he says. "I'm very valuable to Elimination. You can use me as leverage. I think it's safer for you to keep me as your hostage."

"What? You must be crazy to say that," I say. "No, I won't keep you hostage. As soon as we get far enough away, I'm gonna let you go. Just hang out a couple hours, then find a police station and tell them who you are. Every cop must be looking for us already."

"I don't think so."

"Why?"

"You're officially dead," Holtzmann explains. "Nobody outside of Elimination is aware of your existence. They won't have the police issue an APB for you this time. Most likely, Elimination will just use Lena to locate you."

Lena, I think. I've left her, Jessie and Jimmy behind. What will happen to them now? A sudden jolt of guilt burns my conscience.

"I won't be needing your services as hostage any longer in that case," I say. "Sorry for everything you've gone through on my behalf, professor. You're free to go now."

"I don't wish to go back," Holtzmann says. He looks better, his face having returned to its usual pale color and the frantic crazed look gone from his eyes.

"What do you mean, Holtzmann? Are you out of your mind? You can't travel the countryside with me. I'm an escaped convict on the run, and have been given a second death sentence."

"As a scientist I'm very curious to observe a breaker in his natural environment. I've never had such an opportunity."

I temporarily lose my ability to speak, thinking.

"Additionally, you aren't the only prisoner there," Holtzmann continues. "I spent all my days locked away inside the same facility, the same prison if you will. I was never allowed outside alone. Although I do have the right to do so technically, I don't think Elimination would ever allow me to leave."

"Do they keep you against your will?" I ask.

"No, not exactly. I signed a contract with Elimination and I'm well remunerated for my research. But I can't reconcile myself with their cruel methods and I don't share their hatred for breakers. Unfortunately, Elimination is the only institution in our society that can provide the needed subjects and equipment for my research project. I also understand I can't survive efficiently in the outside world and will never have a balanced, normal lifestyle. Nevertheless, I'm still somewhat of a prisoner of my own illusions, being held by my own willingness to cooperate with Elimination. Now having had an opportunity to make observations here, out in the real world, I don't wish to return to the lab. Maybe later, but not now."

"Scientists are a really weird species," I say.

"I'm certain I resemble that remark," Holtzmann agrees.

"Look, I can't take you with me. You'll slow me down."

"As little as possible, and having a ready hostage may come in handy and increase your chances later on," he counters.

I think on my predicament. On one hand Holtzmann is right. Having him is great leverage, considering how precious his work is for Elimination. On the other hand, I still can't fully trust him. We're on opposing sides.

"How can I trust you, Holtzmann?" I ask.

"I helped arrange your escape," he answers. "Rebecca and I created that plan together."

"Why?"

"I owe you a great debt, being my life, as well as Rebecca's. And I also knew that you'd be sent to the Death Camp. I couldn't let them waste such a unique subject."

I still can't tell if he's lying or not.

"It was I who taught Rebecca how to demagnetize your collar," Holtzmann adds.

"How did you know this?"

"I invented them," he answers.

For several minutes I drive in silence. Then I ask, "Did Chase know about your plan?"

"No, he's not the type to break rules or disobey orders," Holtzmann answers. "He's a very loyal officer. He wouldn't help a breaker escape."

A few more minutes pass. I think of Rebecca. She may have already heard of what's transpired. It must have scared her to death. Rebecca obviously loves her cousin and cares deeply about him. Similar to my relationship with Kitty. Then my thoughts wander back to Holtzmann and his illness. I still don't know if it's life threatening or not.

"What's wrong with you?" I ask. "I mean what's the official diagnoses of your condition?"

"I have a variety of disorders," he answers.

"Epilepsy?"

"It's merely a side effect of another problem. I've been previously diagnosed with anxiety disorder, panic attacks and any number of other mental illnesses. Certain doctors even suggested that I may be bipolar, though I can assure you that is not the case."

"Does Elimination permit you to visit other doctors for treatment?"

"They would allow this, yes. But as it happens I've already visited enough doctors and heard enough medical opinions to last a lifetime. There's no cure for my condition, but it's nothing terminal so it's manageable. I suppose these infirmities are the price I have to pay for genius. And I do know how to cope, if not overcome."

"Really? I've just witnessed one of your fits and can tell you, I've never seen anything like that in my entire life. Your so called coping really freaked me out."

"I apologize for frightening you," he says. "I was under unusual levels of stress. It's not every day I become a hostage and foresee my own doom."

I drive with a steady speed down a lonely road, passing abandoned houses and rundown towns that have seen better days. Looks like we're getting closer to the south. I make a mental list of things I need to do. The first order of business is to obtain a change of clothing as this orange jumpsuit is too noticeable. That one shouldn't be a problem. I've got my breaker's abilities back. Next I think of Kitty. I have to find her. As soon as I can, I need to start looking for my little sister. But how? I don't know where she might be. I also need to come up with a way to block Lena. It's almost certainly Elimination will try to use her to recapture me.

Holtzmann seems to have recovered almost completely. He still looks weak, but his mindset of being held hostage has improved. Now,

Holtzmann is smiling as he watches the passing fields, woods and villages out the window.

"It's truly spectacular," he says with genuine admiration.

"Never seen it before?" I ask.

"Long ago," he answers. "I've never spent much time outdoors. I've spent the last few years stuck inside various Elimination facilities, working. When they do take me outside the facility, it's usually via helicopter. And I'm always accompanied by guards, for my own protection. I rather think they're more worried I may run off."

"I didn't know," I say.

"Even when I was younger, I didn't spend much time outside," Holtzmann continues. "I've never gone to regular school due to my afflictions. My parents hired all the best home school teachers for my education. I recall it always shamed and embarrassed my parents when I suffered seizures in public. I was their only son, and my father hoped I could inherit his business. He was truly disappointed when he learned the doctors couldn't control the seizures, and they will always remain a threat to happen at any time."

He sighs, his expression becoming distant. These memories must be painful for him although I don't catch an ounce of self-pity in his voice. Holtzmann talks about himself the way someone might discuss another person, coldly and indifferently.

"I spent the majority of my childhood reading and studying," he says. "Every teacher thought I was exceptionally brilliant. Hard to communicate with at times, yet brilliant. I completed the high school honors program at fifteen. I had my choice of colleges. I chose the best one and received a full ride scholarship. But I had to return home in two months because I couldn't handle being around all those people. Too much stress. It escalated to the point where I was having at least one seizure a day. So, I returned home to complete my studies remotely. My parents were okay with it. I guess they'd already given up most of their hopes that I would ever be normal."

He pauses, smiling unconfidently. Then he continues, "By nineteen I'd authored several works on the human brain. These were published and made me well known throughout the scientific community. Shortly thereafter I signed a contract with Elimination to study breakers. My parents are proud of me now, I believe. And I simply want to make our world a better place."

I listen attentively, wondering why my hostage is telling me all this. We're not friends. And I don't think Holtzmann is trying to manipulate me or wishes any sympathy. For the moment at least, it doesn't matter that he is an ordinary human and I am a criminal breaker on a run. Holtzmann wants to speak.

"What about Rebecca?" I ask. "How does she fit into the picture?"

"My parents adopted Rebecca when she became orphaned. I wasn't living at home anymore but visited occasionally, when Elimination permitted. Rebecca and I became close friends. I felt very sorry for her. The brutal murder of her parents left her in such a deep depression. Rebecca suffered from mental disorders for some time afterward and had some difficulty making friends in school. I was the only person Rebecca could really talk to. We had long conversations occasionally. When she finished high school, I suggested Elimination to hire Rebecca as my personal assistant. They didn't care about her education level. She was resistant and it was enough to get her this job."

"Strange career choice for Rebecca, considering she's terrified by breakers," I say.

"Well, I persuaded Rebecca that it would eventually lessen her fear. She used to suffer panic attacks at the mere mention of breakers. I was correct. Rebecca's fear of breakers reduced once she began working for Elimination. A desire for vengeance of her parents contributed as well. Rebecca wanted Elimination to catch and kill as many breakers as possible. I'm glad she met you."

"Why?" I wonder.

Holtzmann smiles. "I think you've changed Rebecca's opinion about hating all mind breakers."

"Well, Rebecca will definitely hate me now if she didn't already," I say. "I've kidnapped her cousin."

"No," Holtzmann corrects. "You've helped me to escape."

When we finally stop in a small town, Holtzmann asks, "So, what's our plan?"

"There's no our plan," I answer. "My plan is to ditch this car, because Elimination must be looking for it already. Then I need to get a change of clothes. I need the ability to blend in without being identified as an escaping prisoner. While I'm doing this, you're to start walking toward the nearest police station and tell them who you are."

"I won't do that," Holtzmann protests. "I want to make sure this doesn't end badly."

"What are you talking about?"

"When Elimination finds you, and it's just a matter of time before they do, they will simply shoot you. No talking this time. You've made everybody too angry. And that's why you need me. As long as I'm your hostage, you have a card to play."

Having said this, Holtzmann sits tighter in his seat and crosses his arms on his chest, showing he's not planning on going anywhere.

"Fine!" I say. "I'll keep you as my hostage for a while longer. But I still don't understand why you would request this."

"For the sake of science and because I owe you," he answers.

"Okay then. Let's leave the car here. We need to find another one. Let's head over to the store and grab some new clothes."

We walk toward the small clothing store through an empty parking lot. I'm lucky that not many people go shopping this time of day. If somebody sees me wearing my orange prison garb, they'll definitely contact the police. I look around carefully. Thank God, I've got my breaker's abilities back. Today I'll need to hypnotize lots of folks.

Holtzmann follows a couple of steps behind, smiling like a complete idiot. What is he thinking? Does it seem to him this is nothing more than a grand adventure? I've no clue what's going on in his head.

As I enter the store, I take a quick look around, seeing a few customers and a cashier. I immediately project my thoughts, forcing them to follow my will. For a split second I worry that somebody might be resistant, but everything goes perfectly smoothly. Nobody even notices my presence. People continue choosing and buying clothes, even being under deep hypnosis.

"Very impressive, Rex," Holtzmann says with excitement. He approaches a customer and waves a hand in front of his face. No reaction.

"Don't mess with them," I say. "I can't hold them forever."

Wincing from the headache, I quickly grab dark jeans and a hoodie. I take a look at Holtzmann's clothes. He's wearing slacks with a brightly colored shirt and a checkered tie that doesn't match anything. Not wishing him to draw attention, I take an extra pair of jeans and a black sweatshirt. Then we leave.

In the parking lot, I notice a young guy getting out of a pickup truck. I project my thoughts before he spots us. The guy stands still, staring at me blindly. His facial muscles relax. Definitely not resistant, I think with relief.

"Give me your keys," I command. The guy tosses me his keys. "Now go shop for a couple of hours."

Holtzmann and I get inside the truck and I drive away.

"That was perfect! Just a perfect utilization of your unique skill set!" Holtzmann says. "Thank you for affording me the opportunity to observe a breaker in his natural environment."

"It's hardly my natural environment," I answer. "I never stole anything before I tried to stop the bank robbery and became public enemy number one for my efforts."

I can't help feeling guilty. I wonder about the owner of the pickup I've just sent on a shopping spree. What if he's poor and this truck is everything he has? It's gonna be all right, I decide, I'll leave it in good shape and the police will eventually return it. I doubt I'll be able to return these clothes though.

I remember Tim saying that all breakers are evil and can't resist the temptation to use their abilities for personal gain. I still hope I'm different. I really don't want to take advantage of people, but I don't have a choice here at the moment. Elimination is hunting me and I am on the run. That's my reality.

When we stop to change clothes, Holtzmann says, "I've never worn jeans."

"Are you joking?"

"No, it's true. My parents always preferred my wearing something more professional. I never chose the clothes I wore nor the food I ate. They thought I wasn't capable of doing either one suitably."

"Speaking of food," I say. "Are you hungry?"

"I never feel hungry," he says, "which is why Rebecca constantly brings meals and reminds me to eat. I simply forget."

"Well, I'm hungry," I pronounce. "Let's get something to eat."

When we come to the next town, I stop at a fast food restaurant, walk inside and return in five minutes with hotdogs. Of course, nobody saw anything. Back in the truck Holtzmann stares at his food almost in shock.

"These hotdogs have meat inside!" he exclaims.

"You don't say," I answer, rolling my eyes.

"My mother preferred healthier food," he explains. "She was a vegan. And so am I."

"Think of it as an experiment," I suggest.

Holtzmann takes a cautious bite.

"You see? You're not gonna die," I say cheerfully.

"I hope not," he answers.

"Maybe if you spend a few days around me, we'll make a more normal person out of you."

"I doubt it," Holtzmann says. "I'm a freak in this world, just as you are. Maybe this is why I'm so curious about your kind. You know breakers could potentially treat people's mental disorders. It's all about the human brain. In a medical role, breakers would become very useful."

"And then we all live happily together in peace," I say sarcastically. "I don't believe in that nonsense. Breakers will be always feared and hunted."

"I believe that can and will change," Holtzmann says.

After we eat, I drive on for a few hours more, then look for a place to stay for the night. A dilapidated farmhouse comes into view. It appears to be abandoned. I decide to give it a try. We leave the truck far away and walk toward the crumbling structure. It's not too cold in this part of the country. We can spend the night inside of what's left of this building.

It's dark inside and the air is stale. We sit on the floor, each deeply immersed in our own thoughts. I think of Kitty. I can't get rid of a nagging feeling that my sister has gotten herself into trouble.

"So, what's next?" Holtzmann asks. "What's your plan for tomorrow?"

"I need to find somebody," I say. I don't want to give him much information because I still don't fully trust Holtzmann. He understands everything immediately anyway.

"Is it the girl?" he asks. "I've studied the report…it said you had a young female companion as the second member of your party."

I don't answer.

"She must be a breaker," Holtzmann continues. "Am I right? You can trust me. Elimination will never learn about this."

I remain silent.

"How are you planning to find her?" Holtzmann wonders.

"I don't know yet," I admit.

"Use your telepathic skills."

"Listen, professor. I've tried. I can't see things whenever I want to. It happens spontaneously. I don't know how to use those abilities."

"You don't have to know how," Holtzmann says. "That you have the ability is good enough. Believe me, I've studied your kind long enough to understand such matters."

"I don't even understand how telepathy works. I always thought it was another stupid myth about breakers. How is it even possible?"

"Well, nobody knows for sure, but all human thoughts give off a certain vibration of sorts," Holtzmann explains. "Some mind breakers have a higher level of sensitivity to such vibrations. You are included in this group. You can somehow feel or hear them and hone in on their signal. You just need to concentrate on the subject. Having a strong emotional attachment with a subject surely helps."

"How could I connect with Lena then?" I wonder. "I didn't even know her."

"She was looking for you, and your signal is very strong. Consider looking for the proverbial needle in the haystack, only in your case, the said needle is approximately as bright as the North Star. Lena made the connection which subsequently triggered your visions."

"It's all too complicated for me," I say tiredly.

"The science possibly, but the ability itself comes very naturally to you."

"Why does it hurt like hell, if it's so natural?"

"Does it?" Holtzmann asks. "I've never heard about other breakers experiencing pain during the process of hypnotizing or during a telepathic session."

"I must be the lucky one."

"You don't like being a mind breaker, do you?" Holtzmann asks.

"No," I admit. "I actually hate it. Just being a normal human being would make my life much better."

"You may be blocking yourself somehow through your own personal rejection of being a breaker. Most breakers appreciate their special abilities. You're likely causing the headaches yourself. And you may additionally be preventing yourself from seeing visions. You only need to fully embrace being a breaker, believe in yourself and your abilities."

"Tomorrow," I say, "I'll begin believing in myself and embrace being a breaker. But now I just want to sleep."

I lie down and close my eyes tightly, but can't turn my mind off. I keep thinking of Kitty. Looks like using telepathic abilities is the only way to locate her. I try really hard, envisioning her. I don't know if it's gonna work. I just continue thinking of Kitty and hope to catch a glimpse where she might be.

It eventually works but when I do get a vision about my Kitty, she's dead.

CHAPTER 17

My pulse is sky rocketing upon awakening. I've just seen Kitty lying in a puddle of blood.

Holtzmann approaches with a curious look on his face.

"What have you seen?" he asks.

I can only stare at him for a few seconds, unable to speak. I can't fully understand what is real at the moment. Part of me remains lost in the vision. I shake my head to clear my mind.

"She's dead," I answer.

"The girl?" Holtzmann asks. "How do you know? What exactly have you seen?"

"I don't know what I've seen," I answer. "Lots of shooting and then blood being splattered everywhere."

"Where is everywhere?"

"Inside a police station, I guess. I saw cops and people in ski masks."

"And then you saw her."

"Why? What do you care?"

"Scientific curiosity mostly," Holtzmann says. "I've never gotten an opportunity to work with telepaths. Lena was Carrel's breaker and I couldn't properly examine or test her." He pauses, thinking. "Have you fully experienced her death or you've just seen her dying?"

"What does it matter?"

"Well, you don't actually perceive reality in real time through telepathic visions. What you see is just another person's perception of reality. In other words, you see what's happening in somebody's mind and experience the same range of emotions and physical sensations."

"You mean seeing somebody dead doesn't always mean the person is dead?"

"Correct, it doesn't necessarily mean you've witnessed an actual death at all," Holtzmann states with confidence. "You may have seen the girl's anticipation of some future event, her own imagining of possible variants and outcomes. In this case, the subject is considering her own death. If she were really dead you wouldn't just see it. You'd experience the death in your mind as if you were her."

"What have I seen then?" I ask. "It looked like an attack or something. Somebody breaking into a police station."

"When will it happen?"

"I don't know."

"Yes, you do," Holtzmann insists. "Concentrate. Think about it."

I close my eyes, thinking hard. My head is still spinning and I'm shaky. When will it happen, I ask myself. When?

"Tomorrow," I blurt out. "It's gonna happen tomorrow. Wait…Does this mean I can see the future?"

"No. What you saw wasn't the future. It was somebody's thoughts about the future."

I'm trying to understand what Holtzmann is telling me. It's very confusing.

"I have to be there tomorrow," I say. "How do I find the place?"

"You already know where it is," Holtzmann answers. I knew he'd say something like that, and I have no clue where the place is.

"There must be another way," I say.

"There's no other way. You're inside another person's mind. You're connected. You can get any information you want."

"I don't even understand what you're talking about," I say angrily. "I don't have any connection right now."

"You can't turn on and off a telepathic connection. You have it or you don't have it. And apparently, you have a very strong telepathic link with another subject. So, concentrate and tell me where the place is located."

I don't fully believe him, but try anyway. Concentrating, I think of Kitty. I draw her image from the depths of my mind. No vision comes.

"It's not working now, I don't know."

"Of course you know!" Holtzmann shouts suddenly. "Tell me where it happens!"

I think for a few moments and say, "Back in the city where we lived." Then I just stare at Holtzmann in surprise. I can't understand how I know this. I only know that the information is correct. The police station from my vision is back in our city.

"There you go," Holtzmann smiles. "What street?"

I close my eyes and imagine the police station. A few images cross my mind. They're like photographs, moving fast and chaotically. I see a street sign, white distinct on green.

"Maple Street," I read. I've never been there and never known a street with such a name. If it does exist it must be in the different part of the city, not in the area where Kitty and I used to live. "I need to get there by tomorrow."

"Because you think you can find her there…"

"Right. And hopefully, she'll still be alive."

"What are we waiting for then?" Holtzmann exclaims. "Let's go! We have a long road ahead."

"Wait a minute now. You won't be going with me this time."

Holtzmann looks up at me with panic stricken eyes.

"You can't do this!" he objects. "I have to verify our hypothesis and continue my observations. I have to verify whether or not you can locate her. It's important for my work. I have to collect as much data as possible, and to do that I must be present. Can't you understand? This is what I live for!"

He looks like he's about to become hysterical. I sigh. I realize he's right, although it's not for the sake of science I'll be bringing the professor. We're in the middle of nowhere. I can't leave this epileptic psycho out here alone.

"You're the most ridiculous hostage who's ever existed," I say. "All right then, Holtzmann. Let's go."

Surprisingly, we find the pickup truck right where we'd left it. I don't want to use it though. I wait for a lonely car and send my thoughts toward a driver. My head hurts, but to a lesser degree than usual. The car slows to a stop. The driver gets out of the vehicle, wearing a vacant look on his face. I remember Kitty stealing a car with the same technique. What shocked and seemed almost impossible to me a few weeks ago, now doesn't give me even the slightest pause. I'm obviously developing my breaker's abilities. But I still wish I were more normal.

Inside the car I find a GPS and punch the police station on Maple Street in. The thing tells me directions. It's dark outside and I have to drive slowly. My night vision is poor and the road looks blurry.

"You can't go with me everywhere you know," I say. "We'll need to split soon. Do you have any place to go?"

"I could return to my parent's house," Holtzmann says. "But I won't. I'll go back to my work."

"Why? You said you were a prisoner there."

"I don't like the methods Elimination employs," he explains. "But I truly believe the results of my work will benefit all of mankind, inclusive of breakers. I can't give up now."

"How exactly are you planning to save humanity?" I ask, hoping the conversation will help me keep awake.

"First, I need to figure out how breakers and humans can coexist peacefully," Holtzmann answers. "We need to begin with something small, to demonstrate humans and breakers aren't enemies. A community project utilizing a breaker team with you as its leader could possibly be that first small step. I was very disappointed when you refused to participate. It was my pet project."

"Yeah, Browning was disappointed as well. He sent Bulldog's gang to beat some sense into me, and failing that, condemned me to the Death Camp."

"What are you going to do after you find her?" Holtzmann asks, changing the subject.

"Keep her alive," I answer, "even if I have to die again."

"Why do you think you might die?"

I remain wordless for a few seconds and then decide what the heck? Why don't I tell him?

"Remember those terrorists from the news?" I say. "I think she's with them."

It's well past sunrise when we arrive in the city. I worry it may be too late and we won't be able to find anybody.

We find Maple Street easily enough and drive along it. Before long, I notice an old two story building with a lot full of parked police cars. Slowly, I drive past and park at a convenience store with a nearly empty lot. Then I just sit inside the car, thinking. My hands are still on the steering wheel.

"What now?" Holtzmann asks.

I don't have an answer. I only know this is exactly the same police station which I saw in my vision last night.

"Rex, what will happen there?" Holtzmann wonders. "You saw a terrorist attack, didn't you?"

"I'm not sure. Everything happened too fast."

"Maybe calling Elimination wouldn't be a bad idea? We might give them an anonymous call, provide some information and then drive away."

"They would track us down. Elimination is the last thing I want to see here."

"Maybe we could inform the city police?"

"And say what? That I had a vision that they'll be attacked by breakers? We'll be lucky if they just think I'm crazy. Most likely they'll contact Elimination and in the meantime lock me away in a padded cell."

"What are we going to do then?"

I frown, trying to create a plan in my mind. It's harder than it seems. I haven't slept, driving for half the night. My reflexes are slower than normal.

"I'll just go take a look around," I say. "Maybe I'll see something or recognize somebody."

Perhaps the police officers won't pay much attention to me, I hope.

"I'll go with you," Holtzmann offers.

"Not this time. You're staying right here, inside the car."

"What do I do if something happens?"

"Nothing. Just stay away from any trouble and keep low."

"Good luck," Holtzmann says.

I get out of the car and walk slowly toward the police station. The city is waking and a few pedestrians pass by.

Approaching the police station, I notice a large black minivan parked on the other side of the road. Somehow it captures my attention. I walk pass it, then turn and go back for a second look. Part of me still rejects accepting the vision as being accurate. At the same time I have an intuitive assurance that Kitty is somewhere very close.

A police officer walks out of the station, swaying. His eyes are unfocused and foggy. He staggers to the middle of the road and collapses onto the concrete. A couple of strangers offer assistance, but they can't figure out what's wrong with the guy. Although fully awake and visibly unharmed, he can't answer a single question. I immediately understand he's hypnotized. Breakers are already inside the police station. I was right.

I run toward the building, drawing Wheeler's gun that I've kept hidden under my shirt. I slow down when I get inside and walk carefully down the hall, sticking close to the wall. I hear voices coming from different parts of the building. I see a few more officers lying on the floor, others wandering around with the same meaningless expression and unfocused eyes. Somebody has put them deeply under. The officers don't even notice me.

I enter a large office to the sound of gunfire and see several people in camouflage and wearing ski masks. They are well-armed and shooting into the few unlucky officers still in the room. Elimination officers dressed entirely in black, I realize. What are they doing here? A few cops are sprawled across the floor, dying. They must have been directed under hypnosis to attack the Elimination guys and were shot down.

I notice two teens wearing bright orange jumpsuits, sitting on the floor and covering their heads. I spot blocking collars on their necks and understand what's going on finally. A group of breakers have attacked the police station where Elimination was temporarily retaining freshly captured breakers.

In spite of a valiant effort at concealment, I recognize her. A short thin figure all decked out military style. A ski mask with a matching dark gray uniform, tight fitting and tucked into heavy military boots. She's firing a large .45 in direction of the Elimination officers.

"Kitty," I whisper in frustration.

"Damn it!" she curses, as she runs out of ammo. She is definitely in harm's way.

I notice an Elimination officer, gun raised, drawing a bead on Kitty. I don't have time to think. I just shoot, aiming in the direction of the officer. In spite of any consequences, I have to protect my little sister! I miss as he quickly drops behind a desk. I continue firing until my gun is empty. Then keeping low, I crawl through the room toward the officer. I have to stop him. He fires at Kitty, but she's managed to take cover. Risking a bullet, I rise up and charge into the officer, tackling him. It takes him by surprise. I slam my empty gun into the side of his head a few times and the officer becomes motionless. Still not noticing me, Kitty rushes to rejoin the main group of breakers near the entrance.

"Kitty!" I yell. "Wait!"

She stops immediately, turns around and stares at me with disbelief. The same moment somebody shoots me. A burning pain pierces my shoulder as I stagger backward and fall over an overturned chair.

"Rex!" Kitty shouts, running toward me and ignoring the bullets flying by.

"No! Take cover!" I yell. She's not listening. She keeps on running. Kitty will be killed for sure now, I think in horror. And it's going to be entirely my fault. I've killed her by calling out her name.

Miraculously, Kitty makes it to me unharmed. She falls on her knees beside me, pulling the mask off her face. Her huge green eyes are full of tears. She's trembling.

"Rex, Rex," she only repeats. Her voice breaks. She grabs me tightly and kisses several times. "You're alive. How is it possible?" she asks, crying and laughing at the same time. Then Kitty notices my wound and blood dripping onto the floor. "Oh! You're shot!"

"It's nothing, I'm fine," I say. "We need to get out of here. You need to come with me."

"I can't," Kitty says. "I'm in a Retaliation unit. These are the very breakers Jessie was speaking about. I've found them. We're freeing breakers and fighting back against Elimination. You need to come with us."

I'm still on the floor, unable to get up. The wound hurts like hell. I'm getting dizzy and must be losing too much blood.

"No, I'm afraid they've fooled you, Kitty," I say. "They hurt innocent people and they're terrorists. You need to leave them."

"You're mistaken, Rex," she answers. "We're strictly a counter strike unit. Come with us, it'll be all right. We have a medical team who can help you."

Kitty presses her hand firmly against my wound to slow the bleeding.

A man with a burned scarred face approaches.

"Who's that?" he demands. This is a guy from my vision.

I realize that the shooting has stopped and all the Elimination officers must be dead.

"Get away from him," he orders, pointing his gun at me.

"No!" Kitty screams. "This is him!"

"Who?"

"This is Rex. He's alive."

"I can fix that," the guy says, grinning.

"I'll kill you if you hurt him," Kitty snarls, baring her teeth. I've never heard her speak this way before. She's changed, hardened. She looks older than I remember.

I hear sirens outside.

"We gotta go," the guy says, pulling Kitty away. I grab her arm.

"Leave her," I command.

"Let go, loser," the guy says, kicking me in my wounded shoulder. I groan from pain. He manages to drag Kitty away.

"Leave me alone, Hammer!" Kitty screams. "I'll kill you, you're a dead man!"

I make a weak attempt to stand up, but fall back onto the floor. I can't move. I briefly hear Kitty's voice calling out to me in the distance, and then she's gone. The outlaw breakers have taken Kitty and left. A few minutes later cops enter the room. I close my eyes, projecting my thoughts toward them. You can't see me, I suggest. I'm not here.

Surprisingly, it works well enough. My head doesn't even hurt much. The officers don't notice me. They're examining dead bodies on the floor and trying to bring the hypnotized cops back to reality.

I get on my hands and knees and crawl out the door and to the exit, projecting my will upon anybody around along the way.

Holtzmann is waiting inside the car, watching anxiously through the window.

"You're shot!" he exclaims upon seeing me.

"Thanks for the update," I answer.

"You need medical attention."

"It'll be all right."

I continue pressing a hand against the wound. I don't care much about it at the moment. I've got more important things to worry about.

Holtzmann asks about what happened and I briefly summarize the details. I don't mention Kitty, though.

"You're a very strong telepath," Holtzmann says. "You've found the renegade group of breakers Elimination has been looking for. That is truly amazing!" Then he asks, "Have you seen her?"

I ignore the question.

"How likely is it Elimination will locate those terrorists without my help?" I ask.

"It will take longer, but it's only a matter of time. I guarantee Elimination will catch them. Elimination is very resourceful, and they can always use Lena, another telepath."

"And what then?"

"I would expect a death sentence for each of the terrorists."

What a dilemma. If caught, Kitty will be convicted as a terrorist and sentenced to death. How can I save her? I see no way out. Either she is going to be shot during one of the attacks as I have foreseen in my vision or Elimination will capture and kill her.

I still can't believe she freely chose to become a terrorist. She must have been misinformed or fooled into thinking she was doing good. Kitty is still only fifteen and somewhat naive. It would be easy enough to fool her. Those breakers couldn't have told her all they were doing, because Kitty otherwise would have never agreed to join them. They likely presented some type of righteous facade, fighting for freedom and justice. Of course, my Kitty would wish to join them just to take vengeance for my death.

There must be a way out. I have to save her.

I realize I can't protect Kitty from Elimination. It's a very powerful organization and has plenty of ways to hunt down breakers. Alone, I won't be able to liberate her from the terrorist group. There are too many strong breakers among them. My only chance to save Kitty is to join Elimination myself. If I can lead Elimination to the terrorists, maybe I can find a way to free Kitty during the ensuing battle.

How long can I risk everything to protect Kitty? The answer is easy. As long as necessary until she's safe.

"Holtzmann, you'll be returning to Elimination now," I say. "And I'm coming with you to get this shoulder patched up. Afterward, I agree to become the leader of your breaker team."

PART 3

PART 3

CHAPTER 18

I stay inside the car while Holtzmann walks ahead the two blocks to the police station to let them know he's safe, and smooth the way for my arrival. When Holtzmann returns to the car, he asks, "Are you completely positive with your decision?"

I'm not positive about anything, but nod anyway and say, "Only two things really bother me."

Holtzmann waits patiently for explanation.

"First, I doubt Elimination will want me to work for them after all the things I've done," I say.

"Well, under normal circumstances I'd have to agree," Holtzmann answers. "But the situation is far from normal. Browning and Wheeler's careers are at risk, so they're willing enough under these circumstances. The recent terrorist attacks have the government in an uproar and Elimination hasn't gotten a step closer to catching them. Browning and Wheeler are under pressure to get some results."

"Why would Browning need me when he's got Lena? She's a stronger telepath than me. You mentioned earlier that Elimination would locate the terrorists sooner or later anyway."

"Yes, that's true, but later is unacceptable. Browning would definitely prefer the first option, which is only possible with your help. Anyway, Lena is a child. Although she has strong breaker abilities and some experience using them, she's only eight and can't work long hours. Additionally, she doesn't have a mental connection with one of the terrorists, as you obviously do. It's more efficient for Elimination to just make a deal with you."

I take a minute to think. Holtzmann sounds convincing, but I have no guarantees it'll go down the way he suggests.

"What was the other thing bothering you, Rex?" Holtzmann asks.

"How can I trust Browning to keep his word?" I ask. "He and Wheeler are the worst people I've ever met. How can I believe anything they say?"

"Browning is trustworthy as long as he needs you. This recent attack won't be the last. Even when Elimination terminates this group, another one would likely be created in the near future. So, it would be in Browning's best interest to keep you around. He knows that once he breaks your agreement, you'll refuse to work for him."

I take another minute to weigh my options and consider the risks. "I hope you're right," I sigh.

Having accepted the idea of dealing with Browning, all that's left to do is just wait for Elimination to arrive.

It takes only half an hour for a huge Elimination helicopter to appear in the sky. It makes a large circle and then descends. Once it lands, I won't have another chance to change my mind and escape. Elimination won't allow me to slip away twice.

I'm not going to run, though. If I want to save Kitty's life as well as my own, I have to know my enemy and learn any weaknesses. I need to be on the inside to do that, even if that means I have to take extra risks and misrepresent my intentions.

I open the car door and walk slowly toward the helicopter. Holtzmann follows. I expect a furious Wheeler to leap out of the helicopter and charge at me, else just shoot me on sight. Instead I see Chase's mug appear and he's wearing a broad smile.

"You're one crazy breaker," he says. "Why did you suddenly change your mind? And what in the world could you have promised Browning to make him send his personal helicopter for you?"

I ignore the question. "Where's your captain, Chase?" I ask.

"Wheeler? He's getting grilled for letting you escape and taking Holtzmann hostage," Chase grins. "Also, I imagine Browning was afraid to send Wheeler to pick you up. He thought Wheeler would just kill you. That's why he sent me. Well, climb in, breaker."

"No handcuffs," Holtzmann raises his voice. "Rex is my associate now. He is no longer a prisoner, but an Elimination employee."

"Not quite yet," Chase says, although he doesn't handcuff me. There's no need for handcuffs as long as I'm willing to cooperate.

When the helicopter takes off, Chase says, "I've never understood you breakers. What's going on in your heads?" Then he stares at my shoulder wound. "You can't keep away from trouble, can you?"

I don't answer. Chase finds a first aid kit and bandages my shoulder.

I sit silently with my eyes closed during the long trip back to the Elimination facility. I wonder why it took such a short time for the helicopter to arrive to pick us up. They must have been conducting a search somewhere nearby. Then I think about Browning, and what I need to request when speaking to him.

"I'm wondering why your attitude toward Elimination has changed so abruptly," Browning says, giving me a long look across his desk. Chase stands behind, holding his rifle as protocol dictates. I wish Holtzmann could be here to help convince Browning, but he felt sick and had to see a doctor. I'm on my own, again.

"I realize I've made mistakes in the past," I answer. "I can assure you I've come to regret those mistakes, and I want to make amends. I hope to become a useful member of society and earn redemption, if not a full pardon, for any wrongs I've committed. It's my understanding that is the main purpose of the facility here, right? To give bad breakers the opportunity to get back on track and start fresh. That's exactly what I want. To start fresh, and become a good and useful member in a future society where breakers and normal humans live in peace." I finish with a wide grin.

Browning watches for a long moment, keeping silent and thinking. I know he doesn't believe me, but that's not what I want. I only need him to make the deal with me. That's all.

"I'm glad you've finally come around and understand, son," Browning says finally. "But what makes you think that Elimination still needs you for this particular project? We have plenty of breakers in this place to choose from."

"For a couple of reasons," I answer. "First, I'm the strongest breaker you have. Secondly, I'm the only breaker in here who's telepathically connected to the breakers you seek. I've found them once, I can find them again."

"That's all well and fine," Browning says. "But still I doubt we can work together successfully. You've demonstrated very negative behavioral tendencies in your stay here earlier. I don't think we can completely ignore that."

Continuing to smile, I say, "Look, Browning. We both know your career is on the line. If you don't locate and stop those terrorists, you simply won't be warden here much longer. I'm the best shot you have to locate these renegade breakers, and I sit before you offering my complete cooperation and assistance. Accept my help otherwise I walk, simple as that. Take it or leave it."

Laughing, Browning leans back in his chair. "I don't know about that, but what I do know is you're a very brave young man," he says. "So tell me, what do you really want? What's really behind your change of heart and what exactly do you hope to gain? What's your angle, Rex?"

"No angles, warden. Just three small conditions. First, neither my life nor the lives of those in my team should be threatened again by Elimination," I begin. "Secondly, I must be the one who decides which breakers are on this team, and I'm to be the only one who can add or replace them as needed in the future. Third and lastly, there must be no Elimination influence harassing the team, which includes guards and blocking collars. Holtzmann and his assistant are to be the only two non-breaker Elimination representatives who will be participating in our project."

"I can't agree with your last request," Browning says. "You have to have at least one Elimination officer on your team. It's for Holtzmann's protection. And the other deal breaker concerns the blocking collars. You'll be allowed to work without them, but at other times you'll have to have them on."

"Sounds reasonable," I agree. "But I want to pick the guard myself." Browning slowly nods in agreement. "Chase," I say.

"What?" Chase exclaims.

Browning commands him to keep quiet. "Anything else?" he asks.

"One more request seems appropriate," I answer. "After we locate the outlaw group, I want the authority to mark any innocents as untouchable and not to be harmed. This is because I'll be the one in their heads and know the good from the bad."

"You're still trying to save your little girlfriend, aren't you?" Browning laughs.

When I don't answer, he adds, "You really thought I wouldn't realize that she's in their group?"

I guess it wasn't hard for him to come to this conclusion. Knowing how telepathy works, it was the small step to figure out whom I had a connection with in the outlaw group.

"Very true, Mr. Browning," I finally say. "I'll do anything to save her. Let me be perfectly clear, if you do anything to harm her or any member of my team, I'll be done with working for you forever."

"As long as you can locate the terrorists before the next attack it's a deal," Browning says, extending his arm for a handshake. I ignore his gesture.

"Your word is good enough. Don't break your word, sir," I add, leaving the office. I hear Browning laughing.

After making the agreement with Browning, I'm willing to begin working immediately. I don't want to waste time with Kitty's life in imminent danger.

"Negative," Holtzmann says when I come to discuss everything. "We can't start our project today. First, you need to receive medical help."

We argue for a bit, but it's impossible to change his mind. Holtzmann insists on sending me to infirmary for a couple of days.

"Okay, but Browning won't appreciate that," I say.

"It doesn't matter," Holtzmann answers. "You're my subject, not his. Browning isn't even a scientist."

Holtzmann believes that a wounded mind breaker can't perform telepathic sessions or hypnotize as well as a healthy one. Finally, I agree to wait for a couple of days. My shoulder is injured, my head is a mess and I'm somewhat feverish. Taking a short break may not be a bad idea after all.

The doctor readily treats me this time. He must be aware I'm working for Browning. He injects anesthetic into my vein, extracts the bullet and stitches the wound up carefully. Then he examines my head injuries, adding a few more stitches here and there.

I spend the next two days in an infirmary room, resting and recuperating. No handcuffs or chains. Chase is the only guard watching the room.

"I still can't quite figure out why you're doing this," he says. "Is it all because of your girlfriend?"

I think for a long time about his question.

"Not exactly," I answer. "Not only for her."

"What's your other reason then?"

"I simply want to stop them," I explain. "It's terrible what those breakers are doing. Even worse than terrible. Inhuman."

"I don't get it. You're one of them, a breaker."

"They're neither breakers nor ordinary humans, Chase. Most of those people are monsters and shouldn't live. I don't believe anyone who kills innocent people, especially children, has the right to remain alive."

"But you still think she's different," Chase wonders.

"Yes," I answer. "She's just a teenaged girl. They've fooled her." I hope I'm right. I'm certain Kitty wouldn't want to burn those kids and teachers from that school. Most likely, she wasn't even aware of what was happening.

Holtzmann visits me a few times to discuss our coming project.

"Time to choose the breakers you want for the team," he announces.

"All right," I answer, concentrating. "Lena. She's a strong telepath. I'll definitely need her help."

"I agree," Holtzmann smiles. "Also I'm pleased with an opportunity to take her away from Carrel. Lena will become my subject now."

"Can you remove those nasty electrodes from her head?"

"I'll see what we can do. Who else?"

"Jessie," I continue.

"She's not a strong breaker," Holtzmann protests. "She's borderline level 2 at best."

"She's tough and can still hypnotize other breakers."

"I guess," Holtzmann says, thinking. "Who else?"

"Jimmy."

"Jimmy? We don't need him. He's level one. A very weak breaker."

"Listen egghead, according to my deal with Browning, I'm the one who picks the team for this project. I trust Jimmy. Plus he seems like a nice kid."

Holtzmann looks at me carefully and says, "You want to protect Jimmy, don't you? Fine. He's in. Who else?"

I take time to think. Seems like I haven't forgotten anybody. There must be many more inmates who have been falsely accused and needful of protection. I don't know them and am unable to help them out at the moment. "That's all I have right now," I say. "Who would you suggest?"

"I do have one subject I'd like to recommend," Holtzmann says. "His name is Frank. He's a very polite and trustworthy individual. And his situation is unique."

"How's that?"

"Like you, Frank is another breaker rejecting his abilities. I trust him. And he is a level four."

"One more telepath?" I ask. "I thought only Lena and I had telepathic abilities."

"Frank's abilities are undeveloped. He will have to overcome a severe mental block before all his potential can be realized."

It sounds interesting. I agree to meet Frank and see if he can become a member of our team.

One day Rebecca comes for a visit. She seems paler and thinner than I remember. She opens the door slowly and stands quietly in the doorway, looking like a ghost. I sit up on my bed and wait for her to say something. Rebecca just stares at me and I can't tell if she's afraid or just naturally shy.

"Are you okay, Rebecca?" I ask.

"How could you do this?" she finally says.

"Do what?"

"You've almost managed to kill Egbert. He could have died from all that stress you've caused him. And that was after everything Egbert and I did for you!"

"Rebecca, your cousin is stronger than you think," I answer. "Maybe it's time for you and everybody else to stop treating him like an invalid?"

"I don't know what you're talking about," Rebecca says. "How could you use him as a hostage? Were you really ready to kill him? Why do you think you are any better than those terrorists you'll be hunting?"

"Is that what you think of me?"

Rebecca doesn't answer, averting her eyes when I try to catch her gaze.

"I'm not really sure what I think of you," she says, leaving.

"See you during the team meeting, Rebecca," I say coldly before deciding that I shouldn't be angry with her. Rebecca just overreacted a little, worrying for her cousin. What would I think if somebody took Kitty hostage?

When I regain motion in my injured shoulder, Chase brings a fresh set of clothes. Black military pants, heavy boots and a pitch black jacket. The Elimination uniform. At first I only stare uneasily, then decide what the heck and give it a try. Wearing the uniform of my sworn enemy makes me feel really weird.

Chase bursts out laughing upon seeing me in uniform. "That's wild," he says. "Are we really on the same side now? In any case, you look good in black."

I don't answer because I'm not sure what he expects me to say. We have the same goal temporarily, but it doesn't mean Chase and I won't wind up shooting each other at some point in the near future. We can't fully trust each other, and we both realize that.

Chase leads me toward Frank's cell. We meet several officers along our way. One gives me a hateful glare, saying, "Don't think a uniform makes you one of us, you stinking breaker." Chase tells the guy to shut his mouth.

Elimination keeps Frank separated from the other inmates. His cell is large and contains such luxuries as a TV, desk, and even some books. Frank is a big broad-shouldered guy in his late twenties. He wears a dull expression on his wide face. On first impression, Frank seems unfriendly and even somewhat hostile. But then he smiles slightly and speaks in an unusually quiet tone of voice for a guy of his stature. He introduces himself and we shake hands.

"So Frank, why do you want to be on my team?" I ask.

"It used to be my job," he answers, "catching breakers."

"What do you mean?"

"I was an Elimination officer," he admits. "One of the best. Captain Wheeler hand-picked me for the job, and I was really good at what I did. I always knew where the breakers were hiding. Right up until the fateful day I found out I'm a breaker myself."

"Bummer," I say. "And it doesn't make sense. How could you be not aware that you're a breaker? I've known I'm a breaker all my life."

"Lucky you. I realized it only a year ago. I'm twenty nine now. I thought I was a normal human for twenty eight years. Holtzmann thinks it's because I reject being a breaker so much. So you can probably imagine how shocked I was. I mean I hated breakers. I believed they were our enemies, evil incarnate, and I was doing society good catching them. And then I find out I'm a breaker myself."

His career in Elimination was over that same day. Frank turned himself in without resistance, although he now thinks doing so was a mistake. He was just too shocked to think straight. His whole life turned upside down within hours.

Elimination has been keeping Frank in the same prison he used to work as a guard before. Most officers couldn't help from showing their former coworker favoritism. Frank received better living quarters, food, other guards never beat him, and Carrel refrained from performing his sadistic tests on him. Browning initially wanted Frank to become a snitch, but Frank's moral compass wouldn't allow him to accept the offer. He refused beating and humiliating other inmates as well. Frank truly believed in justice, and believed he couldn't abuse others just because they were weaker. So there he was, lost and perplexed. Even Browning and Wheeler couldn't decide what to do about Frank, to keep him locked away forever or simply kill him to put out of his misery.

I listen to Frank's story attentively, considering his strange predicament.

"I want to prove that I'm the same person," Frank says. "That Elimination can trust me whether or not I'm a breaker. That's why I need to be part of this team. I simply hope that one day I can prove worthy enough to become an Elimination officer again."

You can't go back, I think, Elimination will never accept a breaker. You live in a different world now, a world filled with intolerance and hate. Nevertheless, I agree to take Frank as a member of our team. I can't quite decide what to think of him. He's gotten used to capturing breakers and now he's just a very confused and troubled breaker himself. Really odd. At least he seems to be honest. I decide that Frank is all right.

The next morning our team has its first meeting in Holtzmann's lab. Rebecca continues avoiding me, but her expression seems a little softer. Everybody wears an Elimination uniform, even Lena. She gives me a big hug, saying how thankful she is about my stealing her away from Carrel.

"We'll try to remove these awful things from your head as soon as possible," I promise. Lena smiles and takes her seat at a large round table.

Jessie's face is still bruised and swollen from the beating she took in Carrel's lab. She'll probably have scars for the rest of her life and may never completely recover. When I ask her if she's willing to work for Elimination, Jessie answers, "Yes, to protect my parents, you idiot." She sits at the table with her arms crossed on her chest, looking at Holtzmann with unbridled resentment.

Jimmy is the only breaker at the table truly happy and excited to be here. He's telling Jessie about his parent's dogs, making her nauseous. Adding to her pain, he then asks if she's ever flown a helicopter. Jimmy is hoping we'll all get a chance to fly in Elimination helicopters, but he refuses to jump wearing a parachute.

"I saw how soldiers make jumps wearing parachutes in the movies," Jimmy says. "Looks so cool! But I'm not sure I could do that. I'm afraid of heights. Somebody would have to push me out of a perfectly good chopper."

"We're not in the military, stupid," Jessie says. "Elimination doesn't make parachute jumps. And nobody uses helicopters for parachute jumps anyway, they'd be cut up by the blades."

"I saw in the movies that they did," Jimmy protests. Jessie rolls her eyes.

Chase stands aside, rifle slung unthreateningly across his shoulder.

"Let's begin then, shall we?" Holtzmann asks in an official tone of voice. He briefly describes our team goals, to locate the terrorist group of breakers and then call in an Elimination assault team to deal with them. As he begins talking about our pre-mission training, the door suddenly slams open as a very angry Victor enters the lab. He's wearing an Elimination uniform as well.

"What the hell are you doing here, Victor?" I exclaim.

"I've been put on your freaking team," Victor says. "And believe me I like this stupid idea about as much as you do."

The same instant Jessie comes out of her seat and dives across the table into Victor, ready to kill.

CHAPTER 19

"I won't stay on this team if this jerk doesn't leave," Jessie says after being pulled off. "So choose, it's me or him."

"I never invited him in the first place," I answer. "So what are you doing here, Victor?"

"I'm here on Browning's orders," Victor says, wiping blood from his split lips. "I don't have a choice and neither do you. You can't really argue with the warden. He'll simply kill you."

Jessie and Victor exchange a heavy glance. Jessie's face darkens with hatred. Victor is looking at Jessie with sympathetic, apologizing eyes. While Jessie was punching him, Victor didn't strike back. He let her hit him as if accepting the fact that he deserved the beating. Then Chase and I dragged Jessie away, holding her until she calmed down.

"I choose the breakers for this team," I say. "We don't need you here, Victor."

He rolls his eyes. "Are you really so stupid? To think you truly make all the decisions? Wake up, dude. We're in prison and Browning is the guy we all have to answer to."

Victor is right, I realize.

"Why does Browning want you on my team?" I ask.

"What do you think? Browning and Carrel want to know what's going on here. They need to have eyes and ears on your team. That's why they've chosen me."

"To spy on us?"

"Yep," Victor admits. "They've ordered me to be their little snitch and fight a few terrorists along the way. I couldn't believe it. After everything I've done for them, I'd have thought I deserved some respect."

I don't understand why it bothers Victor so much. In my opinion, the role of snitch suits him perfectly. Perhaps, he just doesn't want to risk being shot while hunting down the terrorists.

"We don't need a snitch here," I repeat. "Go back to Browning and say I booted you out."

"Rex, can I speak to you privately?" Holtzmann asks quietly as he walks toward the exit, gesturing for me to follow. When we're standing alone in the corridor he says, "Victor may be useful for us."

"You're kidding me."

"He's got more experience using his skills than any other breaker in this prison."

"He's a snitch," I remark.

"Victor isn't what you think," Holtzmann disagrees. "He was forced to do much of what he did. Besides, I believe Victor would be willing to snitch only the information of our choosing, which might be very valuable at some point."

I don't answer.

"Anyway," Holtzmann smiles. "It'd be nice to steal another subject from Carrel. I recommend you to let Victor stay."

I sigh. Browning is breaking our agreement. While I don't like this one bit, I also realize I have to let Browning think he's in control.

"All right," I say to Victor after we return to the lab. "You may conditionally stay. Everything you snitch has to be run by me first, and if I learn you're snitching any unapproved information, you'll be out the same instant."

"Don't worry, guys," Victor answers. "I hate Browning as much as you do. I don't follow all his orders."

I don't believe him.

"Great, then I'm out of here," Jessie says, standing up.

"Jessie, wait," I say, following her. We end up standing outside in the corridor, arguing for a good fifteen minutes.

"Why do you need me on your team?" Jessie asks finally. "I'm not the strongest breaker. I'm not even really your friend. You hardly know me. So, why?"

"Because I trust you," I answer. "You've helped Kitty and I before. Now let me return the favor."

"Don't make me laugh. I still think you can't help even yourself."

"You may be right," I say. "Maybe everything that I do is just one huge mistake. But at least I'm trying. I've escaped once from this prison. I'll do it again, and next time I'll be taking you, Lena and Jimmy with me."

"Is that your plan?"

"I don't have a plan yet. I just know we need to stop the terrorist group first, and save Kitty. Then we'll see what can be done. Hopefully, we can gain enough of Browning's trust that an escape won't be all that difficult. Maybe we can even take your parents with us."

Jessie thinks for a few minutes in silence. "This terrorist group we'll be hunting, are they the same breakers I've told you about?" she asks. I nod. "I had no idea they were terrorists," Jessie says. "All I'd heard is how they were helping other breakers escape."

"And now Kitty is caught up with them," I say.

"I'm sorry," she answers. "Is that why you came back and agreed to work for Browning now? To save Kitty?"

I nod again and say, "Please Jessie, help me locate and stop them. I know what Victor did to you and your parents. But now we're all in the same boat. We have to do what we can to save Kitty. I've no choice."

"There's always a choice," she sighs. "All right. I'm in." Then Jessie looks at me with a strange expression and says, "I didn't realize you loved Kitty that much."

I don't really know how to answer that. I do love Kitty tremendously, but not quite the way Jessie thinks.

"Okay, breakers," Wheeler says. "In spite of the fact that I hate you and you hate me, we have to temporarily work together now. I advise you to fully cooperate and not do anything stupid."

We're inside the Elimination training facility. Wheeler has been assigned to instruct marksmanship and combat skills to the members of my team. He completely ignores me, probably by a direct order from Browning. There's definitely something ironic about Wheeler and I working together. I'd like to smash his head in, but can't do it now. First, I need to make sure Kitty is safe and we have a means of escape.

"Will we be learning to shoot with real guns?" Jimmy asks. "I've always wanted to shoot a gun! My dad had a rifle, but he never let me touch it and…"

"Jimmy, shut the hell up," Wheeler commands. "That is going to be your primary objective for this mission, keeping your mouth shut."

"I can do that," Jimmy agrees. "No problem. But I just wanted to offer that I think I may become a great shot. I only need a little practice and then I'll shoot all the terrorists…"

Wheeler groans. I can't help from smiling.

"Jimmy, be quiet, please," Holtzmann suggests. He's arrived to watch our training session and make sure Wheeler doesn't kill anybody.

"This is gonna be a really long day," Wheeler sighs.

First, we're tested for marksmanship. At the gun range, each member of my team is checked out a handgun for shooting targets.

"Lena doesn't have to do this," I protest. "She's too young."

"I'm under orders to train all of you," Wheeler answers. "That little rat isn't an exception."

"She may hurt her wrist, Wheeler," I say. "Any injury won't help our mission."

"I don't really care," he grins.

I have a strong urge to punch him in his arrogant face, but I can't do it right now. I can't let Wheeler provoke me.

"I agree with Rex," Holtzmann says softly. "Lena doesn't need to learn shooting. That's not her role within our team."

"Whatever," Wheeler says, giving up.

Frank makes a perfect score shooting. It's no surprise with him being a former officer. I notice Chase quietly exchanging a few words with him. Frank says something in return and Chase bursts out laughing. They may have been close friends before.

Jimmy empties his gun, never once hitting the target. He suggests that something must be off with the gun.

"That firearm is in excellent condition. Something is off with you," Wheeler says. "Why have you picked him, breaker?" he asks me. "It was really stupid of you. That boy is useless."

"It's none of your concern," I answer.

Victor refuses to touch a gun, saying that he's not here for firearm training. "I'm a hypnotist and a memory reader, not a gun slinger," he states as a matter of fact. Wheeler yells at him, but Victor ignores the command, walking away.

It's my turn to shoot and I can barely see the target. I didn't realize my vision was getting so bad. I empty the thirteen round magazine, hitting the target only twice with no bull's eyes. I sigh in frustration.

"You really suck," Wheeler grins. "Now I see why you chose Jimmy. Misery loves company. "

Ignoring his comment, I reload and try again. Pointless. I can't aim well enough. Wheeler laughs, "What are you, blind?"

I don't answer. He doesn't need to know something is really wrong with my vision. I put the gun down.

Jessie is next. She shoots quickly, earning a 98 score out of possible 100. It takes her less than a minute. Seems like Jessie doesn't even have to take the time to aim, and is completely natural with a handgun.

"Damn, girl," Wheeler says. "Where did you learn to shoot like that?" Jessie keeps silent.

"They had plenty of guns back on their farm," Victor answers. "She practically learned to shoot before she could walk."

"Shut your mouth, freak," Jessie growls. Chase steps closer, making sure she doesn't attack Victor again.

Then we all practice firing and reloading rifles. I don't leave when it's time for lunch. I'm staying and practicing. No use. Wheeler was right. I really suck at shooting.

"C'mon, breaker," Chase says. "Let's go eat."

"I used to be a good shot," I say.

"I wouldn't worry too much about firearms if I were you. Who needs a gun with your breaker abilities?"

Even being a breaker, I'd feel safer if I could shoot well. Hopefully, my vision will recover sooner or later. I can't be sure. A long time has passed since the car accident. The damage to my vision may be permanent.

"Anyway, if you wind up in a shootout, it's bound to be at close range," Chase says. "So you should be fine."

I put the gun aside and go to lunch. My team has a special room reserved, where we can eat apart from other inmates. We get juicy burgers with fresh hot fries and even slices of apple pie for dessert. Cooperative breakers really are treated differently around here. Chase and Wheeler eat with us. Holtzmann sits alone, deep in thought. He doesn't touch his salad.

After lunch we spend a couple of hours listening to Wheeler lecture on terrorist attacks and methods for securing buildings. Then it's time for the physical combat training. A few additional Elimination officers arrive to assist. Each member of my team, excepting Lena and Victor, has to partner with an officer. Lena is too young, and Victor is our memory reader.

Frank does great, taking down the officer within a blink of an eye. He may have had previous training in addition to what he learned at Elimination. His movements are quick and efficient, and he uses techniques I've never seen before.

Jessie attacks her opponent ferociously, but the officer blocks her punches and kicks. He's taller and much heavier than she is. The officer takes a swing at Jessie's face, but she manages to duck and then throw herself forward, delivering a nasty head-butt. He steps back, swaying and bloody. Wheeler stops the fight.

"Too bad you're a breaker," he says. "You'd make an excellent Elimination soldier."

Jessie spits on the floor and turns away, ignoring his comment.

When Jimmy steps up on the mat, his opponent asks Wheeler, "Do you really want me to beat this boy, sir? He's only like twelve."

"Shut up and do as you've been instructed," Wheeler commands.

Jimmy moves in toward the officer, swinging his arms in a strange exaggerated windmill style, hitting nothing but empty air. I realize immediately Jimmy has never had a fight in his life. The officer raises his arms hesitantly and then backhands Jimmy hard across the jaw. Jimmy falls down, lying motionless in shock. The officer looks at Wheeler in confusion.

"That's enough," I say.

"This imbecile is gonna die during the first encounter with a terrorist," Wheeler says. "Is that what you really want?"

"My team is chosen, and it did not require your approval then or now," I answer. "If you don't like something, go cry to Browning. I'm sure he'll appreciate your whining."

Wheeler bares his teeth, but doesn't answer.

I'm up next. Wheeler chooses the biggest officer for my opponent and commands, "Go beat the hell out of this breaker."

The officer and I step on the mat. He watches, waiting patiently. I'm still agitated after failing the firearms test. I let my hatred of Wheeler fill me. I remember all the anguish and insult that Elimination has brought into my life. We circle each other, looking for any sign of weakness. I drop down low and charge in, imagining him being Wheeler. I feint an attack on his legs, and as he sprawls down to defend, I throw a knee to his head as hard as I can. He reels backward. We circle again, trading punches. After a couple of minutes, I end up on top of the officer, relentlessly smashing his face, splattering blood across the mat. He loses consciousness, but I can't stop. I realize that I want to kill one of the guys who've made me leave my Kitty, who've destroyed everything I've ever had. I keep pounding his head.

Chase and Frank drag me off of the beaten officer.

"Are you crazy?" Chase yells. "What the hell is wrong with you?"

"Rex?" Holtzmann says in a worried voice.

"I got carried away," I say, wiping drops of sweat from my forehead. "This is an abilities test, right? I thought that's what I was supposed to do. It's nothing personal."

Wheeler smiles. Perhaps he's pleased to have exposed a dark side within me. Suddenly, I feel ashamed. I can't understand what's happened. I've never been so willingly violent before. Something has changed inside me. If Chase and Frank hadn't stopped me, I would have killed that officer today.

In the evening I'm sitting at Holtzmann's desk, checking files on his laptop. I didn't think he'd allow me to do this, but I was mistaken. Holtzmann didn't question why I wanted to see the inmate files. He just nodded, typed in passwords on his laptop and then left me alone. Maybe Holtzmann just knew I had nobody to share this information with anyway, so it was safe for him and Elimination to let me take a glance at their files.

I'm digging into the files and reading about hundreds of breaker's alleged crimes. All these inmates have gone through the same facility I'm in now. Some are still here, many have died and others have been transferred. I don't read their names and don't look at their photographs. All I'm interested in is the crimes they've committed. These files contain the real information, not just what gets presented to the public in a TV reality show.

I find my own personal file and read that I'm accused of being a level four breaker. No word about an alleged bank robbery or killing and attacking innocent people. Other files contain similar descriptions, inmates simply being accused of being breakers. But most files additionally include at least one crime. The descriptions are very official, with no bloody details, but it's enough to send a chill down my spine. I read about robberies, homicides and rapes. I read about dozens of innocent people murdered by breakers. It makes me almost sick to realize most of us are violent criminals.

I can't stop reading.

I don't know what I'm looking for and why I need such information. Maybe I just want to prove myself that I'm right to hate Elimination. I hate the officers the same way they hate and despise me and other breakers. I'm trying to make my own hatred of Elimination bona fide and righteous. Instead, I learn that Elimination is for the most part capturing hundreds of dangerous breakers who really commit horrible crimes. Most of us are a threat to society and can't bear the burden of resisting the temptation to take advantage of our skills. Apparently, Tim was right after all.

I continue reading until my eyes become tired and I get a headache. Then I finally turn away, thinking. The world used to be simple. Elimination was bad and breakers were good. After reading the files, I now understand we're the same. We hate and kill each other. On one side there's Wheeler who enjoys torturing breakers and on the other, there are breakers who enjoy causing pain to innocent people. All the same to me.

Then I think of Lena, Jessie and Jimmy. They've done nothing to be locked away. They're just victims of our violent world.

I don't know what to think of myself. Do I deserve my sentence in this prison? I didn't rob the bank or kill innocent people as accused. But neither am I completely clean. I've certainly committed my share of crimes since Elimination began disrupting my life.

"That's why I joined Elimination," I hear a calm voice say from behind and look back. Frank is standing at the doorway. "To stop the evil breakers from harming innocent people," he says. "I know many breakers believe that Elimination is just a government instrument for abusing breakers. That's not completely true. Elimination prevents a multitude of crimes from ever happening. They're the last defense for normal citizens. You're reading these files and I can tell from the look on your face that you're deeply shocked by what you read. But those files pale in comparison to what you actually see working as an Elimination officer. You can't imagine what I've witnessed."

Frank looks closer at the laptop screen. He sighs, "I used to hate breakers. Now that I'm one of you, I don't really know which side I belong to."

"I thought you wanted to return to Elimination," I say.

"I do, but now I can't know for sure whether it would be a good decision or not. I've never liked the idea of capturing breakers who haven't committed a crime. Now I'm one of those breakers myself."

I remember hypnotizing robbers and cops at the bank and getting the sensation of having my life crumble down around me within minutes. I ask, "How did you learn of your breaker abilities?"

"During my work," he answers. "We were hunting Bulldog and his groupies. They had killed many people before. The bust turned bad and we ended up shooting at each other. Bulldog captured an officer, who used to be my friend. I ran out of ammo. I didn't want Bulldog to kill him, wished very hard for him to drop his weapon and…well, you know."

"You hypnotized Bulldog."

"Right. I'm said to be level four, so I could potentially hypnotize other breakers. I'm still not exactly sure how I did it. Believe it or not, I've never used that ability again after that day. I simply don't have a will to learn. I hypnotized Bulldog, saving my friend's life, and wound up being hand-cuffed and taken to prison along with Bulldog for my efforts. Nobody knew what to do with me."

"Do you have family?" I wonder.

"I used to have a wife. She divorced me when she learned I was a freak. I don't blame her. Who would want to be married to a breaker?"

"No kids?"

"No."

We spend a few minutes in silence. I realize that Frank's situation is even worse than mine. I always knew I was a breaker. I'm used to being one. Frank is stuck between two worlds and rejected by both. Elimination won't accept him because he's their enemy. Most breakers probably hate him for being a former Elimination officer.

"There's no going back for you," I say. "You can't stop being a breaker."

"I know."

"At least you don't have to work for Wheeler anymore. He's a real jerk."

"He's really not that bad. If he mistreated you, it's only because you're a breaker. Wheeler isn't a bad man."

"Wheeler's the worst person I've ever met."

"You only know his tough outer shell, but don't really know him fully," Frank answers. "He's a good husband and a father. And he's a good friend. At least we used to be friends. For the most part, he's only temperamental and mean spirited here at the prison. Outside of here, Wheeler is a nice guy."

I don't answer, trying to imagine Wheeler being nice. I can't. No matter what opinion Frank has, I won't be removing Wheeler from my kill list. He deserves nothing less than death.

It's getting very late. I turn off the laptop and suggest to Frank to go get some sleep. Tomorrow will be a long day, our first attempt to locate the terrorists telepathically.

I get flashbacks from Jimmy's memories in my sleep. I wake, pleading with Elimination to not kill my parents and struggling to remember who I really am. I hesitate to sleep again, because I don't want to risk more visions. It messes with my head. I dress and walk out of my room.

Since I agreed to work for Browning, I've been transferred into another section of the prison. The cells here don't look like cells really, but resemble cheap motel rooms. No locks on the doors. Other members of our team are living in the same section as well.

Victor sits on the floor concealed in shadow, smoking a cigarette. Seeing me he smiles, knocking off ash on the floor, and says, "A gift from Carrel. Like one?"

"I don't smoke," I answer.

"I have some Xanax if you prefer."

"No, thanks."

"Believe me, dude, you'll need some when they make you scan people every waking day," Victor grins. "Helps me not to care or think too much. That's why you're up, aren't you? You can't shake Jimmy's memories."

"How do you know?" I wonder.

"Cause that garbage happens to me all the time. I keep seeing other people's memories instead of sleeping. I no longer understand which are mine and which aren't. I can't tell the difference. A good breaker could probably scan once or twice a week and be fine. But if they make you do it every day, you won't remember yourself after a while." He pauses, smoking a cigarette and exhaling blue smoke. "I may not know who I am," he says slowly, "but I'm pretty darn sure I was not smoking a month ago. Must have picked it up from somebody I scanned."

"I thought you liked working for Elimination," I say.

"I thought so too, but I can't remember why," Victor answers. "I don't know, maybe somebody wiped my memory. What I do know is that I'm really sick of all this." He gives me a piercing stare. "I want out. I'm done with Elimination."

"Why are you telling me all this?" I ask.

"Because I know you're planning something, and I want in."

"I've no idea what you're talking about."

"C'mon," Victor rolls his eyes. "You don't have to pretend with me. I won't be spying on you and your team for Carrel. I'm sick of being told what to do by him."

"Why would I trust you, Victor?"

"Well, maybe because I didn't tell anybody about Kitty."

"What? How do you know about her?" I ask.

"I couldn't read all your memories, but I sneaked a glimpse at a few things before you blocked me," he grins. "Don't worry. I didn't rat you out."

He finishes his cigarette and stands up. "I'll help you catch those guys and find your sister. Then you help me get out of here," he says, walking away. I remain sitting on the floor, wondering whether I can trust Victor or not. Holtzmann might be right in saying that Victor is not what I think. Nothing is certain, time will tell.

I sit back in the recliner with my eyes closed, concentrating on Kitty. I can imagine her in vivid detail, but nothing happens. No vision comes. Lena is in a similar chair beside me, doing the same thing. She's seen Kitty in visions before, but unfortunately, they don't share a connection. Lena's mind is linked to mine, so I'm trying to lead her into my thoughts. I don't exactly know how it's supposed to work. I only follow Holtzmann's instructions. We're in a dark, quiet section of his lab with no distractions. The other members of my team are in a separate section, getting hypnosis training from Victor with Holtzmann watching.

"Nothing," I say finally, sitting up. "Can you see anything?"

"No, I'm sorry," Lena answers.

"That's okay."

We return to our team. Holtzmann gives me a questioning look and I report that we couldn't get any visions.

"That's your own fault, Rex," Holtzmann says. "You're still blocking signals by maintaining a closed mind. In fact, you already know where we can find them. You're getting this information continuously, but you don't recognize it because you don't fully accept and trust your abilities."

"I need a break," I answer, plopping down in a chair and watching Victor hand out candy bars.

"The best and easiest source of carbs for breakers," he says. "Increases sugar in your blood and helps your brain activity. You should eat one too," he says, tossing a candy bar my way. I catch and enjoy sharing mine with Lena.

"We don't have a lot of time," Holtzmann says. "If Browning doesn't see results soon, he'll shut down our project. He'll quickly return to his preferred policy of scanning the entire human population. We must remain focused and methodical in our efforts."

Rebecca brings lunch and eats with us, asking Holtzmann if he took his medicine. She avoids eye contact with me and behaves as if I'm not here.

A bored Chase is pacing back and forth in the lab, paying little attention to us. Looks like he doesn't view our team as a threat any longer.

Lena and I continue attempting to get visions after lunch and don't stop till it's time for supper. Afterward, we try again. Nothing.

I'm losing faith in being able to locate the terrorists. Maybe I've overestimated myself and can't manage any more visions about Kitty. Maybe returning to prison and involving Elimination was a mistake.

Lena's scream breaks the silence. I jump off my chair and shake her, trying to wake her up. A closer look reveals Lena isn't asleep. She's in some sort of trance, her eyes wide open and rolled back in her head.

"Lena, what are you seeing?" I ask.

I know she's having a vision. I need to see it too somehow. I need to know what's happening to Kitty and where she is. I press my forehead against Lena's and close my eyes. Show me, I think. Take me with you.

Images flash rapidly in my mind. They're so vivid and intense that I become dizzy and lose balance.

When Holtzmann and Chase enter the room, I'm still sitting on the floor, gasping and trying to collect myself. Lena looks around and touches the chair carefully as if making sure it's real, not a vision.

"What happened?" Holtzmann asks.

"We've located them," I answer.

CHAPTER 20

"I think I've seen this guy before," Chase says, looking into the face of a dead Elimination officer. "He isn't from our unit, but I remember meeting him once or twice before during an operation."

He turns away as if the scene is too much for him to handle. I don't say anything. It must be hurtful for Chase to see a fellow Elimination officer dead, even if he didn't know him that well.

We're inside a large courthouse with a jail occupying the bottom floor. I've never been here before, but I've seen this exact place in my mind. This time the name of the exact street it's located on didn't come to me, but I was able to describe the place well enough to determine the general area. Elimination provided a spacious aircraft to my team and sent along a dozen officers in support, including Wheeler.

Ascending on takeoff, I stole a glimpse of the prison. It looks like a military base from above, and is located in a sparsely populated area.

Our trip only took an hour, but we were still too late. The outlaw group of breakers had already attacked the municipal jail, freed five inmates and shot several Elimination officers. They had left right before our arrival. What a fiasco. Lena and I both had visions and tracked their location minutes before the actual attack. If I could only have located them half an hour earlier…I groan in frustration.

"Relax, breaker," Chase says. "It's not your fault. You did everything you could."

If I'd received the vision a bit earlier, I could be reunited with Kitty right now. She would be safe. Now I can't even determine whether she's still alive. One of the downed officers could have shot her during the attack.

I look around. Frank stands motionless, studying the faces of the dead officers in the same manner Chase stared at them earlier. He may have worked with them before, I realize, but don't ask. I've had enough of being around the dead and wounded. I don't want to know about these people personally. Victor sits on the floor, smoking a cigarette and smiling. He must be happy he didn't have to fight. Jessie seems as disappointed as I am. Many hypnotized cops with blank stares walk randomly around in the room. Newly arrived police and paramedics are trying to bring them back to reality. They don't succeed. The hypnosis has to wear off on its own.

"Why don't you help them?" Holtzmann asks.

"Can I?" I wonder.

"You have the ability," he suggests, "to snap them out of the hypnosis."

"Can I really do that?"

"At least you might try. It has never been attempted to my knowledge, but I suspect it might work."

"What do I do?"

Holtzmann shrugs his shoulders, saying, "You are a level four breaker, not me. It should come naturally for you. Don't think how you should do it, just do it."

"Thanks for nothing," I sigh. "Your instruction is very helpful as always."

I approach a cop. He's standing stone still as a statue, wearing a silly grin on his face. I concentrate, projecting my thoughts into his foggy mind. Wake up, I think. You're under hypnosis. Shake it off.

I'm not wearing the blocking collar, so my thoughts reach his brain within seconds. The policeman steps back and looks around, disoriented.

"What happened?" he asks in surprise.

"Calm down," I say softly. "You were hypnotized. You're okay now."

He doesn't recognize me because of the ski mask I was ordered to wear as a precaution. With my face being shown on all newscast a few weeks ago, Elimination can't afford to let a public learn my death was a farce.

Paramedics lead the disoriented cop away. Later he'll have to deal with the fact that he shot an Elimination officer while under hypnosis. Fortunately, the terrorists couldn't force every cop to execute their commands. Some happened to be strong minded and just fell into a deep paralyzing trance.

I approach another policeman, doing the same drill. I suggest for him to wake up and he heeds my command. Perhaps Holtzmann was right. The less I think about it, the better it works.

An hour later I stand outside the building, exhausted and experiencing a terrible headache. I helped at least a dozen hypnotized policemen.

"Are you all right?" Chase wonders.

"It could be worse," I answer, wincing.

"Do all breakers get headaches?"

"Not that I know of. I'm the lucky one."

"Thanks for helping with those officers," Chase says.

"They'd be okay anyway," I answer. "The hypnosis doesn't last forever."

"Holtzmann thinks the less time it lasts, the less side effects one suffers. So you did a great job helping them." Chase pauses, looking at me. "Why are you helping non-breakers anyway?"

"You still don't get it, Chase?" I ask. "You still think all breakers are the same and we're all vicious killers and thieves?"

"I've never really thought that way," he answers. "I realize that we often incarcerate breakers who have never committed a crime. It's the least favorite part of my job."

"What keeps you in Elimination then?"

"Money," Chase sighs. "I only have a high school education, so my options are limited. I have to help my parents, they're poor. When I signed up with Elimination, I didn't know about some of the methods they use. In any case, every once in a while we do lock away some really nasty breakers. The killer and rapist variety."

"I know," I say.

Chase grins, "It's kind of ironic, that I spend so much time inside the prison that sometimes it feels like I'm an inmate myself."

I remember what Holtzmann told me earlier about being trapped inside the facility.

"Don't they let you out?" I wonder.

"Sure," Chase answers. "I can take a day off and visit my family if I want, but they don't pay me for that. And my family doesn't care whether I visit them or not. They don't miss me. I have plenty of younger siblings still living with them. They don't care where I am or what I am doing as long as I send them money."

"Why help them then?"

"Why? I don't want my brothers and sisters to starve."

"I can understand that," I say.

"And I don't send all my salary anyway," Chase says. "I'm also saving some for college. As soon as I save enough, I'll be out of Elimination."

"Really? What are you gonna study?"

"Journalism. What? Why are you laughing? I want to become a journalist. What's so freaking funny about that?"

"Sorry, Chase, but I can't imagine you being a journalist," I explain, trying to stop smiling. "Do you want to work with Lola?"

"No Lola, no television. I'd prefer to write about breakers and tell people the truth."

"Chase, you won't be able to write whatever you want in this world. Everybody has their own agenda nowadays."

"I'll try to change that," Chase answers. "I've never gone to college, but I've read some historical books. In times past, people had the freedom of speech. Maybe I can help bring it back."

Good luck, I think. If he continues thinking this way, he'll probably wind up in prison. I don't say anything though. I'm surprised Chase opened up to me about his family and future plans. It actually felt like I've been talking to a human being, not an Elimination officer on duty.

"Chase! Stay away from this breaker," Wheeler shouts, approaching us. Chase sighs, but follows his command. Wheeler glares at him, saying, "What's wrong with you, boy? Why are you making friends with this pig? Don't forget who you are or who he is. Don't let him fool you."

Chase turns away and walks off toward the aircraft.

Time to go back to prison.

"I'm displeased with your team's performance today," Browning says. "I think I may have to utilize other methods to capture the terrorists."

Holtzmann and I are sitting in Browning's office, facing his desk. Browning is studying Wheeler's report on our work and shakes his head, saying, "This project is failing. It's obvious that your team is too slow to react and has no clue how to locate those terrorists before the damage is already done."

"We located them," I protest. "We were only a few minutes late. It isn't our fault."

"You haven't helped capture them," Browning says, "and that's the bottom line. Perhaps, it's time to begin a total scanning of the entire population to identify any unknown breakers. Elimination has to isolate them for the security of our Republic."

"That's ludicrous," Holtzmann says. "Your directive will not lead to safety, but to war. A full blown conflict between humans and breakers. Breakers won't permit you to arbitrarily imprison or kill them without putting up massive resistance."

"Now Egbert, we don't need all that drama," Browning answers. "We must stop those terrorists and other breakers from killing innocent citizens at all cost."

"Give my team more time," I ask. "We'll catch them."

"More time? How can I give you more time while innocent people are being killed?"

It's ridiculous to hear such words from Browning. Many innocent breakers and even their relatives are being tortured and killed under his command.

"It will take months, if not years to scan every person," I say, keeping my voice calm. "And it will take only a few weeks at the max for my team to locate those terrorists. Your career depends on how quickly and efficiently you can destroy them. If you shut down the project now, you'll most likely lose your job. Think about it."

After a long pause Browning finally agrees, "One week. If you don't bring them to me in one week, I'm ordering my officers to begin a total scanning of the population."

Holtzmann and I leave. One week to find the outlaw breaker group or our project will be shut down. I can't know whether I'll have visions or not. How can I locate them again?

"What are we gonna do?" I ask Holtzmann.

"Work diligently," he answers.

"One week probably isn't enough," I say.

"It has to be enough," he sighs. "We have to locate them. We can't let Browning approve total scanning. If we can't stop the scanning, thousands will die."

I remember his prophecy about the war. Somehow it doesn't seem so crazy now.

The next few days I spend hours concentrating on Kitty's image, but the visions just aren't happening. My mind is empty.

Lena helps out as best she can, lying in her chair and connecting to my mind. Holtzmann says she can't track Kitty on her own. Lena and Kitty don't have an emotional link. Lena is usually able to locate a person if she has a picture, but there's no picture of Kitty. And even if I had one, I wouldn't give it to Elimination. That's why I have to guide Lena in my mind, triggering her visions. She's a more experienced telepath than I am, and can get clearer images, but I have to feed them to her.

On the other hand, as soon as Lena sees something, I can easily access her mind and see the same visions. Together we combine our effort, working and thinking as one. Holtzmann explained that during telepathic connection our heart rate synchronizes and body temperatures regulate to become the same. Our brains show identical activity. We actually go through the same experience. If I'm angry, then Lena feels my anger. If she's sad, I become sad too. We even see the world through each other's eyes. Holtzmann seems to fully understand how it works, but for me it's too complicated.

No visions. I sit up in my chair. Lena opens her eyes instantly. She's still wearing bandages after having surgery. Holtzmann had doctors remove the electrodes from her head a few days ago. I wonder if this may be a factor in why we can't locate the terrorists. Lena is still hurting and maybe can't concentrate well enough due to the pain. I know it is affecting her, because I've had a headache since her surgery as well.

"How many days are left?" she asks.

"Two," I answer.

"What if we can't locate them?" Lena asks. "Will I have to go back to Carrel?"

"No, we won't let Carrel take you."

"Carrel always gave orders for the officers to beat me, when I couldn't get visions."

"Why didn't you hypnotize them?" I wonder. "You're level four, right? You can hypnotize the resistant."

"I can't. I don't know why. I'm only good at telepathy. I tried to hypnotize Carrel and the officers, but always failed."

Just like me. I still have trouble with hypnotizing resistant people. Lena may be too young to be able to use all her abilities. Maybe the long months of abuse and fear at the hands of Carrel broke her mentally.

"Anyway, if even I knew how to hypnotize the resistant, I wouldn't dare escape," she says. "Elimination has my mom. They keep her around here somewhere and say they'll kill her if I try anything wrong. I know she's still alive. I feel it. I can see her sometimes."

"Is she a breaker?

Lena nods.

I keep silent for a few minutes, trying to imagine what this child has gone through. I ask carefully, "How long have you been here?"

"Three years."

It means Lena was five, when she was first imprisoned by Elimination. Three years, I think, Lena has spent the past three years among killers and sadists. Three years of pain and humiliation. It's hard for me to remain calm.

Lena feels it, saying, "Don't worry. I'm okay now. I'm really happy to be part of your team and away from Carrel." She smiles.

"We'll escape," I say. "And then rescue your mother."

"Thank you," Lena says, giving me a hug. I'm not sure if it's right to make such promises.

Lena returns to her chair and suggests we try once again to locate the terrorists. I close my eyes, trying to relax. I have to clear my mind, forget who and where I am. I have to envision Kitty, connecting with her mind and seeing the world through her eyes. Where are you, I think, what are you doing right at this moment? Are you still alive?

Nothing.

Holtzmann interrupts our idle attempts around midnight, suggesting we get some sleep. Perhaps he's right, I'm just too tired. I decide we should return to our rooms and get some rest so we can start fresh in the morning.

"Rex! Wake up!" Chase says, shaking me. "C'mon, breaker!"

I sit up in bed and stare at him. My head is foggy. I'm tired and want to go back to sleep. "What time is it?" I ask.

"4 am. C'mon, get up. There's been a terrorist attack at a hospital."

"What? The prison infirmary?"

"No. A regular hospital an hour's drive to the north."

Slowly, I begin to understand what he's talking about. I dress quickly and follow Chase. He leads me toward Holtzmann's lab.

"When did it happen?" I wonder.

"Just an hour ago. Relax, we don't have to go. It's too late. All the terrorists are already gone."

I didn't see it coming. No visions yesterday. Why?

We enter the lab. Holtzmann sits at his desk, watching the news unfold on his laptop. Rebecca stands behind him, looking over his shoulder.

"Rex, they've killed everybody," Rebecca exclaims. "They've burned an entire floor at the hospital. Patients and doctors alike couldn't do anything to save themselves, being under hypnosis. More than eighty people are dead."

My mouth gets dry. I approach Holtzmann's desk and stare at the monitor. I see the large building enfolded in flames, firefighters, people frozen in shock and body bags, rows and rows of black plastic bags spread across the concrete. Something churns inside me. I smell the nauseating reek of burnt flesh. A journalist reports about a group of breakers who broke into the building and set it on fire. Nobody on that floor could react in time. Victims were rendered completely helpless, paralyzed by hypnosis.

"They didn't bother to leave their slogan this time," Holtzmann says thoughtfully. "And didn't bother to leave your image as they've done previously."

"They're now fully aware that I'm alive and not some kind of martyr for their cause," I remind him.

Holtzmann thinks for a moment, then asks, "You didn't receive visions concerning this act of terror, did you?"

"For God's sake, Holtzmann! Of course not!" I exclaim. "You think I would let this happen?"

"I'm just verifying the facts," Holtzmann answers. "Strange. Why didn't you see this? I'd expect you to have very vivid visions, considering it's such a devastating event."

"How the heck can I know why I didn't see this coming?"

Holtzmann turns back to the monitor. We watch news for a long time in silence. I wonder how many people are watching the same broadcast in horror right now. They must hate breakers, associating every one of us with terrorism and believing we're all monsters.

Freaking psychotic terrorists, I think disgustedly.

I begin to realize that I'm somehow guilty for everything that's happened this night. I should have stopped it. I could have located them and prevented all this. But I didn't.

"This is a catastrophe," Holtzmann says. "Browning will certainly request a total scanning of the population now. He's going to want to shut down our project."

"Chase, wake Lena," I suggest. "We're gonna try to locate them."

"Right now?" Chase hesitates.

"We don't have time, Chase!" I shout.

"Okay, calm down, breaker," Chase says, leaving.

Rebecca takes my hand and says, "I'm so sorry, Rex."

"It's not your fault, Rebecca."

She gives me a long sympathetic look. I realize that Rebecca is genuinely worried and that she's no longer associating me with other bad breakers.

"We're gonna find these dudes and stop them," I say. "It's gonna be all right."

"It may be too late," Holtzmann says slowly. "I'm not sure that Browning will allow us to continue working on our project."

"Talk to him, Holtzmann. Make him give us a couple more days."

"He won't listen."

"So, this is it then? Are you really ready to give up?"

He thinks for a long moment before answering, "I'll do everything I can. Actually, I should have a conversation with Browning right now." He walks toward the door.

Rebecca and I are left alone in his lab. We continue watching the news. Rebecca is still holding my hand. Suddenly she's crying.

"What? What's wrong, Rebecca?"

"I don't know," she sobs, covering her face. "The world is just too cruel, I guess. Why do people always have to kill each other? What's wrong with us? There's plenty of room for everyone on our planet. Can't we all just leave in peace?"

I don't have answers to her questions.

"I'm sorry," she says, wiping her tears. "I guess I'm just oversensitive. I was watching the news and thought of my parents."

I end up holding her in my arms and patting her back. I don't know how else to soothe her. No words come to mind and I simply repeat, "It will be all right, Rebecca. Everything is gonna be okay." What else can I say? Nothing that I say or do can bring back her deceased parents.

Rebecca presses her face against my shoulder and slowly calms down. Then she suddenly steps back and turns away in embarrassment. "I'm sorry, Rex."

"For God's sake, why do you keep apologizing?"

She shrugs, "I don't know. I just hate for you to see me like that."

Chase returns, a very sleepy Lena in tow. Yawning, she rubs her eyes and looks around in confusion.

"We have work to do, Lena," I say. "And we have very little time."

Lena nods, ready. We both walk into the dark room used for tele-pathic experiments. Holtzmann suggests that light may be too distracting. Darkness is the best environment for telepathy.

Somehow I understand that Browning won't be giving us more time. He wants Elimination to begin scanning everybody in order to detect all breakers. It means we have to locate the terrorist group immediately. This is our last chance.

I don't have to explain anything to Lena. She's in my mind and knows what I think anyway. I sense a jolt of fear in Lena. "Calm down," I say. "You mustn't be afraid now. We need to concentrate."

She relaxes and calms down. I feel it. I lie down in my chair and close my eyes. Kitty. I need to think of her. I have to figure out where she is. Today. Right now. Tomorrow will be too late.

The minutes pass slowly. No idea how long we spend in the dark room. Maybe an hour, maybe longer. I call out for Kitty in my mind, ask-ing her to help. Nothing. I imagine her as vividly as I can. My head hurts and I'm exhausted, but I keep trying. No vision comes.

"Lena, why doesn't it work?" I ask. "What are we doing wrong?"

"I don't know," Lena answers sadly.

We continue our attempts. Our efforts seem futile. I need to think. Holtzmann said I have a mental block, subconsciously rejecting my being a breaker. I have to accept it on every level, to fully embrace my nature. He said it is as natural as breathing for me to have visions and to use hypnosis.

I take a slow deep breath, concentrating harder. I can do this, I think. I'm a telepath. That's who I am and was always meant to be.

I get a sensation of weightlessness. Then multiple images begin flashing in my head. Kitty, a man with scarred face, a map laid across a table, a large building, other breakers, white sandy beach, the ocean…I gasp. I somehow understand they're planning a new attack to free captured breakers at another police station tomorrow. My head hurts so intensely that I can't bear the pain any longer and sit up. Lena is still lying with her eyes closed. Then she wakes with a jolt, overwhelmed by the visions. Her eyes are open wide and hands trembling. Being telepathically connected, I know we shared the same vision.

"Lena, what the heck was it?" I ask. "What have we seen?"

"It was their main headquarters," she answers. "I think we may have actually seen where they're hiding."

"Can you locate this place?"

Lena shakes her head. "I only know the place they plan to attack tomorrow."

It's something at least. Hopefully, I can find Kitty there. But can we capture all of them at the station? To get them all, we'll probably have to locate their base.

We walk out of the room and see Holtzmann sitting at his desk. He has a dull expression.

"No more time?" I guess.

"No. Browning is skeptical of our team's usefulness, and wants to shut down our project."

"He's too late," I grin. "We've already located them. They're attacking a police station tomorrow."

I describe the place in detail.

"There was a long bridge nearby," I offer. "It was somewhere near water. I could smell the ocean." I search my mind for a sign with a name of the street. "Apple Grove."

"It should be enough," Holtzmann says enthusiastically, turning to his laptop. "Chase, please report to Mr. Browning that we've identified the location of tomorrow's attack," he commands as Chase rushes away.

"We also saw their main headquarters," I say.

"What?"

"Their main base, headquarters...whatever you call it. The majority of them are hiding there."

"Could you recognize the place?"

"No."

Holtzmann keeps silent, thinking. Then he says, "If we want to prevent new acts of terror, we'll have to capture all of them. We need to locate their headquarters somehow."

Easier said than done. I frown. We have no time for conducting more experiments. The next attack is going down in a few hours.

Holtzmann calls for guards and commands them to wake each member of my team. The guards execute his order quickly. Within ten minutes everybody is in the lab. Holtzmann explains the situation briefly and then we're all discussing what we need to do. Victor is smoking, pacing back and forth. He seems bored.

"Why all the hurry?" he asks. "Lena and Rex can get more telepathic visions, after we capture the group attacking the police station. On second thought, why not just interrogate the captured terrorists? They will likely tell everything, especially if we beat the hell out of them. Browning can't shut us down if we succeed."

"The uncaptured group may change their location before we can get there," Holtzmann answers.

This is not the only reason. Kitty is my only link with those evil breakers. Having found her, I won't have any more visions. Afterward, there'll be no further reason for me to work for Elimination. Holtzmann must realize this.

"Too bad we don't have any friends among the terrorists planning the attack," Jimmy sighs. "They could lead us back to their headquarters."

I look at him and then say, "Jimmy, you're brilliant."

"What did I do?" he asks.

"You're right, Jimmy. We'll just need one of us to join the terrorist group."

Everybody stares at me in shock, but then they understand what I mean.

"We could put a tracking device on him," Holtzmann suggests.

"When we arrive, we won't capture the entire breaker group," I say, glancing at a clock showing 8 am. "We'll arrive at the police station and attack them. And then we'll let a few escape. The one of us who helps lead them through our defenses, will hopefully be allowed to join their group and taken along right into their main base."

Holtzmann smiles with approval.

"Why would the terrorists allow one of us to join them?" Frank asks.

"Because I'll have helped a few escape, and besides, I'm their martyr," I offer. "They already want me to join them."

I hope Kitty won't let the terrorists kill me. I can't be sure whether they'll heed her suggestions or not.

"It's dangerous," Holtzmann says, "but bold enough that it just might work. I like the concept."

Looks like I'm going undercover.

Rebecca gives me a worried look and says, "They may kill you."

I shrug my shoulders. I've already died once before.

Chase returns and reports that Browning agreed to give us one more day. "If we don't succeed today, he'll shut down the project," Chase says.

Only a few hours left before the terrorist attack. I'm getting nervous. Today I'll rescue Kitty or die trying.

CHAPTER 21

I'm walking toward the transport aircraft with my team, when I notice Rebecca standing aside and watching us. It's 11 am, three hours before the terrorist attack. I'm wearing the black uniform of Elimination, a bulletproof vest and carrying a rifle. Rebecca doesn't say anything, but by the look on her face I understand she wants to talk. My team has to hurry, but in spite of a lack of time, I decide to stop and give Rebecca a minute. It may be the last time I see her. I don't know if I'm coming back.

I command my team to board the aircraft as I wait for Rebecca to approach. Rebecca hides her eyes. She seems both embarrassed and a bit panicked at the same time.

Anticipating her request, I say, "Don't worry, Rebecca. I'll make sure Holtzmann doesn't go inside the building. He'll be safe."

"He's not the only one I'm worried about," she answers quietly and then keeps silent for a few moments. "I'm also afraid you may not come back. What if those breakers shoot you? No telling what may happen."

"Nonsense," I smile, pretending unconcerned. "Remember, I'm a breaker just like them. Everything is going to be all right."

Rebecca sighs. "I don't know if I should tell you this or not," she says. "It's all so complicated. And I'm confused about what I really feel for you. That you're a breaker, I understand, but now that means little to me. You have a good heart, and I'm better for having met you, Rex. You've shown me how to be strong no matter what. I was living in constant fear, afraid of everybody and everything. But then I met you. It seems like you're never afraid. I admire your bravery."

My bravery? I've never thought of myself being overly brave or strong. I'm just trying to save Kitty, and myself if I can. The things I've done were not acts of bravery, but rather simply following survival instincts. I say, "Thank you, Rebecca. It pleases me if I could help you in some way."

She suddenly reaches for me, giving me a big hug. We stand for a few moments, holding each other.

"Please, come back to me," she whispers. "Please, be safe and don't die. I won't survive another loss. I can't lose you now."

I've no idea what this is all about. I don't know whether Rebecca is just being overemotional or she really does feel something for me. I believe she sincerely cares for me in spite of my being a breaker. And I understand I care for her too.

"Everything is gonna be all right," I repeat.

Wheeler shouts from the open aircraft door, "Hey! Get a move on, breaker!"

"I promise to come back," I say, leaving. Rebecca covers her face.

It's no time for any feelings. No time for doubts. I have to go save Kitty.

I grab a seat next to Jimmy inside the aircraft and it takes off.

"Why do you think they will trust you, breaker?" Wheeler asks suspiciously.

"I don't just think it, I know they'll trust me," I answer. "I was their martyr after all. They will want me to join forces with them. Besides, I'm a fellow imprisoned breaker. They wouldn't kill me."

"It's a stupid idea, destined for failure," Wheeler says. "But be my guest, I don't care if they kill you or not. Actually, I hope they don't because I'd like to have that opportunity myself in the future."

He grins. I don't answer. I just think of the time when I can put a bullet between his eyes or slit his throat. Soon, I repeat in my mind, only not right now. First I need to use Elimination to rescue Kitty from the terrorists. I can't fight them all on my own. I need to cooperate for now.

I must think of what may come next. What am I going to do after I reunite with Kitty? We'll need to escape. We'll have to take Jimmy, Jessie and Lena with us. I should add Rebecca to my list as well. I can't leave her with Elimination. It's no place for her. What about Holtzmann? Elimination isn't suitable for him either, but I doubt he'll agree to leave. That egghead is crazy. Then I look at Victor sitting nearby. I don't fully trust Victor and don't believe I should involve him in my plans.

I decide to worry about all this stuff later. Now I just have to get the terrorists to bring me along to their headquarters. I have a tracking microchip implanted under the skin in my arm. I only need to make it to their main base and then Elimination will come to capture the breakers and hopefully rescue me. We will destroy their organization. No more acts of terror by this group. No more innocent school children being burned alive.

I take a long look at my team. Everyone seems slightly nervous. Lena is biting her nails. Victor checks and rechecks his handgun. Frank is better able to keep calm, but I notice beads of sweat popping out on his forehead. Jimmy can't shut his mouth, mumbling about dogs, parachutes and plane crashes. Only Jessie seems like she really doesn't give a damn. She sits with her eyes closed, napping. I glance at Holtzmann and hope he doesn't have another fit. His left eye is already twitching.

"Worried, breaker?" Chase asks.

"Not really," I answer. He smiles and winks, cheering me up a little.

If things go according to our plan, members of my team, excepting Lena and Jimmy, will go inside the police station to engage the intruders. Elimination soldiers will wait outside as backup. Chase is the only Elimination officer coming with us.

The aircraft takes a sudden turn.

"Are we still flying or falling?" Jimmy asks, grabbing the bench with both hands.

"Shut up, retard," Wheeler growls.

The aircraft is descending. I'm getting anxious and having doubts. What if Kitty isn't with them this time? What if they won't accept me and simply shoot me full of holes? I have to force myself to remain calm. Of course Kitty will be there. I wouldn't have had the visions otherwise. She won't let them kill me. Everything should work out fine.

The aircraft lands in a large square a few blocks away from the police station. My team exits the craft followed by a dozen Elimination officers, who'll be providing backup. It's odd to be associated with them. I notice that they've stopped their offensive insults and now pay little attention to my presence. The aircraft takes off again, heading off to a predetermined staging area.

As we approach the police station, Lena looks around cautiously, saying, "This is the place from our visions. They're coming."

"Why attack during the day?" Jessie wonders. "Night would be safer."

"They want to demonstrate they aren't scared of anybody," Victor answers. "Also these breakers are capable of mind control. What can ordinary cops do against them?"

Jessie gives Victor a piercing glance which falls short of hiding her disgust and hatred. She looks at Victor the way I look at Wheeler. Jessie wants to kill him, I realize. It may turn out to be a problem in the future, although, I can't really blame her for feeling that way.

The Elimination officers take concealed positions inside the nearest buildings. My team takes position a block away from the police station in a post office, waiting for a signal.

I worry that Lena and I were wrong, but finally Wheeler contacts Chase on a radio.

"They're here," Chase reports. "It's go time."

Lena grabs my hand and whispers, "I'll be watching if I can, be careful!"

"Thank you," I answer. "I will."

I realize that should I die, Lena will suffer the same experience in her visions. Just like I died in my mind when Wheeler shot an inmate at the jail.

We walk cautiously toward the police station. I lead while Jessie, Frank, Victor and Chase follow, everyone armed. I see a large van parked on the side of the road. No sign of suspicious looking people. The renegade breakers must be inside the building already.

As we enter the police station, I pass by a few cops standing motionless, peering into nowhere. I wonder why the terrorists put them in a deep stupor instead of using them against those resistant. Possibly, it takes too much effort or those cops are just very strong minded. I pass by them, heading toward the voices coming from the distance. Then I hear gunfire and follow the sound.

Keeping close to the wall, I reach for the door and take a careful glimpse inside the room. A couple of Elimination guards who had been assigned to the jail are shooting. Five people in camo military uniforms are firing back. A few dead cops are sprawled out on the floor. These cops were probably forced to fire at the Elimination officers. Being under a hypnotic trance, they were slow and became easy targets for return fire.

Then I notice a skinny figure dressed in camouflage, shooting a large handgun, too big for her thin arms. Kitty. She's here, only several feet away.

I gesture my team to follow and spread out into the room, keeping low to avoid waist high bullets. Jessie, Frank and Victor are firing above my head toward the intruders.

"This is Elimination!" Chase yells. "Drop your weapons!"

A wall of gunfire immediately returns his direction. Chase drops flat on the floor, emptying a clip in response as I run toward the group of breakers. The gunfire ceases for a few moments and I know, my team is projecting their thoughts toward the attackers. But I also realize Victor and Jessie won't be able to hold them for long, just for a moment. I make it only half way through the room, when the air fills with shouts and gunfire again. A couple of bullets slam into my chest, knocking me to the ground. The bulletproof vest has taken the brunt of the impact. I gasp to regain my breath, then roll over onto my hands and knees. All my attention is focused on a single small figure, holding one heck of a big handgun. I must make my way to Kitty. I'm here for her. Crawling and hoping not to catch a bullet in the head, I continue across the room.

"Drop your weapons!" Chase commands, but nobody heeds his order. That nobody surrenders is fine and everything is going according to our plan as long as nobody gets killed. The terrorists aren't expected to surrender. At least some are expected to escape and take me with them.

"Don't shoot!" I yell. "This is me! Rex!"

"Rex?" I hear Kitty's voice. "Hold your fire!" she commands. "It's Rex, don't shoot him!"

Just as I'm about to reach Kitty, a guy with a scarred face presses a gun to my forehead. Hammer, I remember. The remaining terrorists, with the exception of Kitty, continue shooting at Elimination officers and my team.

"Drop your rifle," Hammer commands.

I place my rifle on the floor and say, "We're on the same side."

"Get away from him!" Kitty yells.

"Shut up!" he growls and asks, "Why are you wearing Elimination black, if you're on our side?"

"They forced me to," I answer. "I'm trying to escape. I'm hoping to join your group."

"Hammer! Don't you dare hurt him," Kitty shouts, reloading her gun.

A long moment passes. I don't know if Hammer will kill me or not. Then he lowers the gun.

"What the hell is going on then?" he asks. "How did you learn of our plans?"

"Elimination has breakers that were able to locate you," I answer.

"That would be you," Hammer says. "You located us and led Elimination here, traitor!"

He puts his gun back to my head.

"Quit it, Hammer," Kitty screams. "Rex would never sell me out. He's with us! He's a breaker!"

Somehow I feel guilty. Kitty is going to be very disappointed when she learns the truth.

"We need to get out of here!" a terrorist exclaims.

Hammer thinks for a moment and then commands, "Put on your masks!" He removes a gas mask from his backpack and places it over his face. The other outlaw breakers follow his lead. Hammer takes out several small round objects from his pockets. Grenades, I realize, panicking. He tosses them as fast as he can pull the pins. I collapse flat on the floor and cover my head, expecting explosions. Instead, I hear hissing noises as the room fills with suffocating white gas. I gasp, choking on the fumes and unable to breathe. My eyes and lungs are burning. The room blackens. I can't see a thing.

"We can't leave him again!" Kitty screams nearby. "Drake will want Rex with our group!"

Somebody's arms pull me up, dragging me off.

I pass out.

Cold water splashes onto my face. Coughing and snorting, I drift back out of the dark and open my eyes. They're still burning.

"It's okay," Kitty says softly, wiping my face with a towel. "You're safe now."

Disoriented, I take a careful look around. We're inside a moving van. I'm on the floor and Kitty is sitting at my side.

"How are you feeling?" she asks with concern.

"I'm fine," I answer, rubbing my eyes. My throat hurts. I'm still having trouble breathing from the gassing. I wonder what's happened to my team and the hypnotized cops back inside the station.

"What kind of gas did you use?" I ask.

My thoughts tangle and my speech is slightly slurred. Kitty understands anyway.

"It wasn't lethal," she answers. "Only good enough to knock somebody out in case our mission failed." She hands me a bottle of water. "Here, drink and wash your eyes."

I drink the water greedily and splash some on my face. It helps ease the burning a little, but I'm still feeling suffocated.

"You'll be fine," Kitty says, hugging me and kissing my face. "I can't believe we're finally together again! Now everything will be fine." She grabs my hand and doesn't let go. I notice her fingers trembling.

"Hey, leave that traitor alone," Hammer says. "Don't waste any more of our good water on him."

Several other terrorist breakers are also inside the vehicle.

"Shut your mouth, Hammer!" Kitty growls. "You shouldn't treat Rex that way."

"He's a traitor," Hammer says matter-of-factly. "He's betrayed all breakers, working for those killers."

"I said shut up!" Kitty shouts. "I can't hear this nonsense."

Kitty has changed dramatically. Her face seems more mature and hardened. Her tone of voice is authoritative. Kitty has developed into a tough fighter and somewhat of a stranger, no longer my sweet little sister. Only when she's speaking to me does her voice soften and her facial expression becomes gentle again.

"I won't let them hurt you," Kitty assures me.

"Where are we going?" I ask.

"Tell him and I'll have to shoot him," Hammer threatens. "He doesn't need to know where we're heading or the location of our headquarters."

Kitty glares at him with anger. "We're going to a safe place, don't worry," she explains.

I try to sit up, but my body doesn't respond. Seems I've lost coordination.

"Easy, just relax," Kitty says. "The effects will wear off in a couple of hours. Just rest now."

I lie back on the floor. My ribs ache from the impact of the bullets slamming into my vest earlier. I'm lucky they didn't go through. Chase said bulletproof vests sometimes fail. I could be dead by now.

"We should shoot him and toss his body," Hammer suggests.

"There's a reason enforcing bad ideas like that are outside your rank," Kitty answers. "Let's wait for Drake to decide what to do next. I'm pretty sure Drake will recruit Rex for Retaliation."

"Whatever you say, Peaches," Hammer says derisively. "Of course Drake will recruit this traitor to join us."

"Don't listen to him," Kitty says to me. "Drake will like you. You were our hero after all."

I remember them leaving my photos inside the police stations they'd attacked.

"Who's Drake?" I ask.

"Our leader, and a great man," Kitty explains. Then she asks, "What happened? We thought Elimination had killed you."

"The execution was only for show. Elimination kept me incarcerated at their research facility to use as a lab rat. They wanted me to join them. I was searching for a way to escape and decided to pretend to be working for them until I got an opportunity."

"You don't have to explain now," Kitty blurts out. "I know you would never join those butchers."

I feel bad lying to her. It lasts only an instant. I remind myself why I'm doing all this, to save Kitty from these terrorists and to stop their cruel and meaningless killing.

"He's lying," Hammer says.

Kitty holds my hand tightly.

"Never leave me again, Rex," she demands. "We need to be always together. You and I."

I close my eyes and rest, thinking of what may be coming next.

The minivan finally stops and we get out. I can hardly walk, but my eyes are no longer so painful and my coordination is slowly improving.

I look around. We're in a desolate part of the country. A thick layer of ash covers the land and ruins of a long abandoned city. Nobody lives here anymore. Everything is gray and crumbling with an air of hopelessness.

The sky is getting dark which means we've been traveling for a few hours. Elimination could have followed us, but I think they didn't. They don't need to pursue because of the tracking device in my arm. Hopefully Elimination knows where I end up.

"Let's go," Hammer commands as he walks toward one of the dilapidated buildings. Hard to know what it was before the Eruption, but I'm guessing it used to be a church. I notice fresh boot tracks in the ash, leading from the entrance to something that used to be a highway many years ago. This probably isn't the headquarters, but only a temporary shelter on the way.

Kitty steadies me, helping me to walk. Other members of the group follow behind, holding handguns on me. They've taken off their ski masks. Most of them look under thirty, stoic-faced and tough. Somehow Kitty now fits in with their company perfectly.

Inside the church, there are several rows of dust covered pews as well as some chairs and sleeping bags set up around the altar.

"Strap him down," Hammer commands.

Two breakers shove Kitty away and grab hold, dragging me toward a chair.

"Leave him alone!" Kitty yells angrily. "Stop this!"

"Shut your mouth, girl," Hammer says.

"Drake won't appreciate this, Hammer," she warns. "He's gonna be mad as all get-out at you."

"Yeah, whatever."

I don't resist, letting them strap me to the chair. It'd be pointless to fight now. Hammer approaches and asks accusingly, "Well, why did Elimination send you to us? What's your mission, traitor?"

"I don't have a mission," I lie. "I just wanted to be with my sister again."

"Your sister?" Hammer looks at Kitty. "She isn't your sister. Kitty told me she was your fiancée."

"Oh," I say and glance at Kitty. Her face flushes red and she hides her eyes. Why in the world would she tell them that? It doesn't matter right now, I decide. "Kitty's my sister," I insist.

"I really don't care where you're at with your relationship," Hammer answers. "It's not my concern. I want to know why Elimination sent you here."

He brings another chair and sits down in front of me. We face each other for a minute. I don't divert my eyes.

"You know you can't lie to me," Hammer says. "You can try to lie if you choose, but it'll do no good. I already know everything. You've been sent here to spy on us. And I believe you led Elimination to us back at the police station. You must be a telepath. How else could you have tracked us otherwise? Of course you're a telepath. And a traitor." He spits on the floor. "You used to be an example for our soldiers, a martyr. Kitty told how you saved her life and died for her. Now I see that wasn't true either. You sold out to survive and made a conscious choice to work for Elimination. You deserve to die, Rex." He speaks very calmly.

"No!" Kitty screams, running toward us. Two breakers stop her.

"If you've already made up your mind, why don't you just shoot me now and quit wasting my time?" I ask.

Hammer thinks quietly, holding a gun on me. He says, "Usually we don't kill breakers. We rescue them. Our main purpose in Retaliation is to free and protect breakers from Elimination."

"I guess burning buildings with innocent people trapped inside is just a secondary purpose," I suggest.

Hammer frowns, shaking his head, "We didn't do that. Elimination misinformed you."

I don't believe him. There's not a second group with terrorist breakers.

"Gimme a knife," Hammer commands and a breaker hands him a long sharp blade. He cuts the sleeve of my shirt, revealing my arm.

"What are you doing?" Kitty screams.

"He has a microchip implant in his arm," Hammer answers calmly.

The cold blade slices into my skin. I don't resist because this isn't my mission. My mission is to make my way to their center. It takes only a second to remove the microchip. Our plan has failed, I realize. Without the tracking device, Elimination won't be able to locate me.

"What's this, Rex?" Hammer asks, smiling and showing a bloody microchip.

"No idea," I say. I don't really expect him to believe me.

"Rex?" Kitty asks in confusion.

"I didn't know it was there, Kitty," I say. I don't care how stupid it sounds. I have to continue my charade.

"Of course you didn't, traitor," Hammer smirks, throwing the microchip onto the floor and smashing it with his boot. "Unstrap him," he commands, pointing his gun in my face. "I'll show you how we deal with traitors." A couple of breakers free me. "On your knees!" Hammer shouts. I don't obey and he nods to his breakers. They come behind and forcefully kick the back of my knees, dropping me onto the floor.

"Hammer, don't," Kitty says. "Please, just let him explain. I've known Rex a long time and I'm sure he can explain everything."

"I'm not about listen to more of this Elimination rat's lies," Hammer answers calmly. "My face bears the scars Elimination inflicted on me," he says, pointing at his scarred face. "I don't want his explanations. I want revenge." He presses the cold barrel between my eyes. "Beg for your life scum."

"Nothing doing," I answer.

"Stop it!" Kitty screams desperately. Two breakers drag her away. "Let me go," she yells, kicking and clawing. "Hammer! I swear I'll kill you if you hurt him! You know I'll do it!"

I don't expect Hammer to take Kitty's threat too seriously, but he does. He holds his gun on my forehead a moment longer, then takes it away.

"She's saved your life for now, traitor," he says.

I can't understand why Hammer doesn't shoot me. I see no reason for him to keep me alive.

A breaker puts a hood over my head and pulls me up from the floor. Then he leads me away.

"Drake will order you to be shot anyway," Hammer says. "We don't forgive traitors where we're going."

CHAPTER 22

I'm barely conscious when the helicopter finally lands. Somebody commands me to get on my feet, pulling me up. Struggling, I make my numb body get in an upright position. They drag me outside.

I can't stop wondering where the terrorist group got money for a helicopter. Somebody must have sponsored them. It's also possible they've just stolen it from the military or confiscated one during a police station raid. They're breakers after all. Only Elimination is a real bother to them, the regular military not so much.

I'm still wearing a bag placed over my head. I see nothing, but smell a mixture of salt, water and fish. We're somewhere near the ocean. The temperature outside is much higher than back in the Republic. As I walk, I feel sand under my feet.

I know Kitty is somewhere nearby, although she doesn't speak anymore. She's been quiet since my interrogation. Hammer is giving me curt commands. Two other breakers hold my arms, pulling me forward. I stumble a few times.

They throw me into a cell and leave. I manage to untighten the rope around my neck and pull the bag off. I look around. There's nothing to see. The room is completely dark. Extending my arms, I take a few steps and find the wall. It's cold and solid. I locate the door and check it. It's made of metal and too strong to pry open. There's nothing for me to do, but sit down and wait.

I think of Lena. Now that I've lost my tracking device, she's the only hope I have of being located. Lena found me once, she may be able to find me again. Maybe I'm too far away. I couldn't see where we were flying, but I get the feeling we're on an island. I'm trying to recall the maps I studied long ago at the library.

Can you see me Lena, I think, concentrating. Do we still have a telepathic connection at this distance? I call for Lena in my mind, trying to trigger a vision. No luck. I don't sense any sign of her presence. I keep trying anyway, having nothing better to do.

In about an hour I take a break. Looks like it's time for a plan B. Unfortunately, I don't have one. It now seems stupid to have been relying only on a tracking device for location, although back at the lab we didn't think anybody would check under my skin. It's my own fault, I guess. It was arrogant to think that the terrorists would fully trust me only because of my being a breaker.

I can't stop wondering how Hammer knew about the microchip. Is he a telepath as well? Or somebody else told him? Anything is possible.

I sigh in disappointment. I may have to escape from here with Kitty by my own means.

Kitty. I'm still shocked by how much she's changed. Only a few weeks ago she was like a sister to me. Now Kitty is almost a stranger, not the same little girl I knew. She suddenly grew up and then became so distant when the chip was found.

I wonder why Kitty doesn't come and check on me. Perhaps she's disappointed with my working for Elimination. Although it's worth considering that I just always needed Kitty more than she needed me. I thought I knew her so well, but Kitty remains an enigma. She has her secrets. Is it conceivable Kitty only pretended being family for food and shelter all those years?

I think on it for a few seconds and decide it doesn't really matter. Nothing can change what I feel for her. I'll always be taking care of Kitty and looking out for her as long as I'm breathing.

Exhausted, I lie down on the floor, unsure if I can fall asleep. I close my eyes, and the next thing I know somebody is opening the door. I sit up, slightly groggy with sleep. The door opens and the light from outside temporarily blinds me. I turn away, letting my eyes adjust.

"Rex, how are you doing?" Kitty asks, walking in.

"I'm all right," I answer.

She approaches and places a plate of food on the floor beside me. "This is for you," she says, handing me a fork. I eat the still steaming plate of spaghetti with meatballs. Delicious. The terrorists aren't starving here for sure.

Kitty kneels to a sitting position in front of me, watching attentively. I sneak a glance at her while eating. She's changed her military uniform for a mini skirt and blue blouse, resembling her school uniform. Her reddish hair is put up in a high ponytail. Even in dim light I notice her bright make up, which makes her older than her years. I realize she's dressed up for me.

"Sorry I couldn't come earlier," Kitty apologizes. "I wanted to stay with you, but I had to see Drake and explain everything. He's willing to meet with you soon."

"What are you doing with these guys, Kitty?" I ask. "Why didn't you stay away from trouble as I asked?"

"I did exactly as you requested," she protests. "I travelled south and found the group of breakers Jessie had spoken to us about. And she was right, they do help out other breakers."

"Don't you know what's really going on? They're terrorists, Kitty. They trap innocent people in schools and hospitals and burn them alive."

Her smile fades. "Don't say that. We're helping breakers escape from Elimination. We don't kill anybody needlessly."

"What about those Elimination officers and cops?" I remind. "You've killed many of them along the way."

"They're our enemies!" Kitty exclaims. "They were trying to kill us. Elimination officers don't deserve to live. I wish I could kill them all."

"They're not all the same, Kitty," I say, remembering Chase and Frank.

Kitty falls silent for a minute. Then she sighs, saying, "They really have done a great job of brainwashing you, Rex."

"We need to escape from here," I say. "You know a way to get out?"

"I'm not going anywhere," Kitty answers quietly. "I'm staying right here because this is my home."

I realize that I'll probably have to drag Kitty away from here against her will. Her belief in this place being home may be a real problem.

"Listen Rex, I truly don't wanna argue," Kitty says. "You should meet Drake and then decide what you want to do."

She turns away, seemingly upset. I finish eating and get on my feet. Kitty looks me over carefully, then says with surprise, "You've changed a lot, Rex. You've become thinner. And what the hell happened to your hair?"

"A psycho doctor had ideas to implant electrodes into my brain," I explain as Kitty covers her mouth.

"Goodness gracious," she mutters. "What have you gone through?! Oh my, all these scars on your head!" She gives me a sympathetic hug. "We'll make them pay for everything they did. I promise."

Then Kitty steps away, saying that Drake is ready to see me if I'm finished eating. We leave the room. Two breakers are waiting out in the corridor, armed with pistols.

"You don't need to hold weapons on him," Kitty says with anger. "This is Rex! He's one of us."

The escorts fall in behind us, weapons ready. I get the sensation that I'm back in Elimination prison. Aside from Kitty being here there's no real difference.

I recognize Drake from the first moment I see him. This is one of the men from my visions. He's tall, wears camouflage clothing and his face is stone cold, lacking any emotion.

"Welcome to our operations center," he says as we enter a large room with soft carpets and antique styled furniture. "I'm pleased to meet you in person, Rex. You were our martyr, a symbol of injustice toward breakers, and gave us purpose for seeking revenge against Elimination."

Not sure how to react I simply say, "Thank you."

Kitty smiles and takes my hand, saying, "Rex is…"

"You've already told me enough, Kitty," Drake cuts her off. "Now, I want to hear what our brother Rex has to say. Please, leave us."

Kitty hesitates for a moment, then leaves. Drake gestures for the two guards to join Kitty. I'm left alone with Drake. I'm curious why he's not afraid of me. How can he be so confident I won't attack him?

"Kitty is an exceptionally gifted girl," Drake says, smiling. "She's one of my strongest breakers. I understand very well why you came for her. I realize how badly you must want her back."

"How can you know what I want?" I ask.

"You're not the only telepath, Rex," Drake answers. "Nor are you the best telepath. I've been inside your head, my friend. I know everything about you."

I feel a sudden jolt of panic and force myself to remain calm. He must be bluffing, I think. If Drake or anyone else tried to read my thoughts, I'd become aware and block them.

"Are you a level four?" I ask.

"My God, son, you even speak like them," he laughs. "No wonder why Elimination didn't kill you and let you join them instead."

"I was forced to join Elimination," I answer. "I was saving my own life as well as the lives of several other innocents being held in that same facility."

"Rule number one, Rex, don't lie to a telepath. I know you joined them simply because you wanted to. Don't feign innocence. You've come here to destroy everything I've created. Additionally, you've come to steal Kitty from us."

Looks like Drake is really reading my thoughts. I don't have to pretend then.

"I don't care what you and your breakers are doing here," I say. "It's none of my business. Just let me and Kitty leave. I swear you won't see me again."

"Kitty won't be leaving," Drake says. "You've lost her. She's one of us now and you'll just have to get over it. You and Kitty aren't a good fit any longer. She needs somebody stronger and more mature."

I look at Drake with disgust. I'll kill him if he touches Kitty.

Drake smiles, saying "Don't worry so much. For the moment, I'm interested in her only as a fighter, a powerful Retaliation breaker. She's very mature for her age, but still a little too young. Although, when she becomes a little older…"

"Shut your mouth!" I growl.

"Why does that bother you so much, Rex? It's a strange reaction considering your so-called brother and sister relationship."

"That doesn't matter now. Neither Kitty nor I have any business with your terrorist organization."

"Why do you think we're a terrorist group?" Drake asks. "After all you've been through, do you really believe all you see on the news? Don't you know how Elimination can distort the truth? I'm disappointed you haven't already learned from your own experiences," he sighs. "Well, we haven't done what you think. Our mission is to help breakers regain their freedom. We are not in the habit of killing innocent people who don't deserve being killed."

I don't believe a word. I say, "That sounds like a noble enough cause, but I'm not okay with risking Kitty's life to fulfill it."

"She's a top notch soldier. Not just some child you have to protect," Drake says. "Kitty will make up her own mind. If you still want to be with Kitty, you need to join us."

"Really?" I grin. "Why do you need a traitor like me among your crack team of breakers?"

"Listen son, I'm not blaming you for joining Elimination. And I don't refer to you as a traitor. We all make mistakes. I'm a very forgiving person. I'd like to see a strong breaker like you join my team of warriors."

I get the strange sensation that I'm talking to another Browning. One sends terrorists to kill ordinary people and another sends Elimination troops to kill innocent breakers. They're very similar.

"If you can read my thoughts, you should already know I'm not interested in becoming a terrorist," I say.

"I'll give you some time to think, Rex," Drake answers. "But let me give you a bit of advice. Don't play games with somebody who can read your thoughts. Do not try to outsmart me. Join us or be killed. It really is that simple, and is the only choice you have to make."

"Thanks, Drake," I say. "I'll definitely take that under consideration."

He sighs, "I must admit though, I liked you better dead. Why couldn't you have remained dead, Rex?"

Drake gestures with his hand, signaling me to leave. I walk out of the room, thinking. If Drake isn't willing to let us leave here alive, I'll have to kill him.

Kitty is waiting for me outside.

"Did he offer to let you join us?" she asks, obviously thrilled.

"He sure did."

"And?"

"Not interested, sorry. I'll have nothing to do with terrorism, Kitty."

Kitty rolls her eyes, groaning, "Oh my! Why do you have to be that way?"

"What way, Kitty?"

"Stubborn and incredibly boring," she answers.

"It's better to be boring and alive than choose terrorism and one day find sticks of dynamite taped to my chest at the local mall," I answer, though it doesn't sound convincing.

Kitty laughs, "I know, staying incognito, unnoticeable and under the radar is the best means for a breaker to survive. That's what you always told me. Well, being incognito didn't work out so well, did it? Everybody knows we're breakers. And guess what? I couldn't be happier! No more hiding in the dark, dreading the day Elimination comes knocking. No more living like cowards. I love my new life."

"Kitty, are you serious?" I ask. "Is this what you call a new life? Attacking schools, hospitals and police stations and randomly killing people? Risk getting shot all the time? That's not what I wish for you and…"

"C'mon, Rex," Kitty interrupts, smiling. "Just relax. Everything is all right now. We're both alive and safe. You don't have to worry about me. I've already told you, I can take care of myself and can even protect you as well if needed. I really mean that." She takes my hand and steps closer, looking sadly into my eyes. "I was so heartbroken after you'd left," she says, changing the subject. "I thought I'd never see you. Please, never do that to me again."

"I won't," I promise without doubts. Kitty and I belong together no matter what. Even being very brave and tough, she's still a child and doesn't fully realize the consequences of what she's doing. She still needs guidance.

She pulls me forward, "Come with me, Rex. Time for a little excursion."

I quickly agree, as learning this place better may come in handy. I follow Kitty. We walk inside an enormous mansion with multiple staircases and corridors. It's old and poorly kept, but still very livable. It was likely built right after the Eruption. Some wealthy people probably resided here many years ago and had to leave it due to the economic collapse. Now, it's used for the terrorist's headquarters. Many strangers dressed in camo pass by, carrying guns and rifles. I'm tense, but nobody pays much attention to us. A few tough looking guys nod to Kitty and she gives a friendly wave of her hand.

"Fellow soldiers," she comments. "We went on missions together."

Some young women with kids dressed in civilian clothing mull about. They all have the same fearful expressions.

"We've rescued most of them," Kitty explains. "We're the last resort for many breakers. They have nowhere else to go. They've all been hunted and captured, some even sentenced to death. Most guys and even a few of the girls joined our missions. Those who can't or don't want to fight just take care about the house, cook food and do other odd jobs around the place."

"Who pays for all this?" I ask, mentally calculating how much money you'd need to feed, clothe and arm this number of people.

"I don't know," Kitty answers. "I've never thought about it."

They couldn't steal so much money, could they? I don't remember any recent reports about bank robberies. They must have a sponsor then. I wonder who might be behind everything.

We walk outside and bright sunlight makes me squint. I see palm trees, white sand and hear the sound of the ocean. It's warm and humid.

"Isn't it beautiful?" Kitty asks. "It's like heaven here for breakers. We don't have to hide or live in fear in this place. Here, we all have freedom to be who we were meant to be. And the weather is really great all year round here!"

Of course she would think this is paradise. Kitty has always dreamt about palm trees and white sand beaches.

"Where are we?" I ask.

"Not sure. Drake never told us. It's an island. But don't worry, Elimination will never find us here."

That's not what I'm worried about. I'm afraid Elimination won't be able to locate us. My last hope is Lena using her telepathic abilities. If she can't locate me, I'm stuck here. I see no way to escape from this island at the moment. I'd have to steal a boat or a helicopter. How can I fight through so many breakers alone?

"How did you find them?" I ask.

"I saw them in my dreams."

"Are you a telepath?"

Kitty shrugs her shoulders, "I don't know. Sometimes I see things, sometimes I don't. I didn't know you were alive. But I kept seeing dreams about you. How Elimination tortured and beat you. I thought they were just dreams."

I believed telepaths were a rare breed. Was Holtzmann correct in saying that breakers are quickly evolving and soon even stronger breakers will develop?

We walk along the shoreline, watching the ocean. It's still and peaceful. Kitty holds my hand, talking about the time when she thought I was dead.

"I was crying for hours and didn't want to go on living," she says. "But then I decided I needed to live for you, because you wanted me to live. I promised myself to make them all regret that they had killed you. Vengeance was the only thing that kept me going."

Great. My faked execution pushed Kitty into the terrorist hands and activities. I'm the reason she's among these criminals.

I see a few meager houses along the shore in the distance.

"They've built them recently for newcomers," Kitty says. "The old mansion doesn't have enough room for all that come. We have to continually build new homes."

Even more money, I think. These terrorists must have a really strong financial support system.

"How many breakers are here?" I ask.

"Don't know the exact number," Kitty says. "More than a hundred, I'd guess."

I suddenly think of all those women and kids I saw back in the mansion. They can't be criminals. They were probably falsely accused just because they are breakers, as I have been. If I direct Elimination here, they'll all be targeted. How can I stop acts of terrorism without putting innocent breakers in harm's way?

"Tell me about Drake," I request. "Where did he come from?"

"Nobody knows," Kitty answers. "I only heard that Elimination was torturing him with bad intentions. He wants to save other breakers from going through all that. When I first arrived here, I told Drake about you and how Elimination had you killed. I don't know much more about Drake, but I could try and ask Hammer if you like. They've been friends for a long time. I doubt Hammer will tell us much though. He despises me."

"Why?"

"He's envious. Before I came, Hammer had been the best soldier here. Now, I'm the best and Hammer hates second place. Actually, I suspect he is envious of Drake as well. Hammer wants to be the leader."

"What's the exact nature of your relationship with Drake, Kitty?" I ask carefully.

Her eyes widen and she giggles. "Are we jealous? I don't believe it!"

"Kitty, just answer my question," I say, raising my voice.

"Whoa! Calm down, Rex. There's nothing between me and Drake. I'm his soldier and he's my commander. That's all."

I look at her suspiciously.

"I can't believe you're so obviously jealous," Kitty repeats, laughing cheerfully.

We walk further along the beach and then Kitty stops, staring out at the horizon. The sky is turning yellow and purple as the sun goes down.

"It's wonderful here," Kitty smiles, taking a deep breath. "And I'm here with you. I still can't believe you're alive. It's like a miracle, isn't it?"

She turns to me, studying my face with a hint of sadness in her expressive big eyes.

"Are you happy to be here with me, Rex?" Kitty asks quietly. "Did you miss me being apart? Did you ever think of me?"

I don't understand why Kitty has doubts. How can she even ask such questions? I want to tell Kitty that I thought of her every single day and night. I was going crazy not knowing if she was alive or dead. I spent hours trying to reach her in my mind. And of course, I missed her terribly. How could it be different?

I remain silent. Something's not letting me express myself. I've always had difficulties finding the right words.

Kitty continues waiting, piercing me with a pleading look. I have to answer.

"Of course I missed you and I worried about you constantly," I say. It seems more than enough to satisfy Kitty. She lets out a sob of relief and wraps her arms around my neck.

"I love you so much," she whispers.

The next moment Kitty presses her lips to mine. I expect an innocent kiss, nothing serious, but her mouth opens. I suddenly realize that Kitty expects something more. She has caught me by surprise. I haven't seen it coming. I push her away and step back.

"What are you doing Kitty?!" I exclaim.

Kitty blinks a couple of times, momentarily confused, then smiles confidently. Her cheeks flush.

"Don't pretend like you don't know," Kitty says quietly, as she reaches for me again. I stop her short.

"What am I supposed to know?" I ask.

She doesn't have to answer. I've known everything for a long time. I just didn't want to admit it to myself. I only wanted Kitty to remain my little sister. I'm not ready for her to grow up.

"I love you, Rex," Kitty answers. "You're the only one I want and need in my life. I fell in love with you from the first moment we met."

"The first time we met you tried to rob me, Kitty."

"Why are you being so mean, Rex?" her voice trembles. "We belong together, always have. Why are you rejecting me now?"

Kitty's eyes sparkle. I realize she's about to cry. I keep silent for a few moments, sorting out my thoughts. I don't know how to behave. Just stay calm, I tell myself.

"Kitty, we've gone through a lot recently," I say. "You're just a little overemotional right now. It's okay. I'm not angry with you. Let's just forget about all this. Like nothing happened."

My words seem wrong and somehow fake even to me. It's unlikely we can forget what's just happened.

"What?" Kitty exclaims. "How can I forget? I've been dreaming about today. I've wanted to kiss you for months, but was scared of being rejected and changing our relationship…"

"Stop it, Kitty."

"No! I won't stop," she cries. "Am I not beautiful enough? Am I too skinny or short for you? I can get fatter if you want."

"Darn it, Kitty!" I almost yell. "You're fine just as you are. And I do love you as my friend and sister, and always will. Isn't that enough for you?"

"No! It's not enough, I'm not your freaking sister and never have been!" Kitty shouts. "Why don't you want me?"

"Kitty, you're fifteen," I answer. "You're still a child."

"I've never even had a childhood, Rex. You don't know what I went through before we met. Trust me, you don't wanna know. I'm not a stupid innocent child. And even if I were it wouldn't change how I feel. I'd love you anyway." She narrows her eyes in suspicion. "Is it because of her?"

"Because of who?"

"That nasty woman with dark hair and the ugly glasses. I saw you and her together in my dreams."

She's talking about Rebecca, I understand.

"She has nothing to do with it," I explain.

"Is she better than me somehow? Do you love her?" Kitty asks angrily.

"Kitty! Just stop it," I say. "You're talking nonsense. And we don't really have time for all this drama. We need to find a way to escape from here."

Kitty listens quietly as tears roll down her face. I know she's hurting.

"I came here for you, Kitty," I tell her. "I agreed to work for Elimination and locate the terrorists. They will spare your life in return. We have to figure out how to contact Elimination."

"Hammer was right unfortunately," Kitty says slowly. "You are a traitor." She steps back from me as if afraid. "I'm not going anywhere, Rex. This is my home."

"They're terrorists, Kitty," I say.

"You are not the guy I thought you were," she says, covering her face. "You were just using me all those years. My goodness! How could I have been so stupid?"

"Where's this coming from?"

"You never really cared about me! You just didn't want to be alone. So you just used me for some kind of pet, you selfish jerk! You never considered the possibility that I may actually feel something for you!"

"Kitty," I say, reaching for her. Kitty slaps my hand away, stepping back.

"Don't freaking touch me!" she yells. "You're a traitor! And you don't give a damn about me! I hate you and wish you were dead!"

Kitty turns and runs off. I remain standing at the edge of water. I won't follow her now. We both need time to recover our senses.

I sit down on the sand, thinking. Does she really hate me now? I don't know. She's so different. Things have grown wrong between us and gotten too complicated.

I hear hands clapping behind my back. I turn to look. Drake is walking toward me, laughing.

CHAPTER 23

"Well done, hero," Drake says, approaching. "I can't believe you've missed an opportunity to have some fun with that little hottie. A very poor decision I think."

I realize Drake is trying to make me angry, but I don't react.

"I hope now you can finally accept the fact that Kitty can never be yours," Drake continues, "unless you choose to join us. So, what's it gonna be?"

"If you could truly read my mind, you would know my answer," I say.

"Is that a no?" he sighs. "Such a waste. I don't understand your continued resentment toward our group here. We're helping breakers."

"By burning innocent children," I counter.

"Not true. I'd never order anything along those lines. I don't know what kind of lies Elimination may have fed you, but I'm really surprised you've fallen for them so easily after everything they've put you through."

Drake walks to the edge of water and stares out at the horizon. I wonder why he denies being responsible for the acts of terror committed at the school and hospital. Is he in denial? Or could be he telling the truth? I don't know what to believe. I only know I don't trust Drake and I hate the way he talks about Kitty.

"I don't blame you for joining Elimination," he says. "Everybody has to pick a side in this war to survive. You didn't have much of a choice. Now there's a very narrow window in which you do. The humans who didn't develop breaker abilities will not be the ones who win this war. Their time has passed. It's our time now. Joining us is the only good option you have."

"I don't believe you are concerned for my well-being," I say. "Why do you really want me to join this group?"

"You're a very strong breaker," he explains. "We need as many strong breakers fighting for our cause as we can get. Besides, every breaker in the country knows your face. You'd be great for propaganda purposes, telling your story and inspiring our troops for war."

"Being the inspiration for war is not something I really want to be remembered for," I say.

"This is a unique opportunity," he says. "We're carving our future from right here on this island. Very soon I'll have enough volunteers to build an army. Can you imagine the power of thousands of breakers fighting together as a single unit? Ordinary humans won't stand a chance against us. We'll destroy the old world and build a new one. A country controlled by breakers, where lesser humans are slaves. If you choose to come in at the grassroots of this struggle, you'll have an opportunity to become one of the leaders of the future. You'll have an abundance of power and wealth."

"As tempting as that sounds, I'm afraid you've got the wrong guy," I answer. "I don't believe in slavery, and I have no desire to be anybody's leader."

"Nonsense. Everybody wants power and wealth," Drake smiles. "We should feel very fortunate, having before us a chance to create something truly great. A chance to grab as much power as we have courage to take. I've had my fill with hiding out and being on the run. There was a time when I hated being a breaker, so I understand all these doubts you're having. We've been conditioned to be obedient and ashamed with being the freaks of society. But we're not freaks at all, but a vastly superior race. Now we can all be really proud of being breakers. I owe a debt of gratitude to Elimination for hunting and killing us, making this war necessary. Where would I be without them? Working regular hours, living an average boring life? Who really needs it? Elimination helped me to become the leader I am. They've empowered myself as well as others in forcing us fight for our very existence."

"The cost of such a war would be too high," I say. "You don't seem to care about all the breakers you'll be sending to their deaths. Are they just a means to an end, acceptable losses for the gain of power?"

"Power is everything," Drake answers calmly. "This is why wars have been fought in the past and will be fought in the future. Do you believe that our current government really hates breakers? Or even Elimination for that matter? They're just trying to hold onto their positions of power. The real problem is that the weak control the strong, but that's about to change."

"I see."

"I'm glad you understand now. What's your decision, Rex?"

I hesitate for a moment. I'm not going to join these terrorists, but I really need to win some time.

"I need more time to think," I say. "You may be right in saying that joining the group here is my best option. I haven't decided yet."

"You're a bad liar, Rex," Drake says. "I'm truly disappointed. You'd be a nice addition to my force." He looks into my eyes and says, "You realize this was the only way for you to be with Kitty. Upon rejection of my offer you're losing her forever."

Drake leaves. I remain sitting on the sand. I'm not sure what to do next. Closing my eyes, I concentrate, thinking of Lena. Where are you, I call. Nothing. No visions. No sense of her presence. She can't locate me.

It's getting dark. I get up and head back toward the mansion to look for Kitty. I need to find her and persuade her to leave with me. It won't be easy. She's always been so stubborn.

I need to be thinking of an escape, but can't stop thinking of what happened between us earlier. This is all my fault, I decide. I should have never let Kitty become so emotionally attached to me. I should have been more strict with her. But how could I? She was my only friend and family. She needed care, being so little and vulnerable. All those years I saw only a child in Kitty and didn't notice her growing up so suddenly. Of course she developed a crush on me. Who else could Kitty choose? She always held ordinary people in contempt and I was the only breaker she knew. She wanted to fall in love. I was the only guy around whom she could trust.

I sigh. Maybe it's not as serious as it seems and Kitty will change her mind about hating me. But somehow I know our relationship will never be the same anymore. She won't forgive my rejection easily. This is awful. It seems like I've lost the only true friend I've ever had.

Approaching the mansion, somebody yells from behind, "Hey, traitor! Where're you going?"

I look back. Hammer and several breakers are walking toward me.

"It's none of your business," I answer, proceeding toward the entrance. Hammer jumps in front, blocking my way.

"We don't allow Elimination dogs in here," he says, smiling.

I stop, looking at him. My muscles tense, readying for the coming fight. Hammer grins, waiting. His breakers form a circle around me. They remind me of Bulldog and his gang.

"About time for you to become dead for real, hero," Hammer says, charging into me. I step to the side, throwing a punch to his ribs as he goes by. Somebody knocks me in the head hard from behind. I sway, losing balance. They attack me like a pack of wild dogs, tackling me to the ground. I cover as best I can, rolling onto my stomach. Somebody puts his boot onto the back of my head, pressing my face into the sand.

"Get what you deserve, traitor!" Hammer growls.

"Hammer! Stop it!" I hear a loud command. A furious Kitty runs toward us. The breakers halt my beating for the moment. Snarling in anger, Kitty jumps on Hammer's back, scratching at his face and shoving him away. "Leave him alone, you moron!" she shouts.

Hammer's surprise quickly wears off and he slaps Kitty. It's enough to knock her down. Almost instantly, she scrambles back to her feet and attacks him again, kicking and clawing. Hammer easily avoids the attack this time, securing her arms behind her back.

"Don't touch her!" I yell.

An enraged Kitty is still trying to bite and scratch. It doesn't help.

"You vicious little rat," Hammer says. "Know what? I might just get rid of you too."

He snatches Kitty up and carries her off somewhere. She's calling for Drake, kicking the air and beating Hammer with her fists. It doesn't have much effect on him.

Multiple hands jerk me up to my feet. A gun is pressed to my head.

"Walk," a breaker commands. "And don't think of trying anything stupid. The last thing you'll see will be your brains being blown out the front of your head."

We follow Hammer and Kitty down the beach. I walk, trying to overcome the pain from the beating I've just taken. My head hurts. I spit blood. I need to do something or they'll kill us both. Concentrating, I project my thoughts toward my attackers. It doesn't work. I'm too weak at the moment. The ground seems to sway under my feet. I'm nauseated and exhausted from the struggle.

We approach an old water well, made of huge stones. I doubt anybody uses it now.

"Let me go!" Kitty screams. "I'll freaking kill you, Hammer!"

Hammer brings her to the edge of the well. He turns his face to me and smiles.

I know what he's about to do. My mouth gets dry.

"No!" I shout. "Don't!"

Hammer throws Kitty down the well. She screams desperately, disappearing in the dark. I hear water splash and then nothing. Kitty doesn't scream anymore.

"Kitty!" I call. No answer.

I stare into the well in shock. I can't move, being temporarily paralyzed.

"What are you waiting for?" Hammer asks. "Jump."

I approach the well and look down. Everything is pitch black. I don't hesitate or think how dangerous it is. I just step up to the edge and jump, dropping into the darkness. A momentarily sensation of weightlessness makes me gasp. My body hits the water hard. It's icy cold and takes my breath away. My momentum slams me down through the water until I collide into the well bottom. Pain shoots through my body and for a few seconds I'm completely disoriented. Shivering and coughing I'm able to stand up on my feet. The water level in the well is up to my shoulders.

"Kitty," I call, searching for her with my arms.

"Have fun down there, traitor," Hammer yells from above. I look up and see him and his breakers closing a solid cover over the well. Darkness.

My hand bumps into something under the surface. I grab her and pull closer toward me. Kitty! Her body is slack and I can't tell if she's breathing or not. I can't perform resuscitation because there's no hard surface to put her on. Only slippery stone walls and water. I realize Kitty may be already dead. Panicking, I yell her name, shake her and slap her face, keeping Kitty's head above the water.

"Wake up!" I shout. "Please, wake up Kitty!"

Kitty gasps, coughing.

"Is that you, Rex?" I hear her trembling voice. "I can't see anything."

"It's me, sweetie," I say softly. My teeth are chattering from the cold. I feel Kitty's body shivering.

"Are we in the well?" she asks. "Rex, what do we do now?"

"I don't know," I answer truthfully.

We look for a way out, examining the walls with our hands. They're slick and impossible to climb.

"Help! Somebody help!" Kitty yells desperately. Nobody comes to rescue us. They either can't hear or just don't care. Nevertheless, Kitty continues calling for help and I attempt to climb the wall. Useless. I can't get a hold.

We stand in the near freezing water, holding each other and shivering. I try to warm Kitty, but I'm very cold myself. I hear her weak ragged breath. We have to get out of here or we'll both wind up with hypothermia. How on earth is the water so cold on a tropical island? It must be coming from a deep underground source, I decide.

"Rex, I'm so sorry," Kitty cries. "It's all my fault. I should have listened to you."

"It's okay," I mumble. I can hardly move my freezing lips.

"I didn't mean what I said to you earlier. Please, forgive me. I can't hate you. You're all I have. You're my whole world."

"Please don't cry Kitty."

She coughs. Her body shudders and sinks down. I hold her, not letting her head go beneath the surface of the water. Kitty feebly grabs my neck. Her feet don't touch bottom. If I lose consciousness and let go, she'll drown.

"I can't feel my fingers," she complains. "Rex, are we gonna die?"

Looks like it, I think. I see no way out. I say, "Of course not. We'll get out of here somehow, Kitty."

"Drake is a telepath," she says. "We need to contact him. He can save us."

"Kitty, I think Drake already knows everything," I answer. "He doesn't want me to live. I believe he directed Hammer to do this."

Minutes pass. Kitty stops talking and trembling. Her body relaxes and I feel her head dropping down.

"Don't fall asleep," I say, shaking her. "Stay awake, Kitty."

She moans, but doesn't answer. I can't see her face in the darkness, but understand she's unconscious. I'm sleepy myself. The water doesn't seem so cold anymore. I'm numb and losing track of time. How long have we been here? Maybe an hour, maybe a few hours. It's quiet and somehow peaceful. Like a grave, I think.

I will my eyes to stay open. If I fall asleep, we'll both die. I don't really care about myself so much. But I can't stand the thought of my Kitty dying. It'd be my fault. If I hadn't come here, Hammer wouldn't have thrown Kitty into this well. If I hadn't revealed my breaker abilities at the bank, we'd still be safe in our apartment.

"I'm so sorry," I say, holding Kitty tighter and listening to her shallow breathing.

I think of Lena. Find me, I repeat in my mind. Save us. We need your help now.

I don't know if it will work or not.

A few times I close my eyes and float between dream and reality. Every time it gets harder to come back. It seems like we've been here forever, surrounded by water and darkness. Nothing changes. Nobody comes to save us. I continue calling for Lena in my thoughts. You promised to find me, I repeat. Please, find us soon.

I'm weakening. Soon I'll be unable to resist the urge to sleep. Part of me knows I need to remain awake. Another part just wants to rest. Frightened, I snap back awake having nodded off momentarily again. I can't last much longer.

The rattling sound of an explosion makes me flinch and look up. The walls of the well are trembling. What the hell was it? An airstrike? My heart is racing. It must be Elimination. Who else could it be? They've found us!

I shake Kitty. "Wake up, wake up." She doesn't move. I put my ear to her mouth. Kitty is still breathing.

I hear gunfire and voices in the distance.

"We're in here!" I want to shout, but can't. I've lost my voice. "Help!" I keep trying.

Suddenly I'm afraid they won't be able to find us in the water well. Or it will take them too long and Kitty will die.

I focus on projecting my thoughts toward Lena. In the well, lead them to the well.

I hear muffled cries, explosions and gunfire. I think of all those breaker kids I saw earlier. Elimination could kill them. But even this thought doesn't bother me much right now. All I want is to escape this well and save Kitty. Nothing else matters.

Somebody removes the cover from the well and daylight floods in. I look up and see a flawlessly blue sky far above. It's morning. We've spent the entire night in this well.

"Rex?" somebody yells.

"In here," I try to answer. All I can make is a wheeze.

A rope drops down. Somebody is descending into the well. I recognize Chase as he climbs down.

"Holy cow that's cold!" he exclaims. "What the hell you doing down here?"

I push Kitty closer to him.

"Take her first," I plead.

Chase doesn't argue. He grabs Kitty tightly with one arm and yells, "Pull us up!" Then I watch him take an unconscious Kitty up. She'll be all right, I think with relief. Kitty is safe now. I don't have to keep her head above the water anymore and I don't have to fight my fatigue. I relax, leaning my back against the wall and resting. My heavy eyelids close. I don't feel cold. I'm not even trembling. Slowly, my body slides down the slick stones. I don't have to resist any longer because Kitty isn't in danger.

Somebody grabs my shoulders and pulls my body up. I awaken, choking and spitting. Was I under the water?

"Breathe, Rex!" Chase commands, slapping my face. "Can you hear me?"

I look at him, but don't really understand why he is so worried. My brain is working too slowly.

"Hold on," he says, gripping the rope with both hands. I put my arms around his shoulders. It's not easy. I can barely move and can't feel my hands.

"Bring us up!" Chase commands as somebody begins dragging the rope up. We're ascending slowly. I stare at the perfectly blue sky and get a bizarre feeling that I'm coming straight into heaven.

I see Jimmy, Lena and Frank standing nearby the water well. Several Elimination officers assist. They're still wired after the fight with the terrorists. One officer smiles and slaps my back.

"Nice job, dude," he says. "We got all of them."

"Man, we thought these terrorists had killed you," another officer laughs.

I stare at them in confusion. Are they making fun of me or what? Suddenly I realize they're not being mean. The officers are treating me like a human being for the first time instead of like some kind of freak. I smile and say, "As you guys already know, I'm not so easy to kill."

"Yeah, we know," the officers laugh. Somebody puts a blanket over my shoulders.

Dressed out in an Elimination uniform, Lena walks toward me and says, "I couldn't locate you for the longest time. But then I heard you calling and I told them where you were."

"Thank you, Lena," I answer. "You've saved us."

We shake hands.

Chase helps me up and leads us to one of the aircraft on the large sandy beach. Frank carries the still unconscious Kitty. I shake from the cold again although it's warm outside.

I look around and see multiple Elimination officers escorting handcuffed breakers away. Some prisoners are wounded and bleeding. Wheeler is standing near several motionless bodies spread out across the sand. He holds his handgun, grinning. Jessie joins us and I notice her limping. Her dull face is spattered with blood. Not her blood, I guess.

"You've missed the fun part," Chase tells me. "These freaks were fighting like hell and even tried to hypnotize us. Thank God we had your breakers on our side. They really helped a lot."

I want to ask him what happened to those breaker kids I saw earlier, but can't speak a word. My entire body is trembling and my tongue doesn't want to move. Symptoms of hypothermia.

Victor is sitting on the sand near the aircraft, smoking a cigarette and complaining. He presses a hand on his bleeding arm, saying, "These freaking pigs shot me! I've had enough. I'm quitting. Won't be doing this stupid job again!" Nobody is paying any attention.

Drake and Hammer pass slowly by, led by Elimination officers. Drake shoots me a hateful glare, saying, "I'll kill you for this, traitor."

Hammer keeps silent and just stares ahead. I notice blocking collars on both of them.

"Don't worry about them," Chase says, helping me climb up inside the aircraft. Kitty is lying on the floor, rolled up in a blanket. I kneel down beside her and listen to her breathing. It's very weak, but steady. "Hold on," I whisper, "you'll get medical help soon."

I sprawl out across the floor beside Kitty, overcome by fatigue. No more fighting. No freezing water.

I hear gunfire and glance through the open hatch. Wheeler is busy outside shooting prisoners. Chase and others out there are trying unsuccessfully to stop him.

CHAPTER 24

I awaken on a hospital bed. A thin needle is inserted in my arm and a long plastic tube runs to an IV bag attached to a metal pole. My body is sore and I'm struggling to breathe anything more than a shallow breath. Kitty is sleeping peacefully beside me on top of the blanket. She's alive and safe. She's with me again. I couldn't ask for more.

Kitty's face seems a little pale, but her breathing is normal. I watch her, enjoying her closeness and warmth. Then I run my fingers through her curly red hair. Kitty awakens with a smile, looking at me.

I suddenly feel awkward, remembering everything that's happened between us. A few weeks ago I wouldn't bother worrying if Kitty slept on my bed. It wasn't a big deal.

"How did you get here?" I ask softly.

"I woke up and went looking for you," Kitty says. "My room is the next to yours. I don't wanna be left in there alone." She reaches for me and wraps her arms around my neck. "We survived the freezing well! You saved me, Rex."

"Kitty, you're choking me," I laugh. "Now go sit in the chair."

Kitty glances at the chair with surprise. "What's wrong?" she asks. "You don't want me here?"

"Of course I want you here. Only perhaps you shouldn't sleep on my bed."

"Why? We've slept together before."

"You're more grown up now, Kitty."

Her face flushes red and Kitty jumps off the bed. "You're weird," she mumbles, plopping into the chair. "Just know I won't be staying in a separate room. We've already spent enough time apart."

I don't know how to answer that. There's some unspoken tension between us. We both remember how she tried to kiss me, but we both pretend not to remember. Right now I'm too tired to sort everything out.

The door opens and in enters a grinning Holtzmann.

"You've saved many lives, Rex," he says and begins a lecture on the importance of preventing an apocalypse. I'm not really listening, but thinking of the innocent kids and breakers who were captured along with the terrorists. I can't shake the image of Wheeler shooting those captives.

"What will happen to the prisoners?" I ask, interrupting Holtzmann.

He mumbles something.

"Elimination is gonna kill them, right?" I ask. "It won't matter whether they're terrorists or just falsely accused breakers."

"I'll see what I can do to help them," Holtzmann answers. But I know he can't really help this time. His power is limited. In a best case scenario Holtzmann would commandeer some prisoners for lab rats.

"I don't trust him," Kitty whispers, after Holtzmann leaves.

"He's all right," I say. "He's just a little bit off."

Kitty gives me a hard look and asks, "What now? How are we going to escape this place?"

I don't have an escape plan yet.

"Let's play it by ear until I can figure something out," I answer.

Browning visits next. He spends a good ten minutes explaining what a valuable asset I've become and how Elimination appreciates my service. Listening to him is making me sick. There's something slimy and untrustworthy about Browning. The way he looks at you and grins always gives the impression that Browning knows something that you don't.

"I guess this little gal is the real reason you're working for us," Browning says, glancing over at Kitty. "As long as she behaves herself, she may become a member of your team. We need strong and cooperative breakers in case there's any further trouble."

"I'm not cooperative," Kitty growls. "And I won't work for you."

"Rex, please explain to this little lady everything she needs to know about her situation," Browning commands as he's leaving.

"They'll torture or possibly even kill you for resisting," I say. "You have to at least pretend to be cooperative. It won't be for too long, we'll figure something out."

Kitty groans. "Why couldn't you just join us?" she asks. "We'd be safe and…"

"And we'd either become terrorists or else be stuck at the bottom of that well," I interrupt her. "That's not what I want for us, Kitty."

"I don't think you really know what you want," she sighs, turning away.

I don't have time to answer because the door opens again and Rebecca comes in. She smiles widely and runs to me, spreading her arms, but at the last moment she stops and holds out a hand.

"Welcome back," she says shyly.

"Come on," I smile and give Rebecca a hug. Kitty makes a choking noise.

"Everybody thought you were dead when we lost our connection," Rebecca says. "But I believed you'd come back just as you promised." She turns to Kitty, "Hello, you must be the little girl Rex wanted to save." Rebecca extends her hand. "Nice to meet you, I'm Rebecca."

"I know who you are," Kitty growls, pushing Rebecca's hand away.

"Kitty!" I say strictly. "Be polite, Rebecca's my friend."

"She's your friend, not mine," Kitty answers. "And I don't like her. She's an Elimination pig."

Kitty jumps from the chair and runs out of the room. The door slams behind her. Rebecca shivers, looking embarrassed.

"Don't worry," I say. "Kitty is just being a selfish child who craves all the attention."

"She's jealous," Rebecca understands. "How old is she?"

"Only fifteen," I answer. "Still believes in Santa Claus." I laugh, trying to clear the air.

"I don't think so," Rebecca says. "What are you going to do now, Rex?"

I shrug.

"I know you are planning to escape," Rebecca sighs. "You hate Elimination, don't you? I want you to know I'll truly miss you should you leave."

I keep silent.

"Back in school the other kids always thought I was strange," Rebecca continues. "I didn't have many close friends. After losing my parents, I stopped going to school at all. I had tutors, but nobody to make friends with. Holtzmann is not a real friend…just a relative needing my care. And if I should die, he wouldn't even notice."

"Of course, he would."

"Holtzmann cares only about his science," Rebecca says. "Maybe you could stay?" she suggests. "Maybe you could be happy here working for Elimination?"

"Rebecca, I'm a convict here, and the task given me has been completed. I have nothing to do with Elimination now."

"You don't have to decide anything today. Just think about it."

She leaves. Nothing to think about. I don't want to spend the rest of my life inside a prison.

For a few days I remain in the prison infirmary, still being feverish and coughing my head off. After experiencing severe hypothermia, I'm on the verge of contracting pneumonia. My lungs make an odd wheezing noise when I breathe. A doctor comes by every day to administer antibiotics. Fortunately, Kitty doesn't have the same problems. She's absolutely well and spends all her time in my room. Every evening I send Kitty back to her room, but in the morning I find her sleeping in my bed. I don't know what to do about it. Kitty behaves innocently enough, not bringing up the recent incident between us. I'm still a little uneasy around her. I've started noticing that Kitty always sits as close to me as possible, takes my hand, always leans against me. I realize I could be just overly paranoid, so I pretend unconcerned.

Jessie visits us several times. Kitty enjoys her visits, telling Jessie about her adventures and how I rescued her in the well.

"What now?" Jessie asks me.

"Now we need to escape."

"I can't," she answers. "They've still got my parents. I'm an Elimination puppet for now."

I understand. We'll have to take them with us. Also I've promised Lena we'll save her mother if she's still alive. And Jimmy. Too many people and too many promises. No idea how we're all going to make it.

Sometimes I think about what Rebecca said. What if I stay in Elimination? Would I be able to change things from inside? I doubt it. At the same time I've grown tired with never-ending fighting and always plotting for an escape. Part of me wants to give up and let Elimination do whatever they want. It'd be an easier way to survive, being their lab rat, a puppet as Jessie called it. Then I despise myself for even considering joining this group. Thoughts of Kitty living locked away in prison make me ill. If it weren't for her, I'd probably give up. She's the reason I have to find a way to regain our freedom.

Holtzmann wakes me up in the middle of the night.

"You need to watch the breaking news," he says in a trembling voice. I glance at him and realize something terrible has happened. Holtzmann looks like he's just seen a ghost, his left eye twitching and face being deathly pale.

"What's wrong, Holtzmann?" I ask.

"Another terrorist attack," he answers quietly.

Still dizzy from sleep, I repeat his words several times in my mind. They don't make any sense at first. We've captured the terrorists.

"That can't be right," I whisper, dressing quickly. "Who did it?"

"I don't know," Holtzmann says.

We wake my team and watch the news in Holtzmann's lab till morning. I'm still running a fever and my eyes are burning, but I can't turn away from the screen. An overexcited Lola in a gaudy pink dress is reporting on the new act of terror. This time a group of breakers attacked a shopping mall during evening hours. Using hypnosis, the terrorists caused the mall customers to fight each other, while they set the building on fire.

"I thought we'd caught them," Frank says.

"My group wasn't responsible for any acts of terror," Kitty answers defensively.

I watch the video, unable to speak. Not again, I think desperately. I've seen it too many times. I thought we'd stopped the terrorists for good. I believed I wouldn't have to watch the firefighters carrying out lifeless burnt bodies again. Lola reports that most of the victims have deceased, while the few survivors are in critical and still unstable condition. The cameraman catches a few vivid scenes: a woman screaming in pain, her face covered in blisters, the little disfigured corpse of a child, people sobbing in sorrow.

My throat clenches. I feel like I'm about to throw up. I don't understand anything. Was Drake telling the truth, saying his group wasn't responsible for acts of terror? It would mean I led Elimination to the wrong target, while the real terrorists were plotting another attack. My head aches.

I see a tall gray haired man on the screen, one of the Fathers. He is making a long monotone speech.

"We have to stop the breakers," he says. "We have to strike back. Our citizens can't be safe and live without fear as long as there are breakers among us."

Lola announces that tomorrow Elimination will begin checking all citizens for breaker abilities. They have a special head scanner that can identify whether you're a breaker or not within seconds.

That's exactly the scenario Holtzmann wanted to avoid.

"Oh, no," he sighs. "This will lead straight to war." He shakes his head and mumbles something, speaking to himself.

First thing in the morning Holtzmann and I march into Browning's office. He doesn't look surprised upon seeing us.

"You can't do this," I say. "You promised not to use scanners on the general population if we bring you the terrorists."

"I didn't promise anything of the sort," Browning answers calmly. "But even if I did, it's a promise I wouldn't have to keep. Terrorists have attacked again. It means you certainly didn't find them all."

"We will find them. Just give me and my team more time."

"We don't have any more time. Innocent people are dying and Elimination has to use more efficient methods to identify the threat."

"This is insanity, Browning!" Holtzmann exclaims. "You'll become the man who ordered the genocide of a population, thus starting the war between breakers and ordinary humans. You'll lead humanity to absolute extinction!"

"The war has already started," Browning answers. "Watch the news, it's the breakers who are the aggressors. We're trying to protect our homeland."

"Those terrorists don't represent all breakers," I say. "They're just a group of haters. You shouldn't make all breakers be responsible of what those idiots do."

"Quit wasting my time," Browning says. "This conversation is over."

Guards escort us out of the office.

I'm watching the news for the rest of the day. Elimination has started their project of total scanning. Everything has been organized surprisingly fast. Seems like they've done some preparing in advance. While my team and I were locating terrorists, Elimination was setting up stations to perform the scanning along with continuing the building of death camps. Browning has lied to me. He never intended to prevent the scanning.

I learn from the news that Elimination will be able to scan the majority of population within a few months. Today they've already scanned hundreds of citizens, having detected sixty breakers. Elimination won't stop until they've thrown every breaker into the death camps. Lola interviews the captives. Scared and in shock, they can hardly say anything.

I change the channel and watch a report about missing people. Hundreds of workers quit showing up at work in different cities. Many children have been held out of school. Elimination has already checked their homes without result. Officials suspect the missing citizens to be breakers, now assumed to be on the run.

Chase enters the lab and joins us watching news.

"You happy now?" I ask.

Chase sighs, saying, "No, and many of the officers don't like the idea. But we have to follow orders."

I suppress a strong desire to punch him in the face. I realize Chase is not the one responsible for everything that's happening, but can hardly overcome my anger toward him along with everybody connected to Elimination.

The next day Elimination captures fifty more breakers. They're all transported straight into the death camps. There's also news about the government increasing its budget for building additional concentration camps to hold all the breakers. They're turning the entire country into a slaughter house.

I hear noises coming from outside in the corridor. Sounds like somebody has stumbled and fallen hard, cussing. I walk out of my room and find Victor sitting on the floor, smoking. His eyes are unfocused and foggy. I detect a sharp scent of alcohol. I'm guessing he's on something else as well.

Swaying, Victor raises his head and says, "I don't deny being a bad person. But I'm not all that bad."

I don't understand what Victor means. He attempts to stand up, but falls back onto the floor. His movements are slow and unnatural.

"Why are you doing this to yourself?" I ask.

"Because Browning and Wheeler think that I'm a terrorist," Victor answers. "And I happen to have no inclination of becoming a terrorist."

He's completely drunk. I want to turn and leave, but something makes me ask, "What are you talking about, Victor?"

"Browning said he freaking trusted me and appreciated my work. He wants to give me a promotion. He's recruiting me for his team of terrorist breakers."

"What?"

"Yeah, I was a little surprised too. Unfortunately, I don't have much choice. They'll kill me if I refuse. They won't allow me to live, staying on the outside and knowing what I know."

I stand unmoving for a moment. I hope he's just drunk and talking nonsense. I never had a high opinion of Browning, but I don't want this to be true. I grab his shirt and half lead, half drag Victor toward the lab. He doesn't resist. I make Victor repeat everything to Holtzmann. The professor listens silently with a distant expression.

"Elimination created those terrorists," Victor tells. "I mean literally. They've sent Bulldog and his gang to perform the acts of terror. God only knows what Browning promised them. And now he wants me to join their little project of horrors. It's my promotion."

"Well, that explains a lot," Holtzmann says calmly. I can't understand how he can remain so indifferent.

"What are you talking about?" I ask. "Why would Browning do this?"

"Elimination had to receive special permission from the government to begin a total scanning of the population," Holtzmann explains. "Also they needed to increase their budget. These latest violent acts of terror are the method Elimination utilized to manipulate the government to get what they wanted."

"What about my team? Why did Browning create it?"

"To terminate a genuine threat to Elimination and replace that threat with their own terrorists, whom they hold on a short leash."

I shake my head. I don't believe it. Nobody would do this. It's too much even for such vicious killers like Browning and Wheeler. They wouldn't let breakers kill ordinary humans, would they? The images of the burnt bodies come to mind. I groan.

"We need proof," I say. "Victor is drunk and could be making it all up. Sorry, but I've never fully trusted you, Victor."

"I can't say I blame you," Victor comments. "But I'm afraid it's the truth."

Holtzmann opens Elimination's top secret files on his laptop, which contain videos from the latest acts of terror. The mall had security cameras, some of which survived the fire. We watch them several times. The terrorists all wear military type clothing with ski masks concealing their faces. It's impossible to identify them.

Suddenly, I notice a guy with only one eye. My heart skips a bit. I realize everything that Victor has said is true.

"That's one of them," I say. "He's in Bulldog's gang. I poked out his eye."

I get the sensation of the floor floating away from under my feet. Drake didn't lie. His group wasn't responsible for the terrorism. They helped captured breakers. And I destroyed them. I eliminated the last defense and hope that breakers had. This is exactly what Browning and Elimination wanted. I've helped those who torture and kill breakers.

"That's why the attacks were so different," I hear Holtzmann's voice. "There were two groups of attackers. One group was rescuing breakers while another was killing innocent people."

I exit the lab and head to my room. Once there I hit the wall several times, then just walk in circles. What a fool! I believed I could outsmart Elimination. I thought I was saving innocent people and fighting against terrorists. Instead, Elimination turned me against my own kind. All this time I've been playing Browning's game without suspecting anything.

Kitty comes to check on me. I tell her everything and she yells, "I've told you over and over my group wasn't the terrorists! You wouldn't listen. Now, they're all gonna die! You've killed them!"

I don't try to defend myself. Kitty is right.

I lie flat on my stomach in bed and press my face into a pillow. This all resembles a bad nightmare. A nightmare I'm stuck in and can't find a way out. Everything I do makes the situation worse.

Kitty approaches, touching my shoulder gently. "Rex," she says in a soft voice.

"Don't touch me, Kitty," I say. "Go back to your room."

Sighing, Kitty leaves. I remain in bed, thinking about everything that's happened. I hate Elimination. I hate myself for being an idiot. I can't accept the fact that I've given a death sentence to all those breakers. Hammer was right. I'm a traitor.

But why did I make this choice to join Elimination in the first place? I needed to protect my own life. I wanted to save Kitty. I did what I had to do.

Stop, I say to myself. There are always options. I always had freedom to make decisions. That's something even Elimination can't take away. And I've made wrong decisions. In believing that I'm resisting, I've never really resisted. I did everything Elimination wanted me to do.

That's enough. I'm not playing their games anymore. Time to do what I need to do. Time to fix all past mistakes as best I can. Kitty was right when she said I didn't know what I want. Now I know. I want to destroy this damnable prison. I want to kill Wheeler, Browning and their squad of terrorists. I want to free all breakers.

How can I go about doing this? I realize I can't accomplish it all by myself. I'll need help. Where can I find help when all the breakers from Retaliation have been captured?

Not all of them. They had good equipment, even a helicopter, so they have supporters somewhere. I need to contact them. They may be breakers too, possibly strong breakers.

I spend the entire night, projecting my thoughts toward someone who may not even exist.

Nothing. I don't know if anybody heard me or not.

In the morning Chase arrives, saying, "Some important people want to thank you for doing a great job. Let's go."

CHAPTER 25

"You're kidding," I say.

"I'm serious," Chase reassures. "Your contribution in terminating one of the terrorist groups is highly appreciated. The government has even sent a representative to thank you in person. Coming all the way from public enemy number one, you're becoming a quite valuable Elimination associate."

I study his face carefully. Does he know the truth about the real terrorists? Most likely not. Probably only Browning, Wheeler and a few Elimination leaders are completely aware of what's going on. At least that is what I want to believe.

Chase leads me toward Browning's office. I'm not handcuffed and Chase doesn't hold his rifle on me. We almost look like two Elimination soldiers, both wearing black. The only difference is that I'm not armed and have to wear a blocking collar around my neck.

A few officers come our way.

"Hey, breaker! You're making quite a career here, aren't you?" an officer asks, passing by.

I don't like it, but make myself grin and answer, "Sure! Maybe I'll even become your boss someday."

The officer appreciates my joke, laughing. All Elimination employees must know that I'm participating in Holtzmann's project. They don't seem to perceive me as a prisoner or some kind of monster anymore. It makes me feel even more like a traitor.

"Making new friends?" Chase asks.

"I'm a breaker and they're Elimination officers," I answer. "We can never be friends."

"If you say so," Chase agrees.

We enter Browning's office. The warden sits behind his desk, studying documents in a thick folder. A man wearing a suit and tie is sitting next to him, greeting us with an official smile. I recognize him instantly. He's the same man whom Holtzmann and I met in this office during Browning's meeting with Elimination executives. I'd seen him somewhere before, but couldn't remember his name or title. He must be the government representative.

"Nice to see you, Rex," he says, continuing to smile. "I'd like to discuss a few matters with you." He looks at Browning. "Alone please."

"Chase, leave us," Browning orders.

After the door closes behind Chase, the man stares at Browning and adds firmly, "I said alone."

Browning hesitates for a moment. Looks like he wants to protest, but doesn't have the guts. Sighing, he gets up and walks out of his own office.

"Take a seat, please," the man says in a most polite manner, motioning toward an empty chair.

I sit down, waiting. He studies me with cold eyes for a moment and says, "First of all, let me congratulate you on performing outstanding work. We're very impressed by your level of skills and eagerness to help others."

"Who are you?" I ask, interrupting.

"It doesn't matter," he answers. "For you, I'm only a messenger. You don't need to know my real name or exactly whom I represent. You're welcome to ask any questions you wish, although I unfortunately won't be able to answer some of your questions. I simply don't have the authorization to do so. You'll be provided with information as you need. Later, you may get an opportunity to learn even more. It will completely depend on your willingness to cooperate."

I'm listening carefully. Something is odd with this guy. He doesn't act like an Elimination executive or government official, being too mysterious. I don't really understand what this is all about.

"I'm working for some very powerful people," he continues. "They've heard your request for support. My singular mission is to let you know that they're willing to help."

"What?" I ask, not understanding.

"Last night you contacted one of us. You asked for our help. We're ready to support you."

"Wait a second," I say, thinking hard. "Are you a breaker?"

"As I've already stated, it's not important who I am."

"How can I trust you then? I know you must be working either for Elimination or the government. Why would they help me?"

His smile fades and he answers tiredly, "I'm not going to try to persuade you in trusting me. I don't have to prove anything. It's up to you what you choose to do next. I only hope you realize that you know very little about the real situation in the world. Everything you think you know and believe today may turn out to be false tomorrow. The people I work for are in power. Don't bother wasting time trying to figure out who we are. You won't be able to. They've been watching you for some time and have selected you for a special assignment in an upcoming mission. You may accept or reject it. They can always find somebody else."

"I wouldn't want to participate in a mission I don't know anything about," I say.

"What if I told you this mission could potentially save breakers from certain genocide?" he asks. "We know you've been wondering who provided the financial support for Drake and his breakers. Well, we did. We actually created Retaliation. Now, we need a leader for our breaker force in the coming war against ordinary humans. We would like to offer you this most important role."

He pauses, waiting for my reaction. I'm trying to sort things out in my mind. Who is he? Why does his group want to support breakers in the war if they are associated with Elimination? There must be breakers among them if they knew what I was projecting. It all makes no sense to me. I can't trust him.

"Why me?" I ask. "I helped destroy Retaliation. I'm probably the worst candidate you could possibly find. And anyway, Retaliation already has a leader in Drake."

"Don't worry about past mistakes you've made," he smiles. "Nobody is perfect. You're a very strong breaker and care genuinely about your kind. Every breaker in the country knows your face. You have the leadership qualities we need. They'll follow you. As for Drake…he's not exactly what we're looking for. He wants power and doesn't really care which side he's on. You know this. Things will be easier when Drake is removed."

"Drake is still alive," I say.

"You could just kill him and take his place," he suggests.

"I don't want to kill Drake," I protest. "I don't really want to kill anybody. All I wish for is to protect and save innocent breakers from Elimination. We don't need a war."

"You can't make an omelet without breaking eggs. If you want to be free, you'll have to fight for your freedom. It's time to decide what you really want and who you really are. If you really want to destroy this prison, then do so. Just let us know when we need to send the transport planes to pick you up."

I stare at him in disbelief. This situation seems unreal. Our government can't support breakers in a war against ordinary humans. It would only mean that our leaders are breakers themselves. But why then did they create Elimination to kill breakers? I don't understand.

The messenger notices my expression and says, "We have the most modern aircraft and our pilots are well trained. We can provide arms, transport and financing, all in support of Retaliation. This will be your only chance to accept or decline this offer. Decline, and there won't be any further assistance."

Who the heck are they? Military?

"If you're so powerful, why don't you help breakers right now? Why do you need me and Retaliation?"

"You already have all information you need. Now, give me your answer. Do you want our help or not?"

I'm afraid to make the wrong choice. He's waiting.

"I need time to think," I answer.

"You have to answer right now," he commands. "Yes or no. Learn to make prompt decisions. It will be necessary in the near future."

"Yes," I blurt out. "I need your support."

"Good. Then you'll have it," he nods his head. No further explanation is forthcoming. He calls for the guards and Chase leads me away. I keep silent, thinking of everything that's happened. Was I right to accept their support? I even don't know who they are.

"What did he say to you?" Chase asks, interrupting the silence.

"Nothing much, just thanked me for my cooperation," I answer, trying to sound bored. Chase seems to buy it. "By the way, this guy never even said who he was," I add. "Isn't that weird?"

"No, not really," Chase answers. "He works in governmental secret service. Those guys are obsessed with obscurity."

That's nonsense. The messenger can't work for the secret service, because he's obviously a breaker. Moreover, he or his bosses must be telepaths, if they were able to receive my thoughts. How in the world can they work for the governmental secret service and be willing to help breakers? I get the feeling of being manipulated again. The messenger was right, I have no idea about the real situation in the world.

It doesn't matter at the moment. All that really matters is how I can save innocent breakers and destroy this prison. I can't do it alone, so I need this alliance with a group I know nothing about.

I ask Holtzmann to call a meeting for all members of my team, except Chase. He's an Elimination officer and I doubt he'll join us in organizing a riot among inmates.

When I enter the lab, my team and Holtzmann are watching the news. Kitty looks away from me, seemingly angry. I take a glimpse at the monitor. Lola reports about a shot breaker. He was exposed during scanning and attempted to escape. They show the concrete spattered with blood and then a dead body.

"He was eleven," Holtzmann says. "They also arrested his parents, though they're not breakers."

"Turn it off," I command. Holtzmann shuts down his laptop and I tell them what I have to say. After I'm done, a heavy silence falls over the room. I understand their hesitation. If we fail, we'll all wind up dead. We speculate about who the messenger could have been, but can't come to a sensible conclusion.

"This is our only chance," I say finally. "We have to destroy this prison and free the breakers."

"Sounds like fun," Kitty says, her eyes sparkling with excitement. I'm not too sure about her. Should I really involve Kitty in this venture? She's no child anymore, I remind myself. She's a fierce and reckless member of Retaliation, and won't think twice about shooting or killing if necessary.

"I'm in conditionally," Jessie says. "I want to see Browning and Wheeler killed. And we have to rescue my parents, even though they're not breakers. Otherwise, I won't do it."

"I don't care whether they're breakers or not," I answer. "We're taking your parents with us."

"I'm sick with this place anyway," Victor says. "I can hypnotize the guards if I can lose this collar."

I can't fully trust him, but I need his abilities to break the wills of the resistant.

"All right," I say. "But if you sell us out, I'll personally kill you."

"Fair enough," Victor sighs.

I look at Lena and Jimmy. They're still kids and I feel bad, endangering them. But they're also breakers and this is their war too. We all have to fight to gain back our freedom.

"Will you help me to find my mom?" Lena asks.

"Of course I will," I promise. "You and Jimmy will be helping evacuate people. We'll try to keep you safe."

"No," Lena disagrees. "You may need my telepathic abilities. I can locate people if you need me to."

"We'll see," I answer.

Frank listens in silence, his face showing no emotion.

"Frank? Are you with us?"

"I don't know," he says. "I really don't know what I need to do. I was an Elimination officer. I know most of the guards. I still hope I can be one of them again. I don't feel like I fully belong with breakers."

"Frank, do you want to be a free man or would you prefer wearing a freaking dog collar for the rest of your days?"

He thinks for a long moment and says finally, "All right, I'm in."

I glance at Holtzmann and Rebecca.

"This will lead to the war," Holtzmann says. "This is all Elimination needs, to commence a war between breakers and ordinary humans."

"Egbert, the war has already started," I say. "You may continue dreaming of saving mankind, or you can help us save a few hundred real people right now. What's your preference?"

Holtzmann doesn't answer, thinking of his dilemma. His eye is twitching.

"We're doing it with you or without you," I say. "But I'd really wish to have you on our side."

"Okay," Holtzmann agrees to my surprise. I thought he'd be more difficult to persuade.

"I want to help, too," Rebecca says quietly. "I just don't know how I can help. I won't be good at fighting." She seems scared.

I hadn't expected Rebecca to be so willing to help. She had suggested I join Elimination recently. The cruel truth about Elimination being behind the real terrorists must have opened her eyes.

"Of course you can help us," I say softly. "And you won't have to fight. You should stay in the lab and keep safe during all that mess, then just help evacuate people."

Rebecca attempts a weak smile. Her face is almost colorless and she looks very fragile and vulnerable. I'll need to get her away from here, I realize. Elimination is not a good fit for her. I still don't know if Rebecca will agree to leave. She's afraid of breakers. Most likely I'll have to make her leave against her will. But how can I be sure what's best for her? I have no idea.

"Well, what's the plan?" Kitty asks. My little rebel can't wait to fight.

I'm still having doubts. Having started the uprising, I won't be able to stop it. Things will get out of control. How can I know where this will lead? And also how will I separate the truly criminal breakers from those falsely accused?

I remember myself a few weeks ago. I used to be a law abiding citizen, living quietly and staying out of the spotlight. I thought keeping under the radar was the best way for a breaker to survive. What's happened to me? Why has my way of thinking changed so much?

It's not too late to give up on the idea of escape. I could continue working for Elimination, and maybe one day gain enough trust to become free again.

No, I can't do that. I can't be their lab rat. I don't want to work for Browning and Wheeler and become one of their terrorists.

Kitty gives me a piercing look, waiting. If I give up, she'll be a prisoner here for the rest of her life.

"Okay, here's my plan," I say and tell my ideas for an uprising.

The next several hours we're discussing the plan, determining the roles and studying maps of the prison on Holtzmann's laptop. Lena, Kitty and I concentrate, connecting telepathically with Drake, Hammer and other breakers from Retaliation. We'll need a joint effort if we expect to survive. I hope they can receive our message.

The night before our mission to destroy the prison I remain fully awake. Kitty sneaks into my room, crawls under my blanket and wraps her arms around me.

"I'm so proud of you," she whispers. "You know I've been dreaming of fighting Elimination all my life."

I don't ask Kitty to leave this time. It may be our last night together. She closes her eyes and drifts off quickly, completely happy and carefree. I watch her sleep, unable to turn off my mind. Tomorrow is the day of our escape.

CHAPTER 26

It's early in the morning as I walk toward the security center. No inmates are allowed in this area. I'm hoping the guards will make an exception for me because they all know I'm helping Elimination. I can't be sure though. They should at least hesitate before shooting me dead on the spot.

I'm trying to move purposely, as if I have full authorization to be here. Jessie, Kitty and Frank follow behind. The collars around our necks have been broken and we're prepared to hypnotize any guards we may encounter, excluding Frank anyway. He still struggles with the concept of using his breaker abilities, but I remain certain that Frank will be very useful in our mission, as he is a strong and skilled fighter.

I'm more nervous about Kitty. I'd prefer her staying behind with Rebecca, Jimmy and Lena in Holtzmann's lab and not risking her life. But Kitty insisted on being at my side during the operation. I know her all too well. When Kitty wants something, nothing will stop her.

Our objective is to locate the security center and open the doors to the cells, while Holtzmann and Victor create a diversion to draw the attention of the guards. Right now, they're somewhere down in the prison basement, rewiring electric generators to start a fire. Just as Browning and his terrorists have taken to burning buildings, my team decided it would be really appropriate to set a nice, big fire for them. These prison walls contain plenty enough flammable materials. We picked Holtzmann for this role, because he's allowed free access wherever he wants inside the facility. Should any guards stop and question him, Victor will be there to hypnotize them.

I sigh, feeling anxious and unsettled. Too many things could go wrong. Our plan isn't perfect, but it's the best one we could come up with on such short notice. We have to rely on Drake and his breakers to help defeat the guards. We also have to trust the messenger to send enough aircraft for evacuation. What if I can't create a telepathic connection with him this time? We'll have about three or four hours, before hundreds of Elimination officers arrive from other prisons to help subdue the uprising. If we can't escape by then, we'll be as good as dead.

I will myself to calm down. This is no time for doubts. I, most of all, have to believe in what we're doing. I've already escaped from here once, even being alone and wounded. Now, I'll have an entire army of breakers following. I'm not on my own this time.

We catch the attention of a group of officers and they walk toward us. I become tense. They're carrying rifles. We don't have any weapons, except our own breaker abilities. I smile and nod, as the officers approach.

"Where are you going, Rex?" one of them asks. He must suspect something, although his voice sounds friendly.

"Browning gave my team a new mission," I answer. "We're looking for Wheeler to get the further instructions. You know where he might be?"

"No, we sure don't," the officer says, passing by with the others. My explanation must have satisfied him.

"Idiots," Jessie whispers when the officers are out of hearing range.

We proceed. I can't believe they didn't try to stop us. The officers must really think I'm trustworthy now. I hate it. I'm not one of them and will never be.

Suddenly, the fire alarms sound throughout the building and I understand that Holtzmann and Victor have succeeded. There's no going back now.

More officers pass by on the run. At first they don't pay any attention to us. My pace quickens, but I don't let myself run.

"Hey!" one officer shouts, stopping. "This area is off limits, you shouldn't be here."

I give him my story about Browning's order, but he's not buying it.

"We're on lockdown due to an ongoing emergency situation," he says, raising the barrel of his rifle. "All inmates must proceed back into their cell blocks at once." Two more officers join him, looking hostile.

I concentrate as hard as I can. My head pounds and I become dizzy from the effort. I've managed to hypnotize the resistant only briefly once before. I still don't know how to do it, but I must overcome my doubts. The lives of hundreds breakers depend on me. I can't allow hesitation to creep in.

I feel Kitty and Jessie joining me in the effort. Together, we project our thoughts toward the guards. The sirens wail. The rifles are still trained on us, but I notice a slight change in the guard's faces. Their expressions become blank. The officers stare through us, not seeing.

I grab the rifle of the closest guard and smash it into his face. Silently, he collapses onto the floor. The same instant Frank charges into another guard, knocking him down hard. A snarling Jessie attacks the third guard. She disarms him and fires point blank into his stomach. He goes down without making a sound. Being under hypnosis he doesn't feel any pain. Jessie smashes her boot into his face a few times, turning it into a bloody mess.

"Ease up, Jessie," Frank says. "Killing the guards is using way too much force. He was already under control."

"At least mine won't be waking up any time soon to come back for seconds," Jessie says calmly.

"We don't have time for arguing," I scold. "If they're holding guns on you, use your own best judgment as to how much force is required."

Kitty grabs up a radio from one of the downed guards. We proceed toward the security center. Now we're armed and can listen to what commands the officers receive.

"They're trying to subdue the fire," Kitty says, pressing an ear to the radio. "I believe most of the guards are in the basement area now."

Good, I think. After we open the cells, Drake and his breakers will hopefully attack the guards. The officers should be trapped between the raging fire and a couple hundred desperate inmates. I smile.

Approaching the security center, we meet more officers. Upon seeing our rifles they open gunfire without warning. Ducking behind a corner, I shoot back and project my thoughts at the same time. It slows the guards only for a moment. Their wills are too strong. More bullets slam into the wall near me. The gunfire doesn't let me focus well enough.

Frank and Jessie are returning fire. A couple of guards go down. Kitty is kneeling beside me, her eyes closed. She's trying to hypnotize the guards. I fire a few aimless shots, just to hold the officers back. Another guard goes down. Then I help Kitty, concentrating and projecting my thoughts. The gunfire suddenly stops. I glance around the corner and see the remaining guards standing motionless like frozen statues. A split second later Frank and Jessie shoot them down.

I approach the dead bodies. Their eyes are still open. Something churns inside me, but I remind myself about the crimes these people have committed. They've tortured and killed innocent breakers. All Elimination officers deserve death.

What about Chase, I think suddenly. I can't quite make up my mind about him. I'm afraid we'll have to face each other at some point. I don't know if I can kill Chase. He's no different than the rest, I tell myself. Unfortunately, I can't quite convince myself to believe it.

Kitty snatches up a rifle and looks at me, smiling. The weapon is too big for her, but she seems to take to it. She's not the same girl I found in the streets four years ago. She has grown and changed into a person I barely recognize now, ruthless and violent. Kitty notices my glance and winks cheerfully. I smile back.

A guard moans, still being alive. Jessie presses the barrel of her rifle against his head and pulls the trigger. I stare at Jessie for a moment. She's very methodical and businesslike in her killing. Frank doesn't bother commenting this time.

"Let's go," I command. "We don't have much time."

We run, sticking close to the wall and only slowing at each corner to make sure it's safe to proceed.

Finally, we arrive at the security center. More guards are waiting for us at the doors. They must have heard we were coming.

I take a knee, shooting and projecting my thoughts toward the guards. Several officers lower their guns. Jessie and Frank put them down with a few quick shots. The guards who don't react to the hypnosis continue firing. We take cover along the wall, just below the level of the windows near the door entrance. I aim in the general direction of the remaining guards and fire a few shots through the window panel. Glass explodes around us, filling the air with dangerous shards. One officer inside the room groans, dropping his weapon. He presses a hand against his neck. Dark thick blood seeps throw his fingers. He rises up to his feet for a moment, then falls over.

The guards are backing further into the security center. Jessie, Kitty and Frank slowly stalk them, taking cover behind furniture and shooting to kill.

I get up to follow too, but a rigid gun barrel presses against my back. I freeze.

"Drop your weapon, breaker," a voice commands. It's Chase. I always knew we would end up fighting each other.

I put the rifle down and look back slowly.

"You won't shoot me, Chase," I say. He steps back, still aiming the rifle at me. I'm projecting my thoughts, but Chase doesn't react. He's too resistant for me. "I don't believe you'll shoot me," I repeat.

"Shut up!" he yells, snarling. He glares at me with obvious hatred. He could pull the trigger at any second, I realize. His rifle is pointed at my chest, but something stops him. I don't think my hypnosis is working. His eyes are focused and clear. Seems like Chase just can't decide what to do.

A stray bullet shatters glass nearby and Chase turns his head momentarily. I use the distraction to slap away the rifle and charge into him. I expect him to swing the rifle around, but he doesn't. Instead, Chase elbows me hard. I grip his jacket, falling. We both collapse onto the floor, grappling for the rifle. He's a well-trained fighter. I knock the weapon away and cover my head, trying to block his punches. Chase hits damn hard. I move forward abruptly and head-butt him. Blood sprays from his nose.

"Stop fighting," I say.

He reaches for my throat. I manage to grip his arm and twist it behind his back.

"Stop fighting," I repeat.

Chase growls in anger, trying to grab the rifle lying near him. I twist his arm harder and something pops inside his shoulder. Chase groans, but continues resisting. His wounded arm doesn't move properly. I slam my fist squarely into his face. Chase blacks out for a moment. I scramble back onto my feet, getting the rifle and training it on Chase. He stares up at me, spitting blood.

"Go ahead and shoot, freak," he says.

"Shut up, Chase," I command. I don't want to kill him, but if he tries anything I'll have no other choice.

Frank approaches us. Together, we pull Chase back up to his feet and head inside the security center. I stare at all the bodies lying on the floor. Jessie walks around, putting a bullet into the head of any she thinks may still be breathing. Kitty is sitting in a chair, watching the monitors. I notice that her hands and jacket are covered in blood. Not her blood, apparently.

"Why is this jerk still alive?" Jessie asks, aiming her weapon at Chase.

"No," I say. "Let him live."

"He's an Elimination killer," she growls.

"Leave him be," I command. I don't fully understand why I hesitate to let her kill Chase. Maybe because I owe him my life. He did save me from Carrel and Bulldog.

Frank and I push Chase inside one of the offices.

"You'll be safe here," I say.

"Go to hell, breaker," he shouts. "I'll kill you as soon as I get out."

"We'll see," I answer, locking the door.

Frank presses a few buttons on the panel. Being a former Elimination officer, he knows how to open the cells. The thought bothers me for a moment. Frank was catching and killing breakers not so long ago. Now, he's killing Elimination guards the same way he used to kill breakers. How can I be sure he won't betray us, if he changes sides so thoroughly?

It won't matter, I decide. Frank is a breaker. He's one of us now. There's no going back for him.

I glance at the monitors. The cellblock doors are all opened and crowds of breakers are freely roaming around. Guards escaping the fire are now trapped and greatly outnumbered by the inmates. They have given up trying to reestablish an orderly retreat back into the cells and are firing into groups of attacking breakers. The breakers can't use hypnosis because of the blocking collars, but they fight fiercely, disarming and killing many guards.

I get a strange feeling that everything I'm watching on the monitors isn't real. It looks like something from a movie, not reality. Pure chaos with plenty of killing. I turn away.

Kitty is listening to the radio. Her smile fades. She stares at me in horror.

"I can't believe it," she says. "Browning has ordered all breakers shot as well as their imprisoned relatives. He's planning to kill everybody."

I stare at her, dumbfounded. I didn't see this coming.

"Why would he order that?" Frank asks.

"Browning must have realized this is the only way to prevent inmates from escaping," Jessie says. Her expression becomes worried as well. She's scared for her parents, I realize.

"The guards won't follow through with this type of order," Frank says.

"Really?" I ask. "Wouldn't you have followed that kind of order a year ago?"

Frank doesn't answer.

"The guards are brainwashed," I say. "Breakers are monsters to them and relatives of breakers are the next worst thing."

A blood chilling image comes to mind: officers shooting unarmed prisoners, whose only crime is being related to a breaker. I shiver and blink the thought away. We won't let that happen.

"We have to stop them," I say. "We need to find Browning and make him give the guards another order."

"I can't go with you, sorry," Jessie says. "I have to find my parents."

I don't protest. She picks up a couple of rifles from the floor. Should I let her go there alone? I look at Jessie. I remember a methodical way she was killing the guards. Jessie should be fine.

We leave the security center and separate. Kitty, Frank and I head toward Browning's office. I hear gunfire and shouts in the distance. The fire alarms are still going off. Suddenly, an explosion shakes the floor, almost knocking us down.

"What the heck was that?" Kitty asks.

"The fire must have reached the fuel tanks," Frank says.

"Let's get moving," I urge them along, calculating how much time we have. I'm worried a reinforcement group of Elimination soldiers may arrive soon.

We run into several more squads of guards on the way to Browning's office. We manage to hypnotize most and shoot the others. Kitty is bringing guards down without hesitation. Her still childish face shines with a bloodthirsty grin. I didn't know Kitty had so much potential for violence and hate inside her. Where did it come from?

I notice Frank closing his eyes when we come in contact. I realize he's concentrating, trying hypnosis. He's a breaker and soon will get used to it. Just as I had to.

We round the corner and run into Holtzmann, Victor and Lena.

"What are you doing here?" I ask.

"We came to help," Lena answers. "Browning isn't in his office. He's hiding in Carrel's lab. I'll lead you there."

I don't bother to ask how she knows everything. Lena is a fine telepath.

"I believe I can persuade Browning to renounce the order," Holtzmann says in a trembling voice. He looks bad. His eye is twitching and he's having a slight tremor. I hope he won't have an epileptic fit.

"I can help with hypnotizing guards," Victor offers. He's holding a rifle.

"All right then," I say. "Let's do it."

Lena leads us toward Carrel's lab. Suddenly, I realize that we may also find Carrel there. Adrenaline surges through my veins. Time for some revenge.

"Carrel has already evacuated the building," Lena says. She must be literally reading my thoughts. I feel disappointed, but overcome it quickly. I'll find Carrel sooner or later. He is on my list to kill.

We finally approach the doors of Carrel's lab.

"Browning is there," Lena says. She squints, concentrating. "He has officers guarding him inside as well."

"Thanks," I say. "Wait for us here."

We shoot the lock on the heavy doors and break into the lab. Browning hides behind Carrel's desk. A row of officers stand in front, holding automatic weapons.

"Don't shoot," Victor says.

Most of the officers freeze, their eyes fixated on Victor. I realize he's put them under deep hypnosis within seconds. Impressive.

"I won't be able to hold them long," Victor warns.

Kitty shoots first, bringing down an officer partly unaffected by Victor. Frank and I join her.

Browning fires his gun. He's not hypnotized. The warden must be even more resistant than the guards.

"Cease fire, Browning," Holtzmann yells, stepping forward. Browning stares at him. "You can't kill everybody in this prison. You have to stop the order."

"I won't allow those freaks to escape," Browning growls. "They belong to me. And I can have anybody killed I wish."

He points his gun at Holtzmann and fires. The professor gives out a short cry and falls. I hesitate, watching in shock. I can't believe it. Browning has just shot his best scientist! If he's not insane, he must be close.

The guards slowly awaken from Victor's hypnosis. Their eyes become clear and they raise their weapons on us. We back away from the lab, Frank and I dragging a bleeding Holtzmann. The guards open up on us. Frank,

Kitty and Victor return fire. I'm trying to reach Browning's mind. Hatred empowers me. I don't doubt myself and don't think. Finally, I completely accept being a breaker. Holtzmann has always been right. This is my nature. I was born to hypnotize and read minds.

I see everything through Browning's eyes, as if we're the same person. I feel his anger, bloodlust and desire to kill as many inmates as possible. The cruelty from the depths of his mind shocks me, but I maintain focus, eventually breaking his will. I force Browning to pick up the radio on his desk. He does it slowly. Order the guards to lay down their weapons and surrender, I project, and cancel your command to slaughter all inmates along with their relatives.

"Get out of my head," Browning groans, raising the gun.

I know he's not going to shoot us. The idea of me being inside his mind and controlling his will disgusts Browning. I sense it fills him with utter horror. This maddening sensation consumes him and pushes his weakened mind to an extreme solution. I know this because I'm going through the same range of emotions, connected to Browning. Put the gun down, I project. Browning resists. My nose bleeds and my head is throbbing. I can't let Browning kill himself, although I'd really like to see him dead. But first, he needs to cancel his command. Put the gun down, I repeat in my mind.

"Get out!" Browning shouts and presses the barrel against his temple. I sense the cold hard steel jamming against my head.

"No!" I yell. He shoots anyway. The room blackens. I collapse onto the floor, holding my head. The pain is so real that I can hardly breathe.

The next moments become a blur. I hear gunfire and screams. I see indistinguishable shadows moving about. I can't understand where I am or what's going on. I can't move or speak. All I can do is to sit in a crouched position on the floor, squeezing my head with both hands. I feel blood flowing from my temple. It wasn't your head, I say to myself. Gosh, it's the second time I've gone through this.

Somebody touches my shoulder, snapping me out of my trance. I look up and see Kitty.

"Are you all right?" she asks worriedly.

I nod, getting up and checking my surroundings. All the Elimination officers have been killed. Browning's body is sprawled in a puddle of blood. He's dead, too. Nobody can cancel his command now. I don't know what to think of this. I'm frustrated by the fact I let Browning shoot himself. I wanted to make him rescind his order, but at the last second I wasn't trying to stop him as hard as I could. I wished Browning to be dead.

I realize that I can be influenced by a personal vendetta just like Jessie.

Holtzmann is sitting on the floor, holding his wounded leg.

"This situation is entirely unacceptable," he mumbles.

I'm surprised that the professor hasn't thrown a fit yet. He's trembling and has uneven breathing, but appears stable enough.

Frank searches the bodies for ammo. His expression is remorseful, but he shows no sign of hesitation for the gruesome task. I have to admit he's holding up very well considering he's a former Elimination officer. He must have known some of these guards, but didn't think twice about shooting when it came down to it.

"Victor, can you assist Holtzmann to his lab?" I ask.

"I can try," Victor answers. I notice his arm is bleeding, but Victor doesn't seem to care. He must be on something, I decide.

I help him pull Holtzmann to his feet. The professor is woozy and close to losing consciousness. Victor wraps an arm around his waist to help with balance. I've no idea how they're gonna make it.

Frank says, "Wheeler's in charge now. He won't stop till every breaker is dead."

"He's next on our list then," I answer, glancing at Lena.

"I can locate Wheeler," she says in anticipation.

CHAPTER 27

Lena closes her eyes tightly, wincing from the effort. I concentrate, hoping to tap into any images coming from her mind. The room fades for a moment and I get the sensation of falling. Then everything returns to normal. I'm too exhausted.

I'm curious how Lena can utilize her telepathic abilities so well. Holtzmann said she's a weaker telepath than me. Yet she somehow has no trouble locating people while I'm still struggling. She's just had more practice, I guess. Maybe someday I'll be as good, perhaps even better.

Lena takes her time, searching for Wheeler in her mind. I don't try to hurry her, waiting patiently. I'm feeling somewhat guilty for letting Holtzmann get shot. I should have never allowed him to follow us.

I think of Rebecca. I made a promise to her to keep her cousin safe. She will be really upset to see him injured. Hopefully, Victor will manage to keep him alive. I don't worry so much about his wound because it didn't look life threatening. But we now have hundreds of inmates on the loose and some of them are hardened criminals. They won't be interested in sparing Professor Holtzmann.

I can't stop wondering how to separate the real criminals from the falsely accused. We simply have no time for this now and will have to allow all inmates to leave with us. That's a bummer. I don't want to set any killers, robbers or rapists free.

I decide to worry about all that later. First and foremost, we need to get out of here alive.

Kitty is kneeling beside me, reloading her rifle. She looks very determined.

"You think the other guards might surrender if we kill Wheeler?" she whispers.

I put a finger to my lips, gesturing for her to keep quiet and not to disturb Lena. Kitty sighs. I know she can't wait to go hunting for Wheeler.

Voices are coming from the hallway. I get up and walk toward the door, keeping my rifle at the ready. Kitty stands up slowly and I signal for her and Frank to remain near Lena. Lena can't protect herself, being in a telepathic trance.

I wait for a few moments, listening. There's a burst of gunfire nearby and I take a quick glimpse into the corridor. Nothing. The sounds of shooting have ceased.

"I saw Wheeler," Lena says, opening her eyes. "I know where he is but I don't know how long he'll be there. I can show you if you're ready."

She stands up and walks toward the exit, swaying slightly. Lena hasn't completely recovered from her visions yet. I know very well how confused and disoriented it can make you. After a few steps her stride becomes steadier.

Lena leads us through the facility passages. She never hesitates or thinks twice which turn to take. Frank follows a step behind, covering her. I don't doubt he'll shoot any guards who appear along the way to threaten Lena. But I can't help feeling a little uncertain going to hunt down Wheeler with Frank. They used to be friends and it may be difficult for Frank to face Wheeler under these circumstances. How can I be sure he won't hesitate at a critical moment or even switch sides?

Lena stops and whispers, "Guards are just ahead. We can't go further."

We have to change our route to avoid guards and other inmates several times. Running into either one would be dangerous. We have to descend a few floors down, walking through smoke and fumes from the fire. It's not dense, but still makes our eyes tear. I really hope the guards have managed to contain most of the fire and it won't consume the entire prison. If it becomes uncontrollable, we all run the risk of burning alive.

As we enter the cellblock area, Lena solemnly announces, "This is where Elimination was keeping our relatives."

I look around in horror. Kitty freezes and presses her palm against her mouth. Frank expels a grunting sound, something between sighing and chocking. Only Lena remains unfazed. She must have seen everything in her mind already.

There are piles of bodies lying on the floor, frozen in unnatural positions, their inmate jumpsuits soaked in blood. I can almost smell the thick sickening scent of death. My stomach lurches and I'm afraid of throwing up. Elimination officers must have used automatic weapons to shoot down fleeing inmates. These prisoners didn't stand a chance, unarmed and unable to defend themselves. They weren't even breakers, just unlucky people who happened to have breakers in their family trees.

I take a long ragged breath, trying to overcome my nausea. I've never seen so many dead in the same place and time. It's overwhelming. I turn away and pause a few seconds, unable to proceed. We have little time, but I can't make myself take a step further.

I knew many would die today, but I couldn't envision such a disastrous outcome. All these people have died for nothing. My mind can't accept the pointless brutality I'm witnessing here. It's something unthinkable, something I wish I've never seen. I know these images will stick deep in my mind to haunt me later. I'll never forget what I've seen today.

"Good God," Kitty breathes out. She looks around, stepping closer to me.

Frank remains silent, but by the look on his face I can tell he's done with Elimination forever. We won't have to worry about Frank switching sides anymore.

I glance at Lena. The little girl is holding up just fine.

"We should get going," she suggests, taking my hand and pulling me forward.

We proceed in silence, carefully picking our way along the massed bodies. I realize they can't feel pain any longer, but I'm scared to step on somebody's arm or leg as if it could still hurt them. Their pale faces wear expressions of indifference, somewhat similar to the vacant stare of the hypnotized. Only these people haven't been hypnotized, but killed. Nothing will ever wake them up again.

These people have all died as a direct result of the decisions I've made, I think gloomily. I began the prison uprising without the ability to protect them. I didn't fully realize the consequences that decision could lead to. I know it will hit me later. Right now, I don't have the luxury of time for worrying about our losses. I have to find Wheeler. We have to destroy the prison and stop Elimination's genocide of the entire breaker population.

"My mom is still alive, I can feel her," Lena whispers. She doesn't dare to speak loudly among the dead.

Passing by, I notice somebody standing inside an opened cell. I raise the barrel of my rifle. It's Jessie. She's holding a handgun and stares blankly at something I can't make out. A few dead guards lie on the floor at her feet.

"They've killed my parents," Jessie says in a hollow voice. "I was too late."

She's not crying and her face is emotionless.

I can't find the right words. Whatever I could say won't help Jessie. I have no clue how it may feel to lose parents you love so much. I've never had real family myself.

"I'm sorry, Jess. We're going for Wheeler now," I say. "We need to kill him."

"I'm coming with you," Jessie answers, taking a last glance at her parents.

We follow Lena.

A thundering explosion shakes the floor. The same instant the lights go off and everything is consumed by complete darkness for a few moments. Then the emergency lights flick on, illuminating the passage with an eerie red glow. We proceed.

Voices and footsteps are coming toward us. I stop and gesture for my group to take cover. We all conceal ourselves in the same cell, preparing to fight. A group of inmates emerge from the dark, carrying rifles. No telling what intentions they may have.

"Hey! Who's there?" an inmate yells, firing his rifle. Others join him. They don't really care who we are.

Jessie and Frank return fire, while Kitty and I are concentrating on projecting our thoughts toward the inmates. Stop shooting, I project, drop your weapons. They're breakers, but being level four I should be able to get into their minds. My head hurts, but less than before. Maybe it's because I understand now that hypnosis can't cause me real pain.

The gunfire subsides. Jessie and Frank leap out of the cell. Kitty rushes to follow, but I hold her back. "I need your help with hypnosis," I say. It's not entirely true, I just can't stomach the thought of Kitty risking her life unnecessarily. She sighs, but remains nearby, continuing to assist with hypnosis. I hear a few rapid gunshots and chance a glimpse into the passage. The inmates are dead. Frank and Jessie are searching their bodies for ammo.

"Why did they attack us?" Kitty asks. "Did they not realize that we're breakers?"

"They were killers, Kitty," I answer. "They didn't care whom they killed."

"They chose the wrong victims this time," Kitty says. "We're killers too." She approaches and spits onto a lifeless body spread eagled across the floor.

She's right. We're all killers here, except Lena. Somehow I feel guilty for using her abilities to locate Wheeler. I tell myself that this is the war and everybody needs to contribute, even the children.

I hear gunfire nearby.

"That's him," Lena warns. "Wheeler."

We proceed, following her lead down the corridor and coming to a large open area with additional cellblocks along one side. I see a squad of Elimination officers with Wheeler among them. A few inmates are lined up, facing a wall. None of them are wearing blocking collars. They're not breakers, I realize with horror, just more breaker relatives. The officers train their rifles on them.

"Stop!" I yell, firing my rifle into the nearest officer. He collapses on the floor. The others spread out, taking cover inside the open cells and returning fire. The inmates look around in confusion, then flee in panic. A couple of them fall, hit by crossfire.

While Frank lays down cover fire, Jessie grabs Lena and drags her inside an open cell. Frank follows them in short order, continuing to hammer off rounds as he goes. Kitty and I wind up inside another cell on the opposite side of the corridor. She's shooting and I'm trying to hypnotize the guards. They're really difficult to break, being very resistant. My head throbs again and the room spins. The clattering of gunfire distracts me, not letting me focus well enough. I know the well trained guards outnumber our group, and without hypnosis we won't stand much of a chance. Stop shooting, I project, stop shooting and surrender.

Although the officers don't follow my command to the letter, the hypnosis is still having some effect on them. They become confused and their shooting slows.

"Frank!" Wheeler yells. "Is that you? Are you really with those pigs now?"

Frank bares his teeth and fires a round in Wheeler's direction. The guards open up in return, and for a few moments I can hear nothing but the rattling of rifles. It becomes nearly impossible for me to concentrate.

"Hey, breakers!" Wheeler yells when the guards cease firing. "I have a gift for you!"

Lena screams and dashes franticly for the cell door. Jessie grabs her shirt at the last moment and pulls her back inside.

"Come on out little girl!" Wheeler taunts. "Come out or I'll put one between your mommy's eyes."

I can't see what's happening out there in the open area. I don't dare to take a glance because I know the guards will be ready to blow my head off the first chance they get. But I have to find out what Lena sees in her mind that's making her so anxious. I shut my eyes and wait, reaching for Lena mentally. I stop hearing gunfire and the images come to me almost instantly, making me dizzy. Probably the intensity of a life threatening situation sharpens my abilities, forcing my mind to work faster. I see everything through Lena's eyes. Her fear and anxiety are overwhelming. Wheeler's holding a short petite woman, pressing a gun barrel against her head. She's wearing inmate clothing and has a blocking collar around her neck. I've never met her before, but I know this is Lena's mother.

"Her last thoughts are about to be splattered across the wall unless you surrender immediately." Wheeler slams the gun into the woman's head.

I experience Lena's jolt of panic. I know she's losing the ability to think straight. She reverts back to being a scared eight-year-old, desperate to save her mother. I already know what Lena's going to do.

"Lena, no!" I yell.

"Don't!" her mother cries at the same time.

While Frank and Jessie are busy firing their rifles at the guards, Lena slips by them and steps into the open area.

"Come back!" I shout, jumping toward her and risking a bullet.

I'm too late. I hear a gunshot and Lena collapses onto the floor. A sharp pain explodes inside my stomach and everything blackens for a moment. I stumble and almost fall. I realize Wheeler has shot Lena. We're still connected telepathically and I can feel she's dying. Jessie and Frank open fire, covering me. I grab Lena with one arm and drag her back inside the cell, keeping low to avoid bullets. I lay her on the floor, not knowing what to do. She's bleeding heavily. My pulse becomes uneven and I kneel down and take a deep breath, trying to overcome the false sensations. I wasn't wounded, I tell myself, it's Lena who's been shot. I put pressure on her stomach wound to slow the bleeding.

Jessie fires her gun at Wheeler. I hope she kills him. It's very hard to aim well in the dim lighting, but Jessie is a great shot.

Lena's eyes are still open, but I know she doesn't see me. My hands are covered in her warm blood.

"I'm so sorry, Lena," I say.

I put my fingers on Lena's neck, checking for a pulse. I don't find one. Her heart has stopped beating. I look at her in a stupor. I'm aware of gunfire, but can't react. I can't project my thoughts toward the officers at the moment. That's probably just what Wheeler had in mind. He shot Lena because he knew it would have a demoralizing effect on me.

I force myself to pick up the rifle. I'll have to wait to mourn Lena's death. Now it's time to fight.

I rejoin Kitty, Jessie and Frank in their gunfight with the officers. They're falling back, carrying an unconscious Wheeler away. Without their captain, they lose their taste for the fight. We follow, then suddenly a group of inmates step out of the darkness. Bulldog's gang. They stand between us and the officers and fire their weapons in our direction.

Taking cover inside another open cell, I project my thoughts toward the gang. They block me. I feel strong resistance. They're really skilled breakers. I see Bulldog coming closer. I aim the rifle at him and pull the trigger. It's empty.

"Drop your gun," I say, concentrating.

Bulldog stops for a moment, seemingly confused. I use his moment of hesitation to charge into him. Bulldog snaps out from the light hypnosis and defends the attack. We fall to the ground, grappling. He's much stronger and more skilled than me. I miss with an elbow and Bulldog slams his fist into my jaw. I wind up on the bottom with Bulldog on top of me. He rains down punches as I try to cover. Everything fades and I know I'm about to pass out. I realize I can't win this fight. Bulldog is a much superior fighter.

I project my thoughts. It's my only chance. I have to hypnotize him.

I remember the crimes he and his gang committed. I imagine the burnt bodies and rows of black body bags. I let the desire for revenge and fierce determination to see justice consume me. No headache distracts me this time. I know I want to kill Bulldog and I have no doubts I'll kill him.

Bulldog freezes. I open my eyes and see he has his balled up fist ready, but he can't understand what to do. His face becomes silly.

I push him away. Bulldog doesn't resist. I pick up the rifle and slam it hard against his head. A crunching sound, then Bulldog sprawls on the floor. I don't stop, slamming the butt of the rifle into his head again and again.

Then I concentrate on hypnotizing the other members of Bulldog's gang. I direct them to cease fire and drop their rifles. Frank and Jessie step out from their cover, holding guns on the criminals.

I'm too exhausted to continue the hypnosis any longer. The criminals awaken from their stupor, looking around in confusion.

"On your knees!" Jessie commands. "Hands behind your head!"

They obey, kneeling down.

"Don't shoot," one of them says. "Bulldog forced us to help Elimination."

"Wait," I say to Jessie. "Don't shoot them."

"What?" she exclaims in surprise.

"They're mine," I explain.

I approach and pick up a rifle. The inmates stare in horror, realizing my intentions.

"No, please," one criminal pleads in a trembling voice. He's no longer that tough, arrogant guy who nearly beat me to death only a few days ago.

I remember the acts of terror from the news and I know I have no mercy left in me.

"Please, let us go," another begs. "Browning put us up to all of this. We're victims, just like you. We didn't have any choice."

"I don't negotiate with terrorists," I answer calmly, press the barrel of my rifle against his forehead and pull the trigger. His body drops on the floor. I feel nothing, but numbness. I know what I have to do and I don't hesitate. I approach the next one and shoot him too.

"Sweet," Kitty whispers.

I kill all of them one by one. I'm not angry and don't even hate them at the moment. I just can't find a reason to let them live. Then I return to Bulldog's body and put a control shot into his brain. Jessie gives me a lingering stare, seemingly impressed. I can't read Frank's face but don't really care what he's thinking.

I walk back inside the cell to take a last glance at Lena. Her mother is sitting on the floor, holding the lifeless little body and crying silently.

I want to explain how much Lena meant to me. We shared the same visions and could see through each other's eyes. Lena has become part of me. She saved my and Kitty's lives. Now, she's dead and I'm to blame. I didn't pull the trigger of the gun that killed her, but I put her in harm's way by bringing her here. I should never have let her step out of Holtzmann's lab. But it's too late to change anything now.

"We should get going," is all I can say. "Above all else, Lena wanted to save you. You need to stay alive for her."

Lena's mother doesn't react to my words and I doubt she can even hear me, being buried so deeply in her grief. I have to physically pull her away from her dead daughter. Finally, she lets her go.

Kitty, Jessie and Frank approach us.

"You think Wheeler's dead?" Jessie asks. "I hit him for sure, but where I can't say."

"I don't know," I answer. "Hopefully, you've killed him. If not, we'll come back for him. I can't let Wheeler live."

I think of Wheeler, trying to induce a vision. Love connected me with Kitty telepathically, maybe my hatred can connect me with Wheeler? I wait. Nothing. No idea whether Wheeler is dead or just injured.

Kitty is listening in on the radio of a downed Elimination officer.

"Elimination support troops will be arriving from other prisons in about an hour," Kitty reports. "We have to hurry."

CHAPTER 28

"Where are we going?" Kitty asks, jogging beside me. She's breathing hard. The rifle she carries is too big and heavy for her, but Kitty doesn't want to give it up. Now, after Lena's death, I'm suffering a heightened sense of fear for losing Kitty as well.

"Most breakers are down on the first floor," I answer. "Holtzmann is trying to open the main doors."

"How do you know that? Have you had a vision?"

"Sort of," I answer curtly. I don't really feel like trying to describe what I've seen. It was a momentary vision, a blur of fighting and chaos. I glimpsed many breakers and Elimination officers bleeding and dying and the intensity was startling. As soon as I saw where we needed to go, I shook myself out of the telepathic trance.

A shadow moves across the wall ahead. I slow down, raising the rifle. An officer is standing along our path in the darkness, arms raised in the air. His expression is something between despair and shock. He stares at us for an instant, then says, "I surrender, please don't shoot me."

He must have run out of ammo, I realize. The officer turns to face the wall, giving us room to pass.

I hesitate. I've never seen this officer before and don't know who he is. He might be one of those who were killing unarmed inmates, following Browning's order.

"Let's move," I command to my group and we pass by the officer, leaving him behind.

"Why don't we cap this guy first?" Jessie asks.

"He surrendered," I answer.

"What's the difference between this guy and Bulldog's gang?"

"I don't know," I growl. "Stop asking!"

It's true. I can't understand why I let him live. Maybe because he looked scared and it was obvious he had no fight left in him. Maybe I just wanted to show him that not all breakers are blood thirsty killers.

As we descend the stairs, I hear a cacophony of gunfire and muffled cries. We arrive to the first floor, a central desk surrounded by a large open space with the main exit doors in the background. Elimination officers and inmates are fighting below. The floor is stained by fresh blood. The inmates appear to outnumber the officers, but many of them aren't capable of firing a weapon or protecting themselves. A lot of them are just kids and a few surviving relatives of breakers. I can almost sense their fear. They're sticking close to the exit doors, trying desperately to keep out of the main line of fire.

Holtzmann, Rebecca and Victor are at the doors doing something with the locks. I'm really surprised to find Holtzmann here. I expected him to remain inside the lab. I see a bloody bandage around his knee. Holtzmann can barely keep on his feet. Rebecca supports him, holding his arm around her neck. Victor is firing his rifle in the general direction of the officers, but above their heads. Drake, Hammer and the remaining breakers from Retaliation are right in the middle of the floor, shooting it out with the guards and trying to win some time for Holtzmann to get the doors open.

I project my thoughts toward the officers. It doesn't work too well. I'm exhausted and the remaining officers are the toughest and the most resistant ones. I can't hypnotize them, but manage to slow their fire for a few moments. Kitty and Jessie are helping, focusing suggestions toward the guards as well. Frank fires his rifle, bringing down a guard. The officers are receding slowly. My eyes are blurry and I can't aim well. I just point the rifle into their direction and pull the trigger till I run out of ammo. Then I concentrate again, lying on the floor and projecting my thoughts. I don't pay attention to the splitting headache and don't let the bullets flying by distract me. I don't care if I get shot. I just have to keep the officers away. If they break through our line, they'll waste all those kids and innocent people who can't even fight.

I'm getting dizzy. The officers are backing off. I have to keep the hypnosis up for a few more minutes. I believe Holtzmann will figure out the locks and then we can all get out of here. I hope the messenger didn't lie about his sending aircraft for evacuation. Otherwise, we're goners.

I don't have time to think about all that. Hopefully those guardians are watching and know that we need help. We don't really have any choice, but to trust them.

An Elimination guard is moving in closer, attempting to flank our position. Instinctively, I grab my weapon, but it's unloaded. I focus harder, but can't stop the officer. He aims his rifle at me.

The same instant, somebody jumps in front of me, taking my bullet. Jimmy, I realize. He manages to fire his handgun, scoring a headshot. The guard falls down, dead before he hits the floor. Jimmy collapses to his knees. Blood pulses from his mouth. Panicking, I lay him on the floor.

"What the hell were you thinking?" I ask with bitterness. "Why didn't you stay with Holtzmann and Rebecca?"

Jimmy's still alive. He's looking at me, but can't speak. Blood oozes from his chest wound. His smiling eyes become hazy and he stops breathing.

One more innocent breaker is dead because of me. I stare at Jimmy, not accepting the fact that he's dead. I wait for him to cough or move, but I know it's not happening.

He caught my bullet, saving my life. Why would he do that? Jimmy was not brave and courageous. Now, I owe him my life and have no way to repay the debt.

Too many dead, I think in frustration. Lena, Jimmy, all those breaker's relatives, inmates, the officers…Too many.

I grab Jimmy's gun and fire toward the guards. When it's empty, I continue projecting my thoughts.

Again, no time for mourning. I have to do what I can to protect those still alive.

The doors to the outer world suddenly open and daylight flows inside the prison. My first impulse is to run, leaving everybody behind. I remain in my spot, hypnotizing the officers. Victor joins me, while Rebecca and Kitty are leading the inmates out. Frank and the breakers from Retaliation are firing toward the officers, holding them back.

It seems to last forever. I've no idea when the support troops of Elimination may arrive. Hopefully later, rather than sooner.

Together with Victor, we force most of the officers to drop their weapons. Drake and Hammer continue firing away, taking headshots at the mesmerized guards. The most resistant flee. Drake along with a few other Retaliation breakers pursue them. I grab a rifle off the floor and join Drake's group, stepping over the bodies lying around.

We wind up at a dead end. The cornered officers turn and fire their rifles at us desperately. They fan out, taking cover inside some empty cells. We do the same, firing our weapons on the go while trying not to get hit. The incoming fire slows as the officers run low on ammo. I recognize Chase among them, shooting a handgun and yelling commands. His injured arm hangs limply at his side.

How the heck he managed to get out of the office where I'd locked him, I think angrily. Somebody must have broken the door and let him out. Why couldn't he just stay where I left him?

"Officer Chase!" I shout. "Enough already! Surrender!"

"Hold your fire," Chase commands and the officers stop shooting.

"Don't shoot," I yell and walk a few steps toward them, keeping the rifle at ready. Chase is holding his handgun on me, watching with obvious distrust. I don't know what he's waiting for and why he doesn't just shoot me. I'm a very easy target at the moment.

"Enough killing," I say. "Surrender and I guarantee your lives will be spared."

Chase looks me over carefully, thinking. "How can we trust you, breaker?"

"You don't have much of a choice," I answer. "But you must remember I could have killed you and I didn't."

My finger is on the trigger. Just surrender, I think, don't make me kill you. I know my hypnosis can't pierce Chase's mind.

Chase waits, hesitating. I notice that I'm holding my breath, waiting for his decision. I truly don't want to kill him or the other guards. I'm sick with killing.

"All right, breaker," Chase says and throws his handgun on the floor, "we surrender."

The officers stare at him in disbelief, but follow his lead, dropping their rifles.

Thank God, I think, it's all over now.

"Nice job," Drake says. "You got these fools to believe you."

I don't understand what he means by that remark. I don't really care.

Hammer, Frank and other breakers leave to help evacuate the survivors, while Drake and I direct the officers into a large cell. I lock the door.

"Thanks," I say quietly. Chase glances at me through the bars, but doesn't say anything.

"Well, it's time to put these losers out of their misery," Drake says, smiling. He walks toward the cell, carrying his handgun.

"No," I protest. "We're not shooting them. I promised to spare their lives."

Drake rolls his eyes, "Who really cares about promises? They sure don't."

"I do," I answer.

"Just whose side are you on?" Drake asks. "I thought you were with us now."

"I am. But these guards have surrendered. If we kill them now, we won't be any better than Elimination."

Drake laughs, saying, "Why do you think we have to be better? Elimination has killed hundreds of breakers, many today. Now it's our turn to kill as many ordinary people as we can. You have to get used to it, boy. This is only the beginning."

His callous remarks remind me of Wheeler and Browning somehow. I realize there's really no difference between them. Drake didn't send his breakers to commit acts of terror, but he's capable of doing that. He doesn't care who he kills as long as they're ordinary humans.

"I won't let you shoot them," I say.

"Really?" Drake smiles. "I'm the commander here, boy, not you." He points his weapon at me. "Retaliation can't have two leaders."

I don't want to be anybody's leader. I'm just tired of pointless killing. What I think doesn't matter because Drake sees a threat in me now.

"I hate wasting strong breakers," he says. "But I do believe you're much more useful to Retaliation being dead than alive. Sorry."

Something is happening. The corridor sways and becomes foggy. Drake is standing in front of me and I'm aiming my rifle at him, but I can't make myself shoot. I'm just staring at Drake in a numbing stupor.

"You have no reason to live," Drake says slowly. "Too many people have died because of you today. This is all your fault. I think you should kill yourself."

My head is hurting. I don't understand anything. What is he talking about? I want to shake off my trance, but I can't. My mind and body seem to be paralyzed.

A bizarre thought comes to the front of my consciousness. I have to kill myself. Lena and Jimmy are dead because of me. Many innocent people have died today. Everything is my fault. I'll be more useful to our cause if I'm dead.

"Put the barrel against your head," Drake commands.

My arms involuntarily move and I find myself pressing the barrel of the rifle under my chin. I suddenly realize I'm about to shoot myself. What the hell am I doing, I think in shock. I try to lower the barrel away from my head and train it on Drake, but can't.

"Rex!" Chase yells. "He's hypnotizing you! Don't do it, you have to fight him!"

I notice Drake isn't wearing a collar around his neck. He must have found a way to take it off. I understand what's happening, but can't change anything. The desire to shoot myself is almost overwhelming. I can hardly resist.

"Pull the trigger," Drake commands. "Now!"

"Don't do it!" Chase shouts. "Think of Kitty! You're stronger than him! Block him!"

Chase's voice snaps me out of the hypnosis. Slowly, I move the barrel away from my face. I still can't think clearly and each movement requires a strong effort.

Drake fires his handgun. The bullet slams into my chest, but still being numbed by hypnosis, I don't feel any pain. My legs weaken and I collapse onto the floor. Everything becomes a blur. I fire my rifle in a desperate attempt to hit Drake. My hands are shaky and eyes unfocused. I miss. Drake approaches and picks up my rifle. I try to stand, but I'm too weak. It's getting hard to breathe. I cough out blood.

Smiling, Drake smashes the butt of a rifle into my face. I still don't feel any pain. The walls and ceiling spin in front of my eyes.

"You're such a disgusting little rat," Drake says accusingly. "I should have killed you the first moment I saw you on the island."

He swings a rifle, hammering my head again. I'm too disoriented and stunned to resist. I don't even have enough strength to project my thoughts toward Drake. I feel blood oozing from my wound.

"Leave him alone, freak!" Chase yells.

Drake steps on my chest, pressing the barrel against my head.

"You'll be our dead hero," he says. "Kitty will be really heartbroken to learn about your death. But don't worry, Rex, I'll help ease her pain."

I snarl in anger. I can't let him have Kitty. I have to do something.

"Rest in peace, hero," Drake says, relishing the moment.

I hear the sound of a gunshot and blood sprays my face. I close my eyes, thinking I must be dead. When I look again, Drake is down on the floor beside me. There's a large gaping hole in his forehead. Hammer is approaching, carrying a rifle. He's just killed his commander.

"Why?" I mumble in shock.

"I've never really liked Drake," Hammer answers calmly.

Now that Drake is dead, Hammer is the leader of Retaliation. I expect him to finish me off, but he just stands there watching, holding his rifle.

I strain to hear more, but fall unconscious as Hammer is speaking.

I awaken to sharp pain. I'm lying on a hard flat surface and somebody is holding my hand tightly. When I manage to focus my eyes, I see Kitty kneeling beside me. Her face is red from tears, but she's smiling.

"Where am I?" I ask weakly.

"We're on the aircraft," Kitty answers. "Don't worry. It's all over. We've escaped." She leans toward me, laughing and kissing my face. "You scared me to death," she says. "When Hammer brought you, I thought you were dead. He said that the officers had shot Drake and were about to kill you, until he showed up and saved your life."

I want to tell Kitty that most of what Hammer says is a lie, but I don't have enough energy. I'm lightheaded and sleepy. My blood pressure must be too low.

"I don't trust Hammer," Kitty whispers. "Now he's acting all friendly, but I'll never forget how he tried to kill us."

Neither will I. Something about Hammer worries me. I'm not buying his new attitude and friendliness. I don't understand why he kept me alive. He must have a really strong motive for sparing me, but we can never feel too safe around him.

Overcoming my weakness, I look around. Rebecca, Victor, Frank and Jessie are sitting on the bench nearby. They all seem worn out. Rebecca is crying silently and looks very lost. Victor is swallowing pills from a plastic container.

"Where's Holtzmann?" I ask.

Kitty doesn't answer and her face becomes troubled. I continue staring at her expectantly and she finally tells, "He refused to come with us. He said he needed to stay with Elimination. Apparently he thinks he'll be more useful there."

Of course he does, I think with disappointment. Holtzmann still hopes to prevent the war and doesn't accept the fact that the war has already begun. I had planned on making him leave with us, but that plan got shot down when I did. The other breakers don't really care if Holtzmann lives or dies. He chose to stay and nobody forced him on the aircraft. I have no doubt Elimination will learn that Holtzmann helped us escape. I can only hope he's too valuable to kill.

Kitty must know that I'm upset and looks away, holding my hand firmly.

I'm surprised Rebecca has chosen to leave without her cousin. She must have witnessed too much Elimination violence and corruption to remain loyal. I'm glad she's with us now. Elimination has never been the right place for her.

I close my eyes, thinking of Lena, Jimmy and all those people who died today. Somehow it seems unfair that I'm still alive and they're gone. I replay everything in my head. We're free now and no longer have to be anybody's lab rats, but this thought doesn't make me feel much better. I want to stop thinking and I can't. I want to fall asleep and never wake up again. It must be a lingering affliction from Drake's hypnosis.

Kitty squeezes my hand tightly. "Please, don't leave me, Rex," she says softly.

Her voice brings me back. I glance at her and answer, "I'll never leave you again, Kitty."

That's the truth. No matter how severe this injury is, I'm gonna survive and recover for Kitty. I have to protect her. A hard time is coming. This is not the end. This is just a beginning of the war between breakers and ordinary humans. There's no going back for us. Our lives will never be the same. Elimination will soon come hunting us again. We'll have to fight back.

I don't know what our future holds. I don't even know where we're heading now or what we will do next. I only know I can't stand by and let Elimination kill the innocent any longer. No more hiding and pretending to be ordinary. Finally, I accept who I am. I'm a mind breaker and I've chosen my side in this war.

THE
MINDBREAKER
RETALIATION

MARINA EPLEY

THE
MINDBREAKER
RETALIATION
MARINA EPLEY

The Second Book in
THE MIND BREAKER Trilogy

PART 1

PART

CHAPTER 1

The constant noise of gunfire is driving me crazy. Our recruits continue their training even after dark. They shoot targets as they jog around the camp yelling out inspirational slogans. The training goes on and on incessantly. All in preparation for the last great war.

"Freedom for breakers!" I hear them shout alongside a sudden burst of rifle fire just outside my shack.

I don't believe they can actually see what they're shooting at in the darkness. Likely, they're only wasting ammunition, hitting nothing but air. But learning how to shoot isn't the primary focus of this training. The main goal is to keep the recruits wired and willing to kill any ordinary human they happen to encounter.

After yet another volley, I give up on trying to sleep. I'm too anxious to rest anyway. It's almost sunrise and our mission will begin in a few hours. This is the day I've been waiting months for. The day when I'm going to capture and kill my sworn enemy, Captain Wheeler.

I crawl out of my sleeping bag, approach a small pile of clothes on the floor and dig out a pitch black uniform. The shirt used to have the hole from a bullet I took in the chest, but somebody sewed it recently. I know Hammer doesn't want his recruits to learn I used to work for Elimination. It wouldn't jive with the version of the story he's already told them about me. Today though, I may need to have the ability to blend in.

As I walk outside, a group of recruits jog by. They all wear identical camo uniforms with heavy military boots, and carry assault rifles seemingly too big for their arms. Their ages range from ten to fifteen. Passing by, most kids salute awkwardly, their lips stretching into wide grins.

I can't help from wincing. These recruits are way too young to be soldiers, but Hammer doesn't give a damn about their age. He thinks all breakers must fight, even the children. Time was when I held the same belief. Not anymore.

The night air is hot and humid. I walk through our compound, stumbling through mud after the recent showers. Puddles of water glisten in the moonlight. I pass several tents and poorly built shacks. More than five hundred breakers live in our compound and the number is growing with each passing day. We don't have enough space for all of them, so some have to sleep out in the open under the stars. It's bearable during the spring and summer months, but we'll have to think of something else when winter arrives. If we're still alive, that is.

Another dozen or so recruits pass by, breathing hard and repeating spiteful slogans against non-breakers. All this hatred in the air worries me. Initially, Retaliation was a sanctuary of sorts, a safe place for mind breakers hunted by the government. But many ordinary people who managed to escape with us reside here as well.

After several minutes, I reach the edge of the compound, stopping in front of a large opening containing several rows of fresh graves. Our cemetery. The nameless graves have no headstones, the deceased fated for oblivion.

I don't really know why I had to come here tonight. Maybe because I feel responsible for these deaths. A few months ago I swore an oath to protect the innocent from Elimination and stop the mindless killing. I've been an epic failure so far.

"What the heck are you doing out here?" I hear a harsh woman's voice coming from behind me.

I don't have to turn to know this is Jessie. She approaches and stops beside me, staring down at the graves. Her face is obscured in the dim light, but I can still see the scars on her chin and lips from the beating she took back in the Elimination prison. Jessie repeats her question, "What are you doing here, Rex?"

"Nothing," I answer. "Just trying to find a quiet place to think."

"You look like death warmed over," she comments. "Have you slept any at all?"

"Just a little."

"You sure you still want to go on the mission?"

I nod.

"Hammer won't like that one little bit," Jessie adds.

"I don't care what he likes," I snap. "I'm going."

"Whatever," Jessie says, yawning as she pulls a pack of cigarettes from the pocket of her camo jacket. Smoking, she says, "You've been sick for months. How are you gonna fight your way out if things go wrong?"

"Just give me a break," I say, causing Jessie to grin.

It's been five months since Drake, the former leader of Retaliation, shot me almost point blank in the chest. The bullet crushed some ribs and lodged inside my right lung. I almost bled to death, waiting to get proper medical care. By the time our mysterious supporters finally sent a medical team, I was close to falling into a coma. The medics performed surgery inside a tent under unsterile conditions, so I wound up with blood poisoning along with a subsequent case of pneumonia. Everybody thought I'd die. I finally recovered after about three months, but had become so weak that I could hardly stand on my own two feet. Hammer prohibited me from participating in rescue missions during that time. So, while other breakers were out risking their lives, I remained cooped up inside the camp.

That changes today. I've become strong enough to contribute and am not going to miss another rescue mission. Not this one, at least.

"Why do you think you have to come with us?" Jessie asks. "Is it because of him?"

I understand instantly whom she is referring to. Captain Wheeler. A burning mass of hatred swells inside me. I can still see Lena falling, then bleeding to death in my arms.

"You don't have to come," Jessie continues. "I'm gonna kill Wheeler this time. I swear it."

"I don't doubt you a bit," I assure her.

"What then?" she insists. "Talk to me."

I hesitate for a second. Jessie waits patiently for my answer. She's one of the few people I trust. She's helped Kitty and I during some of our darkest hours.

"I'm not sure what I've seen," I say quietly. "The visions I've had are weird. I've never been able to locate Wheeler before. And then I suddenly get these really vivid visions. It's just not normal."

"How do you know what's normal?" she asks.

"Exactly," I say. "I don't know, and that's the problem."

"I don't understand."

I sigh. I don't understand either. Being a level 4 breaker, I have an ability not only for hypnotism, but also for reading memories and getting telepathic visions. Unfortunately, I can't always differentiate false visions from the real ones.

"They were flat," I add, taking another try. "Seemed unrealistic somehow."

"So you do think something may go wrong," Jessie concludes.

I nod again.

"Frank will be with me, along with a bunch of recruits," she says. "Isn't it enough? Why do you have to come?"

"What do you care?" I raise my voice, tired with her objections. Jessie doesn't usually care what I do.

"Because your freaking life is too important to waste," she answers. "Without you everything will go to hell around here. You're the only one keeping Roger's killers from slaughtering the non-breakers in camp."

I open my mouth to disagree, but realize what she says is true.

"I'll be all right," I say, changing the subject. "Have you seen Kitty?"

"She's in my tent," Jessie answers, watching my reaction. "What have you done now?" she asks. "She's really pissed at you."

"I wouldn't agree to take her along on this mission," I answer.

"Why not?"

"I have to protect her."

Jessie laughs, saying, "Protect her? I still don't think you can even protect yourself."

I've heard this same statement from Jessie so many times that it's become almost a joke between us.

We share a moment of silence, watching the beginnings of sunrise. The first beams of light reveal the eerie ruins of a long ago abandoned city in the distance. Hard to believe people had once lived there before the Eruption swept away half of the world. Miles and miles of ash-covered wasteland stretches out from our encampment further to the south. A huge lifeless desert. Thick woods surround our camp on the northern side.

Jessie finishes her cigarette, spits on the ground and says, "The briefing will begin soon."

We head toward what passes for our mission center. A large construction made of bare logs, where recruits receive final instructions before going on missions.

A few teens in camo greet us as we enter. They sit along a row of benches, eating cold beans from a can. This cabin is the only one that is furnished.

One eager recruit approaches, offering a can of beans and a couple of candy bars. Canned food, candy bars and potato chips dominate our everyday diet because they're high in calories and don't require cooking. Sometimes I wonder if I'm ever going to taste a homemade meal again. I'm sick with all this junk food.

I hear a high-pitch giggling and turn toward the door. Laughing loudly, Kitty enters as all recruits stare in her direction. She's wearing cut-off shorts and a t-shirt showing off a flat stomach. I've no idea where Kitty gets her civilian clothes from. She probably made an unauthorized visit into the nearest town and robbed a clothing store. Red curly hair falls gently down her narrow shoulders, coming down to her waist. Her face is still somewhat round and innocent enough, contrasting with her apparel. Kitty's only fifteen, but looks even younger.

Jack follows her. Upon noticing me, Kitty grabs his hand and pulls him closer, whispering something into his ear. Then she giggles again, a little too loudly.

I know her game well enough. Kitty's working hard to try to make me jealous. I do feel angry, but the reason is not jealousy. I don't really mind her having a boyfriend. Maybe it would ease some of the tension between us. But I just can't stand her choosing Jack for the role. I don't trust him. Jack is almost nineteen, the same age as myself, a little too old for Kitty.

They sit down together on a bench and continue whispering to one another. I look away.

Hammer enters the room and all the recruits snap to attention, saluting. Victor and Frank follow close by. I smell the sharp scent of alcohol and realize that Victor is drunk as usual. I only hope he'll sober up by the time we have to leave for our mission. We don't have enough medicine and good food here, but there's shocking amount of booze and drugs available throughout the Retaliation camp.

"Turn on the radio," Hammer orders. "Let's listen to what those suckers have to say."

A recruit hurriedly executes his command and we listen to the government broadcast.

The report is about new concentration camps, executions and freshly captured breakers. Nothing specific or special. The government is intent on turning the entire country into a slaughter house. Elimination continues scanning the general population to determine citizens with the capability for hypnotism.

Then I hear a voice I recognize. My muscles tighten and I lean forward, staring at the radio. The most famous journalist in the country, Lola Great, is interviewing Captain Wheeler. The very man I need to kill, and they're speaking about me.

"How did Rex Hunter survive the lethal injection at his execution?" Lola inquires.

"Our investigation suggests that he may have received assistance from a group of terrorists," Wheeler answers. "They replaced the lethal injection with a strong sedative. In short, he faked his own death and somehow managed to escape."

He's lying of course. Elimination controlled everything. They staged the execution for show, broadcasting it over the entire Republic, then forced me to work for them. Wheeler was one of my captors.

"Does Elimination know where he is now or what he may be planning to do?" Lola asks.

"He's the leader of the primary breaker terrorist organization," Wheeler answers. "We haven't located them yet, but we have a team of professionals working around the clock on that. We are on their trail and will find them soon."

Another lie. Our organization has nothing to do with terrorism. We're just trying to protect our future and live free. And I'm not the leader of Retaliation any longer. Hammer commandeered the leadership role while I was ill, and he now has singular control.

The interview ends with Captain Wheeler announcing a generous reward for my capture, dead or alive. The sum of money offered is large enough to buy a mansion and comfortably retire. I'm currently the most wanted criminal in the country.

"Congratulations, Rex," Jack says in a mocking voice. "They've increased the reward again. You must be very proud of yourself."

I'm not. I'm actually afraid that certain members of Retaliation may rat me out. I have more than enough enemies here. Only the youngest of the recruits still think I'm some sort of a hero.

Hammer begins our meeting. He explains how I've finally managed to locate Wheeler. He'll be transporting prisoners to the Death Camp and our main objective is to capture him. This is even more vital than freeing the prisoners. Wheeler is the key to valuable information, and by capturing him, we may get a chance to rescue hundreds more prisoners later.

"We don't expect too many guards on site," Hammer says. "Be advised that the guards who are present will be resistant. You can't hypnotize them. Blockade the road, stop the trucks and shoot the guards. Snatch Wheeler and leave. That's all there is to it."

It sounds really simple, but I still have a bad feeling about this mission. I have to be there to make sure Wheeler doesn't escape. And I have to protect the recruits. They've never seen real combat yet.

"Jack, you'll be in charge," Hammer orders.

"Yes, sir," Jack says, straightening his back. He raises his head, looking proudly over the recruits.

I clear my throat and say, "In all due respect, Hammer, I think you should name me the leader on this mission."

"What did you say?" Hammer asks, although I know he heard me.

"I'll be going with them," I say firmly.

The recruits watch us attentively. Jack frowns. There's no way Hammer can make an argument in front of everybody. He prefers his soldiers to think we're the best of friends.

"Great idea," Hammer says. "Why don't we discuss it outside?"

"Sure," I answer.

Outside, Hammer grabs my jacket and whispers angrily, "Listen you crazy jerk. Don't start with me again. You're in no shape to participate in this mission. You have no specialized training, you…"

"I not only survived the Elimination prison but destroyed it," I say in a calm voice. "What additional training are you talking about? I have more experience fighting Elimination than any recruit here."

"Shut up," Hammer orders in an attempt to keep me quiet. "We can't risk your life. You're the best telepath we've got. Retaliation needs you alive."

It's strange when he speaks about my well-being. Five months ago Hammer attempted to kill me.

"I won't try to escape," I say. "You don't have to worry about that. I just want to make absolutely sure that Wheeler gets captured."

"According to your visions this will be an easy task," Hammer reminds me. "What's wrong? Are you hiding something?"

I shake my head no. Should I tell Hammer the truth, I'm certain he'll cancel the mission. I can't miss a chance to kill Wheeler again.

"They'll bring Wheeler to you," Hammer says. "I'll permit you to do whatever you wish with him. You may beat him, shoot him, whatever. Just don't disobey my orders or I'll have you locked up."

"Listen Hammer, if you don't allow me to go on this mission, I'll simply walk away," I say calmly. "We both know the real reason you need me. I've made a deal with our supporters and they expect me to be the leader, not you. If I leave Retaliation, you'll lose their support. They won't be sending supplies any longer. I'm sure most of the recruits will follow me. You'll have nothing left. You'll be a nobody," I pause. "Or you can just let me tag along on this darn mission and everything remains the same for you. Choose."

Hammer glares at me, thinking. I watch his hands in case he tries to reach for his gun. I'm unarmed at the moment.

"Fine," he says finally. "You're in."

"Thanks." I smile. "See how easy that was."

Before reentering the barrack, he turns his scarred face to me and says, "You stinking Elimination rat. One day I will…"

"I know," I interrupt.

"No, you don't," he says. "Believe me, you know nothing."

We return to the recruits and Hammer announces me as the leader for our upcoming mission. I enjoy watching Jack's disappointed frown.

"What about me?" Kitty asks.

"You're staying behind," Hammer commands.

Kitty abruptly stands up and gives me a long piercing glare. Then her expression changes as if she's about to cry. I expect her to say something, but Kitty just marches away in silence.

I don't have time to follow after her. The next two hours the recruits and I are busy studying maps, going over the details of our plan and checking weapons. I need to concentrate on the mission, but my thoughts are continually coming back to my stubborn girl.

I see her again as we're boarding the aircraft. The recruits are already inside. Jessie, Victor and I are approaching the entrance. A few dozen

Retaliation members have come to watch us leave. They stand gazing in speechless awe.

"Wait!" I hear her yell.

I look back and see Kitty running toward me, spreading her thin arms for a hug, her red frizzy hair waving in the wind. Her green eyes are wild and cheeks flushing red.

I have to suppress a strong urge to run toward Kitty, grab and hold her tightly, soaking up her warmth. I didn't fully realize how much I've missed Kitty's affections. Suddenly I become worried that she'll try to kiss me in front of everybody. And I'll have to stop her and she'll get upset all over again.

Instead, Kitty approaches Jack standing beside me, wraps her arms around his neck and kisses his lips. Jack seems stunned, but well pleased.

"Whoa," I hear people collectively breathe out in shock. Everybody in Retaliation believes Kitty's my girlfriend, although it's never really been true. Rumors of this little incident will spread quickly throughout the whole camp.

Kitty finally lets Jack go and quickly turns away. I'm standing motionless, feeling like somebody just punched me squarely in the gut.

"Let's go," Jessie says, giving me a friendly push from behind. I climb inside the aircraft, and within a few minutes we take off.

CHAPTER 2

I hate flying. It's uncomfortable to think that only a relatively thin layer of steel separates us from a freefall. Kitty believes planes are much like flying coffins, although they have been proven to be very safe. This particular aircraft is a fusion between a helicopter and a jet plane, with high maneuverability and increased speed. The military had begun building them a few years before the Eruption, but had to stop production due to the crisis.

This one looks absolutely brand new, all clean and shiny. Our supporters must have unlimited resources to provide us with better equipment than even what the military has available.

The recruits sit along two benches and I can almost feel the growing anxiety radiating from them. Most of them are level 1 breakers which basically means they can't break the wills of the resistant. It may pose a problem when all Elimination soldiers are resistant, and it takes at least level 2 to twist their minds.

So I'm really thankful to have Jessie and Frank on my team for this mission. They're both great fighters and we've been through a lot together. As for Victor, I'm still not sure what to think about him. Before he conveniently switched sides to join us, he was a snitch and willingly cooperated with our enemy.

Jack sits across the aisle from me, leaning back and showing no sign of concern. His mere presence irritates me. I notice that he's changed his usual camo for a black turtleneck and dark military pants. We now look disturbingly similar. We're the same age, same height, and each wearing black. I'm curious if this is the real reason Kitty chose him. Is she really trying to find a replacement for me? Jack sure seems to be more than willing enough to play along.

A few recruits begin fidgeting in their seats, snickering nervously. I doubt they fully understand what we may be getting into. The war is just a game for them and they still don't realize they are mortal.

A boy sitting next to Jack catches my gaze and his face shines with a happy grin.

"It's a great honor to go on this mission with you, sir," he says excitedly. "I'm very proud to have such an opportunity."

I don't like when they call me sir. That was Hammer's idea.

"How old are you?" I ask.

The boy hesitates for a second and answers, "I'm sixteen, sir."

I immediately understand he's lying. He hardly looks twelve.

"I can fight really well, sir," the boy says very seriously. "We've been training a lot. I won't disappoint you."

"I'm sure you're a good soldier," I answer. What else can I say?

The other recruits grow quiet, watching and listening intently.

The boy asks, "Sir, is it true that Elimination guards shot you four times, but you still continued fighting and killed them all?"

"Not hardly," I answer. "I was shot only once and passed out."

He seems confused for a moment, then says, "But you did survive a lethal injection, right? Hammer told us how you're unresponsive to most known venoms. And you can heal faster than average. That's why Elimination couldn't kill you."

"Can you really explode heads with only your gaze?" another recruit asks. "Hammer mentioned how you're a level 5 breaker. You have the ability for telekinesis."

My goodness. Hammer's lies are becoming ridiculous. How can anybody buy into them? I don't know what to do about it. He wants the recruits to think I'm a hero, a living legend with supernatural abilities, somebody worth fighting and possibly even dying for.

"You shouldn't believe everything Hammer says," I answer. "Level 5 doesn't even exist that I'm aware of."

The recruits nod with understanding, but keep on smiling. Their eyes are full of admiration. They believe I have some truly special abilities.

"We're all ready to die for you if need be, sir," a petite girl from the back of the aircraft says solemnly. She's barely Kitty's age and looks doll-like with blond hair and porcelain skin. I could easily envision her sitting under a Christmas tree, unwrapping a teddy bear. Instead, she holds a rifle in her small hands.

It's sickening. I get flashbacks of Lena and Jimmy, whose deaths were my fault.

"Please try to stay alive," I say.

Jack begins laughing.

"It's all really very touching," he says mockingly. "You're so kind, Rex. You have a genuine concern for us."

I don't understand what he means.

Jack stops laughing, spits on the floor and turns slowly away. His fingers wrapped tightly around his weapon are white from pressure. His posture is unnatural and tensed. It's not hard to imagine Jack training his rifle on me and pulling the trigger.

I'm probably just getting overly paranoid, seeing enemies in everybody. Too many people have wished to see me dead recently.

The aircraft finds a suitable spot for landing a few miles away from our destination. We hike through dense woods for approximately an hour. Overhead, the sun shines brightly and the sky is electric blue. It's still late spring, but the temperature already reaches into the high nineties. The smothering humidity wraps around us like a heavy blanket and steam rises from the damp soil under our feet.

It's getting difficult to breathe and my uniform clings to my skin, soaked in sweat. The recruits march in silence, carrying their rifles and small backpacks packed with food and ammo. Everything seems a little too ordinary, as if we're just going on a hike.

We finally crest the top of a hill and see a narrow muddy road on the other side at the bottom. Frank checks the map to make sure it's the right place. I don't have to check anything. I've seen this exact hill and the road many times before through my visions. It can't be a mistake, even the trees look familiar.

I command the recruits to cut down a dried out oak. Then we drag it toward the road and place it across to block incoming traffic. This road has been abandoned for years and there's little chance a random car will come along. I expect only two Elimination trucks carrying prisoners and Captain Wheeler.

Thinking of him makes my blood boil. I must kill Wheeler today. It's been on my mind for months and I still haven't decided how it should go down. Anything I can think of seems too humane for Wheeler. I want to see him suffer and realize why he's dying. It's going to take a lot of self-control not to just shoot him on sight. Before killing Wheeler, I need to bring him back to our camp for interrogation. He has information about the Death Camp, the largest Elimination prison holding hundreds of breakers. I haven't been able to locate the Death Camp through visions. Something must be blocking me.

The recruits take positions on top of the hill, concealing themselves in a thicket. I lie on the ground, observing the road. The sun is still high in the sky. I'm sure we have a couple of hours before the trucks arrive, but I continue watching carefully.

Jessie and Victor approach. They used to be worst enemies, so Jessie must have finally given up on her plans for vengeance.

"Darn it, where are they?" she asks in a nervous voice.

"I don't know the exact time when they will come," I answer.

Victor pulls out a small metal flask, takes a sip and passes it to Jessie. It must be whiskey, I guess. She takes a drink and offers to me.

"No, thanks," I say. "I should keep my head clear."

"Still can't hypnotize when you're drunk?" Jessie says, smiling teasingly. She can consume unlimited amounts of alcohol and still use her abilities without any trouble. It always amazes me. I have to remain completely sober and it still hurts my head when I use hypnosis.

Victor searches his pockets, pulls out a plastic container of pills and swallows a couple.

"Hey, easy on that stuff," I say.

"Relax," Victor answers. "You know I need it. I won't be nearly as useful should I begin to think clearly."

Elimination overused Victor for reading the memories of prisoners. A good breaker can safely do a memory scanning maybe once a week and be all right. Victor had to read memories on a daily basis. He lost himself in other people's minds, even sometimes forgetting who he was. Now, he's using drugs and sleeping meds to block memory flashbacks.

"We can't rely on these kids," Jessie says, motioning toward the recruits.

"I know," I say. "We need to try to keep them safe. They'll cover us while we take Wheeler. Frank will stay behind as well. He's still a better shooter than breaker. Victor, you're coming with us. Your job is to put the guards under."

"Sounds good," Victor agrees.

"You really trust Frank?" Jessie asks suddenly.

"Frank has proven his loyalty many times," I say. "I don't want to discuss it again."

Jessie and Victor linger around a few more minutes, speculating about when the trucks may come, before returning to their positions to observe the road.

Time drags by slowly. The sun seems to be glued in the same place in the sky. The recruits take turns having a meager supper, then one boy brings over a bag of salted chips and a bottle of water for my meal. I make myself eat.

"You can't fool me," an angry whisper comes from behind. I turn to look and see Jack standing a few feet away. I hadn't heard him approach.

"What the hell are you doing here?" I ask. "Return to your position."

"Don't tell me what to do," he says. "I'm not taking orders from you."

"Really?" I say, getting onto my feet. He takes a step backward. "What's your problem, Jack?"

"You're my problem," he answers.

"How's that?" I ask calmly.

"You don't deserve to be among us," Jack says. "Maybe you can fool those kids into thinking you're some kind of hero, but you can't fool me. I know you're just a coward who can't be trusted. You shouldn't be in charge. This is your first mission, right? I've been on three missions already. I should be the leader here."

I envision myself punching him in the face, then take a deep breath and say, "Jack, insubordination is dealt with by a bullet. Return to your position. I won't tell you again."

"You won't shoot me," Jack says. "You're a coward."

I stare him down, holding my rifle with both hands. He takes another step back, hesitating. Then he lowers his eyes and leaves.

"Hey, Jack," I call. He stops. "When we get back to camp, keep away from Kitty."

"Go to hell," he says. "You don't deserve her either."

"I've warned you, Jack," I threaten.

He walks away, returning to his position. I come back to my spot to observe the road.

The sun is creeping down. Still no trucks in sight. Where are they? Why haven't they come yet? I have to fight an urge to run down the hill and walk along the road, looking for them. I can't stand waiting one more minute, but make myself lie still and keep staring at the road anyway.

It's getting dark when I finally hear vehicles approaching. Two military trucks with oversized tires are cruising down the road. I aim the barrel of my rifle at them. They slow down and come to a complete stop in front of the tree placed across the road.

"Rex?" Jessie whispers nearby.

"Wait," I say quietly.

The recruits give me puzzled looks. I can hear them breathing heavily.

Four guards climb out of the trucks to check out the fallen tree. They glance around cautiously, but don't notice us. A chill crawls down my spine when they look my direction. I haven't seen Elimination officers since our escape. They wear black uniforms identical to mine and carry assault rifles.

"Time to go," Jessie says. "What are we waiting for?"

"I don't know yet," I say through my teeth. "Just wait."

The guards command a dozen prisoners to clear the road. They approach the tree and begin dragging it away slowly as the officers continue to scan the surroundings expectantly.

"They'll drive away," Jack whispers. "You coward!"

"Shut up, Jack," I snap. "Everybody keep still."

I'm not sure why I linger. Something seems off. The prisoners wear bright orange prison jumpsuits with blocking collars around their necks, but no handcuffs. That's weird. Also I recall that guards used to put hoods over our heads during transport. I doubt Elimination has changed protocol that much. Something is definitely wrong here.

"Screw you," Jack growls, standing up. "Let's go!" he commands, running down the hill. His action pushes the recruits over the edge. They all scramble onto their feet and follow behind, firing their weapons.

"Stop," I command. "Come back!"

They don't hear me, overtaken by momentum. I can't stop them. Everything is happening too fast.

The guards take cover behind the two trucks. The recruits approach the road and suddenly freeze, dropping their rifles. The prisoners are standing motionless in front of them, their faces concentrated and tensed.

I understand very well what's happening.

This is an ambush. While we were planning to capture Wheeler, he was setting a trap to kill us. These prisoners are planted fakes. Elimination has created a new team of breakers to use against my squad. They've put all our recruits under.

I don't have time to do anything. I watch helplessly as the guards open fire and the recruits go down.

ABOUT MARINA EPLEY

Marina is an indie writer from Yaroslavl, Russia, where she grew up on and was influenced by American movies like Terminator, Rambo and Aliens. She studied journalism at Yaroslavl University and worked as a journalist for the local newspaper.

No stranger to a blank piece of paper, Marina had begun writing stories to share with classmates by the age of 12, and won district poetry competitions while still in school. Later, she became a laureate in a Russian National Contest for Young Writers Debut. Her two prize winning novellas were subsequently published in a Moscow literature magazine.

Besides having a great passion for writing, Marina loves to read, travel, study martial arts, and has developed quite a taste for tex-mex since relocating to the Houston area. She enjoys nature, animals, long walks with her husband, and competes in 5K and 10K runs as time allows.

Always a natural story teller, Marina has already come a long way since her modest beginnings, both figuratively and literally. From her first serious study of English in 2007 to starting her first novel upon arrival to Canton, Ohio in 2011, Marina demonstrates very well what one can achieve with a strong imagination and hard work no matter the obstacle.

She mostly writes YA dystopian, with plenty of action and adventure, but is a great fan of all good stories containing lots of twists and turns and surprise endings.

Stay updated with Marina's new releases at:

https://www.facebook.com/writerdystopian/
https://twitter.com/MarinaEpley
email: epleymarina@gmail.com